HALLOW POINT

A MICK OBERON JOB

ARI MARMELL

TITAN BOOKS

Hallow Point
Print edition ISBN: 9781781168257
E-Book edition ISBN: 9781781168264

Published by Titan Books
A division of Titan Publishing Group Ltd
144 Southwark Street, London SE1 0UP

First edition: August 2015
1 3 5 7 9 10 8 6 4 2

www.titanbooks.com

A CIP catalogue record for this title is available from the British Library.

Printed and bound in the United States.

For Eugie, who had so many of her own stories left to tell.
I miss you.

A BRIEF WORD ON LANGUAGE

Throughout the Mick Oberon novels, I've done my best to ensure that most of the 30s-era slang can be picked up from context, rather than trying to include what would become a massive (and, no matter how careful I was, likely incomplete) dictionary. So over the course of reading, it shouldn't be difficult to pick up on the fact that "lamps" and "peepers" are eyes, "choppers" and "Chicago typewriters" are Tommy guns, and so forth.

But there are two terms I do want to address, due primarily to how they appear to modern readers.

"Bird," when used as slang in some areas today, almost always refers to a woman. In the 1930s, however, it was just another word for "man" or guy."

"Gink" sounds like it should be a racial epithet to modern ears (and indeed, though rare, I've been told that it *is* used as such in a few regions). In the 30s, the term was, again, just a word for "man," though it has a somewhat condescending connotation to it. (That is, you wouldn't use it to refer to anyone you liked or respected.) It's in this fashion that I've used it throughout the novels.

CHAPTER ONE

Pools of light and waves of shadow.

After hours, the museum's Hall of Africa was a waking dream, and not a good one. Lit only by sporadic fixtures, the light shook and shifted with every running step, so a great mask or bronze statue loomed out of the darkness here, a wave of blindness swept between me and my quarry there.

Jeez, but this cat was fast! I'm pretty speedy when I go all out, and he was still pullin' a good lead on me.

About time to change up the odds a bit.

I had my trusty old Luchtaine & Goodfellow wand already drawn and aimed, so all I hadda do was wait another tick, let him pass from another patch of shadow into what little illumination I had, and…

Bang.

Or *whoosh.*

Abracadabra.

Whatever you care to imagine magic'd sound like if it sounded like anything.

It shoulda torn every shred of good fortune from the sap, sent him stumbling, crashing into all sorts of crap, probably even breaking some bones. I wasn't goin' easy on him. No way he shoulda been able to outrun me, and I don't like it when people do shit I don't expect.

I *missed*.

You got any idea how hard it is to miss with *magic*? Ain't as though there's a bullet involved, as though you need a straight line of fire.

But even as I felt the power discharge through the wand, the bastard leapt like he knew it was coming. One jump, up and over, he tucked his drumsticks under him, and cleared a seven-foot display case holding a bunch of necklaces and those earlobe-plug things and whatnot, made outta stone and hardwood and seed shells.

The exhibit made like it had a bomb in it. Glass shattered with a single caboose-clenching *crack*, thick, ugly shards sailing in all directions. Old twine rotted and frayed, and burst apart, sending pretty little rocks tumbling and bouncing all over the floor.

I didn't even wanna know how much that display was worth. Pretty sure there ain't enough zeroes in Chicago…

Acrobatics like that, and the goofy hombre wasn't done yet!

Me, I'd frozen for just a blink, surprised by the detonating case and having to lean back outta the path of the glass.

He hadn't.

Seemed his dogs barely hit the floor before he jumped again, almost as if he'd *bounced*. Up high, spinning like Newton's laws had been repealed, then kicked off the wall beside him.

And, mid-tumble, he chucked something back at me.

Couldn't tell edge-on what it was, just that it was coming *fast*, and aimed right at my neck. I'd swiped a *lot* of luck from those necklaces and stuff, and I burned *all* of it, and *still* didn't have enough swift to duck completely clear.

Sharp pain sliced through my right ear, and a warm wetness ran down the side of my head, making my hair all thick and matted.

I slapped a mitt to the wound, and tossed the L&G to my other hand. Yep, it had taken a chunk of my ear clean off, right at the pointy part. Hell, if I had human ears, it mighta missed

outright. Hopefully, it'd be one of those details you schlubs—
that'd be humans, for those who ain't payin' attention—don't
ever notice about me. It was gonna be days growin' back!

Then again, without my magic, that coulda been a lot more'n
a piece of skin and cartilage lying flopped on the ground behind
me, beside a bloody...

Shard of glass?

He'd snatched a goddamn shard of glass from the display
case *out of the freakin' air* and hurled it back at me! Who the
fuck *was* this guy?

I still hadn't gotten a clean slant on him, and that wasn't
so natural, either. Even in the pools of light, the darkness
somehow clung to him, trailing off like vapor until he reached
the next patch of shadow. I had seen enough to know he was a
big son of a bitch—not a whole lot shorter than the glass case
he'd hurdled—and that he was wearing something on his head.
Weird hat? Crown? *Something.*

This is when anyone with half a brain in their conk woulda
decided it was time to leg it, but I didn't get where I am by *not*
doing ditzy shit. Anyway, I was way too caught up in the chase,
and *way* too curious.

Figure I was a cat in a past life, and that's *why* it's a past life.

We were in the main hall, now. The place was *huge*,
stretching up through the next story to a couple light fixtures
and skylights with the black of night beyond 'em. Thick pillars
and lengths of wall topped with open arches, that let patrons
on the second floor look in and down, separated it from the
smaller halls on either side. Display cases ran down both sides
of the hall, directing traffic to the final exhibit: a pair of full-
sized African elephants, preserved in eternal combat.

Even *they* didn't reach halfway to the ceiling. They coulda
stuck a whole dinosaur in here and it wouldn't have made the
place feel any less spacious.

Some of those upper arches had banners hanging, advertising
coming exhibits, and that's where my quarry'd gone. I'd come

in just in time to see him bounding like a rubber kangaroo again. From the floor to the top of a glass display, which didn't tremble let alone break when he landed. Then from there to the back of one of the elephants, where he took two running paces to the beastie's head and leapt for a banner just above.

Something to do with a new addition to the Ancient Egypt section. No idea why I remember that.

You know what, though? Don't matter how nimble and tricky you are, you bouncing bastard, you ain't dodging a damn thing in mid-air!

I was running again as I fired, and this time I felt the impact. Wasn't able to hit him nearly as solidly as I'd tried to before—that earlier blast took a lot out of me—but it was enough. The banner, which *shoulda* taken his weight without hassle, tore from its moorings. I heard him slam hard into the bottom of the archway, and then tumble over onto the floor on the other side.

All right, not as keen as if he'd fallen back my way, but between the crash and the entangling fabric, he was down for a minute, if not longer.

More'n I needed, even if I can't jump like him.

Wand back in my right hand, I took a sprinting start at the wall, hit it, and kept going. The stone was smooth, too smooth for you—but not for me. Both feet and left hand carried me up in a roachy climb. Matter of seconds, I was at the arch, leaning over, L&G aimed and ready to—

Urk.

Couple of fists that seemed less ham hock-sized and more like full sides of beef, closed on me, hard and choking. One on my throat held me aloft over the drop; the other squeezed my wrist until it almost quit in protest and went to find work somewhere else. I couldn't even try to aim at him.

What I *could* do, now—way, way too late for me to undo some real poor decisions—was see him clearly.

Heavy riding boots. Thick wools and leathers, older'n my wand. A massive chain wrapped around his shoulders, which weren't *that* broad across, really. Woulda only taken two of me to equal 'em, two and a half, tops.

Heavy beard, dark, not so much trimmed as looking as though it'd just naturally grown into a semi-neat shape. Eyes that were pools of liquid dark, like a stag's. And, of course, his head.

He wasn't wearing a hat. Or a crown.

They were antlers—and they were attached.

Fuck. Me.

"Herne," I croaked.

"Oberon." His voice was the growl of the leopard, the roar of the bear.

"How you doing?"

Yeah, I know. It's called "stalling." Or maybe "panic."

Herne the Hunter. Keeper of the ancient boles of the British Isles. Former and probably future master of the Wild Hunt. And *not*, in general, a mug you want as an enemy.

Up until two minutes ago, we hadn't been. Now?

"Can we just…" I wasn't in any danger of suffocating, but not breathing *does* make bumping gums kinda hard. "Just talk for a minute?"

Looking into Herne's lamps is like trying to stare down a cat. A cat whose best pal, the grizzly, is standing right behind you. I did it anyway.

For a long moment, there was bupkis; no emotion, no communication, just my own reflection. And then…

"No."

Hmm. Mighta started off telling it with me in too deep already. All right, lemme back up a few steps—and a few hours. Pick this up earlier that night…

Voices. Voices and muffled pounding from far away, like somebody hammering his way free of a vat of cotton candy. I grumbled something that wasn't even kissing cousin to a real word, and ignored it harder'n a fourth date.

"C'mon, Mick!" *Pound, pound, pound.* "I know you're in there." *Pound.*

Pound.

"Scram already! I'm sleeping here!"

Least, that's what I think I said. It's what I *meant* to say. But since my whole weight seemed to be on my face, which was pressed into the pillow so tight I coulda chewed through to Neverland, I can't be sure.

"C'mon, Mick," he said again—from a lot closer, this time. Not voices plural, then; just the one. Pete. "Kind of in a jam here."

"Call the cops."

Pete—or Officer Pete Staten, if you'd rather—snorted like a pig inhaling a smaller pig.

"Beat feet, Pete. We're closed for the night."

"Your door was open."

It was? Damn, I musta have been all in when I got home.

"So what the hell you been knocking on?" I asked him.

"Doorframe. Then the desk."

"Well, shit. You mind shutting that for me?"

Footsteps, a loud thump.

"Good, thanks. Beat it. *Now* we're closed for the night."

I think I told you palookas before, I don't have to sleep a lot. Not near as much as you do. But when I'm tired enough that I *do* gotta bunk for a spell, I do *not* take kindly to being woken up.

The fact that Pete was a good friend was the main reason he wasn't wearing my typewriter for a collar already.

He also pretty clearly didn't mean to blow anytime soon. Groaning like a ghost in an accordion, I forced myself to sit up.

"Hey, he lives!" Pete announced all cheerful-like.

"Makes one of us." I didn't bother to knuckle my eyes at all, though I knew he expected me to, and tried to get something close to my bearings.

I hadn't gotten undressed or even crawled under the sheets. Just toppled over in a two-dollar suit and coat, both of which were now made of more wrinkles than sheep. Whole office smelled of wet wool—guess there was still enough sheep in my rags to soak up the rainwater.

Pete leaned back against the desk, half-sitting on it. Judging by the glistening spots on his uniform blues, it was *still* coming down out there.

"Jesus, Mick. What've you been working on?"

"Funniest thing," I groused. "Case of the beat cop who just flat out vanished, right in the middle of bothering a buddy."

"Cute, but I haven't gone anywhere."

"Guess you know what you oughta do next, then, don'tcha?"

My not-so-welcome guest pulled the chair away from the desk and sat.

"Have a seat," I told him.

"I brought milk," he countered.

You might remember that's more or less all I drink—or eat—so of course Pete knew that. Then again, if he'd *really* wanted to suck up to me, he'da brought cream.

"Warm?" I asked.

"Whaddaya take me for? Don't answer that. Yeah, of course warm."

"All right." I reached out, waited for the feel of the glass bottle in my mitt.

"Forgiven?" he asked.

I took a big slug. "Stay of execution, anyway. All right, spill it."

He ran a couple fingertips over his mustache, and I almost groaned again. Now that he had me listening, he didn't wanna sing. No way *that* was a good sign.

"Seriously, Mick, what *are* you working on? I've never seen you this joed."

"Miles Caro," I said.

"Don't know him."

I sorta waved it off. "No reason you should."

Caro was a missing persons job who, the way things'd been going for me, was gonna *stay* missing. He had a worried family—which was how I had gotten roped in—and he had a few regular joints where he liked cutting the rug or whetting the whistle, all of which had proved about as useful to me as a Braille coloring book. Gink owed some trouble boys money, word was, and had either got himself involved in something ugly trying to pay 'em back, or had lammed while the getting was good, depending on who you asked. Since I don't much care for working anything gets me too close to the Mob—you saw how well that shook out for me last time—and since clues were proving about as common as an honest alderman, I'd actually been considering dropping the case.

No, I didn't much *want* to. Hate to leave a job hangin'—and the mystery was drivin' me crazy. But I'd been up to my earlobes in it for weeks, see? Merlin only knows how many other, maybe better payin', cases I'd missed. I had no idea what was up in the world, since I hadn't peeped a news rag in days. Hell, I'd only just started hearin' half-spoken whispers that there were more of *us*—Fae, I mean—in Chicago'n usual, and that's the kinda skinny I usually pick up pretty early on.

I still didn't know if it was true, or why, but least I could be fairly sure that if the Windy City *did* have extra guests, they weren't Unseelie. Newspapers or no, if a buncha the Unfit *had* been runnin' around, they'da been leaving enough blood'n bodies behind 'em that I'd have heard about it for sure.

Anyway, gettin' off-track here. Point is, I'd been putting every smidge of focus I could into digging this gink up, and I had absolute bupkis left to go on. I'd been pounding pavement for days straight without a break, giving the Caro case one last big push before I hadda admit defeat. All of which is why I was so done in.

Also all of which—well, maybe not the "there's supposedly a bunch of us throwin' a shindig in the mortal half of Chicago" bit, but all the rest—I mighta been willing to explain to Pete if I'd been in a better mood.

"Pretty sure you proved you didn't care what I was doing," I said, "when you barged in here and woke me up."

"Aw, don't be like—"

"Pete? What? Do you want?"

Pete sighed. "I need your help on a case."

I glared. "Deduced that much. You mighta forgotten, but I *am* a detective."

"Oh, for the… There's been a break-in at the museum."

All right, on the square, *that* got my attention. "Which one?"

"The Field."

I think I nodded, then, though I'm not sure. Somebody'd robbed the museum of natural history? Christ, that'd be all over the papers come tomorrow! Not sure why the department would bring in an outsider, but…

Actually, that was a damn good question. So. Being as that that's what I *do* with good questions, I asked it.

His answer was an unhelpful, "Uh, well…"

Oh, goddamn it. "They didn't ask you to bring me in on this, did they? You decided to do it yourself."

"Uh, well…"

"Which means nobody's gonna be happy when I show my puss over there, and it may not pay a plug nickel."

"Uh, well…"

Thing is, much as I hated to admit it, Pete *had* got me interested. I may bust his chops, but the man's no fool. If he thought the bulls needed me on this, he had a reason for it.

"There's gonna be a lot of political pressure on the department here, Mick. Even if it turns out to be nothing, the Field's big news and big dollars."

"Yeah, no kidding."

"And the whole force's in a tizzy right now anyway, on account of Judge Meadors."

Huh? I knew the name—local bench-warmer the boys in blue actually considered a pal, since he was a soft touch when it came to issuing warrants. No idea what he had to do with the price of tea in China, though.

"Huh?"

"For heaven's sake, Mick, where you been? Was all over the papers a few days ago. Poor guy stepped outta some burger joint and right in front of a truck."

I decided right now wasn't the best time for a joke about meat patties.

"Point is, everyone's got everything on their plate right now. So I figured, I can help my bosses and my buddy out, if I can get you on this early. Plus, I dunno if the detectives are gonna want to even bother with this one."

He mumbled that last bit quiet as a phonograph without a needle.

"Wait…"

"*Plus*, this one's just *weird*."

Oh, *joy*. "I fucking hate the weird ones, Pete."

"Yeah, but you're good at 'em."

Since it woulda been rude to bump off a guy for complimenting me, no matter how annoying, I decided against strangling him at this time.

"Why wouldn't the cops wanna spend their time on this? Seems like solving a high-profile theft would be good for—"

"Well, see, thing is, um… We're still cataloging'n all, be a few more hours before we can say for sure. There's a lot to go through. But, uh, we're not real sure anything was snatched."

I was starting to wonder if I'd ever actually woken up.

"You're not…?"

"Like I said, there's a *lot* there. But we checked the most valuable stuff first, and, least last I checked in, there wasn't a thing missing."

"Shit, *something's* gotta be gone! Nobody's gonna break into the museum for no reason, unless it was just some delinquents smashin' windows."

"Wasn't nothing, though. Actually, they *left* something. Hidden with some of the other artifacts."

"They… You… You wanna drag me out there to investigate an… an *anti*-theft?"

Pete shrugged. "Guess you could say so."

"You're anti-sane!" I bitched at him.

"Maybe you'll get lucky and something'll be missing after all," he offered through a tight grin.

Thing was, he'd got me, and we both knew it. I was curious enough now to wanna see what I could see.

"You're a bastard, Pete."

"So you've said before."

"Just making sure you were listening."

Pete and I probably jawed a bit on the ride out, or rather he jawed at me, but I don't remember a word of it. Too busy trying to ignore the hornets and hacksaws buzzing around in my noggin to pay any real attention. Pain and itching and irritation got so bad, I started wondering if it was possible to scratch a headache if you stuck a finger in your ear deep enough.

I've told you how much I fucking hate flivvers, right? That's how most of us *aes sidhe* feel when we're all cocooned in metal and technology like that. By the time we turned onto Lake Shore, I was pretty sure I could smell time, and I was damn happy to escape the fucking thing. I know that Pete's beat-up Plymouth wasn't *actually* the corpse-grey of dead flesh, that the headlights weren't actually staring me down, that the red spokes and fading whitewalls weren't really bloody grins, but...

Well, yeah. But.

All right, shake it off, you lug. Got work to do.

Maybe.

Turning my back on the two-door heap, I craned my neck to get a good slant on the scene of the crime—or the *not* crime.

You been to the Field Museum of Natural History? Damn thing's bigger'n a *faun*'s libido. Back in the olden days, in older countries, I've lived in towns smaller than the place.

Up front, where we were, you'd never know anything was hinky. Nobody around but one guy staggering down the street, misbuttoned coat flapping, trying to pretend he *wasn't* lit like a Broadway production.

Windows were dark, building was locked up tight. No tourists climbing the broad steps, or lingering by the fat pillars.

Yeah, the main entrance is supposed to look all Classical and Greek. I *saw* Classical Greece, and they'da scoffed. Parth-anonymous, this place.

Ouch. Sorry.

Anyway, Pete figured they were probably around back, so we went around back. And there they were, gathered around a rear entrance I figure was probably used for deliveries and whatnot. Just a handful of bulls, a single plainclothes dick in rags almost as cheap and wrinkly as mine, and—to judge by the occasional flash and the fact I could taste the detectives' aggravation from *here*—a couple'a late-shift news boys, probably hanging around just in case there was more of a story here than it seemed.

Okay, I know Pete'd said they hadn't yet found anything missing, but I still hadda wonder about the police presence, or lack thereof.

"Looks like a lot of the guys have left since I headed out to your place," Pete said. "All that nothing that was missing? Guess they found even more of it."

"Guess nobody told those last couple reporters about it."

"Maybe—but you don't tell 'em either," he warned me. "No comment on active investigations, you dig?"

"In other words, since you bulls don't like newshawks much anyway, you're deliberately wasting their time."

Pete's smirk was answer enough.

"Keenan in charge here?" I asked.

Pete looked at me like I'd just broken out in a rash of Austrians, and I got a sudden hunch that this was something he'd told me in the flivver, a really dippy question, or both.

"B-and-E, Mick," he reminded me. "Not homicide. That makes this Robbery's case, even if nothing was stolen."

"Right." Jeez, I musta been out of it on the way over. "So who's in charge?"

"Galway. Detective Donald Galway."

I didn't know Galway personally, not to speak of. Think we'd met in passing at the clubhouse a time or two when I was there booshwashing with Pete or Detective Keenan. We'd traded nods, that kinda meaningless hooey.

"He a right copper?" I asked Pete.

"Not someone I'll be inviting over for Thanksgiving next month, but honest so far's I know."

"And how's he feel about the department using outside consultants?"

Pete wouldn't look at me. "He's honest, so far's I know."

Oh, dandy. "So why'd you bring me in on this again?"

"Like I told you, you're good with the weird ones. Besides, he'll be tickled not to have to waste any more of his time on this."

Funny how I heard Pete's *I think* so loud, though he didn't actually say it.

When we finally approached him, Galway—who looked like Charlie Chaplin might have, if he'd traded some height for weight and then forgot to iron his suit for a couple presidential administrations—proved even less happy to see me than I'd expected.

Though of course, it wasn't *me* who caught a faceful for it.

"Staten, what the fuck is wrong with you? You're supposed to be taking Baker's beat while he's here securing..."

I kinda tuned out, right about then. I'd heard these rants before, and it was gonna drag on a while. I tried to nose around some without actually going anywhere, tried to find an angle on what'd happened here. I couldn't tell much from where I was, though, and while I woulda taken some of the heat off Pete if I could, I didn't think maybe getting pinched for trespassing on a crime scene was the wise way to go about it.

Which meant I couldn't accomplish bupkis other'n note

a wet tang in the breeze and figure it was gonna rain again before sunup.

Then I heard every copper's favorite phrase, "have your badge," and figured I'd have to do something after all.

I *thought* about just stepping between the two, snagging Galway's gaze and fiddling around with his noodle a bit until he thought about this whole situation how I wanted him to think. While there weren't an awful lot of people around, though, there were enough. I don't like to fall back on the hocus-pocus with too much of an audience.

So I just needed to get Galway's peepers on me some other way.

Whistling softly, I stuck my hands in my pockets and made straight for the last lonely remaining couple'a camera-wielding reporters.

Got Galway's attention faster'n a priest at a peepshow, I'll tell you what.

"Hey! *Hey!*" he yelled. Almost wanted to ask if he had a bit of mojo himself, given how quick he was at my elbow. "The fuck do you think you're doing?"

"Going to talk to the newshawks, see what's up, since it don't look as if you're gonna tell me." I shrugged. "Why? What's it *look* like I'm doing?"

He tossed me a glare sharp enough I felt I oughta be sitting in a barber's chair.

"Oberon, right?"

"Oberon, actually," I corrected instinctively. *Aw, damn it.* The drive and the interrupted snooze had *really* taken it out of me. I'm so used to people mistaking my name for "O'Brien" in this city...

Anyway, he blinked at me a few times, I blinked back—glad I don't blush like you mugs—until he finally let it go.

"You trying to get arrested?" he demanded.

"Wasn't my *first* goal, no."

"You got any idea how bad you'll gum this up if you start

flapping your yap to the press before we suss out what was stolen?"

"If anything," I added, just to prove that I knew what the hell I was talkin' about. (Figured Pete wasn't gonna get in any *more* trouble.) "Look, detective..."

We still had folks watching, yeah, but now he was right up in my puss. Nobody was gonna glom to anything hinky if I... pushed a little. His peepers went wide as I slipped my focus in past 'em, plucking at his thoughts a bit. Not a lot, just shuffling a few cards around: suspicion and anger to the bottom of the deck, confusion and impatience with the case to the top.

"You and me," I continued, "we both know the department's behind the eight ball on this one. Break-in at the Field? No way the press is gonna buy that nothing, or almost nothing, is missing. You're gonna be chasing more rumors'n crooks. You're gonna have the mayor and the city council climbing up your ass like cheap long johns to shush those whispers. And you're gonna have biscuits for resources, since the force's got better crimes than breaking-and-gift-giving to worry over. So what's the harm in letting me give this an up-and-down? I don't find anything, I go home. I do find something, and you're the genius who thought to bring in somebody to take the heat off the department."

All nice and reasonable-sounding, yeah? Least, it was thanks to the mental nudge. Galway might come out of it later wondering why he went along, but by that point I didn't think he'd say much.

"Okay, Oberon," he said, sounding just a touch slow, scratching under his hat with one finger as though he wasn't quite sure what itched. "You're on. But it's off the books—and off the account—unless you find something."

Sigh. *Fine.* "I'm sure Officer Staten can guide me from here."

I think Galway wanted to argue that one—he was still pretty sore at Pete—but another *aes sidhe*-special push took care of that.

The rest of the bulls gave me and Pete some queer stares as

I stepped up to him and steered us toward the entrance, but nobody said boo about it.

"You called it, Pete. He was just *real* tickled to see me."

"I mighta figured that one wrong," he admitted quietly, out of earshot of the other uniforms. "Guess I don't got Galway worked out as good as I thought. Everything jake now, though?"

"Long as I'm here, yeah. After I make tracks, you're on your own."

"Gee, thanks. You're all heart."

"Oh, and if I come up with anything, it was Galway's idea to call me in."

"And if you don't? Lemme guess."

"Yep. *Then* you get the credit."

"You this nice to *all* your friends, Mick?"

"Hey, you just wanted what was best for the case, right? Now, why don'tcha show me where the break-in happened, before you gotta find a doctor and get that twitch looked at?"

Turned out, though, that the actual point of entry told me squat. Nothing but a smashed window. Not a pro job; anybody with a rock or a brick coulda done it. I was kinda surprised the twit had managed not to bleed all over the jagged glass.

Sloppy. Careless. 'Cept for one teeny problem.

None of the alarms had gone off.

That much, I remembered Pete telling me in that rolling torture chamber he calls a Plymouth. And even if I hadn't, I'd have picked it up from the whispers and conversation among the lingering coppers outside. The Field had some real high-technology stuff, with bells and klaxons, and nobody'd heard so much as the squeak of a goosed mouse.

So what kinda ham-fisted galoot smashes his way in like a caveman but manages not to trip any switches or break any connections? That's a sort of luck even *I* might have some trouble arranging.

I wasn't sure what any of that meant, yet, but I knew it meant *something*.

"All right," I said to Pete. "Lead the way."

Suppose I was kinda unfair earlier. The place actually does a decent job of emulating Ancient Greek architecture, or at least what you lot *think* it looked like. Got your caryatid columns and bas-reliefs and white stone and everything. It's not your fault you weren't around to see the real thing before it was stripped to ruins.

I just ain't inclined to be charitable. I don't much care for museums, see? You might think I'd feel better around all the history and old dinguses and whatnot, and yeah, sometimes I can take comfort in 'em for a few. And they're *bursting* with mojo, or at least potential mojo, thanks to all the luck'n history'n symbolism of everything on display. But there's always this bitter aftertaste of technology to it. All the lighting and alarms, all the science buzzing along downstairs, the echoes of a few million modern souls passing through... Well, imagine a relaxing, soft-handed masseuse suddenly switching to sandpaper, or free-floating globs of cod-liver oil in your cocktail, and you probably get the gist of it.

As I discovered, though, maybe I wasn't gonna have to deal with any of that.

"Not an exhibit," Pete told me when I asked which particular exhibit had been, uh, un-robbed. "Was in the stores, downstairs."

So, after just a wink of the sorta dead lighting and antiseptic smell of museum hallway, we passed through a door with a big warning sign saying "authorized personnel"—sounds like a big deal, but it ain't all it's cracked up to be—and tromped down an open, echoing staircase, which was full of even deader lighting and an even stronger antiseptic stink from below. Guess I shouldn't have been surprised.

It wasn't a long staircase, but we still got interrupted before we made the bottom. Voices, not shouting but sure as shootin' not happy, drifted up to us. Pete dropped a hand to his heater, and I almost went for the L&G Model 1592 I keep in my shoulder holster in lieu of a roscoe, but none of that was necessary. Couple more of the boys in blue appeared on the steps. They were shoulder-to-shoulder with the bird doing most of the yammering: a pale old man with pale bushy hair and a pale beard, in a dark three-piece. He looked like a dandelion undertaker.

"Clancy, Pat," Pete greeted the two of 'em. "How's it figure?"

"Pete," the one on the left—Clancy, I think—said. "I don't… We're not…"

He and Pat gave me a once-over; dunno if they figured I was another plainclothes, or what, but I guess being with Pete was good enough.

"Galway ain't with you, is he?" Clancy asked. They both peered around me, like the fat gumshoe was somehow hiding behind one of us.

"Uh, no…" Pete replied.

"Good. I dunno how the hell we're supposed to explain—"

"Explain? *Explain?*" That was the dandelion squawking now. "You had damn well better do a damn sight more than 'explain,' officers!"

The two flatfeet grimaced pretty much in unison.

"Pete," Clancy said, "this here's Morton Lydecker. Assistant Curator. Mr. Lydecker, this is Officer Pete Staten and… Uh…"

"Oberon," I chimed in. "Mick Oberon. PI and consultant on cases of certain, let's say, historical interest." It wasn't even a fib, really. There was history here, and I *was* interested, so…

"What," I continued, so nobody could ask any questions or whine any whines, "seems to be the problem now, Mr. Lydecker?"

"The problem? *Problem?*"

I swore right then that if he kept screeching, I was gonna drag him up to the African elephant display and dangle him from a tusk.

"The problem, Mr. Oberon," he said, calming himself with a big, deep breath, "is that it's vanished."

In what was already a seriously hinky case, that was *not* what I'd expected to hear.

"What?" I asked, 'cause that was the sort of brilliant questioning that made me a successful dick.

Lydecker nodded, resembling nothing so much now as a frantic feather duster.

"We never strayed far from the room," he swore, though whether he meant himself and the two bulls or some other "we" I couldn't say. "I can't imagine how anyone might have sneaked past us! But why ever someone would break into a museum to *leave* an artifact, someone else must have wanted it. It's gone again!"

A catacomb of winding halls, some brilliant as noon—if noon was, you know, electric—while others were lit by single, lonely bulbs, manmade fireflies dangling and dying in a spider web. Wooden doors with brass plaques, a few of which were even legible. So-'n-so's office here, the department of physical anthropological what's-who's-ery over there; and everywhere the bug-song of halogen lights and the echoes of footsteps I wasn't sure we'd even taken yet.

Yeah, this place wasn't hair-raising at all.

Thing is, I only remember a lot of that in retrospect. At the time, I was too busy gawking bad as a dumb wheat fresh off the bus.

Not at the halls. The rooms.

Rooms? No, more like man-made caverns, even if the rows of metal shelves made 'em feel smaller. Bones, claws, rocks, tools, weapons, dishes, clothes, pelts... A million different gewgaws from a thousand places and a hundred centuries. Some of the crap here was older'n *I* was. And I wanted to study *all* of it, spend a few decades just glomming the whole shebang.

Couldn't help but think of my drawer of curios, back at the flop. All kinds of weird little dinguses, stuff I collected or asked for on whim, payment for my services instead of dough.

Sometimes valuable, sometimes not; sometimes important, sometimes not. But always *symbolic*.

That's the language of magic: symbolism. Everything's got power, from holy relics to a worn-out old shoe, if you got the know-how to tap into it, and you figured out what it means, and to who.

This place? Made my drawer look like... well, a drawer. Most people woulda wanted to study all the goodies and oddities here for the history. Me? I wanted to take it all in for the symbolism. I knew there was power here, mentioned that to you before. But this? A strong enough magician might rule the world with all this.

Then I thought about the last powerful magician I'd met, just earlier that year, and decided maybe I wanted to ponder on something else for a while.

All of which is a long way of bringing me back around to the table we stood around, in the room where we'd finally stopped.

According to Lydecker, the museum staff did a lot of work on their Polynesian exhibits right here. A couple of flat stone faces sneered from a nearby shelf, while a much bigger face made of feathers and wicker and teeth contemplated eating me from another. On the table itself, a bunch of necklaces made of shells and hair had been pushed aside, leaving room for the main event.

A tall wicker basket full of spears lay on its side. The wood was dry-rotted, the tips were stone and scratched up yet good, but it was still plain as day you wouldn't wanna get stuck with one.

"Right in there," the curator was spouting, not for the first time. "I just came into the room, and it was right there."

"What was?" I asked him. I'd sorta already picked up on it, from his rambling, but I wanted to get it all straight.

"A spear! As I've already told you!"

"Uh-huh." I made a show of giving the whole bundle a good once-over. "And you know this collection so well you, what, just knew it didn't belong with the others?"

Lydecker got all huffy, which was what I wanted. I've met the type; you probably have, too. Best way to get 'em to explain anything in detail is to imply they might not know it.

"While neither the Polynesian peoples nor the tools of warfare are my specialty, Mr. Oberon, I can assure you that anyone with even the *faintest* understanding of history would have recognized that something was amiss. I honestly can't fathom how the intruder thought he might hide the thing here. He must have been truly desperate, or—" no mistaking the slant he cast my way, then, "—a true idiot."

"All right." I let him think I'd missed the insinuation. "So how'd you know?"

"In addition to being in much better shape in general—honestly, it appeared expertly restored!—it was *quite* clearly an Iron Age weapon. I couldn't tell you from where, precisely, without closer study or knowledge of *when* in the Iron Age it originated, but I would hazard a Western cultural construction."

"And what makes you think whoever it was stuck the dingus here to hide it?"

"Are you sure you're a detective?" Then, with another huff, "Can you think of any *other* reason for this?"

Sure, I could. "Nah, not really. After you spotted it, then what? Since you didn't make a 'close study' or whatnot."

Yeah, I was probably winding him up more'n I needed to. Whaddaya want from me? He was irritating.

"I *felt*, detective, that it was more important to ascertain the object's origin. It didn't seem to fit with any of the exhibits we currently house, but I still had to check and make certain it hadn't simply been misplaced from another room. Only after that did I discover evidence of the break-in, and I've been dealing with *you lot* ever since."

Amazing how much "you lot" sounds like profanity when you got the right inflection behind it.

I opened my yap to ask another question, but it wasn't my words that came blasting through the room.

"How *the fuck* did you *lose* it?"

Guess Galway'd finally gotten wind of what had happened. He was still making his way down the corridor—I could tell by the echo, voice and hocksteps both—but he might as well have been at my shoulder.

Cat was *loud*, is what I'm sayin'.

"It was in a room full of policemen! In a building *surrounded* by policemen! How in the *ever-fucking-flaming fucking hell...?*"

Actually, it was in a room containing maybe two or three policemen, and there weren't enough of 'em outside to surround a parking space. But I didn't really figure it'd do me, or anyone, any favors to say so.

What I *did* say was, "Pete, I'm gonna make myself scarce a spell."

The *suggestion* I'd made to Galway regarding my participation would probably hold, but the mood he was in? No sense in giving him cause to rethink it.

Pete nodded. I got a puzzled blink from Lydecker as I slipped out into an adjoining room through one door, right before Detective Megaphone darkened the other.

After listening for a tick as he ripped into Pete and the others— seemed to have slipped his mind that Pete wasn't even *here* when the spear went south—I figured I didn't find museum exhibits all *that* disturbing, after all, and made my way back upstairs.

Quietly.

By chance, or so I figured at the time, I found myself wandering through Dynastic Egypt, past a whole mess of stuffed and preserved birds stuck in glass displays or hanging on wires. Eventually I reached the Mammals of Africa. Sure, why not? Gazelles bounded over grassy savannahs, rhinos squatted and glared, lions crept... Ah, fuck it. It was dead, the whole lot of it. Throat-chewing formaldehyde and sawdust and glass eyes and wood-colored resins, in a morbid fever dream of nature.

I finally wound up staring peeper to glass peeper with the taxidermied carcasses of the Tsavo Man-Eaters, one flopped out on the fake rocks, the other standing alert like he was thinking of popping out for a bite. It crossed my mind that these lions ate themselves a few *dozen* workers while the British were trying to bridge the Tsavo River, so maybe preserving 'em and putting 'em on display wasn't the brightest move, savvy? Especially when they're so damn close to Bastet the cat goddess's shrine over in the Egypt department. Just a smidge too much symbolic resonance for my comfort. Most of you mugs ain't exactly wise to the spiritual and supernatural, and no, and they didn't much feel haunted or cursed to me. But c'mon.

And yeah, all of that was me wasting time while my brain pounded away at the real problem in front of me.

It didn't none of it figure. The whole situation made a lot more sense if there was no intruder, no mystery spear; just some drunk kids breaking windows, and an over-tired curator getting his artifacts confused. Or maybe staging some kinda hoax, though I really couldn't noodle out why he would. I really wanted to call it just that way and go take a load off. Okay, yeah, Lydecker seemed awful sure of what he saw, and if the situation *was* on the up-and-up, it was certainly hinky enough to be interesting. But I was tired, I didn't know if this was even an earning gig, I *sure* didn't want to work with Galway, and it wasn't as if any actual harm had been done.

Nah, this was a curiosity, not a real case. Two inches of column space in the city section before the papers moved on to the next bit of urban weirdness. Nothing more to do with me.

Except that was all of it hooey, wasn't it? Pure bunk. And part of me'd known it the whole time.

I hadn't just come up here to escape Galway's huffing and puffing, had I? It wasn't "pure chance" that had dragged my feet through empty, echoing halls to this particular set of exhibits. I'd felt it, sensed it on instinct long before it had busted through my thick skull enough for me to be aware of it.

Whoever he, she, or *it* was, they were packing enough magic to make Circe swear off bacon. And they were really, really close.

All right, then, Mick. Let's see how much swift you still got.

I thrust my hand under my flogger, yanking the Luchtaine & Goodfellow from the shoulder holster. I'd had the hardwood wand for so long, I'd worn the grip down to where it perfectly fit my clenched mitt. I dropped low in the same breath, hopefully clearing the line of any fire—figurative or literal—might be coming my way.

I *didn't* turn away from the Tsavo kitties. No point, since I didn't have anywhere to aim at.

Yet.

Pumping my own magics through the wand, I swept the room, hoovering up scraps of fortune. I mean, think about it. All the artifacts on display in the Field? How long had they survived in order to wind up here? What had they made it through that a thousand other bits and gewgaws hadn't? There's enough ambient luck in any real museum to choke a *sluagh*.

Course, I didn't wanna take too much from any one piece, but that still left me plenty.

In, and right back out again, surrounding me, seeping into me, giving me the luck I needed to punch through any sort of mystic veil, whether shadow or illusion.

I *still* almost missed him. *Damn*, this bird was good! I swear he was hiding between the glass and the reflection of one of the displays, and if you're having trouble picturing that, imagine being there!

He was off like a shot before I was even positive I'd seen him, faster'n most of the animals on exhibit, and it was all I could do to beat feet after him. Whoever he was, I didn't buy he was here by coincidence. He knew something about something, and no way was I letting him vanish without singing first.

If I'd gotten a halfway decent slant on him, enough to even begin to figure out who he was, I mighta rethought some of that.

CHAPTER TWO

So, right. Think that about catches us up to where I left off—Herne dangling me off a damn balcony by a neck that was probably two inches narrower and longer'n it was when this all started.

He didn't so much drop as *throw* me.

It'd be a cliché to tell you time slowed down, but it really felt like that. I saw the pillars reaching up past me, the ceiling receding at a steady, uncaring pace. This was one of those "ain't likely to rub me out but could really, *really* hurt" situations. I used what time I actually had to wrap myself in the luck I'd stolen from Herne's leap, and then...

Wham.

Not the floor, not yet. Lemme tell you, ricocheting off the back of a pachyderm ain't nearly as delightful as it sounds.

That whole "time slowed" thing? I had just long enough after hitting the elephant to think "Howdah, pardner"—I know, *I know*, but it's what I thought—before...

Wham. Again.

Yep. *That* would be the floor. Goddamn *ow*.

I wondered, pain radiating through every limb and nerve, how bad that woulda hurt if I *hadn't* protected myself. I wondered if I'd even still be conscious. I wondered just how far in over my head I was.

I wondered why the light above me had suddenly gone dark. *Oh.*

I rolled, far enough and quick enough, that Herne missed me when he landed—by about the length of a cricket's manhood. A particularly proud cricket, maybe, but still…

He struck the floor in a crouch, fist hammering down where my chest'd been, putting a long hairline crack in the stone. I think I visibly shuddered thinking about how that poke woulda felt if it'd landed, which I'm sure intimidated Herne something fierce.

He rose slowly to his full height, rock powder sifting from his knuckles. I scrambled awkwardly to mine, wand extended like a dueling blade.

Coulda been worse, I guess. One more floor down, and we mighta been close enough for Pete and the bulls to hear from the basement.

Oh, sure, I'd have welcomed help. The coppers, though? They weren't help, not against Herne. They were collateral damage. Maybe sport.

"It doesn't have to go down like this," I told him. I'm pretty proud of how steady I sounded.

"It already has."

Sigh. I knew he'd say something along those—

And just that quick, he was on me.

A freight train of muscle and magic. Trying to take him toe-to-toe was a *bad* idea—but I knew Herne of old. I couldn't match his strength or his speed, but I *might* be able to out-finesse him.

I spun aside—pirouetted, really—when his meat hooks were inches from me, hauling up on my coat with my left hand to make sure the flogger flapped in his face real quick. The museum walls blurred around me, and then I was facing him again, right as he went by. I stabbed out with the L&G like a dagger, punching hard at his side.

I peeled more luck off his aura, but there was no way that'd be enough. Didn't think my chances of messing with his senses were worth a plug nickel, either, not the way *he* sees the world.

So... *Pain.* Every bit of pain in my aching back, my memory of slamming hard into floor and fauna, I channeled it through the wand, an emotional poison to aggravate the wound.

The hunter *roared*, and if you're thinkin' I mean that metaphorically, you go right on and think again. He staggered, almost stumbling to one knee as he flew by me, and I gotta say, I marked that as a small victory. I hadn't been too positive I'd been able to do even *that* much to him.

Course, that also meant he was good'n *steamed*, now, too.

A few almost-crawling steps and he was back on his feet, lunging back at me. Just a touch unsteady, carrying my extra pain, but not a lot slower'n he'd been. The cry had risen in his throat, and sounded more like a hissing cat now. Every running step echoed in the massive hall, until the whole room sounded like the inside of a drum being played by a rhinoceros.

I crouched low, body and wand braced against his charge. It was an obvious move, but we both knew he wasn't enough of a bunny to fall for my matador trick a second time.

Which was why the defensive stance.

Which was why he *did* fall for the matador trick a second time.

No stab on this pass. I spun on one heel, letting the wand slide up a coat sleeve, while I thrust out with both hands. Nice solid grip on his tunic, I helped him on his way, throwing him hard enough that he'n the floor were gonna have to write each other to stay in touch.

I didn't just throw him wild, mind—I ain't a bunny either, I had to end this *fast*, if I wanted to be the guy ending it.

Those fighting elephants? Yeah, the tusks are the real goods. One set of them's pretty well blocked off, since their owner's trying to stab the other elephant, but the second? Got his trunk nice'n raised.

Wouldn't kill Herne, but I figured that dangling impaled on a spike fatter than my thigh would make him docile enough to jaw a bit—or at least stop tryin' to croak me.

But he wasn't hurting bad as I'd hoped, I guess.

Herne crashed hard into the elephant, yeah, but *between* the tusks, not against 'em. Even in mid-air, he'd twisted himself around tight enough to make a corkscrew jealous. Not only steered himself a hair to the right, to less pointy environs, but flipped over so that his goddamn *feet* hit the thing before the rest of him.

Well... Shit.

I dunno how he did it, but he knifed forward when his dogs hit the thing's face, as if he was doing a real back-breaking sit-up. His hands cleared the top of the beastie's head, he flexed his arms, and just like that he was outta sight, somewhere on top of the damn thing.

My crouch was real this time as I swept the wand in a fan out in front of me, ready to fire wherever he appeared from next.

'Cept he didn't.

Nothing. A minute, and more, of nada.

Know how I don't sweat? Good thing, because I think the room woulda been flooded knee-high on the pachyderms if I did.

I didn't wanna go up there after him. I mean I *really* didn't. Coming in that close, with him waiting for me? Recipe for some serious *sidhes* ka-bob. I should wait. Better yet, I should make tracks.

But...

Not even worrying about what he's doing here, if I left this hall, he could come at me from *anywhere*. Way too fast and sneaky. Just stand there like Lady Liberty until he showed his mug? I couldn't see all sides of the elephant display from any one spot. Didn't seem *likely* he'd jumped for one of the archways again without me noticing, but I couldn't say it was impossible.

Unoriginal as it might be to say it: *Shit*. Again.

I really hope I have the opportunity to regret this.

More power through the wand, everything I'd taken from Herne on that first strike, little bits from the exhibits like I'd done in the Hall of Africa. The wood damn near buzzed with the magic current I was channeling through it. I twisted it around, conducting an invisible orchestra, until I'd woven all of that fortune, all that power, around me. If I was sticking my noggin in the lion's mouth, I was at least gonna file down his teeth some.

So where would he expect me come up after him? Same spot he'd climbed? Opposite end?

Screw it. I sprinted over, tumbled beneath the first elephant, and climbed the second with the L&G in my teeth, like some pirate spider.

And whaddaya know, all that extra luck made a difference.

The kick, when it came, was off-balance. He'd been waiting elsewhere, had to jump to this side to hit me, and whatever elephants may be, they ain't the most stable things to land on. So he *didn't* hit me hard enough to crush in a part of my skull, dry-gulch me into dreamland, or even toss me back to the floor.

It *did* make my eyes ring and stars dance in front of my ears, or whatever. I went sliding, spinning sideways, and only a *real* solid fingertip grip kept me'n the elephant acquainted. I tried to turn that spin into a roll, so I could come up onto the creature's back and face Herne proper, but I knew I was seriously behind the eight ball.

Not as though I hadn't known I was in Dutch from the moment I recognized horn-head, of course.

I hadda take a couple of socks from him, rolling with 'em just enough to keep anything from breaking, so I could get a good slant on his patterns. I…

All right, yeah. Bunk and a half. He walloped me a few good ones that damn near put me down then and there, but I was fortunate enough to be able to pluck some useful know-how out of the lesson.

Fast, strong—think I mighta mentioned those a time or two

already—and skilled, but he was wild. Savage. So, back to finesse.

I met the next punch with my forearm, sweeping him down and toward me, yanking him off center. His other hand came at me, I wrapped my arm around his, and for a minute we were locked up, arms making like a cat's cradle.

No way I could *keep* him locked up that way, not with his strength, but I didn't plan to hold him long. We both tried kneeing each other in the breadbasket right about the same time, nearly breaking each other's shins in the process. My whole body went rigid from the shock, and I felt the gink pulling away...

Good. He hadn't realized that one of the fists in the knot of flesh and bone between us held a wand.

I twisted my wrist, painfully, so the L&G pointed right up under his chin, and let loose another blast of agony.

To this damn day, I think my hearing ain't what it was before that scream.

Herne ripped himself free of the arm locks. He was shaky, wobbling, but still *standing*! He came at me, both hands, and I jammed him up again with a different series of locks, this time ending it with my wand jabbing him in the side and pumping ever more hurt into him, and pulling ever more luck out.

He tried to get away. I shifted my grips, and kept going, feeling more of his weight as he slumped. And I remember thinking with more'n a small amount of real wow, *Good gods, I beat Herne the fucking Hunter!*

And then he completely changed it up on me.

Suddenly he threw his strength, his bulk, into pushing *through* my hold instead of jerking out of it.

The first poke wasn't *too* bad; he couldn't get a lotta strength behind it. But it still damn near cracked a rib, put me on my heels, shook me loose.

Which meant the *next* punch had everything he wanted to put into it. And the one after that. And after that.

Mighta been some kicks in there, too. Possibly a headbutt.

I didn't stand a chance. It all came in too fast, too hard, more ordnance than fisticuffs. I knew my grip'd slackened when the L&G clattered away across the stone floor, though I needed a second to even recognize the sound. Only reason I was still on the elephant was because Herne had switched to gripping me by the collar with one paw while trying to make a jigsaw puzzle outta my bones with the other.

When he decided *not* to hold me upright anymore, I only knew I'd hit ground when the room stopped Charlestoning in all directions. After Herne's punches, I didn't even *feel* the floor.

He landed, and loomed over me, one foot on my wrist. Dunno why he bothered. The L&G was a few feet away, and right now it might as well have been on the moon.

I'm gonna tell you something I don't like to admit. If he'd chosen to pop me there, I was dead. I had no tricks left, no cunning sneak to pull. I was done. If he'd given me a few hours to heal, or even just a couple minutes with the wand, maybe… But nope.

He beat me. Simple as that.

I remember thinking, *This never woulda happened in the old days*, though I dunno *why* I mighta thought that. And then I tried to brace myself for it.

But *it* didn't come.

Herne just knelt down, almost crushing my wrist, and hauled my head up off the stone by the collar.

He wasn't even winded, even though I *knew* he still hadda be feeling what I'd fed him. Hell, he was calm. Like Talking Herne and Fighting Herne are two separate Joes.

"We have never been enemies," he said in a low rumble. "Given what's at stake, I am prepared to forgive your assault on me. *This* time."

Mighty big of him, that.

My whole back spasmed as he hauled me up closer, mug to mug.

"*If* you tell me where it is!"

I'd have happily told him, if I had the faintest idea *what* "it" was, let alone *where*.

Say this for Herne, he's sharp. Guess centuries after centuries of hunting'll do that for a guy. Whatever I croaked out wasn't much of a word, but whatever he heard in it, saw in my face, he realized quick enough that, far as I was concerned, he was speaking Greek.

Well, not literally, since I coulda understood if he was, but you know what I mean.

"If you don't have it and aren't searching for it," he said, now more bewildered than anything, "why are you here?"

This time, I managed syllables that actually belonged in the same neighborhood as each other.

"'Vestigating... break-in..."

Herne's lamps went wide, and he chuckled, just the once. Then he shifted his weight off my wrist and lowered me back down to lie flat. As he did so, he leaned in, staying in my face. I had a crazy thought that he was gonna either bite me or kiss me.

"Heed my advice, then, Mick Oberon. Keep your head down for a few weeks. Stay home, or perhaps leave Chicago. You do *not* want any part of what is happening here—and *I* am far from the least merciful of us. Do not stand in my way again, or I shall *become* so."

I didn't really have a smart answer to that. Or even a dumb one. In fact, he'd dusted out before I had the breath and brain to speak again. I didn't even see which way he'd gone.

I lay there for a long damn time, feelin' like a goblin's ass after a double shot of gin and cholera. All I could see was the ceiling, but I wasn't paying any attention to it. I was looking more inward.

You wanna know how come I got licked? What happened to all that extra luck I'd armored myself with? I'd burned through every iota of it not getting pummeled *worse*.

Everything hurt from pate to plates, but other'n a few hairline fractures, nothing was actually *broke*. I could feel the blood of shiny new bruises bubbling under my skin, but nothing important had ruptured.

Hell, the way I heal, I might even be tip-top in just a couple days!

Didn't hurt any less *now*, though. Damn, how bad would it've been if Herne *had* really wanted me chilled off?

It wasn't me wincing and groaning as I staggered to my feet, it was, uh, the elephant, making fun of me. Yeah. Same thing on my second attempt. *Mighta* been both of us on the third.

"Think you're looking at?" I growled at him, wobbling like a stubborn ninepin. "Huh?"

That showed him.

I stumbled over to where my wand had rolled, nearly falling again as I collected it. One knee on the floor and one hand on a display of I-don't-even-remember-and-who-gives-a-damn are all that saved me from a face full of floor.

Display. Shit. I hadda think of a good yarn to spin about the case back in Africa before…

I froze, glaring back at where I'd fallen. Thick pool of the red stuff spattered over the stone. Not as much as you'd expect from a broderick like I'd taken from Herne, but enough.

Hadda deal with that, then, too.

Cost me another twenty minutes, three trips to the washroom, and any tiny bit of hope I mighta had about ever washing the blood out of this shirt. Shoved that wadded, sodden lump in a flogger pocket and gave the mirror another quick up-and-down. The worst of the grime on my face had gone down the washroom sink, and most of the blood on the coat itself was on the inside. Button up tight, make myself walk steady, maybe fiddle with a few people's noodles here and there, nobody oughta see that I was banged up.

Or shirtless.

When I finally got down to the basement—hey, it took a while! Damn stairs were in cahoots with the elephants—the big room we'd been in before had sprouted more police.

Probably the bulls who'd been waiting around outside. Still barely enough people here for a good solid round of musical chairs. Lydecker was hopping, trying to oversee everyone at once, telling 'em where to put things and where not to put things and don't-touch-this and that-dingus-is-worth-more'n-your-house-that. None of 'em had their happy faces on, and I couldn't blame 'em.

I always casually wonder, when people all look up'n see me the way these mugs all did, what they're each seeing. Same basics, yeah; couple knuckles taller'n average, sharp face, dull blond hair—some wiseass once described the effect as a tomahawk wearing a straw toupee.

Yeah, I thought so, too. But I swear to you, that ain't why I killed him. Anyway...

Point is, everybody was giving me the dust, either glad for, or irritated by, having a new distraction, and I knew each of 'em was seeing something just a tad bit different than the others. That's how it always works with you mortals'n me.

"'Fraid there's more work for some of you boys," I said. "Looks like the *gonif* didn't just mess around down here after all. There's a display upstairs been wrecked something ugly. Glass and stone and small whatsises all over."

Hey, no reason our mystery crook *shouldn't* take the heat for it, right? I was only here in the first place 'cause of him.

A few of the coppers bitched and moaned, but that wasn't nothing to Lydecker. His "*What?*" was high enough, I figure he deafened every stray pooch in five blocks.

"That's not possible!" he shrieked. "We have security guards, I looked around for damage after I found the spear missing, there's no way—"

"Ankled the whole museum between calling the police and them getting here?" I asked. "You sure 'bout that, Mr. Lydecker? This is an awfully big place you got here."

"No, of course—"

"Or are you saying you did your looking *before* you called?

'Cause that'd mean you lied about what happened when."

"*No!*"

"Then I imagine it *is* possible, ain't it?"

The gink's jaw was actually twitching; I swear he was grinding and chattering his pearly whites simultaneously.

"How do we know that *you* didn't—?"

I glared. Pete glared. Most of Pete's fellow buttons stared. It was a dumb accusation, and even those who didn't know me personally could damn well see *that*. What *possible* motive could I have?

You know, leaving aside the whole "me and Herne locked in mortal combat" thing.

"You wanna dislike me, Mr. Lydecker, you go right on ahead. I could give you good reasons 'til they're coming out your ears. But this ain't one of 'em."

Reason number one, of course, is that I'm a big, fat liar.

The fuzzy grey curator clammed up and retreated to the other side of the room, where he continued to glower holes through me.

"Where's Galway?"

I'd turned to Pete while asking, but it was one of the others— clean-shaven kid who looked like he couldn'ta been on the force more'n a week—who answered.

"Went upstairs a while ago. Something about finding a phone and making a dil-ya-ble to the precinct. Actually, 'fore he left, he said he wanted to chat with—"

"Oberon! There you are!" The man himself appeared in the doorway, and I didn't much care for what I saw. Galway was still hot under the collar—I'd figured, by now, that "hot under the collar" was his natural state—but it wasn't at *me* anymore. Hell, I didn't have to see it in his mug, hear it in his voice. The *flavor* of his anger had changed.

I don't much like sudden changes, and I think I was more comfortable when he *was* steamed at me.

"I've talked to the station," he said, jerking to a stiff halt in front of me. "They're seriously considering hiring you on as a private consultant." The expression he turned on everyone else wasn't nearly so keen. "Me, I'm hoping they do. Since the officers assigned to me on this don't seem able to keep track of *stolen property*, or catch a thief *in the building with them*, some newer eyes are just what we need. And I'll tell you another thing, I won't be shy punishing any further dereliction or carelessness. You are *not* gonna embarrass me or the department in front of an outsider!"

Oh, for the love of... Just tell 'em all to draw their billy clubs and pound me into hamburger, why don'tcha!

And yep, Pete—and one or two of the others I'd gladhanded personally now and again—all winced or muttered and looked at their toes.

The rest?

Yeah, I'd better not need the boys in blue anytime soon. 'Cept maybe as pallbearers.

"Detective Galway," I began, "I don't—"

He waved me off. "I know, I know. Gotta negotiate fees and all. Come on by the clubhouse tomorrow morning. Assuming they give us the go-ahead, we'll have you John Hancock something."

"But I—"

"Listen." His voice dropped to a rough whisper. "You won't just be digging for an actual burglar. I ain't sure the old man—" he cast a glance at Lydecker that mighta qualified as subtle if it'd been at all, y'know, subtle "—isn't putting us all on. Give him a good up-and-down, too."

"Yeah, but I—"

"Go on and bunk for the night, Oberon. You look all in."

Swell. Even complete strangers could see I was bushed.

Tell you square, what I'd been about to say was that they'd have to do this one without me. Been noodling on that since before I even peeled myself off the floor. I'd wanted nothing much to do with Herne even before he'd gotten himself bound to the Wild Hunt, and he was even worse now that it'd left him behind. I *sure* as shooting didn't wanna get dragged into whatever wingding had brought him to Chicago.

And I couldn't get his little parting speech outta my noggin, either. Maybe he was just being melodramatic—it's a Fae thing—but I couldn't shake the notion that he'd been legitimately trying to warn me off. Off something other'n just him, I mean.

That... wasn't Herne's style. When the Hunter says something's dangerous, wise folks listen.

Fuck it for now, though. Galway wasn't wrong; I was tired. I'd *been* tired, started the night off tired, and that was before I went five rounds with a guy who wrestles bears to loosen himself up in the morning.

And that meant I was too damn wiped to argue with Gasbag Galway. He'd just hafta find out my decision tomorrow.

Over the phone, preferably. And given how I feel about the damn dinguses, that alone oughta put you wise to just *how* bushed I was.

So for tonight, I just jerked him a nod, then a second more friendly one to Pete—poor guy was gonna be stuck here a while yet, with a buncha pals who weren't feeling real pally—and made for the exit.

Actually, sympathies for my buddy aside, I was kinda relieved he wasn't driving me home. Hoofing it to the station and taking the L meant a longer trip, but it also meant not crossing town with an engine right in my kisser, trying to process my brain into cheap sausage.

It was drizzling again by the time I got outside. Of course. The bulls still loitering around the property tried to hide under their caps—the two or three hadn't been called inside—getting cold wet down their necks and cheeks for the trouble, and muttered to each other about how much longer they were expected to stand there.

Miserable as a teetotaler's birthday, basically.

Not that I was a lot happier, but the cold don't bug me as much, and more to the point, I was heading home. I squeezed past with a few polite words most didn't return, and aimed my cheap Sears and Roebuck Oxfords south toward 18th Street station. Should be duck soup to hop the L over to Pilsen, even this time of night, and I could finally get some damn shuteye. Hell, after the wringer Herne put me through, I might just let myself snooze an extra day. Galway could wait to be disappointed.

Whatever the case, I was done. This whole spear thing was curious, yeah, but definitely not worth getting into. I was through with it, and whatever went down next was no skin off *my* nose.

Done. Absolutely, positively done.

CHAPTER THREE

I wasn't done. Learned that as I got to the station.

Smattering of papers danced down the street past me, carried by low gusts until they splatted against the side of this building or that, sticking thanks to the drenching they'd gotten on the way. I could almost read one of 'em; looked like somebody or other was having a huge sale on Ovaltine. I started up the station steps, making a mental note to remember not to care.

Brakes howled, tracks rumbled, shaking oily drops from the trestles overhead, granting the already rain-soaked steps just that little bit of extra slick. Normally it wouldn'ta bothered me much. I could balance on a blade of grass in my youth, I wasn't gonna worry about wet floors. Normally.

Normally I didn't feel like the dance floor on Come Cut a Rug With Your Donkey Night, either.

Staggered once, caught myself with one mitt on the guardrail, and—

Oh, fucking goddamn it, ow!

It was a passing touch, not as though I'd tripped and conked myself on it, so it wasn't *too* ugly. No agony, no shakes. My hand was pan-seared, though, ready to serve up with a side of greens, throbbing to beat the band. And it itched so bad I'd have welcomed ants and mosquitoes to scratch it for me.

(Well, not quite true, since those bastards don't bite me like they do you. Not here in the "real" world, anyway. Totally different story in Elphame, but what's not?)

Cast iron, that rail.

It wasn't the iron that surprised me, though. It was that I'd been dippy enough to touch it. I mean, I take the train everywhere I can't hoof it. Ain't as though this is the first municipal guardrail I've seen.

You getting fed up with me barbering on about how thrown I was, how bushed and how beat, wah, wah, poor Mick, yet? Yeah, me too. Wanted to throw one more example at you, though, since it's important for what comes next.

By which I mean, it makes me look a *little* less like a complete dip.

So I'm sidling away from the rail like it bit me, clutching one hand with the other, spitting enough profanity to make a priest spontaneously combust. Of the tiny trickle of pedestrians actually still pounding pavement at this hour, one of 'em turns out to be a member of an almost extinct species: Good Samaritan, tryin' to wipe drops off his glasses without knocking his hat from his gourd, while shuffling over to see what's up with me. Somehow, I didn't think I wanted him eyeballing my nice new iron rash.

"No problem, pal. Jammed my finger last week, keep forgettin' not to grab stuff with it. Thanks, though," I said.

He gave me a queer look but moved on.

I was gonna have to remember to give Pete a serious sock in the kisser for tonight. I was gonna have to get a better lock for my door. I was...

Being followed.

I just knew it, instantly. Hair on the back of my neck, phantom daggers in my spine, recollections of shapes at the edge of my vision, even tasted the flavor of lurking in the wet pollution perfume this city calls "air." Wasn't any sorta human tang, either. Old, *real* old, and always, always *craving*...

Except... Nah. I was just being goofy again. Stairwell was empty but for me and a couple humming light fixtures, drunk fireflies flickering against a grimy ceiling. Rumble of the train up ahead, echoing patter of the rain. Not even a sign of the Samaritan anymore.

The hinky feeling was gone quick as it crashed down on me, and there sure as hell wasn't anybody around to've sparked it. Not just tired now, but paranoid. Jumping at squat and shadows. Muttering at myself—and nothing nice, either—I climbed the rest of the stairs, growled my way past the few folks standing around on the platform, and slipped between the brown sliding doors. Clunk, hiss, screech, shudder, and the train was chug-a-lugging its way cross town.

Me, I planted my keister on a random seat and leaned my head back against the wall. I'd gotten real accustomed to the steady *clack-clack, thud-thud* of the L by now, enough so that it *almost* distracted me from the damn itch of being inside the whole technological contraption.

Clack-clack. Thud-thud.

The car was empty, 'cept for one gink down at the far end trying to pretend he *wasn't* completely out on the roof, and having exactly zero success with it. He was swaying faster'n the train was, and even one of you mugs coulda smelled the hooch wafting off him.

Couple stations passed. More screeching. More swaying. Boozehound got off at the third, looking unsure if this *was* his stop or not. Nobody else got on, not in this carriage, anyway.

Thud-thud. Clack-clack. My noggin rocking back and forth against the wall, almost a massage, lulling me to...

Wait one goddamn freakin' minute!

I bolted upright, a single step taking me to the middle of the car, already grabbing for the L&G. And all I could think, beyond gunning for a threat I *knew* hadda be near, was *When did I turn into such a fucking twit?*

No way, *no way* do I just suddenly decide I'm imagining

some danger. No way do I get a premonition as strong as the one I had in the stairwell and then just shrug it off. Uh-uh. That ain't me at all, and if you're wondering why I'm just now wising up when you knew something was off from the minute I talked about it, well, that's why I kept hitting the whole "exhausted unto stupid" thing.

I've monkeyed with enough minds to recognize when it's been done to me. Even if sometimes, such as tonight, it's a bit of a belated recognition.

Right. Door.

I was hot enough—with whoever'd been shadowing me and with myself—that I forgot the mortal façade as I made for the next car. I didn't sway with the train anymore, instead adjusting faster, more minutely, than any human. Not a fraction of an inch of wobble in the L&G, now aimed and ready. I wasn't blinking anymore. Faintly, not so anyone else woulda noticed at first, the flickering of the lights started to change. Brighter than they shoulda been, almost daylight; then black as pitch, as if they were *projecting* dark. Slowing until each flicker matched the smack of my heels against the trundling floor. One of the bulbs, the newest and brightest, burst in a shower of sparks and slivers.

Makes me sound all tough and unshakable, don't it? Yeah, I'll come back to that in a minute.

The anger drained outta me just as quickly, though, fading into a sorta resigned futility even as I reached for the door handle. Three stations, with a fourth coming up long before I could cover the length of the train. Even if my tail had boarded the L at all, he (or she, or it, or any combination) could well be long gone. Even if not, well, I couldn't be sure I'd tumble to him (or her, etc.) no matter how careful I looked.

Grumbling some profanities that woulda got me burned at the stake in other times, I thumped back down onto one of the wood benches. The lights'd gone back to their normal stuttering, and I was even blinking again, like a good little human.

Still had my wand in hand, though. If I felt even a *tingle* of magic, someone was getting a mug full of disaster.

All that cursing up a storm, though? Squeezing the L&G until it creaked, lookin' for an excuse to shove some mojo down someone's throat? I was *tryin'* to stay angry, or at least focused.

Because my other option was scared, see? I ain't the toughest thing to ever come outta Elphame, but I got my fair share of power. Wasn't a whole lot out there could muck around in my mind too easy, and even less could do it without me at least suspecting something was hinky.

So who or what the hell had my trip to the Field gotten all riled up?

I didn't even question that this was related to the museum case. Coincidence follows us *aes sidhe* like a begging mutt, but not *that* much.

So who was keeping tabs on me? Herne? Nah, not his style. I don't figure I'd have noticed if he *was* shadowing me, and if I did? His method of handling it wouldn't be rooting around in my senses. Far as I knew Herne, his notion of subtle was a *small* blade through the pump 'stead of a big one.

Well, he did say there were others mixed up in... Whatever there was to be mixed up in.

And I still didn't give a hoot. Let 'em follow. Let 'em all see that I wasn't getting involved. Out of the game. Washing my hands of it, like Pontius Pilate after cleaning the cat box.

I was determined. Absolutely set in stone. I'd learn all about it after, maybe in one of the Otherworld Chicago's news rags. But I *was. Not. Involved.*

Once in Pilsen, it was a couple minutes' walk along wet sidewalks, past dingy brick facades made ghosts by street lights and the gleam of occasional passing flivvers, for me to get from the station to Mr. Soucek's building, where I hang my hat. And rapier. I could tell ya that I *didn't* spend the whole hike nervously tryin' to look over both shoulders at once, but we'd both know it for bullshit.

ARI MARMELL

Turned out, though, it wasn't *behind* me I hadda worry about.

'Bout half a dozen guys and gals, who you woulda thought were human but I knew better, loitered on the doorstep, blending in like Al Capone at a girls' finishing school. They all wore really pricy but totally off-the-rack glad rags—even the women sported suits—and every one of 'em turned to stare me down as I got near.

"You guys practice that?" I asked, then pointed at the fellow on the left. "Jack over here was half a step off-tempo."

I didn't slow. They didn't clear the way. This romp was edging up on interesting, and I had had a belly full of interesting already.

"Whatever it is, I ain't part of it," I said. "Seriously. Go chase your plot or enemy or dingus or whatever somewhere else."

They still didn't budge. At the top step, I actually bumped into the one jackass directly in my way.

"You can be a door," I said softly, "or a welcome mat. I'll give you to ten to decide which. Eight... Nine..."

Hands went under coats, theirs and mine both. If we were human, everyone woulda tensed right then; *we* just got really, really still...

"You really don't want this to get unpleasant, Oberon," said a voice from below.

"It's already unpleasant, bo." I turned to look behind me, edging to one side so I didn't completely lose track of Door-Mat in the process.

Cat standing below on the sidewalk was *aes sidhe*, same as me. I could see it in the expression, the ears, the same wiry build—though his hair was more autumn-leaf brown than sand—but most important, I felt it in the sheer energy gathered around him.

I didn't know him personally—odd, if he lived in Chicago (yours or ours), but not unheard of. He was younger'n me, though, which was good to know.

Course, he also had buddies.

"Then you don't want it to get any more so." He held up a brass amulet in one paw, letting me get a good eyeful as it shifted from a Celtic cross with Gaelic inscription to what looked for all the world like a copper's badge.

"My name is Raighallan—Officer Raighallan—and I am here with legal writ and authority of Their Honors Sien Bheara and Laurelline of the Seelie Court and municipal government of Chicago."

In other words, an Otherworld detective—or a soldier of the Court playing detective, anyway. Fucking swell.

"Take you long to memorize that?" I asked.

"And you," he said, ignoring my quip, "would be the exile currently going by the ludicrous moniker of Mick Oberon."

I kept my fingers from clenching into fists, but it took so much effort they creaked.

"I wasn't exiled. I left. And seeing as how you already called me by name, I ain't exactly bowled over that you know me. Whaddaya want, Raighallan? And also, sorry, can't help you."

"Where is it?" he demanded. "How much do you know?"

"I'm getting right tired of answering that question. I dunno. I dunno where it is, or even *what* it is. I don't *care* where it is or what it is! I'm not involved in any of this!"

"I don't enjoy being lied to, Oberon," Raighallan said, tone dropping toward dangerous. "My boss enjoys it even less."

Boss? None of the others reacted much to that, so I hadda assume he meant someone else, someone not here. Great.

"Think you probably should get used to it, in your line of work," I replied. "But I ain't blowing any smoke here."

He scoffed. I gotta say, the *aes sidhe* scoff real well. We've had a lotta time to get disdainful.

"So it was just a coincidence that you were at the museum?"

"No, genius, I was asked to look at it as a case. Some of us actually have to work to call ourselves detectives. I went, I did a solid up-and-down, I got the piss konked outta me by Herne the goddamn Hunter, and decided I wanted no piece of this action."

Yep, saw it. Just a flicker in his aura before he could hide it. He hadn't known Herne had gotten himself involved.

"Now," I continued before he could open his yap again, "can I go flop already? Or do I gotta get in two dust-ups tonight? 'Cause honestly, those are the only real options I'm offering. I'm done talking about having bupkis to talk about."

I think he mighta actually considered having his enforcers try to pound some additional knowledge outta me, but either he believed that I didn't know from nothing, or he figured there were other ways to find out. Instead, he slipped his badge back into his coat, tipped his hat—his ears hadda make the thing as uncomfortable for him as mine do for me—and turned away. Moment more, the others followed.

Hmm...

"By the way, Raighallan?" I called after him.

He looked back over his shoulder.

"Your people on the train were careless. I'd talk at 'em if I were you."

And there it was again, that flicker I only saw 'cause I'd spent years learning how to spot these things. He had no idea what I was jawing about.

So. Third faction.

"Just remember this is Court business, Oberon. You're making it harder on everyone—yourself most of all—if you stick your nose in. Keep out of it."

"I'm *trying* to keep out of it, if you saps would stop hauling me back *into*..."

Ah, screw it. They were making tracks, which is what I wanted.

I fumbled with the key, staggered inside, and don't even remember the stairs or the hall. I just remember slamming my door, jabbing the lock with the L&G so it *couldn't* open until I replaced the luck I'd ripped from it, and tumbling face-down on the mattress again.

Took me an awful long time to drift off, though. See, no matter how uninvolved I was, I couldn't help but wonder...

CHAPTER FOUR

She slunk into my office like a snake in a fox-fur-and-human stole, dress of forest green rustling and sliding as if it couldn't wait to be shed, and I really can't go on yapping this way, but I always *did* wanna start a sentence like that.

Anyway, lemme back up a few. Again.

For all my big talk about bunking a few days away, my body had other notions, and I'd woken up just an hour or so past noon. Thought about trying to pass back out, but I already had a couple cylinders up and running, and I knew it. Still kinda worn, still hurting from Herne's broderick, but not near as bad as last night. Guess snoozing had done me all the good it was gonna, for now.

So, after another ten minutes of cursing the bed, my body, and the world in general still didn't accomplish anything, I rolled my carcass up off the mattress. First, flick of the wand to patch up the damage to the door lock so I could, y'know, leave if I wanted. Next, quick trip to the not-so-icy icebox and then the not-so-hot hot plate for a slug of not-so-cold milk to get the other half of my motor running—hadda make a note to nudge Ron Maddox, regional manager of the Milkman's Local as they were missing deliveries a lot these days—and tried to suss out what to do with the day.

Long as it didn't involve spears or museums.

Go back to digging for Miles Caro, maybe? That was the only paying job I had just then, yeah, but… Wasn't as though the dead end I'd run up against yesterday had got any less dead. I really had nobody else to grill about him. Even my Mob guy'd come up empty—though, to be fair, he had a lotta stuff on his plate more family than Family right now.

Plus, I was startin' to wonder if I'd let myself get *too* wrapped up in digging for the gink. I shoulda maybe been payin' more attention to the Fae side of things, shoulda chased down some of those rumors I mentioned. Obviously, there *were* more of us in your half of Chicago than usual, and if something big was goin' down, it shouldn'ta caught me so badly by surprise. So yeah, maybe I'd already put more'n enough into the Caro case.

(I probably oughta take the time to put you wise, here. I'm talking about the Caro case 'cause it was on my mind, was what I'd been lookin' into when this whole shebang started. Other'n a quick bit of coincidence, though—which I'll get to later—it ain't tied up in everything else that happened. The whole racket wound up complicated enough; don't go trying to squeeze Caro into your mental map, too.)

Truthfully, though, I was a little unhappy at the idea of going out and sticking my beezer into too much of *anything* right now. If I bumped into Herne again, or whoever else, I didn't much expect them to buy it when I told 'em I was looking for something other'n their missing dingus. Since I didn't know enough to know how scared to be, I'd decided to play it safe and go for "a lot."

Which, since my place looked a lot like the aftermath of a hobo slumber party, left straightening up as my only good option.

Flogger on the coat rack, where gravity oughta tug *some* of the wrinkles out—the ones that were left I deemed the fittest of their species and worthy of survival. Shirt and slacks in a pile inside the compartment the Murphy bed folded into, followed by the bed itself—a few tongues of bed sheet stuck out from around the frame, as usual, but it'd do.

Quick splash-clean in the attached bathroom—can I just tell you, again, how swell it is not to sweat?—quicker climb into an outfit more or less identical to the last one, and I got to tidying.

Started with the nook where a big honkin' refrigerator woulda lived, if I'd owned a big honkin' refrigerator. Instead, it was empty with just a few thick spots of mildew growing in the corners. It was part of the process I used to make the whole niche into a special doorway when I needed it to be, but I didn't want it spreading, becoming too ugly, so step one was to clean around the edges. After that...

Well, you remember my place well enough, yeah? Cheap desk with a homicidal typewriter (I told you, you don't get to hear *that* story), cheaper chairs for me'n the guests, couple chests of drawers and filing cabinets. Not the *same* desk and chairs anymore—I'd been forced to replace those after my dust-up with Goswythe the *phouka*—but close enough for jazz. I'd even managed to scrub the bloodstains outta the rug since then. Amazing what shampoo, elbow grease, and a smattering of magic can do for the décor.

So, wiping and scrubbing and dusting, and I got all of about ten minutes' work behind me when I found myself lingering over the drawer.

The drawer. My collection of curios, bits and gewgaws I'd collected over the years in lieu of actual lettuce for a lotta my cases.

Old books. Old tools. Fragment of a mortar shell from the Great War. The secret last will and testament—and confession— of Ambrose Bierce. Old silverware with patterns of tarnish that *almost* formed legible runes. Of course, the switch to the old electric chair at Cook County, which I'd gotten from Assistant State's Attorney Dan Baskin earlier that year. And a couple dozen other nothings.

The whims of the Fae, I tell ya.

Most useless, all but worthless, to the untrained observer. But like I said before, symbols. Language of magic. Most of these I'd never done a thing with, probably never would. A few of 'em? Saved my life or solved cases.

You never know.

It all put me in mind of the museum again. Yeah, I admit it, I was curious. You blame me? Whatever was up, it was weird and it was big. I wanted to know. And I *really* enjoyed the notion of throwing the Seelie Court's "warning" back in their faces and giving them a notated list of where they could stick it.

I didn't wanna know *enough*, didn't wanna show them up *enough*, though. Probably just as well I—

And that's when the door opened and she slunk into my office like... Well, we been through that.

Just a tiny waft of perfume gusted ahead of her, attention-getting without making you wanna hawk something up. She wore a breezy cloche that matched the green dress so well it hadda be custom, and with that as a contrast, I couldn't at first tell whether her hair or lips were redder. Not that it was the easiest thing in the world to keep my attention on either, not between her deep, almost violet peepers and... other things.

Yeah, I'm dwelling. I know it, I ain't that dumb. But this was a hinky experience for me, dig? She was gorgeous, sure, but I'd seen gorgeous before. Even gone a bit dizzy for a mortal woman before, especially during the old days when I was more like your legends make us out to be, and figured mortals were mostly toys. I ain't proud of that, but I won't make excuses.

Point is, attraction's one thing, but I'd never been quite bowled over this way, not by a human, anyway. Not that I coulda told you that at the time. I wasn't thinkin' clear enough to realize I wasn't thinkin' clear.

Think I forgot to keep up the whole blinking act, but if she glommed to anything weird, she kept it to herself.

"Mr. Oberon?" she asked. Yep, throaty, intense, exactly how she *shoulda* sounded, looking like that.

And hey, she got my name right! That made two in a row, pretty sure I was halfway to tying the record with that.

Not my first thought at the time, though, savvy?

Play it cool, Mick. Just another visitor, maybe a client, no matter how juicy a tomato she might be.

"That's me," I said just a bit too quickly. "C'mon seat. Have an in."

She blinked once, almost languidly.

"Pardon?"

Well done, jackass. Good going. Cool as summer and smooth as gravel.

I made myself grin, flashed some chompers at her.

"Sorry. Caught me in the middle of reminiscing." The drawer trundled along its runners and clanged shut as I shoved at it. "How can I help you, Mrs....?"

"Miss. Webb. Ramona Webb."

Miss. *Good.*

...Mind on business, Micko.

"Please have a seat, Miss Webb."

She did just that, making the chintzy chair look *real* good all of a sudden. Leaning back, she crossed her knees, rested her purse—*also* a pitch-perfect match for the outfit—in her lap, and gave the office a good once-over. She didn't look *unimpressed*, anyway, which was about the best I could hope for with this flop.

"I've never had cause to visit a private investigator before," she admitted, turning her attention to me as I settled opposite her. "Do you all work out of such... intriguing conditions?"

"Nah. I'm classy. Most PIs just live in a cheap mess."

That put a small smile on her button, which was more'n enough to tell me I wanted to see a bigger one. But sittin' at the desk had also helped me gather what was left of my wits, get out ahead of the stupid.

"What is it you need, Miss Webb?"

"Ah. Well, I..." She fidgeted with the purse, not quite as

calm and collected as she was making out. She finally snapped it open, pulled out a pack of Old Golds and a book of matches. She had the snipe in her lips and a match in her fingers before I could manage a word edgewise.

"Ah, I really prefer people not smoke in here." I said it reluctantly, but I said it. Smell lingers for *weeks*, to my schnozz.

"Oh." She paused, peering around once more. "Yes, I can imagine you would."

Then I *did* get a big smile—teasing, apologetic, and mocking all at once, and if you can suss out how she did that, you go right on ahead and put me wise, 'cause I got no idea—right before she struck the match and lit her cigarette anyway.

I couldn't help but laugh, which woulda ruined any further attempt to get her to snuff the thing even if I'd planned on making one. Anyone else woulda gotten an earful—maybe even a snoutful—over it. Not her.

Hell, maybe I'd just been all on my lonesome for too long.

"Not married, you said." It wasn't a question.

One last smile, the tiny one again, and then she got all serious.

"Mr. Oberon, I was given your name by… a source I trust very highly." She inhaled deep, then turned away from me before blowing out a lungful. "I need your help, as much as I don't care to admit it."

Yeah, I imagined she *wouldn't*, at that.

"Gimme the skinny," I said. "Whole thing."

For a confident, classy dame, her story was a pretty mundane one. Disappointingly, even.

Lemme just give you the gist, 'cause the conversation itself—while keen in the moment, given who I was yapping with—really ain't much to hear about.

Ramona's punk of a cousin needed a place to flop, and even though she knows he's trouble, she's too softhearted to give him the brush-off, so he's bunking at her place. He's already loitered a lot longer'n she'd agreed to, but, again, can't bring herself to give him the bounce.

Midst of all this, Ramona's ex-flame shows up. (Yeah, it bugged me to hear that, and the "ex" part only simmered me down a little.) This gink's more of a lowlife than the cousin. Him, she's all set to give the bum's rush, with her cousin's help, but he's begging her, damn near on his knees. He's got some thugs gunning for him over a "bad investment," and he just needs a place to hole up for a few hours, maybe one night.

So, all right. Her place is getting crowded, but Ramona decides he can have *one* night. He gives her any grief about making tracks tomorrow, though, and it's just a matter of whether the coppers or the guys he owes find him first.

Yeah, you've already tumbled to a few dozen ways this could turn sour real fast, ain't ya?

Buncha thumps and crashes and other sounds that just never bode anything positive wake her up a little before dawn. Her cousin's tearing the place up like he's misplaced the lien on his soul and Satan's due for breakfast. The ex-beau is long gone, of course. Took with him a whole sack-full of Ramona's jewelry, some silver, other dribs and drabs, and every bit of cash in the place.

Unfortunately, "every bit" includes a thick wad of rhino that her cousin was holding onto for some of the less savory Joes that *he's* in deep with. Kid throws a complete ing-bing, panics, and takes the run-out, leaving Ramona holding the bag.

"I don't know precisely who my cousin was indebted to," she told me, finishing up her account. "Whoever they are, they don't seem to have any better idea of where he's gone to than I have—but they certainly know where *I* am.

"Mr. Oberon, my car's been broken into multiple times, my home at least once while I was out. I can't prove it, but I'm *quite* sure I've seen the same fellow following me on multiple occasions. I don't think I have enough to go to the police, and, even if I did, I hate the thought of preferring charges on family.

"I can raise the money to pay these people off. I just need some time to do it. I need someone—I need you—to make sure

I have that time. Find either Jeremy or Cliff if you can—feel free to send Cliff right up-river, the louse, but please don't do anything with Jeremy without talking to me first. See if you can figure out who Jeremy owed, who's stalking me. But most of all, I need you to keep me safe long enough to get these hoodlums off my back!"

Judging by how slack her jaw went, my first question caught her completely unawares. "You sure the guys keeping tabs on you are the same ones Jeremy got in deep with? No chance it's something unrelated, something personal to you?"

"I..."

It took her a spell, and a long drag off a newly lit cigarette. (The third, if it matters to you. And yeah, I was counting.)

"I don't see how. I can't think of anyone who'd have it in for me. I have no other recent breakups, and while I have some money, I'm hardly loaded. Besides, don't you suppose the timing suggests...?"

"Sure it does, doll. Coincidences happen, though."

So, what now? Did I wanna take this gig? Felt bad leaving off the search for Caro, but maybe what I needed was a little time away to let that one stew a bit. Sleep on it for a while, so to speak. And it wouldn't hurt my case with Raighallan or Herne any if they saw me all wrapped up in something unrelated to their own shindig. And...

And who did I think I was freakin' kidding? I'd have probably talked myself into working as a live-in maid and trash hauler if she'd asked nice enough. It shoulda bugged me that I was reacting to her that strong, but it didn't. And I liked it well enough that it didn't bug me that it didn't bug me.

That sentence makes sense if you been there. If you haven't, no words in any language are gonna clear it up any.

"All right, Miss Webb. You got yourself a private shamus."

A whole pillar of tension snapped inside her and crumbled away. I swear not just her shoulders, but the cigarette also, sagged in relief.

"Thank you." Not a whisper, quite, but the softest I'd yet heard her.

It made the next bit harder.

"Uhh, Miss Webb..."

"Ramona, please." That smile again. The room tilted.

That was quick, but I sure wasn't gonna raise a stink about it.

"Ramona, we do need to discuss—"

"Oh, of course!" She stabbed out the butt in an ashtray that I only now realized she'd produced from her purse halfway through her story—real observant, detective—and reached for a bankbook. "How much?"

"Ten simoleons a day oughta cover basic expenses," I told her. "After that, we'll call it..."

Boom. Whim time. Came over me just that sudden. They almost always do.

"Any sorta heirloom. Don't have to be worth anything, just has to have belonged to one of your parents."

And whaddaya know, she balked. I mean, I get that it's a hinky demand, and that mighta accounted for the hesitation, but...

"That's rather a peculiar request, Mr. Oberon."

"I'm rather a peculiar detective."

The nail on one forefinger tapped the bankbook, the other the corner of her lower lip. It was easier not to be mesmerized by the first than the second.

"I'm afraid I'm genuinely uncomfortable with that," she said finally. "Surely you can accept more traditional payment? As I said, I'm not *wealthy*, but..."

I wanted to say yes, more'n I'd wanted anything in a long while. Almost *did* say yes, caught the word in my throat right before it made a break for it.

But I been living a good while, and Fae who don't learn to pay attention to their whims and instincts, no matter *what* they're feelin'... Well, they *don't* often live a good while. I could only shake my head, much as I came over blue to do it.

"I'm *real* sorry, Ramona. Gimme a mo and I can jot down some references for you."

Wow, did her face go cold. As in, "I wasn't keen on leaning in any closer in case I got frostbitten" kinda cold.

"You cannot possibly be serious."

So, yeah, not just her expression, then. If she kept talking in *that* tone of voice, I'd hafta thaw out the milk to dip my bill later on.

"They're good guys. More professional'n me, frankly. You'll be taken care of."

She glared, sharp enough to shave with, and I kinda wanted to crawl under the desk and bang my head on the underside 'til I forgot this whole damn day. Upset as I mighta been, though, she wasn't pulling anything over on me. I could taste her uncertainty and, yeah, worry beneath the ice queen "I am accustomed to obedience!" routine.

'Sides, I'd mastered that routine, and a thousand like it, before I'd ever even thought about ditching the Court.

I'd call it a clash of wills, but there was no clash to speak of. She might have me all tied up, turned around, and off my game, but she still had no real chance at staring *me* down.

"I want *you*," she said finally, and I pretended I didn't near trip over my own feet at her choice of phrasing. (Yeah, I *was* sittin' down at the time. So what?) "It was your name I was given. I don't trust anyone else."

"I'm right here, doll. Still for hire and everything."

"But…"

Ramona looked down at her purse, her fingers, and up again. That little quirk of a smile was back.

"All right, Mr. Oberon. You are *truly* odd, but you have a deal. It may take me a short while to dig something up that I'm prepared to part with, though. My relationship with my parents was, ah, complex."

Yeah, I coulda guessed *that* based on her relationships with everyone *else*. Figured that wasn't the most politic point to make, though.

"Mick," I said instead. "If you wanna be 'Ramona,' I gotta be 'Mick.'"

"All right… Mick." She scribbled something, stood—a move so effortlessly sinuous that she *had* to have practiced it—and passed me a check. "Five days' expenses in advance. Is that fair?"

"That'll do me just fine." I slipped the paper into a desk drawer. And pretty much forgot all about it, frankly. "When you get home, it'd be real helpful if you could gather anything either of these cats mighta left behind, no matter how unimportant it…" Why was she looking at me that way?

"Why're you looking at me that way?"

"I thought… Aren't you coming with me?"

It took putting spurs to my brain a couple times for me figure out what she meant, especially since I had a few preferences of my own.

"Miss—I mean, Ramona—I'm a gumshoe, not a bodyguard. I can't watch over you twenty-four seven. I got leads I hafta follow, I got other clients and responsibilities…."

"Keeping me safe was part of the deal," she insisted, knuckles whitening on her purse.

"Yeah, but I *do* that by *finding*…" I hadda sigh, there, even though it's a habit I picked up from you mugs. Like a bad virus. "Tell you what. You got a friend you can visit with for a few hours?"

"I do."

"All right. Gimme your address. Lemme spend the day digging up what I can—" *and what the police have* "—on your boys. I'll call on you this evening, with whatever evidence I've gathered, give the place a thorough up-'n-down, and set up shop for the night.

"In a different room, of course," I added—kinda sorrowfully, I gotta confess. "You got no cause to worry over my behavior, but whatever anyone thinks if they spot me there, that's on you to deal with."

When she nodded at that, I went on. "Once I got a sense of how things are over there, what your situation is, we'll talk about what's necessary to keep you safe and sound. If it looks to me like you *do* need somebody, I'll stick around as much as I can, and I got pals can keep an eye on you when I can't."

Another nod, slower this time. "That... will do for now, I think," she agreed.

"Swell." I put a hand just behind her shoulders, guiding her toward the door. "Don't you fret, doll. I'll figure this out, and you'll be fine."

She'd put one toe through the doorway when she turned, gripping my forearm nice'n tight.

"Mr. Ob— Mick, thank you. I don't understand you, entirely, and I know I got a bit silly about your fee, but... thank you. I feel better already."

Gave me a kinda glow-feeling, hearing that from her, but it *did* remind me of something.

"Why *were* you so set on me personally, anyway? Who recommended me?"

"Someone I trust."

"Yeah, but—"

"Someone who asked me not to involve him, Mick. Please. I'll tell you afterwards, all right? Not now."

I coulda *made* her tell me. She already wanted me on her side, was still juggling worry and relief. Woulda taken almost no emotional nudge at all, a quick dip behind her eyes for a few seconds. Wouldn't need the L&G, and she probably wouldn't even recollect that it hadn't been her notion to sing in the first place.

It wasn't just nosiness tempting me, either. Mystery man sends her my way but don't want me knowing his name? Yeah, that's raising some suspicions no matter how dizzy anyone's got me.

On the other hand, I do know a *lot* of folks on both sides of the law, and both sides of "natural," who have good reason not to want anyone tumbling to their connection with me. Not everyone's as open and good-natured about it as Pete. So this *could* be entirely square.

Nuts to it. Wasn't gonna start this relationship off— Case! Wasn't gonna start this *case* off by mucking around with the client's free will. If it turned out important, I'd look into it later.

I know, I'm usually more curious'n that. Whaddaya want from me? Didn't have enough room left in my noggin for curiosity at that moment.

"Okay," I said, a million years later. "Tell me after."

Grip tightened, smile widened, and I really thought she was gonna plant one on me. Just a peck to the cheek, not full on, but still...

Seems she was just as thrown, since she jerked herself up straight just after startin' to lean in. Her gaze dropped, locked hard on the rug, but her cheeks had gone red as her hair.

I'm a creature outta myth and faery tale. I'm sorta obligated to buy into love at first sight and all that bunk.

This wasn't that, not exactly. This wasn't anything I recognized.

Was I *smitten* with the dame? Was that even possible for me? I'd been in love, been in lust, been purely possessive, but never any of this stammering schoolboy crap.

Schoolboy? For the luvva Shakespeare, I'm older'n most school *subjects*!

Time to behave like it.

I snaked a hand back, yanked my coat off the rack, and pasted an idiot grin across my puss.

"I'll walk you out," I said.

Maybe *tomorrow* it'd be time to behave like it.

When we stepped out into the hustle and bustle of the day—a sidewalk stream of brims dipping, coats and skirts dusting the grime off people's heels, perfumed up the keister by coughing flivvers—we were linked. No, I mean literally. Her right elbow hooked in my left, my other hand on her wrist. All nice and chivalrous and not at all way too personal. Also, I'm really a goblin, and I got an ocean-front property on a bridge to sell you. In Elphame.

You know, I don't even remember taking her arm? I just discovered it, like it was part of the weather waiting for us out there. Cool'n breezy, no rain at the moment, but with sporadic downpours of hand-holding.

She said something by way of goodbye, something I didn't catch. I wasn't much paying attention to the words, more interested in her voice, the look in her—

Oh, goddamn it, Mick!

I *wasn't* paying attention. It took me until she was on her way, that deep verdant dress waving its own real nice farewell, to realize that my distraction came from more'n her feminine wiles, no matter how... uh, wily.

My buddy the shadow was back, and tryin' to play with my grey matter again.

Coulda been anyone in the crowd, wandering by, loitering around, maybe a passenger in one of the passing tin cans. But I felt it, now, and the minute I did, it got worse. Way worse.

Eyes on me, watching, studying. Eyes I sure as hell didn't *want* on me. Or anywhere near me.

More than any of the redcaps or *sluagh* I had stared down in the past, maybe even more than Herne last night, they made me wanna hole up. Hide.

Made me feel like prey.

Which is why I stayed right fucking put, mitt hovering near the holster under my coat, reading everyone who came near like the morning edition. I don't *appreciate* being made to feel that way, savvy?

Whoever it was, he/she/it wasn't gonna muck about in my head again, either. I was set for that, this time. There ain't a real strong border between willpower and magic, and I was doing my damnedest to scuff it out completely. Sure, I suppose they coulda just left and I'd have been none the wiser, but that was their *only* option if they wanted to hide from...

The throng just parted, all casual, dance choreography by Moses, so I could see him across the intersection, standing on the far curb.

He... didn't much wanna hide from me.

Didn't much care about blending in at all, seemed like.

Guy was straight outta news clippings from down south. Brown trousers, lighter brown coat over a shirt white enough to project movies on, and none of that mattered a plug nickel. No, it was the wide-brimmed hat and the ink-black cheaters hiding his eyes—somehow almost reflective in the sun, despite their darkness—that marked him out.

Not sure why, as he wore no visible tin, but something said "lawman" to me. Sheriff's deputy, somewhere in Texas, I'd guess.

'Cept, much as he looked like it, he wasn't that at all, either. I couldn'ta told you why, but I swore I was looking at a façade, a hollow shell over... over God knew what. Like the clean-shaven chops, big friendly grin, and sunglasses were all part of some heavier mask.

He stared at me. Don't ask me how I could tell, but I knew. And everything I'd felt a minute ago came back at me with reinforcements. My stomach curled, fear and guilt mashing into a thick emotional stew.

Not Unseelie. Not Herne. This was something... *else*. Something primal. Something didn't think like we did, want like we did.

Something predatory. I was a rat, starin' down a cobra, and if I blinked...

His smile stretched wide, teeth gleaming from across the street. He lifted a hand to his brim, in greeting, I guess, and turned away.

Between one passing pedestrian and the next, he was gone. I didn't bother racing after him. What'd be the point?

I really wanted to slug someone, about then.

This was bad, *real* bad. Whatever was happening in my city, Herne wasn't even the worst of it. He'd said as much, but who're you gonna believe, yeah?

I'd made the right call, gettin' out of it. Now I just hadda convince everyone *else* of that. I had my own problems, my own case—complete with much more pleasant distractions—and if I got hauled into whatever the fuck this was, I was gonna be *way* over my head, dealing with people I ain't *nearly* big enough to handle. That, or else...

Or else I'd fix things so I *wasn't* over my head, and that'd be even worse. There are reasons—good, solid, *important* reasons—why I'm Mick Oberon now. *Just* Mick Oberon.

I can't afford to let myself *remember* the sortsa things I could do before I chose Mick, let alone actually *do* 'em. Always said I'd die before I let that happen, but... I still didn't know what was at stake here. What the Sam Hill *was* this thing that had everyone so hot'n heavy to get their meathooks on it?

Ah, nuts. I had my own business. Hadda put a temporary bow on the Caro hunt, let his people know I'd hit a wall, and I was happy to keep lookin' but did they wanna keep payin'? Needed to jaw a bit with Pete, too, or maybe Detective Keenan, find if they had anything on Ramo—my client's problem guys.

And I hadda gussy myself up some before I saw Ramona again. It wouldn't do to arrive at her place wearing everyday... Now wait, why not? What the hell made me think *that*?

Well, whatever I was going to be doing, I wasn't in any way hiding from my mysterious southern lawman. It is, on the square, absolute coincidence that everything that needed doing before wandering over to Ramona's digs that night was stuff I could accomplish from inside the office or—uncomfortable as it was for me to use, thanks to the "fire ants in the ear canal" sensation it always left me with—the hallway payphone.

What? No, it really *was* coincidence!

Really.

CHAPTER FIVE

Coincidence or not—close your head, I don't wanna hear anymore about it—I'd wrapped all that up neat as it was gonna get right about the time the sun set. I hadn't dug up anything on Ramona's "gents" at the clubhouse, but that didn't mean much. Lotta cut-rate thugs don't got records, and even if they had 'em, no guarantee they were filed in *this* precinct. It'd take some extra hocus-pocus—don't have the connections there I got with the police—but I'd check the courthouse tomorrow.

As for tonight...

I'd compromised, wardrobe-wise, settling for one of my "better end of normal" get-ups. (Fact that I only had one set of real formals, and I wasn't sure when I'd last had it laundered, mighta played some part in that decision.) I gathered up the L&G, threw my coat around my shoulders, and—grousing—pulled my hat over my hair. I hate the damn thing; always chafes the tips of my ears. (Or just "ear," when one of 'em's still a little shorter than it's supposed to be.) But I figure, out and about on the town at night, when it's been chilly and wet, in a semi-respectable neighborhood like Ramona's? I'd stand out without it, and I didn't think standing out was all that wise.

Gave some thought to toting along a shiv, too—by which I mean my full-sized, centuries-old rapier. This *was* in part a protection gig, after all. But, nah. Little unwieldy to schlep across town, especially with that whole "sticking out like a sore moose" thing I just mentioned. The wand'd be enough; always had been.

Almost always. And if it wasn't—if, say, that thing behind the hat and sunglasses decided to butt in—the rapier sure as hell wouldn't be worth squat, either.

Anyway, I didn't want Ramona spooked anymore'n she was already.

No real rain, just a slick, sopping kiss carried on the wind. Guess the drops'd all gotten too wiped out to travel on their own and had hitched a ride.

Wasn't too late, so the streets weren't exactly empty. I walked past, dodged around, and nodded my head to any number of people, all of whom did the same to me. Footsteps splattered small puddles that had sorta just oozed out of the damp as opposed to accumulating the way water's supposed to. Lamps—head and street—painted the wet roads in yellows and the buildings in shadow. Lots of cats hunched, tryin' to keep the chilly breeze from sneakin' down their collars. *I* hunched away from the itchy buzz around me, doing my damnedest to ignore the power lines and phone lines, the flivvers; the radio waves seemed especially aggravating that evening.

I usually didn't have *too* much bother riding the L all over Chicago, but I was gonna struggle with it tonight. Sometimes I just come over extra-sensitive to all the hooey you guys've added to the world in the past decades. It happens. Those days I stay home, or I suck it up and deal.

I wish I could tell you that my extra sensitivity was *not* due, in any part, to frustration that the buzz and crackle and sting kept me from thinking hard about who it was I was going to call on. Truth is, though, I'd already spent half the day ruminating on that, and thinking about her was a habit I was quickly startin' to enjoy. So yeah, I wish I could tell you that— but I can't.

Funny thing, though? Flittery and fluttery as I was feelin', it didn't feel near as overwhelming as it had when she was actually sittin' across from me. Not like I wasn't eager as a puppy to see her, but it wasn't so all-encompassing. Hell, maybe the distraction of the world around me was even worse'n I thought.

I was still working on the "dealing with it" part when I crossed under the elevated tracks, wincing away from the electricity always flowing through 'em, and saw it.

Almost invisible in the shadow of the trestle, black blending with black—and not just physically, but spiritually. I heard a couple of rough snorts, the scrape of hooves on asphalt, and really hoped it was only horses rather'n something worse.

I could just make out the shapes, if I squinted right. Friggin' full-on four-horse carriage, pretty as you please. 'Cept it wasn't that pretty. The wood of the wheels looked rotten, spokes reinforced by layers of thick twine, and the silver trim on the handle around the windows was tarnished but good.

Polished or not, though, damn thing had about as much business here in Pilsen as I woulda had in…

Well, inside the creepy contraption, where I'd already decided I wasn't going. I turned my path some and kept walking.

Quick snap-sizzle of a matchstick and a small circle of red lit up the front of the coach. I couldn't get a good slant on the driver, up on his perch. Just an eyeful of long, really slender limbs in glad rags that looked better suited to a mortician than a chauffeur. But then, he wasn't the one who'd just lit up.

He wasn't the one I was *supposed* to see.

Lemme tell you, it don't matter how often you deal with 'em, fucking redcaps do not *ever* get any cuter.

Short, hunched, gnarled, and this bastard was even broader of shoulder'n most, meaning he was built like *two* stumps in a cheap suit. Skin was old leather, eyes were beady little coals, mouth was a jagged, craggy, canyon big enough to chomp a Great Dane in half. You figure I'm exaggerating, you ain't ever seen a redcap yawn.

Oh, and his hat, of course. A thick, wet, red, still beading up at the brim's edges and leaving a faint ring on the gink's melon anytime it shifted. The stains were enough for me to see clearly even in the match's tiny flare.

Fresh. *Real* fresh.

Which meant almost certainly human, not Otherworld. My fists and jaw went into a clenching contest.

I kept right on walking.

"You gonna make us get ugly over this, Oberon?" Those hideous chompers scraped across each other with every syllable. I might as well have been booshwashin' with a grain mill.

"Too late for that, ain't it?" I asked.

"You're a riot. Hop in."

"One: No. Two: You guys ain't exactly blending in with the locals in that thing. Three: No."

The redcap stepped away from the coach, enough that the nearest street light brightened him up a hair. Wasn't much of an improvement. It *did* gimme a pretty clear slant on the jumbo-sized meat cleaver hanging at his waist, and the brass Otherworld Tommy dangling loosely from his left mitt.

It had a bayonet on it, too. Nice touch.

"Don't be stupid about this," he growled.

"Uh, if you think the stupid choice here is *not* getting into an Unfit carriage, we're working under a *real* different set of definitions."

They *hate* being called that. The Chicago Unseelie, I mean. Even under the coat, I saw his shoulders tense, heard a creek as the driver—whatever he was—set himself to drop down and come help his pal. Even the horses, if they *were* horses, got agitated, their stomping and snorting taking on a more deliberate, *hungrier* air.

Well, fine.

Wouldn't be the easiest match in the world, but I could take 'em.

Probably.

If I kept on my toes. Hadda be careful of bystanders, though. Still early enough that there were a decent number of 'em, and while not a mug had turned our way—we were hidden by some enchantment on the coach, I'm sure—that wouldn't do anyone a whole lotta good where stray lead's concerned.

Or stray magic.

I was just about to go for my piece, when the redcap straightened—much as his kind can, leastaways—and took a deep breath. Trying to simmer down? Patience ain't normally a redcap's strong point. Actually, I got no idea if it's a strong point, since I dunno if they ever even tried patience on for size. But even as he kept *almost* aiming the chopper at me, and his teeth ground hard enough to crush gravel, he spoke again.

"This ain't a setup, Oberon, and this ain't the time to be muleheaded. It's a sit-down, that's all."

"Oh, is it? Just some friendly gum-bumping with the Unseelie?"

"Yep."

Seriously, of all the friggin' nights... "Sorry. I got another appointment."

"Not anymore you don't."

Calm, Mick. Keep it calm.

"And just who is it wants to talk with me so bad?" I demanded.

"Herself."

Well, shit. I pretty much just deflated.

"She's here in *person*? In the mortal world?"

The redcap's grin woulda scared a crocodile into going vegetarian. "You wanna reconsider that invite?"

"Wish you'd phoned ahead," I told him. "I'd have worn my formal rags; this get-up ain't hardly appropriate."

The attitude was nothing but face-saving, though, and as I hauled my keister up and into the creepy old vehicle, him and me both knew it.

I'd figured on the redcap climbing up to perch next to the

driver, leaving me on my lonesome in the cab, but no such luck. He scrabbled in after me, hauled the door shut—which sounded awfully similar to a guillotine—and plopped himself down on the bench facing me.

Swell.

Always exciting to travel with someone whose strongest emotion is frustrated anger that they ain't allowed to slurp your guts down like pasta.

I'd been in one of these contraptions before. Last one was a two-horse (or two-kelpie, or whatever) deal, with some half-assed effort to spruce the thing up all modern. Whitewalls on a carriage? Just as dippy looking as you'd expect.

Not in here. Whatever else you could say about this thing—and I coulda said plenty—it didn't give a hoot about the fashion of the day.

Some of it was familiar, though. Same pungent scent of cleanser—they probably figured I'd rather take my chances challenging my escort's Tommy than hang around if the place had its usual bouquet—and same super-supple leather seats. Soft and apparently freshly upholstered.

I could tell because someone had missed an umbilical cord dangling down beside the bench, and it hadn't fallen off on its own yet.

Right about then, if someone had granted me one wish, I'd probably have wiped the whole goddamn Unfit from the face of two worlds. Fucking bastards.

Dunno if the gink saw my reaction and was rubbin' it in, or if it was just coincidence, but the redcap laid his Chicago typewriter on the seat beside him—not quite pointing my way, but not quite *not* pointing my way—and started to pick his teeth with what looked to be a *really* small rib bone.

I damn near hadda sit on my hands.

Minute or two of scraping, then he said, "You keep looking at folks that way, Oberon, it's maybe gonna get you hurt some day."

"It's gonna get *someone* hurt," I assured him.

"Would you've mouthed off this bad if you'd made your appointment this morning? Don't figure the coppers took it too good when you didn't show."

He wanted me to react, to get nervous, ask how he knew that. So I didn't.

Took some willpower, though.

We both shut our yaps at that point, just listening to the crack and crunch and thump of wooden wheels over what felt like every pothole, bump, and loose rock in Chicago. Not that I hadda hear any of it, since I *felt* every friggin' one. Damn bench was hard enough, even through the... leather. If I bruised easy as you, I'd have looked like a shaved baboon from the back.

I gotta confess, though, much as I'd rather not... Creepy and stomach-turning as the coach was, it was still nice, even calming, to be traveling across Chicago in something that *wasn't* trying to set my brain on fire.

Speaking of, the cabin was pretty well insulated but it wasn't soundproof. I heard the coughing of engines and the squeal of tires as cans of every make and model passed us on the roadway. Screeching brakes, though? Honking horns? Angry shouts full of impolite and either back-breaking or biblically suspect suggestions? Yeah, zip. I mean, I caught one here'n there from a distance, but nothing in the immediate vicinity.

Nothing to suggest a coach-and-four was trundling, pretty as you please, down a modern street.

"Nice glamour," I offered.

"Yeah, you're cute, too."

And that was the end of *that* conversation. I leaned back, crossed my arms, and realized that even neck-deep in whatever this mess was, I *still* thought mostly about Ramona when things got quiet.

A while longer'n the traffic started to fade. Fewer flivvers, and those there were sounded a good ways away. That bugged me. Wasn't *so* late that traffic shoulda just dropped off like that, and there was no way the carriage had carried us far enough to reach somewhere this quiet. Hell, we shoulda still been within sight of the Pilsen factories' smokestacks. It was hinky, and where the Unfit are involved, I *hate* hinky.

Course, where the Unfit are involved I hate everything, so that's maybe lacking some of the emphasis I meant to give it.

Engines and tires weren't replaced by silence, either. Rain started tap-dancing on the carriage roof. Driver must be getting awful uncomfortable out there. Boo-hoo. Now if the redcap would just go join him...

Tap-dance became a marching band. A charging army. A damn machine gun. The whole contraption trembled beneath what felt like gallon-size raindrops, and shook in the grip of a wind that mighta just been strong enough to pick me up and throw me if I'd been burning shoe leather out there.

"Windy City," yeah, but this was a bit much. I was damn near positive that I'd have heard something if there was a hurricane skulking up on Chicago. Which could really only mean...

Second to the right, and straight on 'til morning.

Not that I guessed we were headed anywhere quite as swanky as Barrie's Neverland.

"Thought you said she was on our side of the real," I accused.

"Naw, *you* said that." The redcap spit out something he'd finally dislodged with the rib. "I didn't say nothing about it."

"Yeah, I said it. And I don't make mistakes, so she's clearly in the wrong place."

Little shit mighta had something to say to that, but he didn't have the chance. Carriage trundled to a stop, and the door swung open all by itself, which is a neat trick if you're nine.

The trick *beyond* the door was more impressive, though, even at *my* age.

There hadda be a world out there—though which one was up for debate. The storm was a *wall*, whipped sideways and made solid by gusts that must've rivaled the first breath of

Creation, painted black by a night so thick I coulda stuck a straw in it and sucked up a few gulps.

It smelled like... after-death. That weird tang when whatever was left to decay *has* decayed, and there shouldn't be squat left to smell at all, but there is? Yeah. That.

My buddy with the bad dentistry said something that was probably rude, but I didn't catch it over the wind.

And that's about when I got wise. *Not* wind, nuh-uh. A gale of souls rotten inside and out, howling and screaming through rains they couldn't feel, rains made poison by the touch—or rather, the *un*-touch—of the profane.

Sluagh. Dead mortal spirits half-born again as Fae, for reasons even the oldest and wisest of us had never really understood. A flock of specters; the Host of the Damned.

One of 'em, anyway. It's a sad and scary fact of life and death in Elphame that the Damned assemble in a *lot* of different hosts. Maybe they get bored easy.

Whatever kinda reality might or might not've been out there, beyond the *sluagh*-ridden storm, it wasn't uninhabited. Two figures coalesced outta the dark, and if you still suppose, by now, that I'm usin' words like "coalesce" metaphorically, you need serious lessons in paying attention.

First one was an old geezer, real grandfather sort. Tall, thin, smooth-shaven, sporting silk duds that shoulda been totally soaked through but only looked vaguely damp. His smile was kind, friendly, which meant he was anything but.

Course, I already knew that. I'd seen him, or one just like him, before.

Boggart. Nasty as they get.

Wasn't him I was worried about.

The boggart held an umbrella off to the side, looking for all the world as though he were taking his granddaughter for a walk, and just tryin' to keep her dry. He scooted forward so his companion could climb into the coach without getting her 'do all ruined. Close enough that I could see the umbrella was made of baby blankets, stitched together over a copper frame.

God, I hate these fucks. And at the time, none more so than…

"Lady Eudeagh," I greeted her, correcting myself to "Boss Eudeagh" at her sideways glare.

"Mr. Oberon." She sat down beside the redcap and waved her elderly escort over to my side of the carriage. I kept my grumbling in my head and scooted over.

"Mr. Téimhneach, Mr. Oberon. Oberon, Téimhneach."

I offered my new seatmate a half-nod.

"I'd say I'm pleased to meetcha…"

The boggart's smile, the twinkle in his peepers, never faded.

"But we would hate to start off by lying to one another, would we not?"

"Something like that."

Eudeagh kept right on talking, as though her goon 'n me had just become best palls. "I trust you and Mr. Grangullie need no formal introduction at this point? He's taken good care of you, I hope?"

I didn't even look at the redcap. I didn't *need* to. You ever been around anyone whose grin you could *hear*? Can't say I recommend the experience.

"He hasn't made me knock him off, so I guess that's something," I said.

"Indeed."

For a few tics we just kinda watched each other, swaying a bit as the carriage started forward again.

Boss Eudeagh. Leader, sovereign, *Capo di Tutti Capi* of… well, not the *entirety* of the Chicago Unseelie, but certainly the single biggest outfit in their whole loco setup.

Most of us called her "Queen Mob," though I'd decided not to say so to her face. No idea how she'd take it. (I occasionally wondered how the real deal, Queen Mab, would've reacted to Eudeagh's moniker, if she'd still been alive to hear of it. Maybe it woulda struck her as funny. Maybe she wouldn't have cared—Eudeagh mighta been a big cheese here, but in the Old

World she wasn't much of anybody—and maybe she'd have hunted down the first gink to've made the joke, flayed him alive, and choked him with the skin of his own elbow. Mab always did make the rest of us look collected and predictable.)

Hell, getcha mind back in the present, Mick. The dead ain't your problem right now.

She hadn't changed much since I'd seen her last, not that I expected she would have done. Mighta come up to my waist, if she was standing in heels. Hair black as her soul, and a whole lotta curves, held in place by a slick violet number that *had* to have been woven around her to fit like that.

And two eyes, for the moment, thank Heaven.

In fact, now that we were close enough for a good up-and-down...

"You hurt?"

She blinked at me, then—when I pointed—she reached a fingertip to feel the smear of dried blood by her left peeper.

"Oh." She spit the glass eye out, letting Téimhneach scramble to catch it before it hit the floor. A fat, wormy tongue excreted itself from between the newly revealed teeth, licking the smear away. "Thank you for your concern, Mr. Oberon, but no, I'm fine. It's not *my* blood."

Think I told you before that the *aes sidhe* don't vomit? Yeah, that's the only reason I didn't. Shoulda just kept my dumb trap shut.

"Kinda surprised the rain didn't wash that away," I said, mostly 'cause I felt I hadda say *something*. "Can't imagine blankets keep you all that dry."

"All a matter of what you grease them with."

"Oh."

Yeah, *really* needed to keep my trap shut around these monsters. Seemed like every time I didn't, I learned something I was a lot happier not having in my head. Part of me wanted her to just get on with it, spill what this was about.

The part of me that already had a pretty strong notion of

what she wanted told that first part to close its head and keep her jawing about *anything* else.

We hit a particularly big bump, making Eudeagh scowl, and I guess she decided on her own it was time to cut the bunk. She squinted her right eye, looked at the glass orb in the boggart's hand, and then spit out the other fake.

Wouldn't want a mismatch, would we? Might not be stylish.

She smiled with all three pairs of lips and started to talk, switching mouths in the middle of sentences or even, now'n then, halfway through a word.

"I require a service from you, Oberon. It may keep you busy for some time."

"I'm flattered, but I'm right in the middle of another—"

"I'm calling in my marker."

Shit. Not unexpected shit, but still. *Shit.*

Short version, for you bunnies with bad memories, is that the Unseelie Court helped me out a short while back, when I needed some leverage in Elphame to find a missing kid. Which meant I owed them—owed her—and shirking a debt ain't something the Fae make a habit of. Bad things happen to us if we try. Real bad.

No point even in arguing it. If she'd decided whatever she wanted was worth cashing in with me to get it, I wasn't gonna sweet-talk her into postponing.

"All right. What do you want?" I asked.

As if I didn't know, what with the timing and all.

Please don't say it, please don't say it...

"I'm quite certain, by now, you've heard something about a spear?"

Fuck. She said it.

"Yeah," I groused, "I heard about it. Already got a good solid broderick from Herne, and a really annoying visit from the other side of your tracks, over the whole thing. I told them all I was out of it."

If Eudeagh was at all surprised to hear of the Hunter's or the

Seelie Court's interests, she didn't show it. Not that I figured she didn't already know.

"Then I fear I'm making a liar out of you, Mr. Oberon. You are most definitely *in* it."

Again I wanted to try to argue my way out, and again I decided it wasn't worth the stress. Not when I already knew it'd be a trip for biscuits to even try.

Instead, I asked, "Why? Why's this dingus got everyone so worked up?"

"It's one of the old relics. Enchanted."

Well, yeah, I'd figured something along those lines. But it still didn't add up.

"They ain't common anymore," I told her, as if she didn't already know, "but there used to be a fair bunch, back in the old days. And I gotta tell you, most of 'em weren't all that impressive, except to mortals without the tiniest knowledge of magic in their primitive noggins. Not even sure how useful most of 'em would be today, honestly. I think the whole lot of you mugs are wasting your time."

And mine.

Didn't say it aloud, but I'll bet you a dime she heard it anyway.

"Unless," I added, leaning in, "there's something you're not telling me?"

Grangullie snarled when I moved, reaching for the cleaver at his belt, but Eudeagh stopped him with a wave. The redcap grumbled, but obeyed.

"Mr. Oberon, you wouldn't *believe* how many things I'm not telling you. And you don't need to know them. In this case, however, there's not a great deal to keep from you. You're quite right that we wouldn't have looked twice at this spear a thousand years ago. And you may well be right that whatever enchantment it boasts could prove of precious little use in this... *modern* world." The revulsion in her tone was thicker'n the storm outside.

Well, thicker'n it had been. Storm had passed a while ago, and I could hear the growl and toot of distant flivvers again. And, almost inaudible on top of everything else, hoofbeats. Not from the horses pulling us along, either, but to either side of us.

Looked as though we'd picked up an escort when Queen Mob climbed aboard.

"If that's the case—" I began.

"Because none of us can allow any of our *rivals* to have it, can we? What if we're wrong? What if the spear's magic yet holds some use of which we're unaware? No, better safe…"

"Than skewered," I finished for her. I leaned back and thought, not bothering to blink or fidget since I didn't need to hide what I am from anyone here.

Mostly I thought about how to take a clean sneak from this whole deal, but, like I said, I had squat in the way of loopholes.

Now, I'm nobody's sap, see? She was feedin' me more lies than a public defender. No way was this just a precaution; no way was everyone goin' to all this trouble for just "some relic." Either this spear was more'n she was sayin', or something else was going down. Maybe both.

But knowin' all that didn't make my current position any less bent-over.

"Fine," I said eventually. "I try to find this pigsticker for you and we're square. Debt's paid."

"Ah, no."

Gotta admit, I didn't expect that. "No?"

"Your task isn't to *try* to find the spear, it's to *bring me* the spear. I don't give a chewed marmot how hard you *try*. You fail? You still owe me."

"*What?*"

I was outta my seat, standin' straight as I could without cracking my melon on the ceiling.

"You'll get my best effort, 'boss,' but you are *not* gonna hold me accountable for shit beyond my control. That's totally friggin' un—"

Grangullie was standing, too, bayonet pressed against my gut. The boggart was somehow looming *over* me, even though my head was pressed against the ceiling. Goddamn shapeshifters.

I even heard the hoofbeats get louder on the street outside, like whatever was escorting us had moved in close. *Real* close.

Eudeagh hadn't budged, hadn't flinched, just looked at me—well, whatever her equivalent of "look" is—and waited.

Well, wasn't this a fine jam of a pickle of a mess?

In a Fae conclave, I mighta been able to make an argument that Eudeagh's demands went too far, that her interpretation stretched the bounds of what I could be expected to owe. Or maybe not. We do a lotta grey areas, us Fae.

Problem was, I didn't think she'n her boys would be inclined to just step aside for me to leave if I demanded an arbiter. In these confines, I didn't think much of my chances in a dust-up, especially not knowing what was waiting for me outside.

But if I agreed... Well, that was it. I'd be bound by her interpretation, even if I didn't think it was legit.

Which left me exactly fuck all for options.

"... Un... unimportant and not worth arguing," I finished.

Pretty sure I'd had to have been three weeks pushing daisies to sound any *less* enthused, and I was so hot under the collar at the whole ugly mess of 'em that I'm amazed my head didn't catch fire. Far as I was concerned, what I owed 'em now was a heap more'n just a debt.

A lot less pleasant, too.

I slump-slid back into my seat, letting Téimhneach find his own way clear before I ended up in his lap.

"Fine. I bring you the spear, and we're clear."

"That," Eudeagh said, like I'd never popped my top, "is indeed what I'm offering."

Heh. "Offering." That's rich.

Yeah, I was sulking. Probably shoulda kept my chin up, made like none of this bugged me at all. Honestly, though, it didn't seem worth the effort. Somehow I wasn't feeling as if I owed the Unseelie much in the way of good manners.

"Yeah. Swell, Whatever."

"Oh, *good*!" The little twist actually clapped, smiling three times over. "I just knew we could come to some sort of agreement."

"Uh-huh."

"I won't be staying to oversee personally, of course. The technology in this world is ghastly, gives me a frightful headache. I've no idea how you stand it."

Now *I* smiled, even if there wasn't a lotta good humor in it.

"I prefer the neighbors here."

"Of course." Pretty sure she caught the insult and decided to ignore it. "Mr. Téimhneach will remain here. You report to him, and should consider his words to be mine."

"So I should ask him to say everything three times?"

She *kept* ignoring. Seemed pretty good at it.

"Should circumstances not permit you to speak with him," she continued, "you'll answer to Mr. Grangullie instead, who will also remain as Mr. Téimhneach's lieutenant—" I couldn't begin to tell you how, what with the whole no eyes thing, but I swear she suddenly focused on me, hard "—and enforcer."

Translation: Step outta line, gum anything up, and my next assignment would be carrying the redcap's bullets for him.

Judging by the smirk on Grangullie's trap, he was looking forward to it.

"You see," Téimhneach said, leaning in to put a "friendly" mitt on my shoulder, "why it would have been *such* a poor idea for us to get off on the wrong foot?"

The only right *foot is the one I'm gonna put so far up your keister you'll be gargling toenail for a week, you lousy...*

"Yeah, I hear ya."

Guess they were done, 'cause the carriage rattled to a halt.

"Last stop," Queen Mob announced cheerfully.

Door creaked open by itself again, which is even *less*

impressive when you're waitin' for it. This time, the dark beyond it was just a normal dark, a shabby side street somewhere in the Windy City, with old newspapers and broken boxes and a busted streetlamp.

Oh, and redcaps. A *pack* of redcaps. A few of 'em had brass Tommies, like their boss, though most of those lacked bayonets (and the one bayonet I *could* see was a steak knife). The rest had empty hands, but bulges in their badly fitting coats announcing *some* kinda gat or other. And all of 'em had cleavers, or similar hacking blades, dangling from their belts.

I stopped myself from looking to see how fresh the blood was soaking their hats. Wouldn't do me any good to know.

Climbed outta the carriage, which gave me a better slant on the welcoming committee, and... Huh. Not just redcaps, either.

Looming behind 'em, near invisible in the dark, were at least a couple of *dullahan*—tall, dressed in horseman's rags, and headless. They *also* cradled brass choppers, but these guns had special baskets built on 'em to hold the *dullahan*'s noggins.

They didn't often miss, I'll tell you.

I thought I heard something whooshing and swooping above, maybe a handful of *sluagh*, but no way I could see for sure without magic. And I didn't think the whole mass of walking psychosis around me would appreciate it much if I made any sudden moves.

"You cats startin' a social club?" I asked Téimhneach.

Damn boggart was *still* smiling, all affable and whatnot. I wanted to sock him one on the chin.

With a girder.

"We just wanted you to see, Mr. Oberon, what sorts of resources you... have at your disposal."

"At my disposal." Meaning ready and willing to dispose of me. "Right. Cute."

Huh. Carriage was gone. Okay, *that* was noteworthy; I shoulda felt *something* when it left, even through the veil.

And it was while I was hunting around for the coach that I

finally got wise to where I was. You'll have to excuse it taking so long. I didn't know the alley, couldn't see real far beyond it, so it took until I got a good whiff of the neighborhood, a solid sense of its aura, and a peek at the stars.

45th or 47th, somewhere between Racine and Halsted, if I wasn't turned around completely daffy by now.

"You mugs know that this ain't where you picked me up, right?" I said. "Least you could do is save me the trip you interrupted, not make it longer."

"But Mr. Oberon," Téimhneach said, sounding more like he was *reminding* me than *telling* me, "you're not heading to the same destination any longer."

"What? Listen, bo, I already told you I got a prior engagement—"

"And *we* already told *you*, no. You don't."

Nuts.

"You're here," he continued, "because we know you have a great many contacts and informants in this area. We wanted to make it as convenient as possible for you to begin tracking them down. Which you will do tonight. *Now*, in fact."

I was gettin' *real* steamed—if that street light hadn't already been broken, it probably woulda popped right about then. But there was still zip I could do about it.

"If you wanna tell us who you're meeting," Grangullie said, grinning, "we'd be happy to go give 'em your apologies."

The other redcaps snickered.

Deal with the goddamn devil.

Knew what I was getting into.

Knew I was gonna regret it.

Did it anyway.

I hadn't thought I had a choice, then, and I still don't. I'd do the same again, if I had to.

But yeah. I regretted it.

* * *

First thought to zip across my noggin wasn't about the case at all, not directly. It was to wonder if I oughta warn Pete'n the cops.

Remember what I said earlier? That I'd known the Unseelie hadn't been in town 'cause I'd have heard about the bloodshed? Yeah. Now they *were* in town. Not just Unseelie in general—even the best of 'em are bad enough—but redcaps. They treat murder the way you treat a pack of cards or a baseball game. And when they ain't mutilating and killing for fun, they're killing and mutilating 'cause they blew their lid over some tiny insult. Get enough redcaps in town, and you know they're on their best behavior if you can count the bodies without runnin' outta fingers'n toes.

If I *was* gonna tell the law, though, I hadda figure a way to do it that they'd actually believe. While I chewed on that, I might as well get to the job at hand.

So where to start? For a while I just sorta roamed the underside of town, tryin' to catch wind of my usual stoolies and gossips. Clubs'n speakeasies, hotels'n alleys, flophouses'n unlicensed fights. I was preoccupied, I admit, but not so much I couldn't do my job.

And I found nobody.

Lenai hadn't been spotted in days. Figured either something'd happened to her, or—more likely—she was just keeping her head down until this whole spear thing blew over. Pink Paddy *had* been to all his usual haunts lately, he just didn't seem to be at any of 'em *now*. I coulda tracked him down eventually, but that woulda been a case all its own. Didn't exactly have time for that.

Which meant, after I'd checked another few off the list, I was down to one.

I hadn't laid eyes on Four-Leaf Franky since I'd pounded the stuffing out of him—in a friendly sorta way—behind a soup kitchen some months back. Hey, gimme a break! I hadn't had time for the runaround he was trying to feed me. *Other* people didn't have time for it.

Anyway, he'd tried real hard to lie to me. Made me think he wasn't reliable as he used to be. And I didn't guess he'd be in much of a mood to help me out, either, so I'd left him alone ever since. Figured that'd suit us both just fine.

No choice now, though. If he had a beef, he could take it up with the Unfit.

It was usually easier finding him than the others. Franky wasn't stupid, it's just he wasn't in the *habit* of thinking, least not when any halfway decent amount of scratch or gold is involved. He's always runnin' something, pullin' something, and always in hock up to his neck with someone.

Which means Franky ain't the sort to lie low for more'n a few days at most. Find all the joints in his area where a cat can make a dishonest buck or ten without committing any "real" crimes—a definition that changes depending on what sorta measures he's been reduced to—and you're gonna catch up with him eventually.

I couldn't really stand to wait for "eventually," so I sucked up enough streamers and slivers of luck, from a hundred different places and people, until the Luchtaine & Goodfellow was about ready to pop, and dumped it all over myself. I swear my aura got so thick, I coulda gotten stuck in a narrow doorway.

It shoulda worked.

Between my new good fortune and what I knew of the gink's habits, I shoulda run him down before dawn.

Nothin'.

All sortsa reasons that coulda been, but the result was still nothin'.

Well, fine. If I couldn't rely on my usual sources, I'd just hafta try an *un*usual one.

The cat I had in mind now probably shoulda occurred to me earlier, really. Not a whole lot of the mystical and mysterious that moved through your Chicago he didn't either have a piece of, or at least know about. He wasn't even too far from where the Unfit had dropped me like a cheap fare. An odd bird, and unlike a lotta my stool pigeons, not the sorta Joe you could just threaten or smack an answer out of. Still, no good reason he shouldn't be willing to steer me wise.

Well, unless he *did* have a piece of whatever was going down.

Or had already been paid off by someone who did.

Or was scareda someone who did, which was a worrisome notion in itself.

Or... Yeah. Any more of this, I was gonna "or" myself outta going.

I took a few turns I ain't gonna describe, wandered along a few streets I ain't gonna name. Wouldn't help you if I did. Hruotlundt's place is always in the same general neighborhood, and you can always find it if you know it's there and it's what you're lookin' for, but it does tend to hop around a bit. I'll get into that in a mo.

So, I found myself in front of a familiar building I'd never seen before, strolled through a rundown lobby I recognized, despite never having being inside, and up a flight of stairs on a route I knew, despite never having taken it.

My feet finally led me to an oaken door, with a big brass knocker shaped like the Minotaur's head with a ring in its nose. It gave off enough fumes to blind a basilisk—way, *way* too much metal polish—and its expression looked more constipated than fearsome.

(And for the record? Yes, it *was* the Minotaur's head, not a bull's. Yes, they really oughta be indistinguishable. They're not—or they ain't on Hruotlundt's knocker, anyway—but damned if I've ever been able to figure out why.)

I didn't knock. Nobody ever knocked. I don't even know why he *has* the damn knocker. I shoved the door open, and for just a second I was falling forward. The world stretched out in fronta me as if it were some big honkin' pit. Gravity got drunk and lost its balance, and the floor under my feet jerked three seconds to the left.

I half stumbled, the way you do when you miss the last step on a staircase, and then it was done. The world was where it should be, inanimate objects stayed put, and I was facing a neat little reception room. Old, sagging sofa, a few dull lamps with age-mottled shades, and a bog-standard desk with a bog-standard secretary behind it.

Well, almost standard. Her hair, blinkers, and blouse weren't just all brown, they were all a *perfectly matching* brown. Real woodsy. It didn't look quite real.

She *sounded* normal enough, though, when she looked up from her nails, smacked her gum twice, and said, "Help ya, mister?"

"Yeah. Lemme see Hruotlundt."

"Ya got an appointment?"

"Never needed one before, doll."

She smacked her gum again. I restrained myself from smackin' something else.

"I'm real sorry," she told me, "but Mister Hruotlundt told me he don't wanna be disturbed for anyone. Maybe come back in a couple days?"

I poked a thumb in the direction of the inner door, opposite where I'd come in.

"He in there?"

"Yeah, but like I said—"

I didn't let her finish, just made for the inner office.

She didn't let *me* finish. I was just layin' a mitt on the doorknob when something wrapped a tight grip around my collar and lifted me not just off the floor but damn near outta my shoes.

"*Like I said,*" she repeated, her voice sounding not from right behind me but as though she was *still behind the desk*, "he don't wanna be disturbed!"

I was too wrapped up tryin' to figure where the sudden odor of wood pulp had come from—and okay, yeah, maybe a bit startled at being picked up like a wayward kitten—that I didn't even realize I'd been tossed back across the lobby, until I cracked into the doorframe.

I was gettin' *real* sick of being thrown around, I gotta say.

Since the skirt was still behind the desk (though she *had* gotten outta her chair), I gave the room a quick up'n down, trying to figure who or what'd just made me a baseball. It took only a second, but since I wasn't payin' full attention to her, it gave her time to get in another sucker punch.

Was a pretty sharp poke, just about doubling me over as it sank into my gut—and she hadn't taken one tiny step to throw it. Her arm'd *stretched*, reachin' across the room to wallop me, and though it got thinner as it got longer, it wasn't lacking for strength.

That wood pulpy aroma filled my schnozzle again, and I could hear she was *still* smackin' that friggin' gum!

And it finally dawned on me what those two facts together probably meant.

"All right!" I growled, hauling myself upright against the doorframe. "All right. I'm going."

Her arm'd snapped back to its normal size and length as if it were rubber, but she was watchin' me close.

And chewing. Good God that was annoying.

I reached for the doorknob, stopped, and looked back, hesitantly as I could.

"Do you... May I leave my card? So that Mister Hruotlundt knows I called, and can contact me when he's ready to see clients again?"

"Yeah, sure."

They can be real effective, real useful, these critters. But they ain't too sharp.

By the time she could see I'd yanked the L&G from my coat, rather'n a card or a wallet, I'd already started power flowing through it. I stripped away not just luck but some of the fundamental magics I knew I'd find soon as I tumbled to what she—it—was. And I knew exactly *where* to hit, to make the whole sequence of spells and formulae come unraveled.

If I'm making this sound easy, it wasn't. Took a *heap* of concentration, and effort, enough I actually staggered when it was over. If I'd faltered for even half a heartbeat, she'da been all over me like cheap rags. Still think she'da come out second best, but I'd have been in pretty rough shape by the end.

Didn't happen, though. I didn't slip. And after a few tics, she just fell apart, disintegrating into a heap of dirt, rotting wood, and quickly melting—and ever dirtier—ice.

The inner door burst open before the dust'd even settled. (Well, soil, in this case.) I'd sorta suspected it would.

"Was that *really* necessary, Oberon?"

Hruotlundt cut a peculiar figure, in two-thirds of his cream-colored three-piece suit. (Slacks and vest, I mean; he'd left his coat in the office.) It somehow didn't entirely clash, nor entirely compliment, his own rock-grey coloring, which was so uniform you really couldn't quite tell where skin left off and beard began.

He also stood about as high as my armpits, which puts him on the tall side for a *dvergr*.

"Don't blow your wig," I told him. "You can replace it quick enough, yeah?"

"Don't blow... Do you have any idea how much effort it takes to *make* a homunculus? Let alone one large and strong enough to serve as a guard!"

I couldn't help it.

I made a big show of looking at the desk, and the heap of muck behind it, and said, "Not the foggiest idea. Do you?"

You ever heard the expression that someone's "eyes went flinty"? Yeah, with the *dvergar*, that's literal. I mean his blinkers really did turn to flint.

See, Hruotlundt ain't like most *dvergar*. He's got no head for crafting with magic or alchemy or all that. He can follow the instructions in a grimoire skillful enough, and he's real sharp at identifying and defining enchantments and relics and what have you. But he don't remember formulae worth a damn, and he's got no imagination for invention.

So he and the other *dvergar* of Chicago'd mutually decided to part ways—so to speak—and Hruotlundt found a new use for his talents.

But any kinda jab at his abilities—or lack thereof—still stung. I thought maybe I oughta be a *little* friendlier.

"The gum was a nifty touch," I said. "Really sold the whole thing. You probably shoulda built her to stop once trouble broke out. Didn't seem natural after that."

"What do you want, Oberon?"

"Just to bump gums for a few."

He snarled a bit—teeth, tongue, lips, all that same precise shade of grey as his skin—and then stomped back into his office. I followed.

Real, *real* plain Jane sorta place. Old, worn carpet. Old, worn desk, with an old, worn ledger sitting on it and old, worn chairs scattered around it. A single lamp. A candlestick phone—guess he was more willing to put up with those than me. No art, no decoration.

Oh, yeah, and two doors in addition to the one I'd come through. One to my right, I knew from prior experience, led to a storeroom and a safe heavier than a whale's grief. And the one opposite me...

Elphame.

You remember that passage I got hidden in my office? One of a whole mess of natural portals to the Otherworld, if you know how to open 'em? Yeah, this ain't one of those—this one's artificial. Hruotlundt created it straight outta some ancient tome or other. That's why the office ain't always in exactly the same spot. He'd anchored it real firmly on the other side, but he had to leave some slack on this one to make sure the damn thing didn't snap.

I've heard tell that the office looks different if you come from the Elphame side, a lot more intricately adorned, a lot more

ARI MARMELL

artistry to the furniture, almost as much a noble's chamber as a place of business. But I ain't ever come that way myself, so I can't swear to it.

Hruotlundt was grumbling—it sounded rather like a rock-crusher—as he slumped hard into his seat.

"Seriously considering billing you for that," he groused at me.

"Look, whaddaya want from me? She wouldn't let me in."

"Uh-huh. And you know what you should have done, instead?"

"What's that?"

"*Not come in!*"

"Talk to me for a few and I'll leave."

He sighed. I'm not sure I ever heard a *dvergr* sigh before. Most of 'em don't live near enough to mortals to bother picking up the habit.

"Fine, but make it quick. You looking to unload something?"

"Not buying or selling," I told the fence—sorry, he prefers *facilitator*. "All I need's some information."

"Long as it's not about a stupid spear," he muttered, so quiet I don't think I was supposed to hear.

I grinned broadly at him. "Well, actually…"

"Oh, god*damn it*, Oberon! This is exactly why I didn't want to talk to anyone!"

"I take it I ain't the first to come nosing around, then?"

"No. No, you most certainly are not!" He pounded a stony fist against the desk a couple times in a near tantrum, leaving some nice, deep gouges in the wood.

"So whaddaya know?" I pressed.

Hruotlundt sighed again—never before, and then twice in one day!—and shook his head.

"I'll tell you the same thing I told the others. I don't know a damn thing of use. If there's an enchanted or holy or otherwise abnormal relic newly come to Chicago, spear or otherwise, I haven't heard about it."

"Oh, come on! You hear everything! You got more ears in the underworld—both underworlds—than a cornfield!"

"Yeah, the others didn't much buy it, either, which is the *other* reason I had a homunculus guarding my door. But it's the truth."

He paused, thinking. Might as well have been a dolled-up statue, until he finally spoke again.

"I heard a rumor a few months back," he said, voice still far away. "From across the pond somewhere. Wales, I think. That someone had dug up an artifact of the old times. From before the Romans, maybe even before the Tuatha Dé Danann fell. And I heard there'd been more than a little blood spilled over it before it dropped out of sight again."

I'd have been holding my breath, if it woulda meant anything.

"I suppose it's possible that it's made its way here to Chicago," he continued. "That it could be this spear you're all trying to dig up. On the other hand, I hear stories of that sort from the Old World every few years, and they're usually either exaggerations or complete tall tales woven of moonbeams and stupidity. So I wouldn't put a whole lot of cargo on that particular raft, if you get me."

I grunted. That was *it*? Yeah, he was right. I wasn't buying it.

"Not really a whole lotta help, Hruotlundt."

"Good thing I never promised I'd be helpful then, isn't it? Now I think it's time for you to go. As you've proved my guard to be less than effective, I think I'd just as soon pack up and leave town until this is over with."

"Could you at least tell me who else has—?"

"You know I don't discuss clients with clients."

"But—"

"It is time. For you to go."

My turn to sigh. I stood, tipped my hat, and—

"Wait."

I froze, fingers caressing the doorknob as though I were tryin' to get her back to my place. "Yeah?"

"48th and Loomis. There's a payphone. Got a call from there asking about all this."

I didn't even ask how he knew where the call'd come from. Who knows what sorta improvements he'd made to his office equipment? "I thought you didn't discuss clients."

"This was no client of mine. I didn't know the voice. And before you tell me it could've been a *new* client, I don't *want* any new clients who are dumb enough to ask me sensitive questions over the phone! And I don't much care for the fact that they somehow got my number in the first place."

Made sense. Guess he figured either I'd hafta tune them up, or they'd tune me up, and either way made his day better.

"48th and Loomis," I repeated.

"Right. Now, you were in the process of going?"

I went.

Horsefeathers. The whole crummy lot of it, horsefeathers, and enough of 'em to build your own hippogriff. Vague rumors of relics from the Old World? Nuh-uh. No way he'da brought 'em up if he wasn't pretty sure they were connected, and *definitely* no way that was all he knew. A fly couldn't break wind in this town Hruotlundt didn't hear about it—not if it happened anywhere near a valuable heirloom or artifact, anyway.

So what the hell was he holdin' back? Why wouldn't anyone, even the people who supposedly wanted me to come out ahead on this, put me wise? Me'n paranoia were startin' to get real friendly.

Well, open and honest or not, my *dvergr* pal had narrowed it down nicely, but I still had a lotta burning shoe leather ahead. Fact that they'd chosen that particular blower to call from *probably* meant they were holed up nearby—but "nearby" still left me more'n a few city blocks to cover. I knew the right pond, but I was still gonna have to go fishing for some real skittish fish. In other words, the next few hours of the night were spent wandering around one of Chicago's less refined neighborhoods, looking for the sorts of people who don't care to be found.

You'd be surprised, considering how often I do it, but it ain't actually all that fun.

I *did* give a few minutes' consideration to taking the run-out, heading over to Ramona's place like I wanted—uh, was supposed to have done. Ain't like I hadn't already put in some work here on Eudeagh's behalf.

'Cept… Could I be sure the Unfit didn't still have peepers on me? I hadn't given 'em her name, I sure wasn't gonna lead 'em right to her doorstep now.

So all I could do was keep on keepin' on.

It was just breezy enough to be chilly, just drizzly enough to be damp. The hem of my flogger and the occasional paper kept huggin' my ankles, maybe welcoming me to the neighborhood. Most of the people I passed were less friendly, keepin' their heads down and their dogs stepping. Couldn't blame 'em. Odds were most had perfectly good reasons for being out and about this late, but it wasn't like they knew that *I* did.

Lights and wires hummed in the rain, resonating with the buzz in my head anytime I got too near or passed under one. I don't agree with Eudeagh on much of anything, but she's onto something about your world being all kinds of irritating.

Passed back by the phone booth at one point, and I suddenly felt stupider'n I had in a *real* long while.

The idea that I mighta left her in danger, or even just let her down, had been sittin' like lead in my gut all night, and it'd never once occurred to me that I had options besides hoofin' it on over. I dove into the phone booth like it was a bomb shelter, and damn near snapped the horn off its cord in my hurry. Much as I hate using the damn contraption, I had the blower in one hand and a nickel in my fingers… And then I felt so much *more* foolish, it made the me of a minute ago look like King Solomon.

She'd had me so dizzy that morning that I hadn't gotten her damn number when she gave me her address!

Smooth, Mick. I was starting to wish I actually *was* the amateur I was acting like. Least then I'd have an excuse other'n "I'm dumb."

Hands stuck in my pockets, head down, and worried as much about Ramona's reaction now as I was about my investigation, I went back to roaming.

And whaddaya know? Hruotlundt's tip—and maybe some of that luck I'd doused myself with—finally paid off.

CHAPTER SIX

The waxing moon winked up at me from every puddle, bright even behind the clouds. Branches, half bare of leaves, swayed in the wind, and the nearby buildings grinned at me through mouths of window with teeth of broken wooden boards. Everything that didn't smell of old dust smelled of old garbage.

Did I mention this wasn't the nicest neighborhood?

Without Hruotlundt's pointer, I might not've searched this area close enough, mighta missed this particular street. Now? Now I was finally gettin' somewhere. My first clue that things'd gone hinky was the vagrants. Or rather, my first clue *wasn't* the vagrants.

See, Chicago's inner-city homeless—and there were a *lot* of 'em—had all been thrown into disarray when the city cleaned up downtown for the Dems' National Convention back in summer. Dunno why they bothered; it ain't as though the politicos, the newshawks, or the listeners at home don't *know* 'bout the Depression. But they *did* bother, and a lotta the outer neighborhoods, like this one, got a whole new influx of citizens without addresses.

Most of that had reversed itself in the few months since, but a small chunk of 'em hadn't bothered wandering back to their old haunts. Not like living in a downtown box was so much ritzier. So these other shabby streets still had some pretty hefty vagabond populations.

'Cept this one didn't. Last block or two, the number of mugs huddled up in alley corners or snoozing under blankets of wet newspaper totaled zip, give or take a zero.

So when I started seeing them again, I knew I'd gone too far and turned back. It was very specifically these couple blocks that'd been emptied, which meant that's where I needed to be.

Oh, and there was a lot to see. More puddles. More sodden trash. More boarded-up windows and buildings sagging like they'd tied on one too many the night before. Good place, overall, if you're the sort who prefers bad places.

If it hadn't been for the frickin' rain, I mighta spotted 'em a lot sooner than I did. As it was, that huge heap of good fortune I'd glommed from my surroundings was still only *just* enough to put me wise.

Footprints. Sorta.

Hardly visible, they were puddles in puddles, tiny spots where an oil or muck of some kind hadn't quite mixed with the water. Only when the light hit 'em just right was it possible to get any vague slant on 'em, and they vanished if you glanced away or blinked. But they left a decent trail, once I knew what to look for, and it was easy enough to noodle out which way they were headed: Go in the direction they get heavier, not lighter.

Keen detective work, huh?

Took me a touch longer to figure out *what* I was following. Don't gotta be an ancient Fae to guess it won't wind up being anything good.

I wrapped the shadows around me, huddling under 'em like a cloak, and shushing 'em when they complained, and peeked around one last corner. Peeked, and then stared, lamps about goggling out of my skull.

The whole street stank like a catfish in a sweatbox. The creature looked for all the world as if someone'd taken a man and a mackerel and just smashed 'em together over and over until they blended. Its skin was a noxious green-grey, fingers were flippery and sharp, its hair and beard looked like weeds in need of a good barber, and its nostrils were two tiny pits directly between its wide, rolling, fishy peepers.

You ever hear of *bagienniks*? Nah, didn't figure most of you would've. Eastern European. Slavic. River Fae. Homely as Medusa's prom date, and while they ain't malicious in any real sense, it don't take much to get 'em stirred up and hopping mad. They got tempers short as... Well, short as you would, if you looked like that.

We didn't have any in Chicago. Oh, they mighta liked the river well enough, but we didn't have many Slavic Fae of *any* kind here. A few in and around Pilsen, ever since so many Czechs moved in. I'd worked with one for a few days, way back when I was tryin' to suss out what happened to Mr. Soucek's wife. I knew all the other Slavs, at least in passing.

And none of 'em were *bagienniks*.

Now I was ogling a trio of 'em, lurking around an abandoned building no different from any of the *other* abandoned buildings.

And that told me three things.

One, we had outsiders, plural, in town. Herne wasn't the only guy come to the Windy City in search of this goddamn spear.

Which led to two, Eudeagh had sold me a bill of goods. (No big surprise, there.) People wanted this dingus for more'n just "keeping their rivals from having it." There was something special about it. Above and beyond being magic, I mean, which—let's face it—don't automatically make it all that special to us.

And three, *Oh, shit! Duck!*

Not sure how he made me—maybe I'd burned too much of my good luck in tracking 'em—but the one on the left spun and spurted a boiling, sizzling stream of oil at me from its nostrils.

Yeah, they do that. Supposedly, if you let the gunk cool and harden a little, the paste is good for muscle aches and excess rheum.

You let it hit you fresh? It'll burn you so bad your shadow'll start peeling.

I dropped and twisted, letting the corner of the building take the brunt. The oil blasted the brick clean and polished, and the few drops that managed to spatter me hurt bad enough I wanted to scream.

I didn't. I whirled back around the corner and broke into a sprint, drawing the L&G from my coat as I went.

They were all coming my way now, burbling and blithering, sounding like a small dog throwing an ing-bing underwater. But for just a few, burbling was about *all* they could do. See, I dunno how often they can pull that searing sneeze thing, but I was sure Fishface Number One would need *some* time to recover. Gotta build up the mucus, yeah? And he was *between* me and the others.

So for just a couple blinks, I was heading straight at 'em. Figured they wouldn't try to hose me down while their buddy was in the line of fi—water. Even if it wouldn't hurt him much—something else I didn't know, and wished I did—it'd be a wasted shot.

They started moving, orbiting each other, but they hadn't figured on me charging out like a rhino with piles. I was on 'em before their footwork did 'em any good.

First shot was a wand-thrust to the breadbasket—or fishfoodbasket, or whatever. I hit hard, more a stab than a prod, and fired off the L&G soon as I felt resistance. Traded him a whole bunch of his own luck and energy for the weight of my anger and the pain from his splattering snot.

He gurgled and knifed forward at the waist, spitting up watery blood. He was probably already out, but I caught him with a sharp left to the chin, just to be sure.

Then I *literally* caught him, with both hands—wand hooked through one finger—and, using my own strength and some extra *oomf* I'd just ripped from his aura, tossed him at his buddies.

They scattered quick, giving me the opening to take shelter in an old, cobweb-choked doorway. I leaned out, ready to squeeze off some more magic...

No bunnies, these lugs.

The two of 'em spread out, both facing my doorway but far enough apart that I couldn't have gotten 'em both, even with a chopper. Not before one of 'em could turn me into a lobster dinner.

Even worse, two *more* of the scaly bastards came flop-stomping from around the building their pals had been guarding. Guess they were standing watch on the other side.

Four-on-one odds. Didn't suit me very well. I could try to pick 'em off one by one, but I didn't think I could keep 'em at bay that long. Hadda deal with the whole crew in one throw.

I chuckled to myself. I was so far behind the eight ball, I could actually have used some of those "resources" Téimhneach said I'd have at my...

Huh. Now *there* was a notion.

Follow me on this. *Bagienniks* don't spent a lotta time away from their rivers. They dry out something ugly. Night like this, though? No big deal. They just absorb the moisture they need from the rain and humidity. Be out here 'til the cows come home, wouldn't bother 'em.

Know what we got a lot of here in Chicago, though? Whole *heaps* of pollution. Crap gumming up the air so you wouldn't believe. Car exhausts, factories belching up God-knows-what... It's all over.

Odds of any thick pocket of it gathering overhead right here and now, heavy enough to seriously taint the rain falling through it? Not good. Real not good.

But not impossible. Would just take some wacky amount of luck.

Got the idea from the *sluagh* in the storm. Thanks, Eudeagh.

They closed slow, unsure what I might do or what I could throw at 'em. That did me just fine, since I needed every second

I could get. The amount of chance and fortune I was playin' with, they'd have been able to fight me off if I tried glomming it all from them, and I didn't want any of these buildings teetering over and collapsing, so...

Yep. I had long enough.

My whole body was tense and quivering as I concentrated through the L&G.

Two of the fishfaces had just gotten me in their sights and prepared to—uh, blow—when the weather took on a faintly greasy smell.

Not a lot, not strong. Dunno if I'd even have noticed if I hadn't been looking for it. Smelling for it. Whatever.

Don't get the wrong notion, it ain't as though the *bagienniks* suddenly dropped or anything. It'd take a lot more'n an extra-thick layer of pollution to really poison 'em, and it'd take a *much* longer exposure for 'em to absorb enough to be real harmful.

But if you suddenly sucked down an unexpected mouthful of gasoline, you'd be sick pretty quick, even if you spat it back out. Same here. The fishfaces reeled, staggered, started to look—if you'll excuse me putting it this way—kinda green around the gills.

No need for a play-by-play at this point. I had one of 'em down before I even got up close, draining enough from his aura to put him out hard. I won't say the last three were duck soup, but when it was over the only pains I had to handle were a couple claw-tracks on one arm and an ache in my knuckles.

Hem of my flogger was oily and hot to the touch, where it took a splatter meant for me, and it reeked like a seagull's leftovers. I'll tell ya, though, grease aside, it probably hadn't been that clean in weeks.

No sign of who or what they were protecting. Not outside, anyway. Which left the obvious option. L&G held ready, stepping lightly enough I don't suppose a leaf woulda crinkled underfoot, I moved through the shadowy doorway into the building they'd been guarding.

* * *

Dust. Cobwebs. Carpet made outta more mildew than actual carpet. Smelled like a *leshy*'s bathroom after the morning fertilizer.

Some of that dust and mildew was scattered, some of those cobwebs broken and dangling. No big shock there; I'd already guessed somebody else had come this way.

But then there was the singing.

High, crisp, clear. This canary had a set of pipes, for sure. Even without any kinda musical accompaniment, she was flawless. Every note, every trill. No words, just melody, beautiful and distinctive enough to make Blanche Calloway give up in disgust and go learn to type.

This? This was a *bad thing*. When the Fae are involved and you hear someone belting it out that way, it's *always* a bad thing.

I felt it tug at me. Velvet fingers reaching through my ears, gently cupping my thoughts and trying to drag 'em forward— and the rest of me along with. It was a real pleasant touch, soothing, promising to brush all your troubles away like so much lint, if you'd just let it…

Nuts to that. I been around too long to fall for it. Ain't *nobody* capable of making all *my* troubles go poof.

It wasn't the only magic I felt, though. Behind the song was something else, something faint and lingering, like old cigar smoke. Whoever my songbird was, she hadn't picked this building by chance. Spear or not, *something* with genuine mojo had been here recently, though it was up and gone now, and I couldn't figure why it mighta been here at all.

Well, I'd work that part out later. First, I hadda face the music.

I followed the tune, yeah, but fast, at a hard run, wand at the ready. Dust and spores kicked up behind me in a filthy wake. Webs flexed, stretched, and fell apart, never meant to hold back anything resembling the L&G or the meathook holding it.

Shabby door up ahead. Old wood, rotted and sagging,

rusty hinges, screws hangin' onto the frame mostly through determination and habit.

Didn't need the mojo for this one. I just turned a shoulder into it. Didn't even really break stride.

Big open room that stank just like the hall. Old, stained sheets flopped like lazy ghosts over decrepit chairs and a table or two. Whole room was lit by a soft, somehow aquatic glow, not coming from any lamp or bulb or even magic gewgaw that I could see.

In the middle of it all, a couple danced. Slow, graceful steps, old steps, nothing you'll find cutting a rug today.

And shoot my hat off and call me a dandelion if one of the pair wasn't Four-Leaf himself!

You remember how Franky was on the bad end of a broderick when I first dug him up during the Ottati gig? Yeah, that ain't exactly an uncommon occurrence. Franky got himself beat more'n your average bongo.

This time, though, he'd caught something worse than a few bruises from a thug trying to collect his dough.

He *looked* normal. Wrinkled suit so cheap it mighta actually cost less than my socks. Couple gold necklaces hanging off him, 'cause Franky *always* had something gold. It's the leprechaun in him.

But his peepers were nearly as round as the glasses in front of 'em. Glazed as a doughnut and focused on what I hadda guess was the twenty-second century. Oh, yeah. Take it from a guy who spends a lotta time plucking the strings in other people's heads, they don't come much more entranced than Franky was right then.

I was a bit more concerned with his partner, though.

I could talk about her slim, exquisite features, the gams that'd make a man long to be a stocking, the snow-white dress, all that. But those ain't the important details.

No, *those* would be the radiant blond hair—held in place by a gleaming silver comb—that still sluiced water everywhere, even though the rest of her was dry; and the green fire in her eyes that, I realized, was the source of the room's lighting.

Rusalka.

Call 'em what you want. Siren, river nymph, nereid, mermaid... They're all the hell over. Little different, one culture or family branch to the next, but all basically the same shtick: hypnotize passersby with song and/or dance, then drown 'em and suck up their life essence in the final bubbles.

Nasty twists, the lot of 'em.

'Cept this *rusalka* wasn't looking to drown Franky, not this far from the river. My guess? Once she figured she had him well and truly wrapped up, there'd be a few questions.

About a spear, probably.

I glared at her, and she at me. Gotta admit, to an outsider, her glare probably looked a lot more intimidating. Green fire and all.

She spun, swaying the wrong way and breaking the rhythm of the dance to put Franky between me and her. The poor lug stumbled, almost toppling completely but for her grip on him. He was still pretty well under, though. Guess she'd already been working him a while.

I circled the other way, stepping around or occasionally climbing over the furniture, keeping a close watch on the dame, trying to draw a bead that wouldn't risk hitting Franky with whatever magics I threw at her.

Her voice rose, shifting from the breathtaking melody into a sustained, high-pitched note. Sharp, piercing. I clutched at my ears—didn't even mean to, just instinct—and I was actually pretty surprised that they didn't come away bloody. Someone was hammerin' a chisel into both sides of my noggin. Thinking was an uphill battle, if you wanna call Everest a hill.

I dunno what it was—maybe a mirror in a nearby room, or some tableware leftover someplace, but I heard glass tremble and crack. Oddly muted, though. Guess my hearing wasn't gonna be up for a lot more of what she was dishing out.

So, fine, Mick. Don't think. Just *do*.

The L&G discharged, not at the *rusalka* and her meat-puppet, but at the cloth-draped furniture close behind them. Old legs creaked and then snapped as bad luck seeped deep into the wood, wiggling in through a smattering of rot. The whole kit'n caboodle collapsed, sliding and spilling sheets, a couple chairs, and a newly mangled table out onto the makeshift dance floor.

Wasn't much, really. Slow as the furniture-avalanche was, graceful as *she* was, it was eggs in the coffee for her to dance through the mess even as it came lapping at her heels.

But it caught her off-guard, startled her, made her split her attention. For about the length of a hiccup, she clammed up.

My Oxfords sounded a lot like a typewriter, pounding against the floor as I took off. Quick as I was, I still almost blew the whole job. She'd caught her breath and kicked up that goddamn screech before I reached her, but by then it was too late. I don't think I coulda stopped if I'd tried.

Pain lanced through my head, yeah—but then through hers, too. Haymaker to the button'll do that.

She flew back, stumbling over the same junk she'd just avoided, blood pouring from a schnozz now more crooked than a politician's smirk. Only sounds the *rusalka* was makin' now were an ugly pained gurgle and a few grunts and gasps as she staggered over bits of broken wood.

No chances. I ain't always sharp as I oughta be, but I'm no idiot. I aimed and fired, blasting power and luck from her aura while pummeling her with the pain she'd inflicted on me with her squealing.

She dropped, limp as—well, as a fish—flopped over the heap of broken furniture, and landed real still on the floor.

I shot her again, just to be sure. Much luck as I'd torn from her now, she'd probably impale herself on a broken table leg if she sneezed hard.

I turned at the sound of a mild *thump*. Franky was doubled

over, one mitt against the wall where he'd caught himself. I'd seen guys hungover after being tight for four days straight who looked better'n he did right about then. If he'd gasped any harder, he coulda gone moonlighting as a vacuum cleaner.

All right, he wasn't going anywhere. Back to our foreign guest. I wanted her to sing a few verses—uh, not literally—before I got into it with Franky. Figured she might spill something Queen Mob had decided to keep to herself.

Gotta say I was impressed with her gumption. She was struggling to stand, hauling herself upright on the broken furniture. What I at first took to be a low hum of some mechanical gewgaw or other from outside the building turned out to be coming from her, a sorta guttural ululation in the back of her throat.

She was using what she had left of her own mojo to try and gum up mine, or at least ward off the worst of the bad luck. Probably the only reason the whole heap hadn't collapsed on her at the first tug.

Still, she didn't have a lot left, and she knew I knew it. She saw me looking, socked me with a glare of pure, contemptuous hatred that somehow struck me as *very* Russian, and tried to run. More of a staggering limp, really, and I coulda caught up with one foot tied behind my back, but I hadda admire the attempt.

Yeah. Shoulda spent less time admiring. If I had, I mighta been in a position to do something 'bout what happened next.

Or maybe not. She was having a *real* unlucky night.

Basically, the *rusalka* sprouted a small flagpole, went briefly stiff, and collapsed bonelessly enough that I didn't need to be a doctor to know she wasn't getting up again.

I was at her side in a jiff, not that I thought I could do much. The spear sticking straight up from her chest was old, thick. A whole bundle of trophies or fetishes, bones and teeth and that sort, hung from right below the tip.

Yeah, I thought it, too. But no, I got wise quick that this wasn't *the* spear, not what I was looking for. I didn't feel any magic, any power, from this thing—or at least, none of its own, just some lingering traces it coulda picked up from its owner, nothing close to the aura I'd already sensed hanging around here. Also, I didn't figure Herne woulda stuck around this burgh once he had what he wanted.

Oh, yeah, didn't I mention? A glance in the direction the spear'd come from showed me Herne standing in the doorway opposite the one I'd come in through. Big and glowery and real unhappy-like. Dunno if he'd been following the *rusalka*'s crew, following me, or if he'd felt those same traces of power I had, but either way, he was here.

Just swell.

"They're easier to put the screws on if they're alive," I told him. "Most dead folk don't talk, and those that do ain't friendly company. In case you didn't—"

"I was aiming," he growled, brow lowering even further, "for her shoulder. *Something* threw me off."

Yeah, that'd be an extra dollop of extreme bad luck. Didn't figure I'd mention that, though.

"Well, goody for us, we still got…"

I turned yet again, but there was no sign of Franky 'cept another door hanging ajar.

"Goddamn it, Franky." It woulda just been a polite conversation, but now? Now I hadda be mean to him next time we met.

Principle of the thing, savvy?

"Maybe not. All right so we…" I began.

Not sure how to imitate the noise that spear made when Herne pulled it outta the stiff's chest. *Schleeurchk!* maybe comes close.

Which woulda been unpleasant, but not alarming, if he hadn't then started toward me, leavin' a trail of spattered, dribbling blood to mark his path.

"Uh…" I said. "So, who leads the Wild Hunt right now? It was Gudrun last I heard, but—"

"You told me you had no involvement in this, Oberon. You told me you were not a competitor."

"…but none of us really have any idea how you guys cycle in'n out, so—"

"You lied."

I started backing away, not that I woulda had much success if I tried to run.

"Actually, I didn't. I sorta got roped into this after we talked."

"I don't believe you."

The spear dripped.

"No, really! I owed people." I didn't really want word of my deal getting around, but I wanted Herne's spear in my heart a whole lot less. "They called it in over this. I can't begin to tell you how much I *don't* wanna be here."

"Oh, no fear. I'm about to demonstrate." He *did* pause, though. "Who?"

Sigh. "The local Unseelie. Eudeagh's crew."

A long, slow blink. Like a mickeyed lizard.

"And the fact you've debased yourself to serve the *Unseelie*—" Wow, but he could cram a lotta disdain into that one word. "—is a reason I should *spare* you? Your logic escapes me, Oberon. Pity you can't accompany it."

Somehow, *This isn't my fault, taking it out on me ain't fair!* didn't seem likely to convince him. But…

"You're better off with me on this, Herne."

Again, the hunter stopped. I tried not to sigh with relief—I was runnin' outta room for retreat. I took that halt as demand for explanation, so I explained.

"How many of the local Unfit do you know by sight?" I asked. "By name?"

"Few, being a stranger to Chicago. As you well know."

"Exactly! You bump me off, Eudeagh's just gonna send someone else. You'll still have just as much competition, only you won't know who to watch out for. Won't know how to predict 'em."

Truth was, I didn't buy for a second that I was the only one the Unseelie had searching. No way they were gonna put all their eggs in the Mick Oberon basket. But so far as I *knew*, with genuine certainty, it was just me. So I wasn't really lying or omitting anything, see?

"And," I said more softly, "you won't be able to count on 'em fighting even as fair as me. You know I got lines I won't cross. You may not think much of where I draw 'em, but I got 'em. You think whoever else the Unseelie might send would say the same?"

"That… is actually a point worth contemplating." The hunter lowered his weapon just a bit, and I almost sagged in relief.

"Very well," he said. "I'll kill you *after* this is all done."

Less relief-sagging. "Gee, thanks. Your kindness and generosity are truly boundless."

"Don't try me, Oberon. And do not *dare* cast me as the cruel one here." He pivoted and started to walk away. "I've no idea what they hold over you, but the power you seek to put in the hands of the Unseelie is far more damaging than *I* ever could be!"

I'd caught up to him before he reached the door, and though I thought for a minute he really was gonna off me when I reached out to grab his arm, I stood fast.

"What power? What're you talking about?"

Again, he seemed to sense that I wasn't trying to pull anything. His blinkers stretched wide when he realized I really had no idea.

"They didn't tell you what you're seeking?"

I shrugged. "Old spear. Enchanted, one of the few remaining."

"You…" I could *see* the thoughts chasing each others' tails around his noggin, watched him consider not telling me, watched him decide otherwise.

"Gods, man, this is not some toy you hunt! Not some curiosity your Unseelie mistress wants for her collection."

I decided to let that bit pass. I'd already known Eudeagh hadn't told me everything, but this was starting to put me on edge.

"So, what? What *is* it, then?"

"Gáe Assail, Oberon. The Spear of Lugh has come to Chicago.

"And you have agreed to deliver it into Unseelie hands."

CHAPTER SEVEN

"Spear of what now?" Pete was nearing the bottom of his second mug of joe, and still sounded deeply groggy. Then again, I didn't think he'd be making a whole lot more sense out of this if he were fully awake. "Spear of Lou?"

"Lugh," I corrected, even though he probably couldn't hear the difference. Woulda helped if I hadn't had my head between my hands like I was trying to compress it into a pancake. With brain jelly. "The Spear of Lugh. Alias Gáe Assail, alias Ahreadbhar. One of the four hallows of the Tuatha Dé Danann."

Pete peered at me through bloodshot peepers.

"Okay, so I know some of that was words…"

Just so you know, you mugs look even sadder when you're confused in a bathrobe than when you're just confused.

Pete's flop was exactly what you'd expect, if you knew the guy. Small but comfy, redolent of cheap aftershave lotion and slightly burnt beef. Spick'n span where it counted—clean kitchen, creased blues hanging behind the wide-open door of the closet—and, ah, let's call it *informal* everywhere else. I'd hadda move a pile of books and a light bulb off the chair before I could plant my keister on it, and my heels were resting on a wadded-up pair of pants.

Oh, and the bird himself, of course. Worn grey bathrobe,

mustache half-matted to his lip from sleepin' on his face, and clutching his coffee like a holy icon.

"Okay," I said. "Short version, since you ain't gonna live long enough for the unabridged...

"A long time ago—no, longer'n that—longer'n that, too—the *aes sidhe* and few of the other Fae races were a lot more'n we are now. We were beautiful, and we were *powerful*." I wondered if he could hear the regret and resentment. I wondered if I'd ever manage to ditch 'em. "Magics of a sort this world hasn't seen since. Your ancestors worshiped us as gods, and they had reason to."

"Well, long as it hasn't gone to your head..."

"I'm serious here, Pete. You got no idea."

He blinked over the rim of his mug, nodded, threw back a swig.

"Our power was a lot more concentrated, then. You gotta remember, this is before any significant human technology, before a lotta the Fae and semi-Fae races even exist—"

"'Semi-Fae'?"

"Damn it, Pete, you wanna hear all this, or don'tcha?"

"You're the one came to me at four in the A.M., Mick. I think I get as many questions as I want."

"Yeah, remind me not to do *that* again." He was right, though. I'd come knocking 'cause I had to hash out my thinking with *someone*. (Fact that *he'd* woken *me* up the night before had no bearing on it. No payback here. Nuh-uh. None.) He deserved to understand what I was yapping about.

"What you call the supernatural," I said slowly, trying to couch it all in terms he *would* understand, "is either human—mortal sorceries, ghosts, whatever—or Fae."

"Wait, all of it?"

"All of it."

"Vampires?"

I jerked him a nod. "Fae spirits, real dark ones, inhabiting human corpses."

"What about... me?"

Shouldn'ta surprised me that he asked. Especially since the full moon wasn't even two weeks away.

"Creature of the wild, way back when. Primal, savage, from the woods of Elphame. Something in its essence, its blood, corrupted a guy, he carried it to someone else, and... well, Bob's your uncle."

"Gotta say, Mick, I'm not sure I buy it. Sounds kinda... propaganda-ish."

I shrugged. "Could be bunk. It's how we're taught, though. Can I get on with it, now?"

Pete wandered into the kitchen, poured himself a third cup, and strolled on back.

"Now you can go on."

"Oh, *can* I? Swell.

"Point is, at the height of our power, the Tuatha Dé Danann crafted a lot of powerful devices and fetishes. When I say we put part of ourselves into it, I mean it. Our power, our essence.

"The greatest of these were the four hallows, and one of those was a spear, granted to one of our finest warriors."

"That'd be this Lou guy?"

Oh, for... "Lugh. Lugh mac Ethnenn. Lugh of the Long Arm. Father of Cú Chul..." I actually *heard* Pete's eyes starting to glaze over. "Ah, nuts. That 'Lou guy,' yeah. Anyway, the hallows saw a lotta use for centuries, especially when our other power started to wane. We couldn'ta conquered the Firbolg without 'em. But eventually, after we'd faded to just 'the people of the mounds,' the hallows were lost. One or two've popped up here'n there—we're pretty sure *Claíomh Solais* resurfaced for a while with the name 'Excalibur'—but never for long."

He didn't say anything, do anything, just stood there and held his cup while it steamed. He was wakin' up fast, though. I could see it in his expression and his aura both.

"All right, so this spear thing's here. That really such a big deal? What's it do?"

"Eh, nothing much. Always strikes its mark, punch through any damn thing, returns to the hand that threw it, glows with fire hotter than the forge, no man may stand against its wielder in battle. Focuses and channels the wielder's own magic in a way that makes it a howitzer if we assume my wand's a friggin' Daisy BB gun! That sorta spiel."

"Is… is all that true?"

I wanted to shrug, decided I couldn't be bothered.

"Some of it? Nobody ever got the full use outta it that Lugh did. Whether that's 'cause some of it was him, instead of the spear, or just 'cause nobody else knows properly how to use the dingus… No idea. But even at its weakest, it ain't something I want the Unseelie getting their grubby mitts on. Or the Seelie, for that matter. Or Herne. Or any-damn-body."

"Fuck me." Pete upturned a splash of milk into his joe, then handed me the bottle. Bit chilly for my taste, but I threw back a few slugs anyway. "What're the Unseelie gonna do if they get hold of it?"

"God knows. There's a good chance it'd be enough to win 'em Chicago in the Otherworld. If they decided to play with it *here*… Pete, you'd be surprised how many of your unsolved cases are down to them. When they visit the real world, especially the Unseelie, most of the time people die. And that's in small numbers, *without* ancient magical hardware. If this goes down bad, it'll make the city's worst gang war look like a bridal shower."

"And you're just gonna hand it over to them if you find it?" he demanded.

"Whaddaya want me to do?"

"How about, let's see, just a quick thought off the top of my head, *not* handing it over?"

"I swore an oath, Pete."

"I think your conscience can shoulder a fib or two!" He was so animated now, gesturing this way'n that, I think more of his coffee ended up on the rug or his bathrobe than in his belly.

"Ain't a matter of principle. It's a matter of…" Shit, how could I even try to put a human wise to what a Fae's word means? What kinda chance I took, what kinda fears I had, when I bonded myself to Eudeagh?

Damn the Unseelie, anyway! No-win decisions, pickin' the lesser evil, hurting some to save others… That's why I abandoned the Court, locked so much of myself away, in the first fucking place! I promised myself long ago, after the last time, that I wouldn't…

Guess an oath to oneself doesn't carry the same weight, huh? Fuck.

"Okay, look," I explained, about a year later. "One of us violates an oath—the right kinda oath, anyway—we lose all Fae protection for a year and a day, see? Legally, anyone can do anything to the foresworn, with no repercussions. Nobody can start any family vendettas over it, either; though it's not like I have a family to avenge me."

"Okay, yeah, that don't sound good, but…"

"That's just the legal bunk, Pete. The real kicker's mystical. You seen what I can do to random chance? That'd turn against me, but swift. I'd have better luck if I broke a mirror'n used the pieces to skin a black cat under a ladder. And I'd be a damn *beacon*. Anything within miles'd feel it. *Vulnerable* aes sidhe *here!*"

"What do you mean 'anything'?"

"There are things out there, see? Things that normally leave the rest of us Fae alone, things worse'n the Unseelie, worse'n you could even… They might not suss me out, *probably* wouldn't, there ain't many of 'em. But they *could*. I might be willing to die to keep the spear outta the wrong hands. But I'm not willing to risk my *soul* for it. Even at my best, I was never *that* brave."

Took him near on a full minute to absorb it all. He finally dropped into another chair, didn't seem to notice he'd planted himself on top of a crumpled—and now gettin' more crumpled—magazine. (Me, I decided to pretend the quick peep I got of a brown breast, as the pages folded up, meant it was a *National Geographic.*)

"Loopholes?" he asked more quietly.

"Nada. Dame I bargained with, she's sharp. Wouldn't let me get away with anything like that."

"You sure?" He smiled, a little. "Could ask a lawyer."

"Nuts to *that*! The Unseelie's one thing, but let's not push it!"

We both chuckled, and we both knew full well that neither of us was really feeling all that chipper.

Was another minute before he opened his trap again. "Don't that mean it's a good thing, though? That you can't find it?"

"I gotta get out from under, Pete. 'Sides, if I don't, one of the others will, sooner or later. We'll all still be behind the eight ball anyway."

I shook my head, kept on yapping, as much to myself as my buddy. "Gotta be veiled somehow. Something that potent, that much mojo? Me and the others, we'd feel that across town. Maybe across worlds. Nah, it's hidden, contained. I'm gonna need actual clues."

"Anything I can do?"

See? There's a reason Pete'n me are buds when I usually got no time for mosta you.

"Anything more you can sniff up about the museum, uh, not-robbery, that'd be swell. Hmm. And try to dig up everything you can on any unexplained or hinky deaths in the past few days."

Like I'd told him, with Unfit and outside Fae stalking Chicago, it was a fair bet there'd be at least a handful of… unfortunate bystanders. The Unseelie ain't *all* full-on psychotic, but even the stable ones… Well, the fact that there wasn't a newsworthy amount of blood in the streets *already* had me pretty well astonished. If I could learn some about the deaths that *had* happened, maybe I could at least keep a peeper on where everyone was'n what they were up to.

"Can do."

"Thanks, Pete. Um... Maybe don't go through Galway on this, yeah? Kinda doubt I'm in his graces after my no-show yesterday morning."

Few more minutes of polite jawing, a few more snorts of lukewarm cow juice, and I was off. Hadda let Pete catch some more winks before his shift; and me? I decided, since I still had a couple hours before sunrise, that there was time for me to have one more conversation.

If I was right about who it was I was tryin' to talk to. And if he'd take my call.

Assuming you want something bigger'n a beagle, there ain't a lot of full-on predators in or around the Second City, unless you're talking about the kind with two legs. Suppose I coulda snuck into the zoo, but what I had in mind might attract attention there that I *didn't* need.

Still got a *few* options, though, even if they're as much scavenger now as hunter. This close to dawn, most of 'em had already slunk back to their dens, but once I got to the outskirts of town, it wasn't *too* hard to find a handful of coyotes still out and about.

I crouched in the dirt and weeds, and waited. I don't smell human, not to them. Between that and a touch of long-distance mental coaxing, I got one to come near enough for some peeper-to-peeper communication.

Pushing into an animal's mind is weird. Different than a human's or another Fae's. It's duck soup in some ways; they don't got the same will, same innate resistance, as you schlubs. But they also don't think like we understand it. They're all emotion and instinct. It ain't easy giving 'em instructions, making 'em understand what you're encouraging 'em to do. Ain't even a language barrier so much as a... concept barrier.

End of the day, though, after a whole dance number of sniffs and yipping, I got through. Wasn't as though I was asking it to do anything unnatural—just a smidge, uh, differently than normal.

Drawing a whole lot of perked ears and confused stares from the rest of the pack, the coyote howled.

Short. Long. Short, short. Long. Short, short, short. Long.

Up to five shorts, then counting back down.

Didn't mean anything, really, but it was a *blatantly* artificial pattern. No coyote, no animal, was gonna call out like that of its own accord.

Most Fae would probably notice but not much care. I could get a few of the local wilderness enthusiasts—a *ghillie dhu* or faun, or maybe even a *huldra*. Didn't think it too probable, though, with everyone either tracking down the spear or lying low.

I coulda gotten Herne, too, I suppose. He'd have noticed the odd call. But he'd also probably dismiss it as a ruse.

No, the guy I was looking for, if I was right, would notice the call and *wouldn't care* if it was a trap.

Yep, he showed. And yep, he didn't give one good goddamn if it was a trap.

He appeared from a nearby copse of trees, sorta ghosting outta the dark beneath the canopy. Branches didn't rustle when he passed, grass and leaves didn't crunch where he stepped.

Just about pitch black out here, and he still wore the sunglasses and the wide-brimmed hat. His teeth glinted in the darkness.

And it was all I could do not to dust out of there, to run until my legs were worn to bloody stumps. Not because he was so frightening, though he was that, but because he *knew*. I could just sense it, feel it in the air around him. I didn't even know *what* he knew, only that it included every crime and every sin I'd ever indulged—and so much more, besides.

"That's a mighty peculiar telephone you got for yourself there, son."

Voice sounded regular enough, not counting the deep Texas twang, but something in it put me on edge. I swear, hidden beneath the words, I heard the echoes—the *shadows*—of growls and screams.

"I didn't have your number," I said. He just smiled wider, so I went on. "Whadda I call you?"

"Oh, let's go with… Sealgaire."

Sealgaire. "Hunter." Real cute.

But it did more or less erase what few lingering doubts I still had about who he was. And yeah, now I was *real* glad I'd decided against bringing a blade with me tonight. He'd probably've found it funny. Or, just maybe, he'da taken offense.

I don't wanna think about what he'd do if he got offended.

"Okay. Tell me something, Sealgaire. Who's Master of the Wild Hunt these days, anyway?"

That damn smile got wider still, and I tell you, it didn't much look human anymore.

"Don't rightly matter, now, does it?"

In a way, I supposed that was true. Whoever the Master was at any given time—Herne, Gudrun, Hereward the Wake, Arawn himself, or a dozen others—they shaped the Hunt: their targets, their methods, to an extent even their appearance, though *where* they rode also impacted that.

Another glance at Sealgaire and I had a sudden image in my head: a few score like him, wielding spears and rifles and six-guns, pounding along endless roads atop massive, hideous horses, following behind a pack of demonic, slavering, fire-breathing bloodhounds. A sheriff's posse from hell, damn near literally.

I don't shudder often, but… yeah. The Wild Hunt takes a lotta forms, but something about that one bugged me in ways I still can't quite explain.

What's the Wild Hunt?

Oh, just a ravening horde of Fae, unnatural beasts, and worse, who charge through the world taking lives and souls, sometimes one by one, sometimes in whole villages. We don't know where they come from, what causes certain Fae to just abandon their lives to become goddamn hounds. Nature's backlash against some of us abusing our magics? Deal with the devil, if you believe in the mug?

No idea.

All any of us really knows is that they are implacable, constant, and uncontrollable. They don't take sides, and they don't do "friends." This right here, this mighta been the most neighborly talk anyone's had with one of the hunters in decades, if not centuries.

Where was—? Right. Master of the Hunt. Yeah, the Master shaped the Hunt some, but he was still swept right along with it. Still carried on a primal wave of instinct and bloodlust. He led, but he wasn't in charge. In some ways, wasn't really even himself for the duration of...

A prize buzzer went off in my head so loud I'm stunned Sealgaire didn't hear it.

"That's why Herne wants the spear! He thinks he can use it to keep control, keep *himself*, next time his turn comes around as Master of the Hunt!"

Got no agreement or even a nod from the Hunt's emissary, but that wolfish smile did slip, just a hair. The coyotes bowed forward, noses on the earth between their paws, and whined. A breeze kicked up, sending leaves scurrying around Sealgaire's feet, bobbing like religious postulants.

Actually, they were *all* blowin' around him, from every direction, as if the wind was sucked his way directly. Didn't much care for that. Still don't.

I needed to keep this moving along, I decided.

"So you're sure it's really here? Not just chasing rumors and whispers?"

"We don't cotton much to rumor, Oberon."

My surprise that he knew my name coulda been measured at exactly zero.

"But there's been a right heap of 'em," he added. "Goin' on for a long time now, longer'n your average hogwash gossip."

Shit. I'd *really* let myself get too sucked into the Caro case, if they'd been makin' the rounds for that long without me getting' wise to 'em. Still, it explained why so many people—well, "people"—took 'em serious.

"Could Herne actually do it?" I asked. "Use the spear to shape the Hunt to his desires, instead of vice-versa?"

"I reckon ain't nobody gonna be happy with the consequences if he gets hisself a chance to find out."

"And you're here to stop that?"

"I'm here to watch, son. See who, if anybody, gets holda Lugh's pig-sticker. There's a whole mess of folks we'd rather not come out on toppa *that* little contest."

That actually worried me worse'n if he'd said he was here to take a direct hand. I didn't think I much wanted to ask, but...

"And if one of them does?"

Leaves spun faster, 'til they crackled like cooking grease. Branches creaked, turnin' against the wind to reach his way, and the coyotes—though their whining never ceased—began to bristle and snarl between whimpers.

No smile at all, now, and the growls beneath his words were louder. Like I was listening to something with a much deeper voice talking *through* him.

"If we don't like where the spear ends up, boy... then we're coming to Chicago to fix it. Whatever it takes."

The pack screamed in unison, turned tail, and fled into the night.

"That..."

I was havin' my own trouble with words, now. The Wild Hunt in *Chicago*? It'd be a fucking massacre, human and Fae both! Even the Unseelie—even the Unseelie *with the Spear of Lugh*—could maybe be fought. The Hunt? The Hunt was a force of nature, and I mean Elphame nature, not your silly nonsense. You don't fight it, anymore'n you fight a twister. You just hope you can get out of its way.

But I never yet heard of a place you could hide from 'em indefinitely.

And at least all the Unseelie could do was torture and kill you. The Hunt wasn't near that gentle.

"That… won't be necessary, Sealgaire."

Dancing leaves dropped, branches snapped back to their proper angles, wind faded to a gentle breeze.

"Fantastic to hear. See that it ain't."

"You *do* know I'm foreswearing myself if I just hand the dingus over to you, don'tcha?" I challenged.

"Yep. Don't worry, son. The Hunt won't come after you for that."

"Swell. And how about everyone and everything *else* that'll come slaverin' for my friggin' soul? You gonna protect me from *them*?"

Just another predator's smile, a tip of his hat and he was gone, striding off—whistling "The Yellow Rose of Texas," believe it or not—'til he and his music both were lost in the early-dawn shadows.

I coulda tried to stop him, put him wise to exactly who I was (reluctantly) working for, that expecting *me* to make sure the wrong guys didn't take home the prize maybe wasn't the best idea. Somehow, though, I didn't figure that'd change his mind any—and *that's* assuming he didn't already know.

Grumbling all kinda profanities in Old Gaelic, I started the trek through the wilderness, back to civilization and the L that'd eventually carry me home.

CHAPTER EIGHT

Not that home was my first stop, more's the pity.

Between the rain and the tussle, I didn't exactly look my finest. Thought about going home first to slip into something a little less vagrant, but heck with it. The clubhouse was on... Well, all right, it wasn't on my way at all. But I knew that after a night like this, once I'd reached my flop, I wasn't gonna want to leave again.

And if you're thinkin' "Ain't he forgettin' about someone?" the answer is, yeah. Turns out that no matter *how* taken you are with a dame, a face-to-face with the Wild Hunt's gonna pretty well occupy your spare thoughts for a while.

So, clubhouse first.

The police station wasn't just made of bricks, it basically *was* one. Just a big heap of hardness squatting on the corner. I've seen more graceful architecture from cultures still working out the kinks in this brand-new invention called "the hammer."

Wasn't too packed yet, not at this hour. Most of the owls had already called it a night, and the day folks wouldn't start showing up to file their complaints in numbers for a while yet. I actually hadda open the door to walk in; usually it's just held that way by an ongoing current of flesh and sweat and cheap rags.

Know what, though? It was *still* loud enough inside to

drown out a couple locomotives making whoopee. Whole place echoes like a big cave—which is what it is, come to think.

I waved at the desk sarge as I pushed into the bullpen, flashed him a gleaming grin when he glared at me for not signing in. Gink knew me by sight, but he still wanted my John Hancock every time. Well, he was too busy right now to fuss—or at least to fuss anywhere near me—so I strolled right on in.

Typewriters clacked; blowers rang; impatient, grumbling voices gave way to impatient, *shouting* voices. You know, cop sounds. I scooted around a couple desks, made my way toward the offices on the far side.

See, after everything that'd gone down last night—and especially now I knew what could happen if the wrong cat wound up with Gáe Assail—I'd decided I was gonna have to choke down my pride and take whatever Galway wanted to scream at me for missing our sit-down. I needed in on the official case after all, needed every damn resource I could get. If I hadn't already gummed up my one'n only shot.

I was maybe three paces from the office doors when one of 'em swung open and I found myself mug-to-mug with a detective—just not the one I'd been looking for.

"Morning, Detective Keenan."

"Oberon."

The homicide dick looked like the contents of a clogged drain. Stubble was even thicker'n normal, hair didn't so much need a brush as a sedative, and his outfit—brown, everything always brown, as if it was a uniform—had more wrinkles than Baba Yaga's backside.

"I hope you're just comin' off an overnighter," I told him. "Otherwise I think you need a hospital."

Me'n Keenan weren't close, but we'd worked together a few times, and we had a mutual buddy in Pete, so normally joking around with him that way shoulda been fine. Today, though, he scowled.

"You can't be here," he said. "Not right now. Not for a while."

"What? Now wait a minute. I get that Galway's pretty steamed at me, but—"

"Not about Galway. Not anymore."

"What then?"

Keenan's scowl frowned—don't ask me to explain that, it just did. He spotted an empty desk, and half-guided/half-dragged me over to it. He sat. I couldn't help but notice he didn't ask me to do the same. Once we were there, though he didn't seem to know what to say.

"Lemme guess," I said. "Galway rescinded the job offer? Keenan, I can help with this. I know things. It's—"

"Not only is the offer off the table," the detective said, "but nobody in the department's supposed to work with you until further notice. Pete'll be *personally* ordered not to talk to you for the duration."

I think, if I *had* sat down, I'd have been up again in that moment anyway.

"*What?* What'd Galway—?"

"Not him, Oberon. Not any of the boys." He cocked his head to one side, back toward the offices. "Order from the chief. And *he* got it from…"

Another office door opened.

"…him," he finished, sounding even more tired.

The "him" in question was tall, almost painfully slender as best I could tell, given the tailored suit. Oh, yeah, and "he" was also a "she." Hair was gold as a good pancake with a thin layer of syrup, and unfashionably long. Down-to-the-backs-of-her-knees long.

She also had no eyes. Just dark, empty hollows where her peepers shoulda been.

I may or may not have jerked Keenan a nod in farewell, I don't really remember.

I walked over to her, slow and steady. She just crossed her arms and waited.

"Oberon." Voice was deep, musical.

"Áebinn. Been a while."

"Some would say not long enough."

I call what I did next *smiling*, but some mighta described it as *showing my teeth*.

"Some, but not you, right?"

"Oh, of course," she said in a dull tone that translated loosely as "Fuck off. Preferably in front of a fast-moving truck."

So, all right, quick skinny. I met Áebinn years ago, back when I was working as hotel detective at the Lambton Worm. She's *bean sidhe*, or "banshee" to you. Feed on proximity to death, though not normally the sort to cause 'em.

Most *bean sidhe* are tied to a specific bloodline; it's why you hear 'em howl when one of the family's about to croak. It's sorta a wail of anticipation. But the bloodline Áebinn was linked to died off some time ago. I mean, completely. I dunno the full story behind it, but rather'n find another to attach to, she wound up here in Chicago. Well, the Elphame side of Chicago. Been using her ability to sense imminent or recent death as an investigator for the Seelie Court.

In other words, she's basically a cop.

Well, Raighallan *had* told me he had a partner…

I chucked a thumb over my shoulder.

"So what're they seeing when they look at you?"

"Generic mortal male. With the proper documentation to convince whoever I need to that I'm a high-ranking agent of their 'Bureau of Prohibition.'" She shrugged. "Simple charm, and it excises a great deal of hassle."

"Yeah, I'll bet. What're you doing here, Áebinn?" Then, at her raised eyebrow—which is a *weird* thing to see when there ain't any accompanying eye—"Pretty sure we're out of your jurisdiction."

"We're making an exception."

"Uh-huh. So what're you doing *here* here? Not the mortal world. I mean *here*. The clubhouse."

"Inconveniencing myself," she sniffed. "To avoid greater inconvenience later."

"You mean cutting me off from police resources."

"I told you, Oberon," Raighallan's voice came from behind me. "Stay outta this."

I hadn't heard him approach. Managed not to start, though. I think that's something to be proud of.

"Lemme guess." I was still talking to Áebinn. "Your partner agent from the bureau?"

"This is the last time we're going to make a point of keeping this polite," she said. "If you interfere with us again, I'm going to have to treat it as criminal behavior. Potentially even enemy action."

"Gosh, I've never had enemies among the Seelie Court before."

Áebinn leaned in so she could whisper. This close, her pipes were potent enough that, even though she wasn't wailing, her words carried a chill.

"Make me one of them and you'll never have any again, either."

She straightened, smiled, and fluttered her fingers in the general direction of the door.

"You may go now."

You're in public, Mick. And she's an official emissary of the Court. And she ain't alone.

It was still *almost* worth it to sock that grin off her mug.

Almost.

I kept my mitts at my sides and made for the door, brushing Raighallan aside with a stiff shoulder on the way.

More rain. More train. Dripping, buzzing, cold, painful. I trudged up the steps to the door of Soucek's building, stabbed the lock with the key a couple times until I finally hit something vital, and lumbered inside. Each step left a rainwater footprint to soak into the carpet, but honestly, it woulda taken *two* of me, both not caring, to care any less.

Grouchy, is what I'm getting at. I don't call this the end to a good night, or the start to a good day.

I took the basement stairs, stomping on each one like I was mad at it. Finally I threw open the door to the hall...

And got myself such a smack across the chops, I wished someone would answer my ears already, so they'd stop ringing.

"You *louse*! You crummy, two-bit, no-good conman!"

Ah, shit.

The outfit was much the same as yesterday's, 'cept mostly in blues instead of greens, but it wasn't near as immaculate. Not sloppy or anything, just a little wrinkle here, a bit crooked there. Her hair was kinda frizzy, too; she hadn't spent much time on it, for sure.

Or she'd got caught in the rain, in which case it was right on the line of a miracle she still looked as put-together as she did.

"I was followed again this morning, for almost an hour! And where were *you*? They said you were *dependable*! They said you could be *trusted*! You've got everyone pretty well fooled, haven't you?"

I hadn't thought of her for hours, but now? Now the notion of her bein' this steamed at me, this *disappointed* in me, made my stomach knot. I felt like I'd just discovered my last big glass of milk had actually come from a bull, and it took some struggling to remind myself how words worked.

"Ramona, I—"

"Oh, *no*. That's 'Miss Webb,' to you! I want my money back! I want to see your license so I can file a complaint with the police! I want... Why do you look like that?"

The rain had washed away a good bit of the dirt and the mud, but my coat was still singed from acid-fish-juice, I was still kinda banged up from everything, and I still had a headache coming and going from the *rusalka*'s killer shriek.

"Got into a pretty ugly scrape last night, doll. I only just got done dealing with the bulls." Both statements being true, just... kinda incomplete.

"Oh!"

I swear she shrank about a foot and a half as her temper evaporated—or maybe I was just standing straighter, with its weight off me.

"Oh, Mick, I'm so sorry." She was redder than her hair, now. Her emotions smelled like she wanted to cry, but wasn't about to let it happen. "I'm such an idiot!"

"Nah, don't say that." It irritated me some that I was so keen to reassure her. I mean, *I* was the one who'd just been given what-for! Couldn't help it, though. "You had fine reason to think the worst. Don't even worry your—"

"Hush. Now unlock your office so I can clean you up!"

"Miss Webb—"

"I said *hush*. And it's Ramona."

More weight offa me. I tried not to let her see me grin.

So, inside. Hat, coat, jacket all on the tree, and then I was stuck in a chair while Ramona ran back and forth to the bathroom with a wet handkerchief and tried, real gentle and tender, to wipe my face off the front of my noggin.

I really don't dig why you people do that when there's nothing open and bleeding. It ain't as if you're gonna get a *bruise* any cleaner. Maybe it just makes you feel like you're doing something? Nuts, I dunno.

The attention was nice, though. *Real* nice. I even forgot to hurt for a few.

Anyway, after that, nothin' would do other'n her pouring me a snort. Gave me the most peculiar look when I assured her that, no, really, all I got is milk, but she rolled with it.

Only then, as I was leaning comfortably back with a glass of the white stuff, did she settle herself in the other chair.

"Mick…"

I've heard people sounding less nervous on their way to the gallows.

"Yeah?"

"Was this…" She held up the kerchief she'd used to play

nurse, sorta waved it back at my flogger and jacket, hanging all forlorn across the room. "Was this because of me? The people who are after me?"

I smiled at her, genuinely moved that she felt guilty at the possibility. The old me—I mean real, *real* old me—mighta strung her along on that for a while, used it to manipulate her some.

I told you before, there are reasons I ain't the old me anymore. And even more now than before I'd met her.

"Nothing to do with you, kid. One of my other cases. Promise."

The first twitch of what might grow into a return smile was a ray of sunshine through the clouds. And yeah, I know how cornball that sounds. I knew it *then*. Still how I thought of it.

"Well, *most* of it might be nothing to do with me," she said softly. She *did* grin, now, but it was mostly outta embarrassment. "I'm sorry."

"Ah, no big deal. I been slapped a lot harder'n that," I assured her.

"I don't doubt it."

I stared at her a minute, until we both busted up laughing. Think we both needed it.

"Ramona," I said when we were finally done, "I *do* think you mighta had the right idea, even if for the wrong reason."

She rooted around in her purse, found herself a cigarette and lit up. I didn't bother protesting, especially since I didn't much mind the opportunity to watch her lips working.

"How so?" she asked.

"I think maybe you *should* find yourself another shamus. This other case—"

"No! Mick, no. People I trust, trust you. I don't want... I mean, there isn't anybody else."

I shook my head. I mean, I didn't really *want* her to go find someone else, but I didn't want her hurt, either.

"Appreciate that, but being around me ain't safe right now."

"Oh, sure," she scoffed, blowing a short plume in my direction. "Because I'm *so* safe on my own. Not a chance, especially not after this morning's news!"

"Wait, this morning's—?"

"If you *must* keep dealing with this other case, I'll stick with you until it's done."

Now I didn't just shake my melon, I leant over the desk, like I was grilling her for classified info.

"No way, sweetheart. Forget it. These people are rougher customers than anyone you might have gunning for you. Ain't happening."

I mighta come off kinda gruff, yeah. But the idea of her gettin' mixed up with my world scared the crap outta me.

Ramona matched my gaze and didn't look too impressed.

"You'll have to tie me to this chair, Mick."

"That can be arranged."

She gave me an eyebrow, and I gave thanks—again—that, like sweating, blushing ain't one of those things I'm usually subject to.

"Look," I tried, pleaded, "you gotta understand—"

"I do. I get that you're trying to protect me. But I'm not going away, and I'm *certainly* not hiring anyone else! If you manage to ditch me, you really will be leaving me *alone*."

My poor, put-upon chair squeaked a complaint as I folded hard back into it.

"You're crazy. Wacky in the bean." And God, I was grateful for it.

Damn it, I was beat up, steamed as a Maine lobster, and gettin' on towards tired, and her smile was still radiant.

"You wouldn't be the first to tell me that," she told me.

I still dunno what my final answer woulda been in those circumstances. My trap opened, and I had no idea what I was about to say. Whatever it might have been, I never found out.

The both of us started at the muffled thump of the stairwell door.

"Expecting someone?" she asked.

No. No, I wasn't. Coulda been someone else with a place in

the building, coulda been a new client, but... Well, there ain't that many of either.

I froze a sec, reaching out. Couldn't always tell, but...

Yeah. Fae.

"Sorry 'bout this, babe."

"Huh? About wha*aaaaaa*...!"

I hauled her outta the chair and steered her by the shoulders into the bathroom, more or less with one move. (Thankfully, the Old Gold flared and went out as she dropped it, rather'n trying to set my carpet on fire.) She'd just twisted my way, furious as an aching badger, when I slammed the door shut between us. I pretty well *dove* for my coat, yanked the L&G out, and fired it, before she could twist the knob to get out. Couple small bits stopped working inside the lock—sudden and drastic loss of luck—ensuring that latch wasn't unlatching anytime soon. I'd fix it later.

Now, I got my moments, but I ain't as stupid as I look. I'm sure you remember the *last* time I had a dame stuck in that bathroom—*I* sure as hell did.

That time, I'd used a bit of the old magic to make sure the sound in the room carried *to* her. This time, well, I flipped on the rotary fan that hadn't been used in a dog's age, turned it away from the desk, and made sure that was all any bathroom eavesdropper would hear.

Quick rap on the door, impatient, and not the first one.

"All right, already!" Wand in hand, I stepped to one side of the doorway, reached out, and clicked the lock. "It's open!"

Old Man Téimhneach, my least favorite boggart—and there's competition for *that* title, make no mistake—shoved the door open and peered in around the jamb with that wide, empty smirk I was already good'n sick of.

He had crooked grandpa teeth and breath like an old, musty library.

"You appear a bit jumpy, Mr. Oberon."

"And you appear to be standing in my doorway like a lump.

You coming in, or should I start trying to coordinate you with the rest of the furniture?"

"Amusing." He wandered inside.

I stuck my head out quick, got a good slant on Grangullie—damn redcap waved at me from beside the stairwell, and I just knew his hat was leaving blood smears on the wall—and then sat down with his boss and, for now, mine.

"Okay, you're here, and I suffered a sudden drop in brain pressure and let you in. So whaddaya want?" I demanded.

Téimhneach reclined, crossing his legs at the knees *and* ankles—frickin' boggarts—and steepled his fingers together.

"Why, a progress report, of course, Mr. Oberon."

I forced a chuckle. "Funny. No, really, why—?"

His expression didn't change. Mine dropped far enough to taste shoe.

"You can't be serious! I ain't been on this job much more'n one night! What the hell do you expect me dig up in *that* timeframe?"

"A magic spear."

"Oh, go climb your thumb." Then, after a second noodling over whether I wanted him to know I knew, "Well, I found out what your 'magic spear' actually *is*, for one thing."

He waved a few fingertips. "We assumed you would."

"Then why...? Ah. Because your teeny tiny boss thought that if I knew what it was before I'd agreed to find it, I mighta tried harder to find a way outta taking the gig."

"You'd have failed," he said, the words slithering through those ugly teeth. "But it would have wasted time and energy that neither of us—"

"Yeah, fine. I'll add it to the list."

"Surely you've learned more than *that*. Are you not supposed to be some astonishing detective?"

"Nah. On a good day, I'm supposed to be an *adequate* detective." Then, since that clown-smile was finally slippin' a notch, "I found out about some of the other parties after your gewgaw of Lugh. You already know about the Seelie, I figure. And I told you about Herne."

"We had already heard the Hunter had come to Chicago before you informed us."

"Yeah, whatever. More outsiders? Comin' at least via the river, probably others?"

"You're still not telling me anything useful, Mr. Oberon. I'd hate to have to—"

"How about the Wild Hunt?"

Ha! I knew there hadda be *something* that'd wipe that greasy leer off his mug!

"Here?" He didn't look like he looked like an old man anymore; he looked like he *was* an old man. (If you spend any time around the Fae, that'll make sense to you.) "The Wild Hunt is *here*? How could we not know? We'd have heard—"

"Not here, exactly. Not yet. They got a good slant on us, though, and if *they* ain't happy with the outcome of this snipe hunt, *nobody's* gonna be happy with it. You dig?"

"Then why are you wasting my time?" he shrieked, rising from his chair while still seated, and then straightening his legs to reach the floor. "No more stalling, Oberon! I want progress! *I want that spear!*"

My turn to recline. Even steepled my fingers together the way he had.

"You *got* progress, bo. More'n you had any right to expect after just a few hours of—"

"Do better! It would be in the best interests of all three of us if you were to... accelerate your efforts."

Three? He hadn't somehow sensed Ramona, had he?

"You got a mouse in your pocket, bo? Maybe you're soft on Grangullie and want him to be—"

Téimhneach blinked, long and languid, which wouldn't have been a big deal 'cept the lids on his left lamp snapped shut vertically this time, instead of horizontally.

"Why, you, me, and Officer Peter Staten, of course."

Think my blood went so thick'n cold it coulda doubled as mortar.

"What?"

I'm surprised I got the word out. Just as surprised I didn't immediately put the nearest sharp thing through the boggart's map.

"Yes," he yapped on, "I think the next full moon's as good a deadline as any." His cheeks actually extended to fit his nasty grin. "We're quite aware of Staten's unfortunate condition, Oberon. It hasn't been worth our time to interfere, as we had little to gain, and slaughtering a lycanthrope in the wilds of Elphame is a, ah, tricky proposition.

"But it *is* quite achievable, with the proper motivation. And we both know you cannot afford *not* to bring him."

"If you go anywhere *near*—"

"Oh, is it threat time now? How tiresome."

My hand was shaking some. Yeah, that's a tic we share with you lot. *If* we get angry enough.

And he was *still* jabbering on! "Fortunately, such threats are, in addition to meaningless, quite unnecessary. The full moon is still a couple of weeks away. I have *every* confidence that you'll have results for us well before then.

"Good day, Mister Oberon, and good hunting."

That ugly grin got wider, curled back around until the corners of his lips touched in back and he flipped his whole head open.

No, really. Opened his trap wide, and *kept* on opening it, 'til the top half of his head fell back like it was hinged, leaving his mouth one great big honkin' hole, a ring of flesh, bone, and crooked teeth.

Then that ring dropped to the floor, his body vanishing through it, and he was gone.

Say it with me, now. *Goddamn boggarts.*

Still, hinky as it was, even for me, it was probably a good thing he'd pulled his vanishing act instead of just hoofing it outta here. If he'd turned his back on me, I really mighta stabbed him. I knew I hadda calm down when the bulb over my head started to shudder, and somethin' in the icebox cracked itself open.

He'd picked the right leverage. I was gonna work a lot harder'n faster with Pete in danger, even if I'd never admit that—to Téimhneach or Pete, either. But you do *not* threaten my people.

I ain't got many of 'em as it is.

Attacking Téimhneach woulda meant starting a war I couldn't win, which is why I *hadn't* shanked him something good.

But he'd regret today; I got a *long* memory.

I went back to the office door, flicked the lock, and stuck my noggin into the corridor again.

"Your boss just took a powder," I snapped.

Grangullie sighed, shot me a look that said "What're you gonna do?" no matter which side of Chicago you were, and scurried back toward the stairs.

Probably shoulda just let it go at that, but I was too hot under the collar.

"Tell him something for me, Grannie," I shouted after him.

He froze, his whole back clenched as he tensed, but I wasn't gonna give him time to get a word in.

"Tell him if he—or you, or any of your jolly mob—hurt Pete, I don't give a fuck what oaths I've sworn to who, or what it costs me. I *will* end him."

Even more shoulder work. I think I coulda blunted an axe on his spine in that moment, and it wouldn'ta broken the skin. But it wasn't anger making him tense up like a piano wire with stage fright.

"Threatened Staten, huh?" He was tryin' to sound nonchalant, but the surprise in his voice was unmistakable. He hadn't been expecting that at all—and he wasn't too thrilled with it.

He was gone, though, before I'd decided if I could risk pressing the issue. Plenty else to worry about, and now I got to add warning Pete and tryin' to keep him not-dead to the list.

Not that the *rest* of the list was lookin' any more fun. Shame the bloodthirsty, mobbed-up redcap *wasn't* the scariest conversation I needed to have.

Took an extra few minutes—putting off the inevitable, maybe—to handle a few lingering details. First, a quick call on the horn to warn Pete about his new fans. The tirade that followed proved that my friend had some creative but wildly inaccurate ideas of Fae physiology and sexual practices.

Then, when that lovely conversation was done, I popped on out to the corner and dropped a few coins on a newsrag. (I didn't *see* Sealgaire anywhere, but the centipedes in fuzzy slippers playing hopscotch up'n down my spine made me think he was probably somewhere close.) Quick skim told me a whole lotta nothing immediately relevant. People were still celebrating Roosevelt's election; the Bears were lookin' like they might go all the way this year; couple of shopkeepers got shot in a robbery spree up on the north side; one of our aldermen slipped in the shower and cracked his conk open on the side of the tub (between him'n Judge Meadors, this hadn't been a good week for city officials); over a dozen dead in Switzerland after the army opened up on a buncha protestors; a car bomb, which—this being the Windy City—hadn't even made the front page; lotta different fairs and carnivals were heading our way for the next few months, since nobody expected to be able to compete with the "Century of Progress" exposition come May; unsolved murder this; bank robbery that; and so on, and so forth, and enough already.

Lots and lots of "definitely not." A handful of headlines that Ramona *could've* been talking about before, sure, but not any I could put my chips on.

Meant there was nothing left but to do it. I think I'd have rather tussled with Herne again.

I shut off the fan, poked the bathroom doorknob with the L&G until the bits and whatsises fell back into place, and carefully cracked the door open.

"Um," I explained, hoping I didn't come across near as sheepish as I felt.

Ramona stood in the middle of the room, arms crossed, and *glared*, fierce enough to make a Gorgon blink first. Hell, maybe to make a Gorgon's *victim* blink!

"Uh," I apologized.

She stormed past me out into the office, managing to brush by—hard—without actually knocking into me. Dunno how she managed *that* in the bathroom doorway.

It woulda been easier if she'd gotten hysterical, screamed, threw a full on ing-bing. At least then I'd have *known* how upset—hurt—she was. Instead, she advanced on the desk like it'd called her names and snatched up the newspaper.

"Look, doll," I tried again, trailing after her. Just one big puppy, me. "You gotta understand—"

"Here." She stabbed the paper with a finger, hard enough that I winced.

Can't say I was much surprised that she'd all but punched a hole in the car bomb story. Picture showed the burnt-out wreck of what'd been a real nice (if you go for that sorta thing) Cadillac, with an engine the size of Dearborn Street station. Not my area of expertise, but given the damage to the engine and the front seats, I figured on "dynamite wired to the ignition" even before the article got there.

Considering just how many types of hatchetmen actually use car bombs, I was about equally surprised to read that at least some of the victims were made men. Maybe they all were, but the boys in blue hadn't IDed 'em all yet. One of the names they *had* released—hoodlum by the not-at-all-Italian-sounding name of Giancarlo Manetti—was ringing bells in the back of my head, though they were so faint I couldn't tell if it was Vespers or a streetcar crossing.

After a moment, I said, "All right. What's it gotta do with you, though?"

She looked at me like she was counting the different varieties of stupid. I wanted to crawl behind the Murphy bed and close it up after me.

"Not wanting to wind up that way, for one."

"Well, sure, but c'mon. We don't even know for certain the people you're mixed up with are Mob. Even if they are, the odds that they're directly linked to *this* crew—" I tapped the paper "—or the guys who whacked 'em, are pretty damn small, savvy?"

She added another stupid to her tally. "Mick... the various organizations, the... what, Outfit?"

"Yeah."

"The Outfit, North Side, all of those... It's all been fairly quiet lately, hasn't it? Not a lot of warring between them?"

Depends what you mean by quiet. If you count magic...

But, "Yeah, fairly."

Again she poked at the paper. "So isn't this rather brazen? For 'peacetime'?"

Maybe not so much as she thought—the Mob, they don't tend to go in for subtle—but I hadda admit, she had a point.

I mean, it didn't *have* to be the Outfit. Coulda been any sorta smaller criminal endeavor, or something personal. Even wondered for a sec if this mighta been a sign of that violence I was lookin' for, but a car bomb ain't really the Unseelie style. Too technological and too impersonal for 'em, especially for redcaps.

"I don't know what's what in the underworld," she concluded. "I don't *want* to know. But if things are heating up for whatever reason, and there's even a chance the people who think I owe them could be caught up in whatever's about to happen..."

"Ramona, probable as it is, we don't even know for sure that whoever's gunning for you *are* the same mugs your cousin owed." It was a reflex protest, though. She was right; there were a lotta *ifs* and *maybes*, yeah, but they weren't that far-fetched.

"Mick... Please. I need this. I don't... want to be alone. And besides," she added with forced cheer, "you know I'll just follow you anyway."

"Oh, for... Fine!" I agreed.

Why the hell did I agree? I knew better than to agree. I didn't *want* to agree!

Except, it seemed that I *did*.

"You stick by me," I continued. "You do what I say *when* I say, and you don't ask questions."

"I'll give you the first two."

Why was I not surprised?

"Whatever. I'll just hide you back in the bathroom if I need…"

Ding-ding-ding! "Hide." That was the trigger I'd needed in order to remember where I'd heard of that one guy before.

Manetti's a smuggler and bootlegger. It was the cat's specialty, moving illegal or stolen goods into or outta the city. I'd come across his name a few months ago, doing some follow-up digging after the mess with the Ottatis. See, I'd gotten wise that Vince "Bumpy" Scola, a rival of Fino Ottati's, knew something about magic. Not a lot, maybe barely anything, but he knew it existed and wore a couple charms, just in case. So *also* just in case, I figured I'd better dig up some more about him. I'd read about Manetti among Scola's known associates.

Big deal, right? Ain't like bootleggers are a rare breed around here, and a *lotta* trouble boys know Scola in one way or another. No reason to guess this meant anything about anything.

Except… Lots of bootleggers, yeah, but not nearly as many who *specialize* in it. Who make a point of hiring out to multiple crews specifically as a top-notch smuggler.

Now he'd gotten himself zotzed in a big way, right after one of the world's oldest pieces of contraband had been snuck into Chicago.

Coulda been coincidence, but it felt worth checking out, at least.

"Hold that thought, sweetheart," I said, even though I'd been the last one jawing. I collected a nickel from a desk drawer and wandered out into the hall.

"Okay, pal. I don't like you, you don't like me, so let's just get this done fast as we can."

Having said my piece, I picked up the blower, dropped in my nickel, and waited for the operator.

No sure way to reach Pete. I'd been lucky to catch him earlier; by now he was probably out on his rounds, pounding the sidewalk flat. But Keenan... Yeah, they weren't supposed to give me anything, but I figured I could sweet-talk a little knowledge out of him. I mean, all I wanted was info on a couple mobsters. Shouldn't be too tough.

When I hung up a few minutes later, my ears burned like I'd been shoving matchsticks in 'em, and, for once, it *wasn't* 'cause of the horn itself.

"Guess Keenan takes his orders pretty serious," I muttered, trudging back to the office. "Impressive vocabulary, too."

I stepped in, made a quick rummage through my drawer of oddities, and then slung my jacket and flogger off the rack. Ramona, who'd just seated herself in my chair, promptly stood.

I enjoyed watching her more'n I had the boggart, just for the record.

"Where are we going?" she asked.

I didn't even argue the *we* anymore. Just didn't seem worth the energy, and we both knew I didn't really wanna ditch her.

"If one side of the law won't talk to me," I answered, "I'll just have to talk to the other."

"Huh?"

"Never mind. You'll see. Do what I say, when—"

"When you say it, yeah." Ramona collected her purse and coat, a fur-lined thing, awfully nice but with its best days behind it. "You told me already."

"Wanted to make sure you heard." I held the door open and she ducked out around me—then stopped.

"Mick?"

"Hmm?"

"You could've just told me you needed me to hide in the bathroom. I'd have gone."

"With or without asking a million questions first?" I asked.

She turned and headed for the stairwell door, but not before I saw the knowing smirk trying to slide its way across her face.

CHAPTER NINE

"Are you *nuts*?" she hissed.

What it lacked in volume it more'n made up in intensity.

"Hey, I figured this neighborhood would be to your taste."

"The neighborhood *is*!" Ramona snapped back. "The *neighbors* aren't!"

See, thing is, I hadn't let on *exactly* where we were going. We took the L south, hopped out somewhere in the mid 60s-eth streets, and hoofed it on up Calumet. Nice area, here, especially for the far-south side. Not too swanky, but the grass was still mostly green, the windows glinted despite the overcast skies, and the red-brick houses were more'n big enough for comfort. Pedestrians ankled on by, friendly enough. The cans chugging past in the street were kept well enough that the exhaust was only *almost* enough to choke a goat. Ramona'd been in pretty good cheer over it all, especially for someone with the curse on her, until I told her who we were calling on.

(Uh, I guess I oughta clarify, I don't mean a literal curse, I mean someone'd put out a contract on her. Metaphor and slang and all that. Given where we were headed, and what happened here a few months ago, figured I better lay it out clear.)

"How do you know these aren't the people who are after me?" she demanded.

"'Cause I know 'em, Ramona. He ain't gonna take home any awards for kindness, and people who cross him occasionally seem to walk in front of really tiny, really fast-moving objects. But he don't hurt people without good cause, and he owes me. Big. Hell, if I *did* have to muster up some guys to protect you, I could probably count on his more'n most of the cops.

"Plus, his wife's real friendly."

Considering that she spent the rest of the walk up to the door grumbling about the idiocy of bringing her to a gangster's home, I'm gonna go out on a limb and suppose she didn't buy the reassurance. I tried not to take it personal, and *mostly* succeeded.

Raised some knuckles to knock, and froze. Always did, just for a blink or two, even though I'd been here something like five times since it all went down. No matter how much I *knew* Maldera's wards were long gone, I couldn't forget the burning, the sickness. Approaching that house, stepping across that threshold, was an act of will every damn time.

Suck it up, Oberon.

If I hadn't already been wise to the birds watching us through various windows, the door opening about a second and a half after I knocked woulda told me. Lug tryin' to stare me down wasn't one of the boys I'd met before, but he definitely came off the same assembly line. Big, not real sharp-looking, and draped in a suit that did bupkis to hide the heater he was packing at his left shoulder.

I was sure he could have it in his meathooks in a heartbeat if he decided he didn't care for me.

"Yeah?" he said.

I couldn't help it. "Would you kindly tell the lady of the house that the representative from Credne Household Device Repair—and his, uh, assistant—would be grateful for a moment of her time?"

He blinked, and the already limited intelligence shining in his peepers dimmed another notch. It was like the shadow of a cloud passing in front of a slightly whiter cloud.

"Look, pal, this household don't need any kinda—"

"Hey! Jerry!" This from a guy inside who was basically a conceptual twin to the doorman (Jerry, apparently). He, though, was a crew soldier I *had* met on a couple prior visits. "Let the man in already! He's right with the boss."

Jerry's forehead and cheeks turned into wrinkles. Guess he didn't enjoy being showed up.

"What about the dame? You didn't say nothin' 'bout her!"

Ramona reddened. "I beg your—!"

I shook my head, and she sullenly bit her lip.

The other guy sighed, tossed me a halfway apologetic look. "So check her before you let her in, you *gavone*!"

The doorman turned back with a leer, and I decided I was done playing nice. I was just about to slip in behind his forehead and dance an impromptu samba in his noggin. Turned out I didn't need to.

"I want you to think really hard," Ramona said—nah, *growled*—"about what's going to happen if a friend of the boss complains to him about wandering mitts."

Jerry might be dumb, but he wasn't *that* dumb. He nodded so hard I think it slung the smile off, and proceeded to pat Ramona down—politely and professionally. I figured it'd ruin her performance if I applauded, so I held off.

As I figured, I hadda force myself to pass through the door, and also as I figured, it was the memory of Maldera's magics, not the new ones, that did it. The Ottatis got their own wards up, now, but they'd worked in a free pass for me. Not that it made no nevermind anyway. The new wards wouldn't keep out a determined pixie. Pretty clear the talent for witchcraft didn't run in the family.

Felt something else, too, though. Something spiritually hinky. Something that, far as I knew, was unique to this house. Or rather, to the girl lying dead to the world upstairs.

And then there I was, back in that same sitting room. The same table, the same chairs and sofa with the same paisley upholstery and cushions so overstuffed you could build wings for an entire choir of angels with the feathers.

(Given what I already told you, I guess I better clarify again. If angels exist, I never seen one. Just me being poetic. Go with it, savvy?)

Ramona gawped, and I couldn't figure why—place wasn't *that* ritzy—until she said softly, "My, they're *very* Catholic, aren't they?"

I chuckled at that. "Votaries outnumbered the crucifixes and portraits together, last I checked. But that mighta changed by—"

"Mick!" The woman was first through the door, wrapping me in a hug that I'd really rather have avoided. Her hair was ink-black, and she was startin' to look her age—worry lines, mostly—but carried it well.

Her husband was right behind her, and their daughter— well, one of 'em—behind *him*. Block-jawed and heavy lidded, Fino wore dark brown, and combed his hair like he was still trying to pretend it wasn't going away. And the girl... Well, she looked a lot like her mother.

All one happy, *normal* family, if you didn't know what the guy did to earn his lettuce. Or his ancestry. Or the girl's history. Or... Yeah, not a normal family at all.

"Hey, *amico*!" Another hug, damn it. Couldn't the guy just shake hands? "How you doin'?"

The daughter didn't come close enough to hug or slap palms, just hung back and jerked me a nod.

"Keeping alive, Fino. Guys, Ramona. Ramona? Fino, Bianca, and Celia Ottati."

Then, of course, I hadda sit through another round of handshakes and half hugs and the *good-ta-meetcha*s and the *any frienda*s. Almost as bad as being back home at the Court.

Another five minutes or more, until everyone who wanted a snort of something had a glass beside 'em, and we'd all staked out a seat somewhere. Few *more* minutes of gum bumping that nearly had me pulling my hair out with my teeth, until finally we passed whatever that magic line is where it's not rude anymore to talk business.

"Are you here about Adalina?" Bianca whispered, as though she wasn't sure she wanted to hear herself ask.

I opened my trap, but her husband beat me to it. "Nah, *tesora*, he ain't here for that. He'da said so right off, same way he always does. So, what the fu—uh, heck—" he corrected himself, gaze ping-ponging between Ramona'n me, "*does* bring you all the way cross fu—uh, cross town?"

I might notta been at my sharpest just then, but I ain't *that* slow. It only took me a shake to figure out what his dancing eyeballs were asking.

My soul sank into my stomach so hard, I figure it was lookin' at real estate down there. It hadn't even crossed my noggin to watch what I was about to blurt out. And not just my own secrets, but the Ottati's, too.

I trusted her. I just… did. And that, that didn't sit right. With my job, my history, my life? I gotta have months, if not years, before I'll let my guard down around someone. Ramona was different—and she shouldn'ta been, no matter how taken I was.

Could I really be *that* much off my game?

I loved what I hadda do next even less, though. I wanted to squirm in the chair, maybe crawl under the cushion.

"Hey, Fino, I wonder if someone could entertain Ramona for a while. I don't think she'd have much interest in what we gotta say."

"Sure. Hey, Celia, you wanna show our guest around a little?"

Whatever muscle it is that adolescents got that let's 'em roll their eyes farther'n adults can, Celia's was well developed.

"I think I'd prefer to stay." Ramona's voice woulda frozen a hot cuppa joe solid through.

Oh, God, I was gonna suffer for this. Hell, I already was.

"Ramona, we got things to…" I began gently. "Confidentiality issues, you dig? If it was just about me…"

Ramona said nothing more, didn't even look my way, just followed when Celia stood—with a sigh *just* quiet enough for her parents to pretend they didn't hear—and blew the room.

"The Shark," as they called him in Mob circles, studied the door, studied me, and grinned.

"That's one hot number, but you maybe shoulda left her at home. You're gonna fucking pay for this, later."

"Tell me about it." And sure, I didn't much enjoy the thought of Ramona hot under the collar, but... I'd hurt her pride and her feelings, both. I felt like a heel for it, too.

But damn it, why *hadn't* I thought of it? Why'd Fino need to remind me?

"How's Celia doing?" I asked, then, tearing my attention from the empty doorway—and circling questions I knew I couldn't shoo away right now.

They both frowned, and Bianca began sliding a rosary between two fingers.

"It's been hard," she admitted. "Six months is a good while, but not enough to recapture a lifetime. We... still don't really know who she is, sometimes."

"But she's still here," I pointed out. We'd all figured there were decent odds she'da taken the run-out by now. "She's tryin' to be your daughter."

"I dunno," Fino said. "Maybe."

"She spends most of her time alone," his wife continued, "or else taking care of—of her sister. I think she's a lot more concerned with Adalina than becoming family with us. Still, we talk. We eat together. There's less distance than there was. That's something."

"Yeah. Yeah, that's a lot better'n it coulda gone," I agreed.

"I think she's still a little afraid, too. Any sign of him?" she asked.

The "him" in question was a miserable, abnormally cruel *phouka* by the name of Goswythe. He was the bastard who'd raised Celia in Elphame, telling her that her family hadn't wanted her, teaching her to obey and steal and otherwise be his damn slave-puppet. Me'n him had had it out, and I think I was gettin' the better of him, but last I saw of him was right before a witch's spell had knocked us both completely loopy. Hadn't heard hide nor hair of him since; when a shapeshifter wants to stay hidden, they can, but I'd have expected him to come after me—or her—by now.

'Cause, y'know, we none of us had enough to worry about.

"Not a peep," I told them.

They weren't surprised.

"And Adalina?" I asked. "How's she?"

Bianca's rosary occupied *both* hands, now. "Nothing's changed, Mick. She still won't wake up, no matter what we do."

I winced at that—I'd told 'em more than once not to *do* anything until we knew more—but it woulda been a trip for biscuits to try to convince 'em yet again.

"The muttering *has* gotten worse, though," she continued. "It's almost constant, now. It keeps her tossing and turning for hours and hours..."

The muttering was a new symptom, started about a week ago. They'd called me in a panic, and I'd been stuck with that damn horn in my ear for an hour.

"All right. Don't think it means a lot, but I'll look in on her before I go. Eating?"

"Yeah." Fino shook his head. "We put food in her mouth—well, Celia does, mostly—she chews and swallows, but... *Maddon'*, she *still* don't seem anywhere close to awake! Just, mouth movin', lifeless, like a fucking industrial—"

"Stop!" Bianca sobbed.

"Yeah," he said again. "Sorry."

"I'm doing what I can," I assured them. Which I guess wasn't technically true: I *coulda* been spending all my time in Elphame, instead of just popping in now and again, trying to suss out what the hell the changeling actually was. But I got my limits; *nothing's* worth spendin' any more time in the

Otherworld than I absolutely gotta.

Besides, I *did* have other cases. Speakin' of…

"Look, guys," I said. "Reason I *am* here is, I got this thing I'm working on, and I think you could do me some good."

"Anything," Bianca said quickly. "We owe you that."

Fino answered a bit slower, bit more thoughtfully. "Whatever we can do."

"Swell. You can start by singing me a couple verses about Giancarlo Manetti."

"Ha!" Fino declared. "Anything I sing about *that stronzo*'s gonna be 'Amazing Grace.' Maybe Chopin."

"I'm gonna use my brilliant gumshoe deductive powers," I said, "and guess that, one, you already know someone knocked him off. And two, you and he didn't exactly drink outta the same bottle."

"I mean, it ain't like we had a real beef or nothing. Guy was just a fucking ass. Hang a gondola from his ego, you'da had yourself a fuckin' zeppelin."

"I'll bring you by the Seelie Court sometime. You wanna see ego… So, yeah. Bootlegger, right?"

Fino nodded, throwing back a quick slug of whatever eel juice had been poured for him.

"Bootlegger and smuggler of anything you care to fucking think of. Booze, sure, but also stolen goods, hop, mescal, even people didn't want nobody wise that they were in—or leaving—Chicago."

Bianca lightly toe-kicked him under the table.

"All right, already!" he snapped. Then shrugged at me. "Gink was the worst kinda *gavone*, but I gotta admit, he was good. One of the best. Think that's why everyone put up with him. 'Til now."

His wife glanced my way and smiled. "You have to prod him, sometimes."

The Shark muttered under his breath. I didn't catch most of it, but there were a *whole* lotta words that rhymed with "duck."

I let him simmer down, took a slug of my own drink—they knew to keep extra milk for me by now; sweet of 'em, really—and went on. "Any notion of who he's been working for, or with?"

"Hmm. Well, I can tell ya who got zotzed in the car along with him, for starters. I got a guy in the coroner's office, and I just got the lowdown myself. Lessee…"

Fino rattled off a trio of names, the first two of which meant zip to me. Name number three, though…

Pretty sure I leaned forward sharp enough to slice the cushion under me.

"Gimme that again?"

"Uh, Caro. Miles Caro. Say, wasn't that the guy you were askin' around about the other day?"

Well, dunk me in the river and call me Ophelia. How'dya like that? Guess the poor idiot *had* gotten into something over his head. Least I had an answer for his family, even if it wasn't the one they wanted.

(And yeah, that's the slight overlap I mentioned earlier. Big case gave me the answer to a little one, is all. Sometimes weird coincidence really is just weird coincidence.)

"Any idea who Manetti'd been running for, lately? Any chance it was Scola?"

"Shit, what do I know, Mick? It *coulda* been, sure. That bastard hired him often enough. But it coulda been any one of a couple dozen others, too."

The upholstery *fwoomped* under my head as I leaned back, staring at the line where wallpaper met ceiling. Tiny grey spider in one corner paused in his web-building to stare right back.

Then, since "web" made me think "Webb," and I really needed my focus right now, I ignored it.

I sighed, really for their sake, not mine. So they knew I didn't wanna do this.

"You guys know of anyone else in the, ah, business might also use some of the… special tools you do?"

Didn't either of 'em look happy I'd asked. We were startin'

to tread on some uncomfortable ground.

It was Bianca who answered. Guess he'd given up trying to keep any of the business from her.

"You already know about Scola—" she began.

"Right."

Now Fino jumped in again. "Guy called Eli Housemann. North Sider. Rumor has it he uses that, uh, whaddayacall? That Jewish hocus-pocus?"

"Kabbalah," Bianca and I said at once.

"Yeah. That. He ain't been around much last couple years, though."

No shock, there, since I was *why* he hadn't been doing much. Got into a case involving him back in '29, though I never met the guy. Wasn't able to get anything the state could use to convict, but Pete'n me'd managed to gum up his magic safeguards enough that his operation sorta fell to pieces. I called it a win.

Didn't seem worth getting into right now, though.

The both of 'em tossed a couple more monikers my way. Ricky Kincaid, Saul Fleischer, Finn Skelley...

Two things, right off the jump.

One, while it wasn't exactly a phone book they were givin' me, it was more names than I expected. Really didn't care for the notion that so many of Chicago's low-and-mighty even knew magic existed, let alone used it.

And two...

"Can't help but notice," I said, "that, other'n Scola—who I already knew about, and who you guys wouldn't mind seeing pushing up daisies—there's not an Italian name on your list. How much you wanna bet that, if I dig into it, I'm gonna find out real easy that everyone else you've named is a North Sider, not Outfit?"

Bianca, at least, had the grace to look a little embarrassed. Fino just grinned—friendly enough, but with some real bite behind it if you got a close enough slant.

"I owe you. *Maddon'*, there ain't words for what I owe you. But I got other loyalties, too. I can't rat one to satisfy the other. I won't."

I coulda *made* him. Right there. But the both of 'em would know what I'd pulled, and right now I was a lot better off with Fino "the Shark" as an ally, not an enemy. Still, I was seriously considering it when he continued.

"I'll tell you this. There ain't a lotta guys in the Outfit have any truck with the kinda shit you're talking about. Those that do, least according to rumor? None of 'em been real busy last few weeks with anything but normal business. I'd have heard otherwise."

"You sure about that, Fino?"

He was all stone, now. "Sure enough for this conversation, Mick."

"*Capisco*," I said. He'd just told me I'd pushed that question 'bout as far as it'd stretch, and if he hadda tell me again, it wouldn't be so politely.

It'd do, for now. If I hadda come back later and make him sing louder, well... I'd deal with the troll under that bridge when I came to it.

"Thanks."

I stood, and the pair of 'em scrambled to do the same.

"I'll pop in on Adalina real quick, and..."

Huh. Now *there* was a thought. I didn't wanna worry 'em any more than they already were, but I didn't want 'em caught by surprise, either.

"Fino, Bianca... I can't much go into what's happening, but there's a *lot* of Fae in Chicago right now. Far more'n usual, and that includes the Unseelie. They all got a particular reason for being here, but that don't mean one of 'em might not try to grab Adalina while the gettin's good."

Bianca gasped, clutching at her rosary. Fino's breath seemed stuck in his throat.

"I'll try'n strengthen the wards," he said finally.

I nodded.

"Do that."

It probably wouldn't help. As I said, Fino didn't have whatever his mother had had, when it came to witchcraft. But it couldn't *hurt*.

"Don't worry about leaving a back door for me. We'll deal with that after. And remember, *iron*. Your boys' heaters would probably hurt whoever or whatever came after Adalina, but not enough. Iron knives, pipes, fireplace poker, whatever."

"You got it, Mick. *Grazie.*"

"Yeah. Watch your backs, kids."

I got two steps towards the stairs and stopped.

"Y'know, now I think about it…"

They both waited. Think they could see the wheels spinning.

"You been hearing about any spilled blood that *ain't* related to the Outfit at all? Anything private or outside?"

You could tell the Ottatis'd been hitched for a good while: their headshakes coulda been choreographed.

"Nothin' jumps to mind," Fino said. "I mean, usual small-time shit you see every day in this burgh, but nothin' outta the ordinary. Kurtzman, maybe, but everyone's pretty sure that was a accident."

"Kurtzman?"

I knew the bird he probably meant; even worked with him myself a time or two. Martin Kurtzman, an accountant who often consulted with the cops when goin' over Mob books. Since you can imagine how well the Mob liked him for that, the guy had cops stationed far enough up his keister they could brush his teeth. Last I'd heard—though it'd been a spell, I admit—guy was doin' just great.

"Yeah. *Gavone* made a bad left and turned himself and his flivver into a fucking tree ornament. Lotta made guys'd love to take credit for it, but like I said, it was probably an accident."

Another one.

That was, what, the third time an unrelated "accident" had

come up over the course of this job? And every one of the poor saps was important in some capacity or other. My "this ain't kosher" bump was startin' to itch.

Then again, accidents happen, and I was payin' more attention to things than I had been, so who the hell knew what was what?

Took me a sec to realize the Shark'd followed up his answer with: "Why'd you ask?"

"Curious. Tryin' to figure what the Unseelie are doin' and where. It ain't like them to be this quiet." I briefly pondered the notion that there was some connection between the two—the Unfit and the accidents—but I couldn't get it to track.

Aw, hell, what was one more hinky wrinkle to add to this whole shindig?

I didn't figure either of 'em was planning to just shake hands, and I really didn't care to hassle with any more hugs today, so I just turned and resumed the long and arduous trek across the room to the stairs.

"Oh," I added at the last, "tell Archie I said 'hello.'"

"Sure."

"Actually, tell him I said, 'hello, hello.'"

"Right, 'cause he ain't ever heard *that* one before."

I already knew which door was hers, but even if I hadn't, I would've. Not even 'cause Fino always had one of his torpedoes standing guard outside, just in case. I *felt* it. An aura, a presence. Fae, sure, but not any kinda Fae I could recall ever meeting.

Last couple times I'd set foot in here, I'd *almost* thought of something. Something about that sensation poked at the ol' grey cells. Not a memory, even, but a casual thought about a memory. I felt it trying to catch my attention; trying to catch my eyes across a crowded ballroom, sorta.

But I never could grasp it. Couldn't even be sure it was real; the "memory" might not exist at all. Might just be that the familiar-yet-alien feeling was mucking with me, makin' me think I recognized something I didn't.

I dunno. Whatever. I nodded to today's gorilla and pushed the door open.

Place was neater'n when I'd first seen it. Emptier, too. All the books and stuffed animals and other girl stuff had been picked up and put away. Big honkin' radio was gone, at my suggestion—Adalina didn't need anything that technologically advanced lurking nearby while she recuperated.

Bianca hadn't wanted her to be without music, though, so she'd replaced the radio with an old wind-up music box. Most days, she was the only one who bothered to key it up.

And there in bed, surrounded by pink and lacy everything, was Adalina.

She'd seemed human, once. Not what you'd call a looker, but not abnormal. Now? Her eye-sockets had drifted to either side of her head, her lips thinned to almost nothin', her skin tight and whiter than any stiff in the morgue. Her hair was still healthy'n thick, oddly. I think that made it worse.

Oh, and the stink. Not bad—you hadda be close, or have the senses of a Fae, to notice—but definitely there. Fishy and fruity. And lately kinda burning, like alcohol fumes.

Already told you that Adalina was a changeling, left with the Ottatis almost seventeen years ago, now. What I *still* didn't know was what the hell she was turnin' into. It didn't resemble any kinda Fae I knew, and it wasn't followin' the pattern of those swaps where the "kid" is just an enchanted doll or a lump of wood.

She'd been ensorcelled to hide her nature, exposed to Orsola Maldera's witchcraft, and God knew what else. I couldn't even be sure this is what she was *supposed* to look like. For all I knew, all the competing magics had queered each other until nothin' was working right anymore.

I pulled back the sheets for a quick up-and-down. Physically, she was good, healing. Months ago, she'd almost died. *Shoulda* died. Her body'd been scoured by dust and sand and *iron filings*, in some places to the bone. I don't think I'd have survived it.

Now? No trace of it, 'cept for a couple light spots where the skin still looked new. (Yeah, light spots, pale as she already was. They were more or less translucent.)

But she would. Not. Wake. Up.

She tossed. She turned. She muttered in her sleep. Like the Ottatis said, she ate when you fed her. But no more.

We'd long since tried all the herbal remedies, and I even snuck an elixir or two outta Elphame that weren't ever supposed to cross to the mortal world.

Nada. Zip. Jack and bupkis.

I'd told the Ottatis I was still workin' on it, and that was basically square. I *was* still lookin', still listening, when I could.

What I *hadn't* told 'em was that I was hunting blind. I'd long since run outta ideas.

I put one mitt on her forehead: she was cold and wet, almost slick, like even her sweat was sick. Nothin' new there. She turned at my touch, flopping over on one side, kicking her feet under the blankets. Her muttering rose almost to a shout for a minute, before it faded again.

And I almost fell back from the bed, startled like I ain't been in some time. Not by the shout.

By the *words*.

We'd all thought she was muttering bunk, but now I heard it *clearly*...

She was speaking Old Gaelic!

Which didn't automatically make it any *less* bunk. Nonsense in an ancient language the speaker's got no business knowing is still nonsense, and most of what she was spouting made about as much sense as a glass cabbage. After a short while listening, I was about ready to chalk it all up to just another curiosity on the grocery list that was Adalina; fascinating, maybe a potential clue, but nothing of any immediate use.

And then, "Ahreadbhar..."

Plain as day and twice as clear. Maybe five or six times as clear, given the weather we been having.

I leaned in, whole body rigid, probably close enough that it coulda given anyone who happened to barge in a *really* wrong idea. Absolutely still: I didn't fidget, didn't blink, didn't even *breathe.*

Just listened.

Not a mistake, not a coincidence. It surfaced again, and again, one bit of value in the flotsam of her delirious nonsense.

"Ahreadbhar," multiple times; "Gáe Assail" once or twice. Enough so I couldn't doubt it if I wanted to.

She felt it. Deep in a sleep she hadn't come outta for months, across Danu only knew how much of the city, while the damn thing was *veiled from mystical detection...* She knew. The Spear of Lugh was near, and through all that, she sensed it.

"What are you, doll?" I ran a gentle palm over her forehead, brushing some stray, clinging hairs back into place. I dunno, but I like to think it calmed her a little, that she wasn't muttering and tossing quite so much after.

From a flogger pocket, I came up with the reel and string from an old fishing rod. That was what I'd grabbed outta my drawer, back when Ramona and I left my office. See, I'd picked it up on a case where... Eh, don't matter. Point is, guy who owned this is dead—twice—but during his life, fishing had been his only escape from the rest of the world. It'd brought peace, and a lot of it, to a troubled man.

Powerful symbolism, that.

I put the old hunk of junk on Adalina's night table, held a hand over it, and let just a bit of magic flow through it. Sorta crank-starting the symbolic power it held, if you wanna think of it that way. Still no guarantee it'd do squat, but just maybe she'd sleep a bit more soundly.

But me, I didn't look to have any rest in my immediate future. All this new stuff I'd learned about the girl was amazing, and maybe useful in the future, but for now? Now I still had a job to do, and this wasn't gettin' me any closer to done.

* * *

"Look, Ramona…"

"No, you were right." She sounded distant as we walked through the blustery gusts back toward the L. Distant, but not angry.

My heart sank. Think I mighta preferred angry, frankly.

"We've only just met, really," she continued, makin' a real close study of the sidewalk ahead—obviously too important for her to look at me. "And while we may… understand each other… Or I *thought* we did…"

My gut made like I just got punched. With a tree trunk.

Don't think she noticed.

"…you *don't* have good cause to trust me yet. I shouldn't have expected it of you."

Oh, shit…

"Ramona, sweetheart, we just need a little more time to—"

"Isn't this the station? We wouldn't want to miss our train."

I bet you can guess how pleasant the ride was for me, so I ain't goin' into it. Suffice to say, we got where we were going.

CHAPTER TEN

Between multiple hops on the L, and some deliberate stalling on my part—cat I was searching for wasn't gonna be as easy to find in the daylight—the sun pulled the western horizon up to its chin like a blanket before me'n Ramona reached our next *real* stop. And lemme tell you, she was just thrilled as all get-out when I put her wise to where that was.

"*Wonderful.* More gangsters. Do you protect all your clients this way, Mick? Or are you charging me the Judas goat special rate?"

"Relax, doll. Nobody's gonna hurt you."

"Oh, I'm *so* relieved. Was it the guns or the criminal records that convinced you?"

I decided nothin' I might say was gonna make the situation any better. Though sarcastic humor was still an improvement from the *no* humor she'd been tossin' my way.

I'd been here before. Kenson's Fine Smokes, which was exactly as much of a cigar vendor and club as I'm a human. We swept past the cases and containers of cigars, cigarettes, and enough pipes to build an organ. A few of the rooms off to the side even had people actually smoking.

Not fooling anyone, though.

Last time I was here, with a slightly different face, there'd been a line to get through the seriously heavy door in the back of the shop. It was a lot earlier in the evening this time around, and on a weeknight, so Ramona and I just strolled right on up to the two lunks in off-the-rack suits standing nearby.

I dunno, maybe the Mob buys 'em wholesale. And no, I don't mean the suits.

"Once we're inside," I whispered, "follow my lead. Don't make like you like me *too* well. And if anything goes down, don't try'n help me. Just get outta the way. Most trouble boys won't treat a skirt as an enemy unless you give 'em real good reason."

Her blinkers were big as doorknobs. "What happened to 'nobody here will hurt you'?"

"That's what I'm making sure of. Ain't you been listening?"

"I should have hired a Pinkerton."

Since I couldn't tell if she was putting me on or not, I decided to assume it was a joke. Safer for me that way.

I was all ready to crawl into their heads if I had to, but for the most part it wasn't necessary. They asked the usual (and the same as they'd asked me last time): who I was, how I'd heard about the place, was I packing, and so on.

They found my wand when they patted me down, of course, and then I *did* fiddle with their thoughts a bit, just to make 'em a tad more gullible. I fed 'em my usual spiel—about how I don't carry heat, but use the "stick" to fill out the holster so it bulges as if I did—which is really pretty dumb.

Course, this was also the first time Ramona'd seen that what I had in the harness wasn't exactly a roscoe. She couldn't seem to settle on any one expression.

"What?" I asked as we stepped on through.

"I... you..."

"Both of us, yeah. You havin' second thoughts?"

"Mick, I passed 'second' so long ago, I'm well into double digits."

Real encouraging, I found that.

Wasn't much happening on the dance floor, this early. They didn't even have anyone actually playing yet, just an old record-player blurting out some Wayne King for about three couples to romp to.

The bar, though, was already flowin' strong with people and hooch.

Imagine that.

I felt fingers tighten around my arm, and tried to think through the faint electric hum that seemed to flow through me at the touch.

"You okay, doll?" Then, when she didn't answer, "Don't tell me this is your first time in a speakeasy?"

"No," she breathed, clearly distracted. "Not first, but... first since I was a girl. What if there's a raid?"

"Won't be."

"How do you know?"

Not sure I bothered to shrug. "Just know."

"Anyone tell you lately that you can be surprisingly reassuring?"

"Don't think so."

"Do you suppose there might be a reason for that?"

Couple minutes spent wandering the place made it pretty plain the boss was out. I figured as much when I saw his private booth was empty, but wanted to be positive.

I watched everyone, for a while. Dancers danced, drinkers drank and waiters waited. Finally spotted an older guy dressed a lot like the servers, but better, and figured he might be important enough to know something from nothing.

"Hey! Bo!" I called out to him. Then, as he sniffed and turned, "They train you on the job for that sneer, or is it a required skill for being hired?"

He sniffed again. "Can I help you... sir?"

"Yeah."

He waited. Gink was irritating, so I waited, too.

"Well?" he finally demanded.

"Well, what?"

"How can I help you?" It wasn't loud enough to be a shout, but it had enough volume, if you dig what I mean.

"Thought you'd never ask. Mr. Scola gonna be in tonight? And if so, you know when?"

"Mister…"

Huh. It was *mister* now, not *sir*.

"Even if I was privy to my employer's schedule, I don't see how it would be any business of—"

Sigh. Into the noggin I go, then.

I asked him again, this time with more'n just words.

"He told us to have his table ready at half past ten, though it wouldn't surprise me if he's a bit later than that."

"See? That wasn't so hard."

I left him wondering why the hell he'd just sang to me like that. Then again, I didn't want him noodling *too* hard on it, and he *was* an obnoxious son of a bitch, so before I'd completely withdrawn from his mind, I planted a convincing image of a dribbled wine stain down the front of his coat.

Have fun washin' that out, pal.

"You dance, sweetheart?" I asked as I took Ramona's arm.

"Uh, not often…"

"Good thing I ain't askin' you to do it often, then."

I half guided her, half pulled her out onto the carpet. Current tune was pretty soft, and there didn't look to be any musicians winding up anytime soon, so we kept to slow, simple steps.

Just as well. Not sure I coulda concentrated on complex with an arm around her and her hair against my face.

Then she turned her head just a bit, her cheek against mine, lips right by my ear, and yeah, then I *knew* any kinda concentration was a losing proposition.

"What are we doing, Mick?" she whispered.

I lost a step and almost stumbled. Asking her if she could dance, and *I* was the one making a cement mixer of myself.

"What?"

"Here. Dancing. Why?"

Oh. Not sure if I was relieved or sad that that's what she'd meant.

"Waiting. Couple of tunes, and we'll grab ourselves a table and a cheap snort. Gives us an excuse to be here." Then, lying through my teeth, "It's just to help our cover, that's all."

"How long?"

"Maybe 'til ten-thirty. Maybe later. Long as it takes, doll."

She sighed and said nothing more. When she tightened her grip, round about the third song, I hadda bite my tongue to keep from asking some fool questions I knew I'd regret.

Yeah, I know, I'd said we were only gonna cut the rug for two or three tunes. Wound up being, I think, seven. Whaddaya want from me?

Right about the time the last record stopped with a quick scratch, and a stocky but graceful black woman in a sapphire-blue dress started makin' love to the microphone, I saw him walk in.

Looked much as he had last time, though his tux jacket was tabby-cat grey instead of the white he'd worn then. Same rodent-tail mustache, and while I ain't sure if it was the same ceremonial blondes on his arms or the same Mob soldiers around him, they were damn close enough.

I barely waited until they'd planted themselves in the booth and ordered a round.

"Go sit over there," I said to Ramona, pointing to an empty table. "Don't come near that booth."

"But—"

"Ramona, I told you nobody'd hurt you, and I hate being made a liar. So go already! Please."

You know how to scowl at someone with concern? Not sure I do. She did, though. She muttered something I didn't catch, on account of the noises the musicians were makin' as they set up shop—all black, of course, 'cause God *forbid* a white man play backup to a black woman in this day and age—and stomped off, lighting up and taking a deep puff from an Old Gold as she went. Seemed to be heading for the bar, not the table. But hell, maybe she just needed a shot or a sandwich.

I wasn't halfway to the corner booth when two of Scola's boys got up and cut me off.

"Private," one of 'em rumbled at me.

See, when I'd done this months ago, I'd had this whole rigmarole planned out to gimme an excuse to see the guy. It was real clever and everything. Tonight? Tonight I was gonna have to be more direct with the big fish, so I figured I might as well start with the small ones.

Soon as I was sure the first gorilla was looking at me real good, I sucker-punched him. In the brain. A quick meeting of the eyes, a shove of willpower and magic—not to convince him of anything or make him see what ain't there, just to overwhelm him a few ticks. Didn't much wanna have to bother finessing both of 'em. Gink rocked on his heels and proceeded to drool some.

Now, the second goon, *he* got a more controlled dosage. I shuffled his feelings, sliding suspicion to the bottom of the deck and the boredom and monotony of standing guard in this speakeasy—night after night after night, where nothing happened and he almost never had cause to give any troublemakers the bum's rush—to the top.

Then I just smiled politely and walked on by. He acknowledged me with a grunt that woulda had to pack on twenty pounds to qualify as a syllable, only just remembering to walk with me back toward the table.

"Hell is this, Donny?" Scola asked, scowling. "I been here ninety seconds, and already you let someone in here to bother me? Didn't even see you pat 'im down."

I didn't have to look close to see that he and his other guys'd taken precautions 'cause the first mook hadn't. Figured at least three heaters were aimed my way under the table. Maybe four or five, if either of the girls was carrying.

"Don't give him too hard a time, Bumpy," I said, taking a seat opposite him. Every one of 'em had that "guy's scrambled worse than an egg" look on their mugs now. "I just convinced him how important it was that you and me barber some."

"That right? So why don'tcha convince *me*?"

Quick sideways glance, and down, and sure enough, he was wearing that same charm—slender chain with silver'n iron tokens—on his left wrist. Didn't figure it was too strong, or I'd have felt more from it, so I could probably get into his head anyway, but... I didn't much care for that "probably." I was *sure* I could poke on through with the help of the L&G, but if I went for something under my jacket, the joint was gonna have a sudden surge in the slug population.

So instead, hands on the table in front of me, I pointed at that wrist.

"Because they're easier for me to *persuade* than you."

Fella's peepers blew up so big they shoulda been floating at the end of a string at the fair, and I didn't have to get behind 'em to see the wheels turnin' in his head. So now it was all down to what he knew about the supernatural, what he *thought* he knew about the supernatural, and what he thought about what he thought he knew about the supernatural.

Uh, by which I mean, it was an even bet whether he'd jaw with me for a bit, or just try to fill me full of daylight right then and there.

Pretty certain he gave some real consideration to both.

"Everybody outta the booth," he ordered. "Go get yourselves a drink. *One!* Any you bastards get lit, it's your ass." Then, when they reluctantly stood, "Not you, Gina. You stay."

One of the blondes, a tall glass of water in a black dress so tight I wondered if she shed it monthly and grew a new one, sat back down. Curiouser and curiouser. She smiled at me, nice and empty-headed, but behind the simper I saw something deeper. And darker.

No Orsola Maldera, by a stretch and a half, but she knew

some of the old ways. Clever way to hide a witch, I hadda admit.

The other moll, though, didn't seem wise to it.

"Why's Gina get to stay, Vinnie? Why can't—?"

"Get outta here, already! I wanted to hear a broad whine at me, I'd have brought my wife!"

Last time I talked about this guy, I said something about "store-bought class." Guess he hadn't gone back to complete the set.

"All right, pal," he growled. I couldn't help but note his mitt—and the roscoe I'm sure was in it—was still under the table. "First off, we ain't business partners and we ain't friends, so next time you call me 'Bumpy' you're gonna wish you hadn't."

I almost did, right then, just to annoy him, but I decided I didn't need to be quite *that* childish.

"Second…" He paused long enough for the waiter to approach, deliver his drink—and the witchy chippy's—and scram again. He hefted the glass in the hand he *wasn't* keeping hidden. "We met before? I know faces, and I dunno yours from a dog's ass, but you still seem familiar."

Well, guess that charm bracelet wasn't complete hooey. One time we *had* met, I hadn't much resembled me. That I was even ringing a bell meant he had some real mojo going.

"Pretty sure I'd remember if we had," I said carefully.

"Huh. So who are you?"

"PI," I told him.

"What kinda PI believes in the occult?"

"Kind who's been around enough to take in the sights, Mr. Scola."

Couple drops of his booze sloshed outta the glass as he absently tried to toss one back and nod at the same time. I pretended not to notice.

"What makes you think," he asked me, dabbing at his kisser with a napkin, "I wanna talk with *any* dick, private or otherwise?"

I leaned forward, right about as far as I could without getting threatening.

"Look, you're wise to some of what's out there. You mighta heard there's a lot goin' down in the city right now, the sorta stuff you ain't gonna find in the papers or police reports. If your pet witch here ain't a complete ringer, odds are she's sensed something hinky lately."

Wasn't as if so many Fae converging on Chicago wasn't gonna leave *some* footprints in the ether.

Two of 'em traded furtive glances twice, first when I'd identified the dame for what she was, and then again a second later. Oh, yeah, she'd felt something, sure enough, and she'd mentioned it to him.

"So what if she did? What's it gotta do with you?" Scola demanded.

"Client's got me mixed up in it, is all."

"And what's it gotta do with *me*?"

"Not much, if we both play it right. You trade me some information, and I trade you every effort to get what's going on done and gone before it starts interfering with... local business."

He took another snort, a long, slow one, watching me over the rim of the glass. His chin took on all sortsa weird shapes through the hooch.

"What kinda information?" he asked, and there was so much suspicion in his voice I could taste the doubt in each individual word.

"Giancarlo Manetti."

He didn't make us go through the whole "I dunno who you mean" song and dance, thankfully. "What about him?"

"Wondering if you know who he's been running for lately. What he's been moving. Which fences he works with."

Scola's glass was back on the table with a thump, and his glare was *not* what you might call chummy.

"These don't sound much like occult questions, bo. These sound more like cop questions. I start to think you're giving me the third degree, maybe I decide to take you someplace I can give it back. A lot harder."

"Why don'tcha ask Gina," I said, smiling real friendly at her, "why that ain't such a swell idea?"

And I let her see.

Just for a second, I drew a huge swathe of what I am—not all of it, not close, but enough—up into my eyes. Didn't use it, didn't try messin' with their thoughts or their luck. All I did was something I usually don't: I let it show.

The witch gasped, rocking back in her seat, one hand covering lips that looked *real* red against her sudden pallor. Bumpy's own peepers did that whole balloon trick again.

"I got no beef with you, Scola," I said. "I'm trying to do this polite and friendly. You don't wanna gum that up for me, do ya? It'd be rude."

Mighta pushed him too far with that one. Pride and anger got into a slap-fight with fear, and I could see on his mug that he was pondering violence. I grumbled inside, and did this the Otherworld way. I hit him hard, fast, through his eyes like a shiv. And yep, I felt his protections—they were real enough—but they didn't amount to much. Didn't even slow me any.

"Abe Rosen."

Not sure which of my questions he meant to answer with that, but it was a start. I wanted more, though.

And I'd have probably gotten it, even with his charm and his witch. Wouldn'ta made me any friends, and maybe Gina mighta surprised me, but I'm pretty sure I'd have come out on top. Can't tell you for sure, though, 'cause that's when everyone in the gin joint heard the keening that definitely did *not* come from the singer's pipes.

Most of the folks there, when they thought back on the parts of that night they could recollect at all, would remember it as a police siren. A weird one, something they'd never heard before, but a siren just the same.

Not me. I knew what it was then, and I know now.

A scream? A wail? I'm tryin' to describe a flood to someone who ain't ever seen a body of water bigger'n a bathtub. It was those, and it was more, and it was less. Deep enough to rattle your guts, high enough to hurt your ears. All of this, and none of this, 'cause you really heard it more with your soul than your ears.

This wasn't anything close to the *rusalka*'s cry. That'd been bad, sure, but it was just pain. This... This was nothin' as ordinary as pain.

Empty, cavernous, desperate want, need beyond hunger, need that crossed over into a burning, passionate lust that was nothing to do with sex. And at the same moment, an icy chill, a contemptuous, unemotional disregard for anything of light and life.

Some of the patrons had fainted. Learned later that one old man croaked of a heart stroke. My own shoulders were bunched tighter'n rocks, my hands shaking. I don't much do "dread," but yeah, it was absolutely dreadful.

Oh, I knew what it was, all right. Heard it before—back in the Old World, and once on the battlefields of the American Revolution—and hadn't wanted ever to hear it ever again.

Banshee.

Door busted wide open like God'd just stubbed his toe on it. Whole buncha uniformed bulls spilled into the room, pieces aimed, shouting all kindsa orders. Some of 'em might even have been real human coppers, minds fogged and fuddled. I could see that others, though, were definitely glamours over creatures that weren't in any way mortal.

Which wasn't to say they weren't still the law, in their own way. Just not *your* law.

The "federal agents" followed 'em in. Raighallan all pompous and pretentious, barking orders at the bulls who barked orders at the civilians. And behind him...

His partner wasn't doing too keen a job keeping her work face up. Áebinn looked jittery, anxious, as she ankled through the door—and I don't mean "a little fidgety." I mean like something cruel and *real* hungry strainin' at the leash. Her breath came fast'n sharp, and she couldn't seem to keep her gaze on any one spot for more'n a few seconds.

She'd worked up an appetite, building that scream. I hoped nobody was gonna die here who didn't have it comin'.

Even through all this, though, don't you even *think* that I couldn't also feel Ramona's glare chewin' into my soul from the moment the first "cop" appeared in the doorway. I wasn't building up a lotta credit with her, that's for sure. (I wanted to kick myself square in the rear when I realized that was bothering me even more'n the damn *bean sidhe* did.)

Maybe they'd found the place, learned about Bumpy's occult dabbling, on their own. I kinda hoped they had, because it wasn't impossible I'd *led* the damn Seelie here. They'd hafta be pretty low on leads themselves to bother shadowing me, but—preoccupied as I'd been with Ramona—anyone with a smidgeon of talent coulda done it without me being any the wiser.

Sloppy. *Again*. I ain't been this careless since before you lot invented stirrups. I needed to get back to something vaguely approaching competent.

Well, the situation wasn't as bad as it looked. I didn't know if they were here for me or had the same idea of grilling Scola as I had, but I should be able to blow the place. Even if they meant to take their "You'll pay if you get in our way again" hooey seriously, they wouldn't wanna get into a magic fight in front of a whole crowd of mortals. No, I could talk or sneak my way over to Ramona and then outta—

Either Bumpy's charm or his pet witch twigged to the fact that the raiders weren't human, and the whole place went to hell.

The boss shouted an order of his own, and suddenly the room was sprouting gats like a bullet garden after the rain. Every one of the thugs he'd come in with, the other blonde, about half the wait staff, and of course Bumpy himself had steel in their hands. And the steel was *loud*.

Lead flew, ears rang, more people screamed than were even *in* the damn joint—or so it seemed, anyway. Gina crouched down by the bench, waving one hand, and drawing glyphs in chalk on the floor with the other, and chanting under her breath. I felt a sudden discomfort, a vague notion that I wouldn't wanna get near her or her boss, but that was *all* I felt. Woulda been duck soup to ignore it: if that was the best she had, she wouldn't even slow down Raighallan or Áebinn.

The Bumpy turned his Colt on me—guess he figured I hadda be wrapped up in all this—and I was too busy diving across a table and turning it over as a shield to worry much more about his precautions, or why he'd been so quick to panic.

Nah, he wouldn'ta killed me, but those slugs *hurt*. And I was runnin' outta non-ventilated suits.

Since I *was* pinned behind that table, I didn't see where it came from, but the smaller roscoes and a lotta the screams suddenly vanished under the roar of a Tommy. Quick peek around the edge and I saw bulls fall beneath the metal hail, before I had to duck back or get a mug full of splinters. I had no way of telling how many of 'em could shake it off and get back up the way I could.

Another look showed me Bumpy, Gina, and a couple of his guards scurrying around the edge of the room in a huddle, squirting lead at the police and making for the door to the kitchen...

Guy in a coat and hat—guess he'd come running in from outside—in that kitchen doorway, was writing a letter to the whole room with a Chicago typewriter that seemed like it'd *never* run outta ink...

Most of the civilians lay flat, hands over their heads, below the lines of fire. I was glad to see that much go well, at least...

Raighallan pressed one hand to a gut wound that really hadda sting, his other hand waived a fat cylinder of oak, a wand I recognized as stronger but slower than my own model...

And Áebinn just stood in the middle of the room, ignoring

the bullets, basking in the deaths that'd already occurred. This can't have been what she wanted or expected outta the raid, but damn if she wasn't gonna enjoy the opportunity to feast!

Bumpy and crew made it through the doors and the chopper finally fell silent. Guess the hombre carrying it had gone with the boss to cover the retreat. And since it wasn't too tough for some of the faux-cop Fae to close on the cats with the smaller guns, most of the shootin' gave way to the grunting and groaning and smacking and cracking of hands, bottles, chairs, and nightsticks.

And I almost didn't care about a whit of it.

Oh, holy fuck me, where's Ramona?

I raised my head over the table again, just in time to see her peekin' up from behind the bar, whole face slack from shock. I swallowed a surge of relief and jerked my noggin toward the kitchen; figured Bumpy making his sneak that way meant there was a back door. She took a moment, but nodded.

I drew my L&G, stood, and ran.

With every step I squeezed power through the wand, yanking luck from this guy here and tossing it Ramona's way, or winding it around myself; throwing random pain at that group over there.

I heard Áebinn shout my name, saw Raighallan start to elbow his way through the crowd toward me, and kept going. A blast of power burst against me, ripping away a lotta the good fortune I'd just glommed, but not touching me directly.

For a moment I lost track of Ramona in the chaos, but she showed up pretty quick. I reached the kitchen door at the same time as one of Raighallan's glamoured goons—and he was clubbed down before I hadda deal with him. Ramona stood behind him, clutching a stool by the seat—she'd just walloped the gink with the legs.

"Mick?"

I couldn't help it. I needed a second, had to absorb what I was seeing, what I was *sensing*. Something was wrong, she shouldn't have—

"Mick!"

"Right!"

I grabbed her hand, dragged her through the kitchen door. She dropped the stool as we ran.

By the time we'd got ourselves clear, I didn't even remember that something'd been bothering me, nagging at me, let alone what it'd been. Of course, that mighta had something to do with who *else* we bumped into in the process.

CHAPTER ELEVEN

He was loitering, calm as you please, watching everyone fleeing every which way as we burst through the back door and down the alley into the street. I'd have recognized the hat'n sunglasses even if he *hadn't* been standing smack dab under a street light. To say nothing of the urge to recoil, find the nearest hole, and pull it in after me.

Sealgaire was still keepin' close tabs on me, and he wasn't being shy about it.

I'd rather have gone back in and faced down the Seelie. I do take some pride in the fact that I still stepped in fronta Ramona, though.

Brave, but unnecessary. He just smiled that crocodile smile and vanished again.

None of which was as startlin' as Ramona clutching my arm and whispering, "Mick! That's the man who was following me this morning!"

If you'd shoved a snowball up my... nose that minute, it wouldn'ta melted.

"He must work for whoever's after the money! Mick, we should try to catch—!"

"He don't work for anyone you're involved with, babe."

I wish to hell he did.

"Then who—?"

"C'mon. We're going."

She probably woulda argued, if I wasn't already dragging her off by the hand. I sure wasn't gonna just hang around there and jaw about it!

Sealgaire. Why the fuck would…?

Don't be a bunny, Mick. You know exactly why.

Message received, you bastard.

"Where are we going?" Ramona asked impatiently.

I still held her hand, and was steering her along the sidewalk at a pretty good clip. I didn't answer, 'cause I wasn't entirely sure. Also, something kept eating at me like a whole hive of ants, something I'd noticed back in the club, something I couldn't put my finger on…

Damn it, how could I be so completely off my game? It couldn't *just* be her, could it? I'd known Ramona for a couple days, and in that time I'd gotten twisted up into a pretzel worse'n I had in *centuries.*

Finally, I just grunted and said, "To get some answers from somebody who *doesn't* wanna kill me."

"Do such people exist?"

An hour ago, I'd have chuckled at that.

"What about the raid? The people? When the news—" she continued.

I shook my head, didn't say anything. There wouldn't be any news, other'n maybe a small article about a run-of-the-mill raid or maybe a shooting. Most of the humans there hadn't seen a thing they could make any sense out of. And if a few had, Raighallan and the other *aes sidhe* could scramble those memories easy enough.

I grunted again, and that was all the answer I was offering for the moment. Pretty sure I actually *heard* her scowl behind me, but she stopped makin' with the questions, so I could think.

Not that I cared much for anything I had to think about.

So. Local Seelie. Local Unseelie. Outsiders of Ogma knows

what city or what Court. Herne the Hunter. The Wild Hunt.

And now, at least sorta, Bumpy Scola. 'Cause there was no way he was gonna let this go, not after what'd just happened to his place and what he already knew about the supernatural. Probably he'd never learn anything of use, would just waste his time poking around the edges of the whole shindig, but... He was another wild card in a deck already full of 'em.

If Lugh wasn't ages dead, I coulda strangled him.

We didn't end up in the ritziest neighborhood. Not "broken bottles and boarded-up windows" bad, not like where I'd found Four-Leaf Franky and his aquatic playmates, but not the kinda place you wanted to wander alone after sunset.

Well, *most* people wouldn't.

"Mick Oberon!" Ramona finally snapped, yanking her wrist outta my grip. "I am not taking one more step until you tell me what the hell we're doing here!"

I stopped, turned. "Not one more step, no. Three more, actually. Maybe four if you stumble."

"What? What on earth are you*uuuurk*!"

I'd snatched out, grabbed her arm again, and dragged her between two thick, lumpy greystones with delusions of building-hood. One of 'em had a fire escape that looked as though it actually might *not* fall off the wall if a toddler jumped on it.

"Stop manhandling me!"

She sounded sincere enough, though I couldn't help but note she hadn't jerked away from me again.

"Manhandling? You're a woman."

"I..."

Wasn't the answer she'd expected, obviously. Her kisser twisted, tryin' to find a comfortable position, and her shoulders slumped.

"You're impossible."

She said to the former Seelie Court prince.

"You got no idea."

"We're in an alley."

"Hey, and here I thought *I* was the detective!"

"Do you spend a great deal of time in alleyways, Mick?"

"Nah, but I been meaning to take up a hobby."

"It stinks."

"Beats collecting stamps, though."

"No, I meant..." Her sigh was more exasperation than it was actual breath. "Forget it."

That sure sounded like a conclusion, but barely twenty seconds'd passed before, "Mick?"

"Uh?"

"What are you—what are *we* involved in? This is about more than money, or some other everyday case you're working on."

I didn't have the slightest idea how to answer that. The *truth* sure wasn't an option.

Silence for a while. Well, except for the humming wires and the passing flivvers and the shouting of the radios from a couple windows, and the distant buzz of the parts of the city that don't sleep... So, y'know, silence-ish. Chicago silence.

Until we heard the *fwop-fwop* of approaching shoes.

I hadn't needed any extra luck for *this* search, though I'd sucked up a bit of mojo on the way just to speed up the process. I already knew his beat, see?

"Hey, officer! I wanna report a suspicious figure lurking in an alley."

"Jesus, Mick!"

Pete jumped so hard I thought he might change even without the full moon. Then he stared at me, stared at Ramona, glanced around like he was planning to knock over a bank, and finally stared at me some more.

When he finally opened his yap again, it was just to repeat, "Jesus, Mick..." in a brand-new tone.

"We're friends, Pete. Just 'Mick' is fine."

"You oughta know better'n to make me jump after everything you've told me! Besides, I ain't even supposed to be talking *about* you, let alone *to* you! If anyone spots us—"

"In the middle of your beat? Middle of the night? Ain't likely. Most cats still awake around here are gonna head the other way at the first glimpse of your blues. Be even less likely if you step on over here and outta the street, though."

He headed my way, though he might as well have been trudging through mud.

"Hell, Pete. You look like Sydney Carton after a change of heart."

"Syd... What? Who're you...?"

"Seriously? Guillotine? *A Tale of Two*... Ah, forget it." Then, when he finally *had* entered the damn alley, "Thanks. You know I appreciate this, right?"

"You damn well better. Who's this?" He nodded at Ramona.

"Ah. This is my... a client of mine." I half-glanced back at her, felt a flicker of a smile cross my mug as I did.

Ramona beamed back. I felt about seven dozen emotions, all of 'em at war with each other.

"You sure she can be trusted?"

"Manners, Pete. Since when did you get so paranoid?"

Hey, it was easier than explaining how I trusted her, but didn't know *why*.

Pete's mug scrunched up in a way that suggested I was a truly impossible variety of idiot.

"Uh, maybe since you phoned'n told me the Unseelie Court might try'n bump me off?"

Huh. Yeah, that'd probably account for it.

"Besides," he added, "I thought someone was tailing me earlier tonight. Dunno if it was them or not, but it got me pretty antsy."

And there I was, colder'n that snowball again.

"You get a good look?" I asked.

"Tall. Cowboy hat and sunglasses. At night. Weird, huh?

Figure that's why I noticed him at all, but he didn't actually bother me, and he vanished soon enough. Guess I was probably imagining things."

"Yeah."

Damn it, Sealgaire, I fucking *get it! I'm already getting enough of this shit from the Unfit, so leave my friends out of this!*

"Yeah, probably."

"So look, just tell me what you need, quick, in case I come down with a sudden case of common sense and walk away."

"Ah, don't worry, Pete." Forced another smile I didn't mean. "Pretty sure you got an immunity."

He glared, but there was no real anger in it, and we both knew it.

"What. Do you need?"

"Guy named Abe Rosen. Maybe a fence, maybe a made guy, may or may not ever've served time. Need whatever you can tell me about his recent activities."

"Oh, is that all?"

"No. Need an address, too."

"Mick, do you see any room in this uniform for a filing cabinet?"

"Well, maybe if you dropped a few pounds—"

"Now you're pushing it."

"All right, look. I know the pressure you got comin' down on you, and I know the hot water you'll be in if this gets back to the wrong people. I been running around all evening, and what I got for it is beans—or at best confirmation of what I already knew. I wouldn't ask you if I didn't *have* to. But I'm fresh outta options."

"I hate when you do this."

"Yeah, me, too."

"I *still* ain't carrying a filing cabinet."

And now it was *my* turn to sigh. I see why you mugs do it so often.

"Call in, Pete. Secretaries ain't gonna ask why you want 'em to look this stuff up."

He extended a hand, palm up.

"You kidding me?" I demanded.

"I'm making this call for you, I'm making it on your nickel. Seems only fair to me."

"Me, too," Ramona chimed in.

In the end, of course, I made with the coin. A couple, actually, since there was some calling back for extra detail. Got me what I needed, though.

Rosen was indeed a fence, or at least a suspected one. A few charges, no convictions. Guy kept his head down. Looked to be a complete freelancer—no strong ties to any particular side of the Chicago Mob. And whaddaya know? His place was in Pilsen, albeit multiple blocks from mine. No way to suss out whether this was his flop, his office, or both, though. Not without paying a visit.

"Thanks, Pete. Really. You just saved my bacon on this one."

"And don't you forget it. Will there be anything else this evening, or may I bring you the check?"

"Cute. Actually, come to think of it…"

"Oh, goddamn it, Mick!"

"Nah, this'll just take a mo."

And it did, but I ain't gonna go through it word by word, 'cause it's a conversation you heard already, more'n once. Any news on unexpected bloodshed? Violence, especially non-Mob related? Everything I been wondering about, everything I asked him to look into when I was at his place.

And nope. He had more or less the exact same amount'a bupkis to give me as everyone else.

Just for giggles, and since my bump was still itchy, I asked about that trio of accidents, too. Figured I'd find out if the cops thought it was as hinky as I did, if they'd learned anything.

Well, yeah. For one, they knew of a fourth death: an old-money heiress and frequent political donor who'd taken a header down her fancy stairs.

"And sure," Pete told me, "a few of the department dicks got to wondering. I mean, three of the four were friends of the force in one way or another. But nobody found nothing suggesting foul play, or even the thinnest string connecting 'em all. Really does just look like a run of bad luck."

Then there was nothin' for it but another round of appreciate this and goodnight that. He was just movin', to resume his beat when he said, "Hey, maybe if Rosen's building's neat enough, you oughta consider moving your offices there."

"Why in the name of Shakespeare would I wanna…" A sudden suspicion came over me. "Pete?"

"Yeah?"

"You know I don't pack heat, right?"

"Uh… Yeah. But why—?"

"If this is a setup so you can tell me 'good fences make good neighbors,' I will *find* a gat to shoot you with."

"I'll just get back to my beat, now," he said with a Cheshire grin.

"Yeah. Yeah, you go and do that."

He went one way, we went the other, and for a while we were back to the city's notion of quiet. Leave it to Pete'n his dippy jokes, though; I'll be damned if I wasn't smiling, just a little, while we walked.

When Ramona *did* talk again, it was to observe, "He must be a very good friend to you," and that smile melted away like a runny milkshake.

I couldn'ta said why, but something about the way she said that really, *really* bothered me.

Now this? *This* damn well coulda been the work of the Unseelie.

"Is… is that Abe Rosen?"

Ramona'd had to swallow hard a couple times, force the words through clenched throat and lips, and I can't say I blamed her any. I don't do queasy, 'less there's magic involved—certain wards, for instance—but even I was feelin' a tad heavy-stomached.

"Think it is, doll. Someone sure didn't want us to be too positive, though."

"Then... who was *that*?"

I smiled, though I sure as hell wasn't finding much funny.

"That, if I ain't mistaken, is *more* of Abe Rosen."

She slapped a hand over her lips and gagged. Actually, I gotta confess, I was impressed she could still breathe without taking the run-out or keeling over. Carnage has this real particular stink right when it's starting to congeal... You may not take my opinion of her as unbiased, but nobody could deny she was one tough cookie.

Place was an office, and looked very much like... an office. So typical it coulda been a set and props. Interior: office; our heroes enter stage left. Yeah, it was *that* typical.

Almost as if the owner didn't wanna attract attention. Imagine that.

So, yeah. Desk. Chair. Other chairs. Bookshelf. Filing cabinet. Doorway to the back rooms where he kept his merchandise and a cot for nights he couldn't make it home. I knew all this because, well, I could *see* it. Notice I said "doorway," not "door." *Was* a door there, not too long ago. Now? Broken hinges and firewood.

The front room was decorated... Actually, I can't tell you how the front room was decorated. It was sorta obscured right about then. I dunno if Rosen was the kinda guy to really put himself into his work, but *somebody* had.

"What the hell did they *kill* him with?" Ramona wheezed after another few breaths. "A mortar shell?"

That'd be about where Pete woulda said something about "finding the mortar weapon" or "first-degree mortar." Pete woulda, but I wouldn't, so I hadda figure he was still weighing on my mind.

"Nah," I said. "Wasn't any explosive. They didn't do Rosen like they did Manetti. Even if they'd made him swallow the damn thing, any boom that shredded him this bad woulda damaged the room. You see any blast damage?"

"Who could tell?"

"Saw a guy who'd fallen through an industrial fan once..." I mused.

"Stop. Just... Stop."

"All right." I ran a finger over the desk, leavin' a smear in the blood and other fluids, more double-checking my guess on how old it was than actually looking for much. "All right, chew on this for a while, then. Forget how. *Why?*"

I mean, if this'd been redcaps or somethin' of that sort, they might not've *needed* a "why." But we didn't know it *was* Unseelie work. And if it was, why'd they gone all Jack the Ripper here, on Rosen, but nowhere else?

All this dashed through my noodle even before Ramona had finished answering my question.

"I assumed he knew something they didn't want anyone else to—"

"You're smarter'n that, sweetheart."

"Uh, thank you?"

I wandered over to the shelves, but they had nothin' much to show me other'n various gewgaws and doodads, and more bits of old man. Was a flap of skin stuck to the wall, kinda resembled a Picasso. I decided not to point it out.

"I don't mean why'd someone knock him off," I told her. "I mean why this way? Quick stab, or a bullet, or a bomb, or hell, I dunno, catapult a rabid badger through his office window."

"Catapult a...?"

"It takes effort and some sharp, heavy blades to take a bird apart this completely. So why do it?"

Ramona steadied herself, took another hard look around.

"To encourage people not to look too closely? Distract them from whatever else is in here?"

I couldn't help but grin.

"Not bad. Not the only possible answer, but a fine place to start."

Her return smile lit up the room—for about three seconds, before it shattered like a porcelain golf ball.

"But that means we have to…" Her complexion had gone sorta waxy and green; she coulda almost been related to the *rusalka*.

"Yep. Pick a side, sweetheart."

"What are we looking for?"

Good question. No way the spear was here, but maybe there'd be some sign it had been? Or evidence of… Well, anything else hinky? It coulda been *anything*, so what to tell her?

"Anything looks outta place," I said. Then, at her expression, "*Other*'n the pureed body."

We both wound up scouring the entire room, just in case, but we didn't find anything important except more of Abe Rosen. Ramona looked even more all in by the time we were through, but she hadn't thrown up.

Or refused to search anywhere.

Or even taken that much longer'n me.

I was starting to question how put off by the sticky mess she really was.

The filing cabinet was locked up tight, of course. But thanks to a small blade and a smaller sliver of luck, it didn't stay that way. The prize for that particular endeavor was a whole stack of shipping invoices that told me nada about nada.

Well, huh. I mean, no real shock that the fella'd keep anything incriminating in the back, outta public view. But it kinda put the kibosh on our theory that the poor sap had been turned into bolognese to prevent people from searching the room.

So, back we went. Storage room, with various jewels and artwork and bonds and a few bottles of fine hooch, and a nice radio, and basically everything you'd expect. Bedroom was a bedroom, even more'n the office was an office. We *did* find a couple binders and a ledger with files that might actually not be bunk, stuck in the wardrobe on a shelf behind a handful of floggers that'd been hangin' there long enough for the cobwebs to get dusty.

I decided to let Ramona have first crack at flipping through 'em, mostly because I was startin' to get really goddamn annoyed. This didn't make sense, none of it. I hate it when clues don't make sense. The *mystery* ain't supposed to make sense. The *pieces*, though...

Hell, we weren't even positive Rosen was a lead! I mean, obviously he'd ticked someone off but good—unless this was the fanciest suicide in history—but while I knew of some creatures that would do this to a man, we'd found no proof that the Fae were even...

Waaaaait a minute!

I trudged across squishy, sticky carpet and sat down in one of the chairs that wasn't too soiled. Then I closed my eyes, concentrated for a tick, and...

Yep.

Nice little double-blind. Figure out you ain't supposed to search the room, so you search the room, find squat, get frustrated, move on. And then, even if you got the know-how to do it, you don't think about *other* ways to search.

Now that I reached out, though, I felt it. Not a lot, just a faint trickle. A lingering aura. Something with a touch of the magic had been here, not long, and not long *ago*. It was a weak enough echo that most people in my position—well, most Fae in my position, 'cause there wouldn't *be* anyone else—woulda probably assumed it was a trinket. Some small, mildly enchanted dingus of no real significance.

Except I knew the spear was partly shrouded somehow, didn't I? And it felt exactly the same as the sensation I'd felt when I'd bumped into Franky and the *rusalka*.

So, I had been onto something. Rosen was involved. I mean, that he mighta been a red herring I could believe, but that he'd been a red herring who *happened* to have something *else* magic here recently? Not on your life.

I leaned back, blinkers still shut, to think.

Okay, so it made sense the thing was harder to find if it was one of you mortals who'd been holding onto it, not Fae. You can't access its magics, and you got none of your own for it to react to, so it wouldn't flare up the way it would if one of us held it. But, obviously, even between that and whatever else was cloaking it, the spear's magic was leakin' through, or I wouldn'ta felt it twice now, and Adalina wouldn'ta somehow sensed it clear across town. So how come I'd gotten zip at the museum? I'd felt for magic then, and came up snake eyes (not counting Herne).

There were possibilities, sure—maybe the concealing magics were breakin' down, for instance; ain't like this was some toy here—but none of 'em felt right. It'd only been a few days since the museum. If I was feeling something even this potent now, I *shoulda* felt somethin' then!

Could I've just *missed* it at the Field? Did Herne's mojo, not to mention fists, block it out? I mean, I hadn't known what the dingus was yet, hadn't been looking *too* hard...

Ah, nuts. Wasn't gonna put it together sittin' here.

I heard more squishy steps—it was as if Ramona'd sensed I was done with the whole "deep thoughts" thing.

"I think there might be something here, Mick," she said, stepping through the bedroom doorway with her gaze on the folder she carried. "Didn't you say that...?"

She'd stopped when she looked up. And it wasn't 'cause she was bowled over by my baby blues.

Which could only mean one thing.

Real slow and careful, keepin' my mitts away from my pockets, I scooted the chair around.

A tiny number, she was, even though I'd have pegged her at mid-twenties. Woulda had to stand on an upturned shot glass to reach five foot. Dark hair, dark clothes, and tanned.

She sorta gave the impression she'd tried to doll herself up as a Doberman pinscher. Even as I watched, though, her skin paled. Lips quivered, like she had somethin' to say but'd forgotten how.

Tiny as she was, though, I don't suppose it was just contrast that made the .38 she held two-fisted—fists a *lot* steadier'n her kisser—look real friggin' big.

Figured we had about two seconds before the shock wore off and she started slingin' lead, and if she really was going into shock or hysterical, she'd probably get a few shots off before I could get any kinda angle on her thoughts. I was gonna have to try the mortal way.

"If you look careful," I said, grabbing air over my head so she could see both hands, "you'll see we didn't do this."

"You... you *bastards*!" I dunno how she normally sounded, but this worked up, she was shrill enough to crack sugar candy. "What'd... what'd you *do*...?"

"Just told you, doll, we didn't do this."

"You're lying. *You're lying!*"

I didn't need my *aes sidhe* ears to hear the hammer clicking back on her revolver, but it sure added an extra splash of drama.

"Look at me!" I stood, quick as I thought I could pull off without catching a slug for it. "Whaddaya see?"

"Blood... So much blood..."

"Yeah. On my hands and shoes, where I been searching and walking. You see any anywhere else on me? On her?"

"N-no..."

More gently, I said, "You think anyone coulda done this without getting' covered, doll?"

The roscoe started to drift, then firmed right up, aimed back at me.

"Who are you, then? Why are you here? Planning to rob an old... an old..."

"I'm Mick."

Geez, it was like coaxing a feral kitten. A feral kitten with a gun.

"This is Ramona," I continued. "We ain't robbers. We just came to ask some questions, see? We're after the same thing as the monsters who did this—but not the same way."

Again the gun started to droop, and the girl swayed where she stood, but she still wasn't totally convinced. It was Ramona, actually, who sealed the deal.

"If we're telling the truth," she said, "and part of you already knows that we are, then, if you shoot us, whoever did this will get away with it."

The heater dropped to the carpet with a wet *schpludd*. Ramona and I both winced, but it didn't go off. The girl sagged against the doorframe, which was probably all that held her up.

"What's your name, doll?" I said, gently.

She didn't even look my way.

"Leslie. Leslie Rosen."

Hmm. *Coulda* been Abe's daughter, if the old goat stayed frisky into his twilight years, but I guessed *grand-* was more probable. Given the situation, I think I can be excused for not noticing any family resemblance when she strolled in.

I stood, put a hand on the back of the chair. Then, when she didn't seem to understand—or much care—what I meant, I went over, softly took her by the shoulders, and guided her back to it. She sat, I think, entirely outta habit and reflex. Once she was planted, I scooted the chair around farther, so she'd be facin' me direct if I stood in the doorway. Meant she didn't have to look at the bulk of the... mess.

"What're you doin' here at this hour, Leslie?"

Nothing. Not a word, not a blink.

Ramona smiled at her, knelt, put one hand on Leslie's arm and whispered in her ear. Even with my hearing, I couldn't make out a word of it, so I dunno if it was what she said, or how she said it, or somethin' else. Whichever, Leslie jerked once as if she'd sat on a live wire. When she *did* look up, then,

I could taste in the air and see in her aura that a swathe of grief'd been pushed aside. Not all of it, and not gone, but overwhelmed.

And to tell you square, what I got from her in its place was... inappropriate for someone sitting in the middle of a newly remodeled relative.

Well, ain't *that* somethin'? Maybe Ramona just knew the right thing to say, and Leslie had what you lugs'd consider "unconventional" tastes. Or just maybe...

I realized I was getting jealous and shoved it aside. Later, Mick. Handle it later.

Ramona repeated my question from a minute before, and Leslie answered without pause.

"I work here, with... *Worked* with..." One quick sniff, and she went on. "Came in to help with some inventory. Grandpa was... He'd let the books slip a little recently. He... he lost a few important customers a little while ago, and it hit him hard."

"Lost?"

"Yeah. Just... bad luck and a couple of accidents. They weren't friends, but they were important to the business..."

I'd stopped listening.

All right, Fate. I friggin' get it. You can quit with the jumping up'n down and flapping your arms. It all meant something: these "accidents" were important. I just needed to suss out how they fit into the rest of this wacky jigsaw.

In the meantime... "Inventory one of your regular gigs?" I asked. When she jerked me a nod, I said, "Spear come through here recently?"

"A... what?"

"Spear. Long stick for poking people. Woulda had an iron head. Or maybe just a box, tall and thin? Woulda been fairly... recent..."

Well, shit. I'd caught myself right after I'd spilled way too much. Ramona was gonna have all *manner* of questions now, questions I didn't want to...

Except, her expression hadn't so much as twitched. *Hmm...*

"I can check my notes," Leslie told me, though she was already shaking her head. "But I'm fairly sure we haven't had anything like that."

Oh, swell. This just kept gettin' better. If she was right, then what the hell had I been sensing when I...?

I honestly damn near threw an ing-bing right there, and a Fae temper tantrum ain't anything anyone wants to see. Every time I thought I had a handle on exactly what was goin' down, the rug got yanked out from under my feet—and then shoved up my backside.

Was the spear even fucking *in* Chicago? Could this whole thing just be some kinda sick hoax, maybe...

Nah. I dismissed that thought soon as it came to me. Why would anyone go to that trouble? Besides, I'd already seen— felt—evidence it was close.

Hadn't I?

Ramona interrupted that particular train of thought before it reached the station.

"You can help us with more than just that," she coaxed the other woman—almost purred. She flipped open the binder she'd been clutching since Leslie came in, and turned to a page she'd dog-eared earlier. "Mick, you said the museum break-in was the day before I first came to your office?"

"Uh, yeah."

"There's only one scheduled appointment for the day before that." One graceful finger thumped the page in a less-than-graceful point. "But I can't read it. It's some sort of code or shorthand. I was hoping you," and here she turned her attentions back on Leslie, "could translate for us."

The girl chuckled even as she wiped away a tear with the back of one hand.

"It's not shorthand. It's just that Grandpa's handwriting is absolutely appalling." She barely glanced at the page. "It says 'C.C., O'Deah, 6:30.'"

"And that's *not* shorthand?" I asked.

"Well, I don't know who C.C. is, but O'Deah is the name of a restaurant a few blocks down. It's one of his favorites... *Was* one of..."

Whatever Ramona'd said to her wasn't lasting. Leslie buried her face in her hands and sobbed, her whole body and even the chair shaking. I took Ramona's wrist and quietly guided her out of the room.

"Are we just leaving her there?" she hissed at me once we stood in the hall, door carefully shut behind us.

"We've heard all she's got to sing. Ain't too long until dawn. If he was a regular, shouldn't be too hard to find out who he was sharin' a table with. This CC bird's our next—"

"I meant literally! In the middle of her grandfather's remains? She can't handle that!"

"That's what the cops are for." I tried to sound gentle but unmovable, which ain't the easiest combination to pull off. "Ramona, whaddaya wanna do? Tidy the place up for her? Sit around with her until the bulls show?"

"Well, no, but..." I waited while she worked through all the options we didn't have. "It just doesn't seem right."

"No, it doesn't. Not a lot does, these days."

We tromped down a couple flights of stairs and echoes, each of us lost in our own heads. Dunno what she was pondering on, but me? I was startin' to feel the tug of strings on my arms and neck. I mighta dismissed the idea that this whole thing was a flim-flam, but I was *definitely* being played somehow, by someone.

Maybe a whole lotta us were.

I also couldn't help diggin' at the array of bad luck that'd zotzed a whole handful of the Windy City's high'n mighty recently. Had a thought budding, one I didn't wanna let sprout. I hoped like hell Pete'd found out something more, something I could go on. Because if he hadn't, if I hadda follow that beanstalk-thought as it grew, it meant I'd have to go somewhere—metaphorically and literally—where I really, really, *really* didn't want to have to go.

Distracted by all this as I was, it wasn't 'til Ramona shoved the stairwell door open that I sensed the trouble waitin' for us in the hall.

I got plenty of swift, but both of 'em already had gats in their meathooks.

"Take your hand outta your coat, O'Brien. Real slow. Piece in two fingers only."

"O'Brien?" Ramona whispered, reaching skyward.

"Happens all the time, doll."

The two thugs—and that's definitely what they were; if the cheap glad rags hadn't given the game away, the pair of choppers sure did—both gawped when my hand came up holding a stick instead of a roscoe.

"This a gag?" one of 'em asked. "This here's funny to you?"

"In order: No, and Ask me again when it's over."

"Mick…" Ramona warned from the corner of her lips. "You *did* catch the *machine guns* pointed at us?"

"Yeah. I'm a detective. I notice subtle little details like that."

"You might wanna think about acting that way, then!" one of the trouble boys barked. "Unless you *wanna* be filled full of daylight!"

"It's night time. And we're inside," I pointed out. Then, when all three gawped at me like fish at a burlesque show, "Oh, don't blow your wigs, any of you. Ramona, they ain't gonna shoot us."

"No?" The guy on my right, bit taller'n the other, adjusted the brim of his hat with the barrel of the Tommy and then aimed it back my way. "How you figure that?"

"Well, first, 'cause you coulda opened up when we came through that door. And second, Scola wants us alive so we can talk."

Hadn't been a tough nut to crack, though I let 'em go on staring as if I'd just pulled off a magic trick. They weren't Fae, they weren't cops, Fino's boys wouldn'ta started the conversation with me in their sights... While it *coulda* been someone else I didn't know was wrapped up in this, odds favored ol' Bumpy, and their expressions said, "Yep."

"Sharp, O'Brien," the shorter one said. "Was still a bunny move comin' into the boss's place like you did, though. You figure nobody there'd know who you were?"

I shrugged, which is an odd thing to do with arms sticking straight up.

"So what's the story?" I asked.

"Story is, boss wants to finish the conversation you was havin' in more... comfortable surroundings."

Meaning surroundings where gunshots'n bodies wouldn't attract attention.

"Appreciate the invite, boys, but me'n the lady got a prior engagement. Now..." I put my hands down and advanced on 'em. "If you'd care to just blow, we can forget this ever happened."

I got a few seconds of bluster'n threats, and then a pair of triggers got pulled on a pair of Tommies.

One of 'em went *clink* and jammed up tight. The ammo drum fell off the other.

Yeah, did I mention the L&G don't have to be aimed right at somethin' if I'm slowly siphoning the luck outta it? Helps, but ain't required; I mean, it's just channeling my own mojo, after all. And machine guns are complex dinguses. Ain't hard for the mechanisms to go wrong.

First guy was just standin' there, clutching his gun and lookin' about ready to cry. I figured I'd give him a reason.

A quick grab and twist, and we were both holding the gat— vertical, now, the stock right under his chin.

Then I drove my knee up into the barrel.

Teeth broke, bone cracked, and a rubbery something or other bounced off my right shoe, leaving a smear of blood behind. Wonder if it still counts as circumcision if it's a tongue.

Gink toppled and stayed down. You'd almost think that'd maybe hurt a little.

His partner was also on the floor, crawling after the disobedient ammo. His fingers were just stretching out to grab it when I kicked it across the hall. Bad guy said a lot of bad words, then lunged to his feet with a switchblade *snick*ing open in his fist, because most of these trouble boys are dumb bunnies who don't know when to quit.

I let him take a few wild stabs, then pinned him up in a joint lock, my arms through his, and took the knife away.

I dunno what he had to complain about, though. I mean, I gave it right back.

I took Ramona's elbow and escorted her out, leaving one cat writhing on the floor, the other using one mitt to try and gingerly remove the blood-slick knife that pinned his *other* hand to the wall.

What can I say? I didn't wanna kill 'em, but I wanted to make sure they'd be crossing the street anytime they saw me comin' for a long, *long* time.

Best I could tell, nobody in the building'd even bothered to call copper. Either they were *real* heavy sleepers, or they weren't any of 'em real anxious to nose into anyone else's business. In this city, who could blame 'em?

"Wasn't that dangerous?" Ramona asked once we were outside and moving on down the sidewalk. She sounded sorta absent, distant, and she didn't seem keen to look my way. "Is Scola the sort of guy you want angry at you?"

"You mean like he already is, after the ruckus at the club? Trust me, doll, if the other choice was goin' along with those guys to somewhere Bumpy feels comfortable using negotiating tactics measured by caliber, tuning his goons up some was definitely the wise move."

"Oh. Okay."

Right. Nice talkin' to you, too.

CHAPTER TWELVE

No, nobody else tried to jump us that night. Yeah, once we found O'Deah's, I was able—after some asking around and a mental nudge here'n there—to find out who Rosen'd been with that night.

Our C.C.'s name was Clint Clanton. I assume his parents were drunks. Hadn't been too hard to track Pete down again and cajole him into digging up some more info for me. Turns out Clanton was an art thief—so just the guy you might wanna give a ring if you were planning a heist in, oh, say, a museum.

And yeah, he was dead.

Car "accident" two days ago. Right. *Suuuuure* it was.

All that'd taken the wee morning hours, so the rising sun was right in our faces on the walk back to my place, and in all that time, I don't think Ramona'd uttered any two words near enough together to dance. I thought about tryin' to squeeze more out of her, figure what was eatin' at her, but I had more'n enough of my own contemplation to do.

No big mystery how those lugs had found me, either. Scola might not know *why* he'd spilled Rosen's name to me, but he knew he *had*. Didn't take a genius to figure that his place'd be one of my next stops.

Nah, what bugged me was a lot bigger'n that. Namely, this

whole thing was starting to smell so bad it'd give a redcap the vapors.

No magic—well, other'n Herne's—at the museum. I hadn't sensed a thing. On the other hand, I *had* sensed it downtown and in Rosen's place. On the *other* other hand, not a one of us, 'cept maybe Adalina, had any sense of it elsewhere in the city. (Or at least not enough for anyone to actually *find* the dingus.) So where was the damn spear? Who had it now? Where had it been, and where hadn't it? Was it shielded, or not?

The mundane clues weren't sitting much better with me, either. Manetti to Rosen to Clanton. It was *way* too pat. Too neat. If Manetti'd smuggled the thing into Chicago, why the stopover at the museum? If Clanton had broken into the museum, why the obvious broken window? That hadn't been a pro job.

And then, maybe not first but certainly, in my head, foremost, was our radiant Ms. Ramona Webb.

Had she somehow not *heard* what I'd asked Leslie Rosen? Had the night gotten so weird that she didn't figure me lookin' for an ancient pig-sticker was at all hinky? Or was there something more to it? Every time I looked her way, it all felt like a bunch of hooey; no reason to be suspicious at all. But then, I'd find myself peepin' elsewhere, and... it was as if, for just a second, I could think.

I'd fallen for her, hard. Been tied up in a pretty little bow. It felt right. Sometimes I couldn't even question it, anymore'n I questioned the ground under my plates, or the existence of my left arm.

It felt right.

But I was finally starting, just starting, to think *maybe* it wasn't.

We were comin' up on Mr. Soucek's building, and I still hadn't decided whether to come out and say anything about all of this—or even if I *could*—when she made the choice for me.

"I'm going home for a time." She said it real quiet, so that with the workday-morning traffic around us, I'd have just barely been able to make it out if my ears were human.

I turned, leaned one shoulder against a street light.

"What're you talking about, sweetheart?"

"What am I...? Good God, Mick, did you actually *see* any of last night? I've had more guns pointed at me with you than if I'd just stuck around to deal with Jeremy's, ah, *associates*! You were supposed to keep me *safe*!"

"Simmer down. Nobody's fittin' you for a pine overcoat yet."

"And Rosen? God, I don't... I will never, *ever* get that out of my mind! The sight, the... the smell..."

She choked up, and you know something? I wasn't entirely sure I was buying it anymore, not after she'd managed to give that room a thorough look-see despite the gore. Yeah, maybe she was just real good at putting her feelings aside and doing what's gotta be done—some people are—but it was one too many "maybes."

"You firing me?"

"I... No. Well, not yet, anyway. I need some time to think, and... Frankly, after all this, I don't think I'm likely to be in any more danger on my own, or with friends, than I've been with you. I'll call on you tomorrow one way or the other, let you know what I've decided."

"Uh-huh. And if I *don't* hear from you?"

She smiled, first time in a while, and damn it if it still didn't make me come over giddy.

"Then," she said, "I expect you to remember that I *haven't* fired you, and to come looking for me to make sure I'm okay."

"Right. Got it. I don't think this is a keen idea, Ramona. But if it's what you need..."

"It is. Thank you, Mick."

Ramona turned one way, back toward the nearest train station, and I went the other, heading home.

For a minute. Until she'd turned the first corner. And *finally*, when I couldn't see her anymore, when so much about her felt hinky, it came to me. What it was I'd seen in those last minutes at Bumpy's place. What'd been bothering at me ever since, like ants in my brain.

It was the stool. The one she'd picked up as a makeshift club. A stool from the stage, where the band had been playing. Plenty of bottles and bar stools where she'd been crouched that she coulda snatched up in a second. Yet she'd gone *back*, farther into the mess and chaos, because for some reason she'd wanted *this* stool for her weapon.

This stool, which—unlike the fancier, shinier numbers by the bar, with their stainless steel—had legs of *iron*.

She knew.

I spun and went after her like a lion on a three-legged gazelle.

If I'd been sure she was just a normal one of you dolts, I'd have counted on skill alone. But I wasn't much sure of anything, anymore, and I wasn't gonna chance it.

In my wake, as I ran—then walked—after her, people were havin' a bad morning. Some tripped, stumbled, getting dirt on, or putting tears in, their work rags. Briefcases, purses, and newspapers slipped from what shoulda been secure grips, and I heard a woman shriek as another pedestrian's dog slipped its leash and stuck its cold, wet nose somewhere she never really wanted a cold, wet *anything*.

Almost as though something was just sucking the good luck from 'em as it passed.

I didn't take too much from anyone. Nobody got hurt, beyond maybe a skinned knee. But I didn't have time or patience to do it any more slowly or gently than that.

And I'll tell you what, it's a good thing I did. Ramona never *looked* to be watching for shadows, but she sure *acted* as though she was. Extra trips around the block, switching lines at the gates and counters, even boarding the "wrong" train and hoppin' back off at the last minute.

But I always found a spot, behind a barrier or in a crowd, where I could watch. Always managed to duck behind one of the other commuters if she looked too hard my way. Lucky I had so much... uh, luck.

I knew straight off she wasn't heading home. Right general direction, but wrong line, especially when she switched trains somewhere around Englewood.

When we approached the Loop, I suspected. When she disembarked on West Washington, I knew. Y'see, I think I mentioned a while back that a few of Chicago's politicos—an alderman here, a secretary there—know something about what really goes on in their city. Not a *lot*, mind. Usually they're no better informed than, say, Bumpy seemed to be. But some do know that much, and a real tiny handful know *more*.

And the Loop is—among other things—the Windy City's government and financial center.

Still, even knowing that, even having sussed out the sorta Joe she was likely calling on, I was startled when, after some extended weaving through the downtown crowds, she finally ended her hike at a towering, inflated ego of a structure. Granite and a bit of marble and all the usual rocks. All squared corners and classical-style pillars that weren't actually all that different from the ones I'd seen at the museum a few lifetimes-slash-nights ago.

Yep. She'd stopped in at LaSalle and Randolph. That's City Hall, to you.

Which narrowed down the list of who she could be seeing to about a bazillion. Between the city of Chicago in one half of the building, and Cook County in the other, there were hundreds of offices, thousands of officials and employees, to pick from. And that was assuming she was actually meeting someone in the building; City Hall's got exits that open up into a whole collection of other government office buildings. *And*, of course, the place was busy enough that she could be meeting with someone else just passing through, and nobody'd bat an eyelid.

I thought real hard about following her in, but even my

luck'll only cover so much. Odds of me finding her in that mess were about zip, and the odds of me staying unnoticed if I *did* stumble across her were even lower. No, better to call it done here, work at diggin' up more details later on.

For now, I had a pretty solid notion of who, or at least the *kind* of "who," she was having a sit-down with. You'd think I'd be used to being lied to by now, and maybe I am from most people, but she wasn't "most people" to me. It hurt. A lot. Intestines-removed-with-an-ice-cream-scoop kinda hurt.

So be it. I was gonna get my answers, goddamn it. And not just from Ramona, either. No, she could wait. I had errands to run before I got back around to my so-called "client"— starting with a line of investigation I couldn't avoid any longer, and that I'd rather chew off my own kneecaps than follow.

CHAPTER THIRTEEN

I got wrapped up enough following my train of thought that I could ignore the rocking and thumping of the more literal train around me. You wouldn't think I could get lost in my own head, given how often I been visiting the place lately. Guess I still ain't accustomed to it.

Look, you were gonna say it if I didn't.

So, what did we have? Ramona—and we both know it'd be a helluva fib if I pretended it didn't hurt just to think her name—was workin' for someone else. Someone who was probably a pretty big cheese in Chicago. Politico, fat cat, or both. Money'n power really ain't much different in your world, not that you need me to tell you that. I couldn't be *totally* sure; as I said, the City Hall meet coulda been one of convenience or anonymity. But I figured that was the less likely option—and also the option that didn't give me any kinda lead to go on—so I went with the more obvious notion.

Plus, I just couldn't see Ramona working for a nobody. Assuming, then, that her boss was a highbinder of some sort, what'd that get me?

Well, for one, it meant he fit the profile of the poor schlubs who'd kicked off in those "accidents" that kept poppin' up like toadstools everywhere I looked. That wasn't proof of anything, but it was an interesting bit of circumstance I wasn't willing to write off.

Second, it made him one of the Windy City elite who had dealings with—or at least knew about—us Fae and the Otherworld. I mean, Ramona obviously had some knowledge of us; I hadda assume the boss did, too. So, that narrowed down the suspect field a whole bunch, but it also made the guy more dangerous than your average mortal, rich'n powerful or otherwise.

Could be all kindsa repercussions to that, but those weren't what I was digging into right now. See, realizing that "my client's" boss fit both those categories had reinforced an idea I already had bouncin' around my noodle like a rubber kitten. Namely, the reason the cops had found bupkis connecting the different accident victims to each other just might be because the connection lay in a *whole different world.*

That was why I'd been so desperately hoping Pete'd come up with something, see? If he didn't, it'd mean—for my sake, for his, for a lotta other people's—I was goin' to have to start hunting elsewhere.

Yeah, *that* elsewhere. I *hate* that elsewhere.

But needs must, and all that. I leaned my head back against the whisper-soft woven cobweb seat, and tried to ignore the grunting and stench that occasionally seeped up from the goblin and *brounie* oarsmen in the galley below, enough for the rocking of the train to relax me a bit.

Oh, yeah. I didn't actually mention where I was, did I?

Brass car on bronze wheels on brass tracks carried me'n a few others—a couple *aes sidhe*, a small group of leprechauns and *coblynau* commuting in to work, a greasy-looking *gancanagh* chortling over his latest feminine conquest, but mostly human servants with their vapid, fruit-and-wine-drugged smiles—to, and through, Elphame's reflection of Chicago. Here, I was home. Here, I belonged; I could rest; I no longer felt the constant screech of technology in my head, or the itch of nearby iron on my skin.

It still didn't make me any less anxious to dust out, back to your half of reality.

It wasn't all that far a walk to the city proper from where my little rabbit hole opened up into Elphame, but I really didn't wanna spend any longer here than I had to. Also, it ain't real pleasant bein' outside for too long in winter, which'd come earlier to our world this year than yours.

So I'd taken the train, instead of walking, and I'd spent most of the ride, while I was ponderin' this whole mess, staring out the window. (It's funny. So much of our more modern buildings—the ones that try to mimic yours—is made of glass. We like glass. But the windows on the train? *Not* glass. Wind, captured and packed into solid slabs. Nobody ever accused us of bein' either efficient or consistent.)

Anyway, yeah, starin' out the window, watching the world go by. The thickly falling snow hid a lot, but since the light here is ambient—no sun in this part of Elphame, just a general daytime glow—it didn't cast any shadows, so it wasn't as obscuring as it woulda been in your world. I couldn't see any of the pixies from here, but I knew the floral bunch had gone into hibernation for the winter, transforming into their icy and somberly cruel seasonal alter egos. Fields which were usually covered in grasses'n flowers of every color of the rainbow were now a thousand different shades of brown, where they weren't coated in gleaming white drifts.

And yeah, there *are* a thousand shades of brown. Nothin' blends, here. Every color, no matter how subtly different from any other hue, stands out in sharp contrast. It's beautiful when it's beautiful, and it's *real* ugly when it's ugly.

I hoped it'd leave off snowing by the time I hadda disembark.

Then the fields'd given way to the outer neighborhoods and "slums" of our Chicago, apartments and warehouses built either of or in trees—and by in I mean *in*, not just among the branches. Factories, too. We don't *need* an industrial area, since we got no real industry, but you folks have 'em, so we gotta have 'em.

Fuckin' Fae.

And no, I haven't forgotten that includes me.

Bad neighborhoods gave way to better, downtown to up, and I couldn't help but notice the streets were largely empty. We ain't exactly packed in here to begin with, and a lot of Fae felt the same way I do about the snow, but still, this was deader'n usual.

Hinky.

Skyscrapers and rich business fronts, now, edifices of stone or glass—supported by trees, magic, or both—rising from the lower floors in the thick earthen mounds that gave the *aes sidhe* our name. Roads paved with bricks from the lost, torn-down, fallen, and discarded places of your world, some of the smoothest footing you'll find in Elphame, and *still* almost no foot traffic. A scrambling servant here, a rubber-tired coach creeping furtively behind a team of nervous horses there, and that was it.

Hinky. Again. As if I didn't have enough cause to be jittery.

The train's horn blew twice—no steam whistle, but a small fragment of storm run through a Pan flute—and the whole thing shuddered to a stop. The passengers weren't supposed to be able to hear anything from below, but I could make out just enough to tell that the rowers were exhausted and not happy about havin' to start up again anytime soon.

It's a rough gig, keepin' the brass highway moving.

No real train station, here, just a ticket booth manned by a leprechaun on a tall stool, and a comfortable cottage where important Fae passengers can wait for the next arrival. Less important Fae, and human servants? They wait out in the weather. Comfort's a privilege, not a right, right?

Ugh.

And no, it hadn't stopped snowing. Damn it. I stuck my hands in my pockets, hunched my shoulders, and waded into the flurries.

The snow here? It's all white. No shades of grey or cream, no pickin' up dirt or pollution in the air, or even on the ground. Not just white; WHITE.

It's also more'n a little pungent, and it tastes even worse. Legend goes that every tear of grief shed by a human in one world becomes a snowflake in the other. I dunno if that's literally true or not, but I *do* know that the snow here is tinged with salt and somehow oppressive.

Also, unlike our rain, which you can just wipe off once you get indoors, 'cause it doesn't soak into clothing, the snow sticks.

No, it doesn't make any sense by the laws of *your* world. So what? I'm still bewildered by basic chemistry and time zones.

The few pedestrians I passed shot me some dirty looks, full of mistrust and buried fear. A couple even crossed the street to avoid me. I ain't a popular guy round here, but I don't normally provoke *that* kinda response, and there was no way every single one of 'em coulda known who I was. So I hadda figure they were reacting that way to everyone.

And now I'd had that thought, I could feel it in the air, see it in the buildings I passed. Businesses closed, or so empty they might as well be. Pedestrians' steps were short'n shuffling, trying to move quick while stayin' as inconspicuous and seemingly harmless as possible. Windows were shut, and I saw rifles and bows and brass Tommies behind more'n a couple panes of glass.

Even without all that, though, I'd have felt it sooner than later. The tension in the air was thick enough to taste, and us bein' Fae, I promise you I ain't speakin' metaphorically. It was everywhere, cloying, sickly-sweet and acrid all at once. Like sweaty molasses.

I hadn't felt an Otherworld burgh this uneasy in a black dog's age. Don't think I *ever* felt it in Chicago before. Guess maybe it mighta been this way over in Unseelie territory when Capone finally got pinched, but there'd been celebrations over on this side of the tracks.

So I'm told. I wasn't here.

Point is, our Chicago wasn't a city under siege, but... maybe adjacent to siege. Lotta people were expecting one.

Which fit, really. Enough of us were searching for

Ahreadbhar over on the other side, enough stories and rumors and whispers floatin' around about it, it hadda be common knowledge by now. Everyone here musta known the Spear of Lugh was in play.

And yeah, that meant open war between the Courts could be lurkin' around the corner. If the Unseelie got hold of the thing? Might just have enough power for 'em to make a play for the whole city. Seelie win the race? Wasn't too far outta the realm of possibility the Unfit'd try to strike first, bring down their enemy before the Seelie could gather their forces.

Either way, it was gonna be trouble with a capital Q—not just bad, but bewildering.

Even more motivation for me to find a way outta all this that didn't involve just handing the damn thing over to the neighborhood monsters. I might not be fond of this place, but that don't mean I wanna see it torn apart.

Most of the time.

All right, and that was about enough wool-gathering to get me to my destination only *moderately* miserable with snow. Anyone could tell it was an old building; it was mostly stone, not glass, but polished marble, not the cheap granite of poorer streets. A small grove of trees—oak, ash, and hawthorn, because why the hell would they be anything else?—formed a winding walkway to the front door, and not a one of 'em had lost a single leaf to the changing seasons, or sported even the tiniest patch of snow.

Wonder how expensive it was to renew *that* enchantment every year?

Place was… whaddaya wanna call it? An archive? A library? A depository? A Domesday Book writ large? Let's just say it was our Chicago's Hall of Records, since that's as close a definition as any.

Also because we called it the Hall of Records. Score another one for Fae originality.

So, okay, if the rash of dead humans *were* connected

through the Fae, as I suspected now, odds favored the Seelie over the Un-. Not that Eudeagh and her ilk never worked with humans—far from it—but the sorta high-class Joes who'd been chilled off were more Seelie style.

And if any of 'em *did* have connections to a member of the Seelie Court—if it was a *formal* connection, an actual alliance or patronage as opposed to somethin' more personal—I just might find a record of it here.

That sound thin to you? It should. *If* they were formal, and *if* they were of the sorts of agreements that'd be put down in official documentation, and *if* they were even connected via the Seelie at all... Even assuming I found one or two of 'em, no way I'd be able to connect the whole bunch this way.

That was just jake with me, though. I wasn't tryin' to pin the whole web together, not yet. For now, I just figured, if I could find those one or two links, I'd know if this was all a trip for biscuits or not. If so, I could take the run-out without ever having to ask anyone anything.

If not, if there really was some meat to this wacky theory, it could mean a lotta unpleasant sit-downs, and I wasn't about to start in on that until I *knew* I was on the right track.

Hall of Records it was, then. I'd just pop in, spend a few hours eyeballing the paperwork, and move along to my next step.

And if you believe for one heartbeat it was that easy, you oughta get your noggin checked for termites. They've eaten the important bits.

The front door was newer'n the rest of the place, made up of expensive glass in a hardwood frame. The *brownie* doorman offered to take my coat. I told him where he could take it, and which orifice he could store it in for the trip. We agreed to politely part ways with my coat still on my shoulders.

I'll tell ya, it don't matter which world you're in, or whether the carpet's made of shag or woven rose petals, or the walls covered'n paint or colored residue scraped from the trailing edges of dreams. Don't matter if the folks sittin' around on their keisters waitin' are mortal or *sidhe*, and it don't matter if the lousy background music is piped in through a chintzy speaker or played by a small orchestra of low-rent pixies on lower-rent miniature instruments. A lobby is a lobby is a lobby.

Was only four or five John Hancocks on the sign-in ledger ahead of mine. And it was still a couple hours—when I was long past wantin' to rip up the rose petals and break a few tiny musicians—that I finally heard my name called.

When I heard the greasy contempt wrapped around every syllable, I just knew me'n the crumb weren't gonna hit it off real well.

The guy behind the counter was what you guys call a *nisse* or *haltija* up north, or *lares* if you're, y'know, an ancient Roman. Guardians and protectors of farms and households, most of 'em are decent enough, long as you don't try to harm anyone or anything they're attached to. (Or otherwise rile 'em up; short tempers, those guys.) Every now'n again, though, you'd get one decide he was too lazy for any kinda real post, and end up workin' a counter or a door, something you could call "guarding" if you got drunk enough and squinted right, but really just made 'em another bureaucrat.

This one looked to've taken to bureaucracy like a buzzard to carrion. He was smug, smarmy, and… I dunno. Somethin' else unflattering that starts with "sm."

An old wrinkly face peeped up at me from behind a beard that was probably bulletproof. Three foot'n change is about average for these guys, but he was standin' on something. An apple box, probably.

And he knew me. I couldn'ta said how, but I heard it in his voice.

"Well, Mr. Oberon. You've not been home in quite a while, have you?"

"Uh, no. Guess not."

"What might I do for you, now that we're again graced with your illustrious presence?"

Oh, boy. "Yeah, I'm tryin' to find some information on—"

"I'm sorry, we don't seem to have any records on that. Will there be anything else?"

Well, then. "Look, bo, you could at least let me finish before pretending—"

"Of course. By all means, please finish."

I ain't dumb enough to have expected it to go anywhere, but I gave it one last shot.

"Tryin' to find some information on—"

"Oh! My mistake. We *do* have those records, but I fear they're unavailable at the moment. Perhaps you might try back in a week or two?"

Throttling him woulda been a lot tougher'n it sounds—small but *real* damn strong, *haltija*—and it wouldn't have done me any good, either. I *sure* as hell didn't need to be gettin' in hot water with the Seelie Court right now; at best I'd spend a few days cooling my heels in a magic cage, while a whole swarm of people who hated my guts argued over who got to throw away the key.

It was still real damn tempting, though.

"You wanna at least tell me what you got against me, you bastard?"

I thought his beard was gonna just fall open like a stage curtain, he smirked so wide.

(Smirking! There's the other sm.)

"I'm so sorry," he gloated. "I don't believe that information's available in our records."

Yeah. I decided I'd better blow the joint before I lost my temper'n added "smacked" and "smothered" to the list.

I was openin' the door, feelin' the first cold and salty fingertips of the dancing snow, when he called after me.

"Oh, Mr. Oberon?"

Here it comes. I stopped but didn't turn.

"His Honor Ylleuwyn offers his warmest regards."

I wasn't gonna give him the satisfaction of seein' my curse, so I waited until I was out in the cold white and a good half a block away before letting loose a string of profanity that woulda had a longshoreman slapping his momma.

The name explained everything to me, but for those of you with shorter memories…

Judge Ylleuwyn—or Earl Ylleuwyn, dependin' on which of Chicago's rank'n royalty system you were usin'—was a politico I'd butted heads with last time I was in the Otherworld. Yeah, back on the Ottati job. He'd been standin' between me'n the straight dope I needed to get on with the case. I'd eventually gotten the better of him, but it wasn't easy, and he really, *really* hadn't been happy.

Course, that was also how I'd gotten in deep with the Unfit, dropping me in the jam I was in now, so I gotta say it hasn't really made me happy, either.

Anyway, there was no way he knew I was back in Elphame, or what in particular I was gunning for. But tellin' each and every friend, ally, and worker he had to keep a peeper open for me, and to gum up anything they possibly could for me if I showed? Yeah, that was not only entirely possible, but completely in character for the Seelie high'n mighty.

Buncha goddamn babies, the whole friggin' lot of us.

It was a nuisance more'n anything else, but it was a nuisance at a real bad time. Weren't a whole lotta official trails I could follow to what I was lookin' for, but what few there were? I'd basically just lost all of them. No, Ylly didn't have his fingers *everywhere*, but he had more'n enough pull to make any kinda official inquiry take about a zillion years. And while he may not've known I was in town to begin with, I'm sure my good pal at the Hall of Records would be spilling the beans before long.

Hell, even if he didn't, mosta the city's *other* officials'd be happy to give me the runaround, too. Most of 'em didn't have a grudge as personal as Ylleuwyn's, but none of 'em ever drank outta my bottle, if you get me.

All of which meant I had no option but to go to one of the few people here who *did* like me, and as a reward for helpin' me out, they'd probably get in all kinda dutch with Ylleuwyn and Ogma only knows who—

"Hey! Oberon!"

—else. Goddamn it.

The empty street around me wasn't so empty anymore. I twisted back the way I'd come, but I didn't need to. The bear-choking-on-sand tenor told me what I'd see.

I admit, though, that I hadn't expected to see *three* of 'em.

Big dark blots against the white of the snow, they were all jet-black fur'n scissor-length claws and jagged chompers in mouths so big you'd expect to see miners pickin' away for gold on the inside. They smelled like wet dog, and their breath... Well, it also smelled like wet dog. The inside of one.

Bugganes. Distant relatives of trolls, *phouka*, and black dogs, they were basically all malice and hunger. Might surprise you to hear, but most of 'em ain't Unseelie. Not Seelie either, mind. Mostly they got no time for the Courts, or much of anything civilized. They're happy to work for anyone, though, if the price—or the meal—is right.

These? Almost definitely workin' for the Unfit.

"What're you doing here, Oberon?" It was the middle one talkin', not that it much mattered. "You've got a job you should be doing. People don't like it when you don't do your job."

Yep. Definitely the Unfit. I'd only been here a few hours; Eudeagh must be keepin' real tight tabs on the place. Normally she'da sent redcaps, or maybe *dullahan* or a troll, to deliver this sorta message, instead of hired goons. Guess either her people were all busy, or she knew what'd happen if a buncha Unseelie traipsed over to this side of town.

Seemed as if *these* guys *hadn't* thought about it, though. *Bugganes* ain't stupid—lotta people make that mistake, and most of 'em are rewarded with a one-way fare through a mystical digestive tract—but they're creatures of instinct and emotion first. They *can* think; they just usually don't want to.

So I was gonna have to push 'em into it, and then hope I could steer 'em in the right direction before somebody decided to use my hair as a toothbrush.

"Lemme save you some time," I said, locking my gaze with the *buggane* in the middle—less as a challenge or signal that I wasn't cowed, though I hoped he'd take it that way, than as a way of avoiding starin' at the teeth or claws. "This is the part where you make it real clear Queen Mob sent you, without ever usin' her name, and then you tell me I'd better get myself back to the mortal world and tryin' to suss out the spear, or else."

The beastie on the left grumbled something unintelligible; the one I was yappin' at just scowled, which made me think of a disappointed bandsaw.

"Something along those lines," he admitted sullenly.

"All right. So, first off, I'm here followin' a lead. Second—"

"Bullshit. We all know the spear's not here, Oberon. Don't treat us like we're dumb." The other two snarled agreement, claws screeching as they rubbed together.

"I didn't say the *spear* was here. I said the *lead* was here. Or did you think that every line of investigation about a friggin' *Fae artifact* was gonna keep itself neatly on the human side of reality?"

"Uh..."

"That's what I thought."

Funny thing, it wasn't even a lie. I *was* still hunting for Gáe Assail, and I *was* following a lead. I mighta just forgotten to mention that the lead wasn't exactly part of the hunt.

"All right, fine." The rage in his voice was pretty clear: he was tryin' to keep control of the conversation and his temper both. "What's this lead?"

"Complicated. You wanna stand around climbin' your thumb while I explain it? Not really an efficient way of gettin' me back to work."

More growling and grinding of stalactites disguised as teeth.

"You said 'first off,'" he demanded. "What's second?"

"Or else what?"

"Huh?"

"Your threat. 'Get out of Elphame or else.' My second point is, or else what?"

"You don't really—"

"Eudeagh probably sent you creeps because of your reputation. Nobody messes with a *buggane* if they wanna keep all their skin and organs. And we all know I can't take three of you." Though I bet I coulda held 'em off long enough to set some new Fae sprinting records. "Guess she figured I wouldn't question it.

"But really, what're you gonna do to me? You tune me up a little? Ain't gonna change anything. You put some real hurt on me? I'm outta the game for days, weeks, maybe even longer. Can't really get back to diggin' up her majesty's trinket if I'm laid up, can I?"

In case you've forgotten, since Elphame's my "natural" world, I don't heal mystically here the way I do among you mugs. My own magics may be more powerful, but I'm a lot easier to hurt—and I *stay* hurt a lot longer. Never thought that'd actually come in *handy*, but at the moment...

"Same with killing me," I pressed on. "You're just takin' me outta the hunt completely that way. No way Eudeagh wants that, and I figure she told you as much in no uncertain terms. So really, other'n looking big'n mean'n intimidating, trying to make me yellow the surrounding snow a little, what've you actually got to threaten me with? Because right now, by my count, you're right at zero. Maybe, if you're real creative, twice that.

"You've delivered your spiel. I've heard it. Now scram."

I worried I mighta poked a touch too hard when Grumbly on the right started to howl and lunge, but *buggane*-in-the-middle shoved him back with a paw. Not that he was a whole lot calmer: I could see his paw shakin'.

"And what if you get us mad enough," he bellowed, "that we forget ourselves? It happens. A lot!"

"Then you get to explain to Eudeagh why you gummed up her assignment—and just maybe, why you queered her chances at getting the Spear of Lugh."

Even the snow was holding its breath, or that's how it felt; air got less cold and less salty for a few seconds. Then, grinding their not-so-pearly whites so hard they actually drooled shards'n powder, the trio of *bugganes* turned away and trudged back outta sight.

I couldn'ta *really* held my breath all the way to my destination, but recollectin' now, it sure as hell felt that way.

As I've said, I didn't have a lotta friends here in Otherworld Chicago. Of the few I *did*, I'd already called on one for help within the last year. As a result, she'd had one of her best rooms shot up, an official investigation in her place, and almost certainly landed on the bad side of Ylleuwyn and his not-insubstantial political network. I'd definitely caused her enough grief for a while. So whatever else happened, no matter what other dead ends I ran up against, I was absolutely determined to steer clear of the Lambton Worm.

About three hours later, I arrived at the Lambton Worm.

Shut up. I don't wanna hear it.

You remember the Lambton Worm, right? I ain't wastin' my breath spinnin' you all these yarns, am I?

Fine, real quick, then. The Lambton's one of the best hotels in our Chicago. Caters to any and every kinda Fae. You got yer modern-style hotel rooms, your castle bedchambers, your hollows in the trees, your tunnels in the mounds, each in its own section of the joint. You've also got the massive stone serpent wriggling and winding its way around the entire building, which the owner says was a real dragon until a basilisk caught its eye, and everybody else says is just a damn statue.

Same swanky glass revolving door. Same carpeted pathway winding between forests of decorative columns and actual trees, both. Same menagerie of every kinda Seelie you could imagine—staff'n guests—same counters and tables, same array of hotel bars servin' the same array of a million kinds of rotgut.

And, as it happened, the same pain-in-the-ass spriggan sittin' and drinkin' in one of 'em. With the same beige overcoat, pixie-puke-orange fedora, and bushy red beard that didn't need a trim so much as a good brushfire. He was six foot tall at the moment, which ain't his tallest or his shortest, but the height he tends to favor when dealin' with us normal-size folks. I knew he could break nine when he got good'n steamed, if not even taller, and the sight of me was always enough to stoke the boiler.

He'da given you a whole heap of reasons he didn't care for me. Me, I figure he was just threatened. I worked as the Lambton's house dick for a while before him, and I've got a solid hunch he's afraid I was better'n he is.

Wouldn't surprise me if I was, either.

"Goddamn it, Mr. Oberon, didn't y'make enough trouble fer us last time y'were—"

"Slachaun, I got no time to play today. Can we just skip right to the part where you stomp off all sullen and resentful to tell Ielveith I need to see her? I promise, we can compare pecker sizes *twice* next time, to make up for it."

"First off," he shouted, puttin' on about five inches, "that's *Mrs.* Ielveith to ya, boyo!"

"It really isn't."

"And second, why'n the name'a any god y'care to invoke would I—?"

"Come over here'n search me."

"—even want to—What the hell'd y'just say?"

"Search me. You know what you'll find?"

With his jaw workin' that way, even Slachaun's beard looked bewildered.

"Uh..."

"You'll find that I got nothin' on me but my wand, identification, and a list of names."

The clatter of glasses and chatter of conversation at the bar had completely stopped. The spriggan was just sorta scratchin' under his blinding hat. He'd faded back to about six feet again, too.

"Fine'n dandy, but—"

"What you will *not* find," I bulled on, "is anythin' of value. No wad of cash. No shiny jewelry. No pretty magic gewgaw. In short, you'll find exactly squat that I could offer Ielveith as a gift. So c'mon." I patted down the sides of my coat. "Let's get this over with."

"Nah, I'll… I'll take yer word fer it. But I never *asked* if y'had—"

Would you believe me if I said I wasn't gettin' a certain kick out of interrupting every last thing he said? 'Cause I sure as hell wouldn't.

"Now," I said, "you're supposed to be a detective, yeah?"

"I *am* a—!"

"So let's try some inductive reasoning. You know how much I hate comin' home, so why am I here? In Elphame, and specifically here at the Lambton? I don't have enough scratch on me to bunk here for the night."

"Y'need Ms. Ielveith's help. Same as always, leanin' on the hard work o' others ta—"

"Right. And we both know my last visit wasn't a lotta fun for her, so it ain't too probable she's gonna help me just outta the goodness of her heart. Not on anything heavy, anyway, and we also both know I wouldn't be here for anythin' small. Since we just established I don't come bearing gifts that might buy me some consideration, what's that leave, Slachaun?"

I've said it before: for all his temper, and people skills to make Vlad the Impaler blanche, the spriggan actually ain't too shabby at his job. He understood the song I was singing.

"Either what y'need's big enough that ya'd put yerself in

debt for it," he grunted sourly, "or it's somethin' y'figure she'll help y'with for her own interests."

Bugganes and spriggans. Like everything else bigger'n me, it was all about knowin' how to handle 'em.

"Not bad. Now, in either of those cases, you wanna be the one to explain why you didn't give the boss the chance to hear the skinny'n make up her own mind?"

He just sorta deflated back to his normal three feet'n change.

"I'll go tell Ms. Ielveith yer here."

"You stomp off sullenly and reluctantly do that."

Ielveith'd greeted me friendly enough, but she also didn't make too sincere an effort to hide her suspicion. When I'd gotten into some of the basics of why I was droppin' in on her, she started shakin' her head.

"You cannot *possibly* be serious," she said when I'd finished.

"Well, I *can*. I just usually make a point of avoiding it."

If Queen Victoria'd risen from the dead right then and spouted her "We are *not* amused!" routine, she'd still've gotten more of a laugh outta that than my fellow *aes sidhe*.

Ielveith was straight-laced, beautiful, kinda severe, and her office matched.

Yeah, I was in another office.

I'm so damn sick of offices I could scream. And no, I'm not gonna describe it in detail. You know what the Fae aesthetic looks like, you know what an office looks like. Paint your own damn picture.

She was ensconced behind the desk; I was plunked in a chair opposite; and Slachaun sat rigid on a sofa to my left, almost quiverin' with the urge to do... something. I couldn't say what, but if someone'd offered odds that I wouldn't find it pleasant, well, I wouldn't bet against it.

"Look, Ielveith—" I started.

"No. Mick, I've had enough trouble keeping out of

Ylleuwyn's sights since you were last here. The Lambton doesn't play favorites, and in exchange, we don't have enemies. Or we *didn't*. I know what you're looking for on the other side. A lot of us do. I wish you luck, but I'm *not* going to stick my neck—"

"Just take a gander at this, would ya?" I shoved the list into her hands before she could protest. "Any names ring a bell?"

"I just said I'm not—"

"This ain't just for me, Iel. This is bigger'n me. Might even be bigger'n the Spear of Lugh."

That got me an eyebrow, but her blinkers flicked down to the paper.

"I recognize a few," she admitted, after a brief pause. "I've had a few dealings with Mr. Horton, here, actually. How is he doing?"

"Dead."

Ielveith shrugged, let the paper drift down to her hardwood desk.

"Ah, well. They go so quickly. I still don't—"

"They're *all* dead, Iel. Every name on that list. All within the last few weeks. All in 'accidents.'"

Her fingers scrabbled to recover the list, audibly crinkling the paper.

"Lemme guess," I said as she went over it again. "In addition to your pal Horton, every name you know has some tie or other to some Seelie or another."

"I only recognize a few, Mick."

I decided to take that as confirmation.

"Sure. You wanna wager a free week in the presidential suite that the others do, too?"

The spriggan leaned forward on the sofa.

"What're y'suggestin', exactly?"

"I'm suggesting that the Unfit are workin' some kinda Chinese angle. You know how much extra violence the city's seen with all those redcaps in it? Zip. Bupkis. They're keeping a low profile, and redcaps don't *do* low profile unless they absolutely gotta. Meanwhile, a whole truckloada mugs got themselves chilled off. All rich'n powerful. And the only connection I found so far between *any* of 'em is the Seelie Court. So whaddaya *think* I'm suggestin'?"

"What you're describing," my host said slowly, her fingers clenched and nails scraping against the desk, "comes perilously close to an act of open war."

"Yeah, I'd noticed that."

"*If* it's true," she added. She wasn't pacing, given the whole "seated in chair" thing, but she managed to convey the impression of it. "The idea of the Unseelie using the search for Gáe Assail as a diversion to target mortal allies of the Seelie Court is…"

"Pretty tough to swallow," I finished for her. "And as soon as we find out that the rest of those names ain't connected to the Court, or you can offer me a better theory that fits all the facts, we can just leave that ridiculous notion behind."

"Slachaun?"

"Right, Ms. Ielveith."

He didn't even look resentful, now, just took the list and slipped from the office. Guess he saw clear as she did: if I was right, no matter how off the chance, this wasn't just about me, or even about the spear. Not anymore.

The pair of us sat'n waited, sipping on dew-sweetened fruit juice and thinkin' our own private and mostly unpleasant thoughts.

Even Ielveith's connections weren't gonna let her private dick dig into the whole friggin' list, especially not over a couple hours. But between the Lambton's important guests, her own political allies, and Slachaun's drive—I'll give him credit where he earns it, sure—they ran down a solid handful.

Enough that nobody coulda even tried to pretend it was coincidence anymore. Nah, they weren't *all* allies or servants of Seelie Fae, but most of 'em were. And even those who weren't?

Were still among the ranks of Chicago's elite who're wise to our existence. They just hadn't hitched their wagons to either Court.

"Explain something to me, Mick," Ielveith asked. We were both packin' up to leave, me to get my tail outta Elphame, her to go finish up identifying the Fae connections to the rest of the list. We figured, solid as our evidence was, it'd take *overwhelming* proof to cut through the political bullshit that'd otherwise entangle the whole damn Court when she tried to warn the rest of 'em about this.

"Sure, if I can."

"Why?"

I halted in the middle of the room. "Why what?"

"The Unfit. Sure, this is clever, if this really is the first step in a bigger play. Except... They risk losing the race to the spear by splitting their attention this way, don't they? Bad as it's going to hurt us to lose so many of our mortal connections, isn't Gáe Assail a much greater prize?"

Fact is, I'd had that exact thought. And it weighed on me, heavy, that I didn't have an answer.

What were the bastards up to? Why escalate hostilities now? Why risk the grand prize pursuing an honorable mention?

What the burning, flickering hell did they know that I didn't?

CHAPTER FOURTEEN

"Heya, Franky." I spoke soon as he clicked on the lights, since the place was curtained up tight enough to be where nighttime slept. He'd been out when I showed, but I don't mind waiting.

Actually, that's hooey. I *hate* waiting. But I'm pretty good at it.

I never seen Four-Leaf freeze that way. Pretty sure Medusa woulda moved on, figurin' she'd already given him a once-over. Handful of roaches, who'd scattered when I let myself in but slowly re-emerged during my wait, scattered again, fleeing the light. Even motionless, Franky managed to give me a pretty strong impression he wanted to do the same.

"Don't do anything rattle-brained," I told him. "I'm just wiped out enough that chasing you down would seriously sour my sunny disposition, but not so much I wouldn't catch you up."

Franky gulped hard enough to swallow a bowling ball, and took a step away from the door.

"How'd you live like this?" I asked him. "I seen cleaner walls in a nuthouse, the roaches just got done dialing pest control to deal with the silverfish, and the carpet don't need to be vacuumed so much as aerated and tilled."

"I—" he started, quivering.

"Yeah, I know. You're lying low. And I gotta say, this was a pretty solid choice. Ain't even any gold stashed away. Nobody'd think to look for you in a dump like this, and if they did, they wouldn't find anything to suggest you'd been here."

"That… That was the idea. So how—?"

"I'm a detective, Franky. Nobody hides from me if I don't like for 'em to."

By which I meant I'd gone to one of our mutual low-life acquaintances and did the whole "shake him down then bribe him" dance, but I didn't figure he needed to know that.

"Mick…" He raised both hands, in a way some woulda described as "beseeching" and others as "pathetic." In the sickly yellow light of the lone bulb, his skin was sallow and his green glad rags looked to be dyed with pond scum. "You gotta understand—"

"You ran out on me, Franky-boy. That ain't mannerly."

"Jesus, Mick! I'd just been ear-mickeyed by a *rusalka*!"

"Which I saved you from," I reminded him, slowly rising from my seat (a moth-eaten chair with less stuffing than a soup-kitchen turkey).

"Come on, pal!" His back bumped up against the door, hard enough I could see my reflection in his glasses start to shake. "You know what kinda mess it is out there right now! I didn't want any part of that! I just wanna keep my head down until this all blows over, you know?"

"Sure," I told him, nodding. "I know. And I want a cow that gives pure cream and plays the harp. We're both just gonna have to soldier on."

"Mick…"

I was right up on him, now. I'd hafta either crush him against the door or kiss him to get any closer.

"What's gonna happen here," I said softly, "is that you're gonna answer a whole *heap* of questions. In detail, and without even *thinking* of pulling my leg. About *anything*. Then, depending on what kinda song you sing, you might maybe run a few errands for me.

"After that, *maybe*, if everything's gone how I need it to, and you've gotten through it without queering anything I need done, I might forget that you ran out on me."

For just a sec, he got mad. I saw it in the clench of his jaw, heard it in the rasp of his breathing. On the square, I think I'd have developed a dollop more respect for him if he'd taken a poke at me.

End of the day, though, Four-Leaf Franky's basically a coward, and he knows I know it. He sagged, so me'n the door were all that kept him upright, and nodded. I went back to the chair, if you wanna call it that.

"We'll start real simple," I said. "Even when you're lyin' dormy, I know you keep an ear to the ground—when it ain't got a *rusalka*'s fishhooks in it, anyway. Tell me about anything big been going down the last few nights."

I almost didn't even bother to ask him. At this point, I was pretty well convinced that, no matter how out of character it was for 'em, the Unfit were keeping a low profile. So I was pretty well expectin' his answer.

"Umm…" Franky wandered to a nightstand, pulled a bottle of something pungent from the built-in cabinet, and took a swig. "Mick, you're talkin' the loud stuff? Fireworks?"

"Anything attention-grabbing, yeah. That tough for you to understand?"

"No, it's just…" He sat hard on the nightstand, which creaked a loud protest. "Mick, other'n your impromptu clambake with Áebinn at Scola's place—and, well, the incident with me'n the *rusalka*—Chicago's been pretty quiet. I mean, not the whole city, of course. Just, uh, our half of it. Been some gang violence and all, but I ain't heard of anything else involving Fae."

"And what's that tell you?"

I let him work it out. Franky don't always make great decisions—in the same way I "sometimes" don't like cars—but he's no bunny. Once I got him thinking about the repercussions of what he'd just reported…

"But that makes no sense!" He sounded almost put out, as if it were my fault things weren't adding up. "*Maybe* the outsiders mighta managed to keep outta the Seelie's way, but if the Unseelie are out in force, looking for this thing... There's no *way* they dodged *everyone*, and no way they didn't... Mick, there oughta be a trail of human and Fae bodies a mile long!"

"Give the man a cigar. So how do *you* explain it?"

"Maybe I just ain't heard about stuff—not *everything* comes to me, you know?—but it's hard to figure anything too big woulda slipped by me." He frowned, didn't seem to really believe his own words; started to shrug, discovered he was sloshing perfectly good rotgut from the bottle, and took another gulp instead. "Maybe they coulda hidden some of it in the human gang violence, but not all of it. Beyond that..."

"Yeah." Didn't figure I oughta spill about the so-called accidents just yet. "'Beyond that'... How long's the talk about Gáe Assail been crawlin' the grapevine?"

"Jeez, at least a few weeks? Maybe a couple months? Honestly, though, I think most of us—even those who were out lookin'—only sorta half believed at best. The search was pretty well dyin' down until the museum break-in."

Well, well. And could that maybe have been the point?

Oh, and that reminded me: I hadda quick detour I oughta take before headin' home, once I was through here.

"Tell me everything out of the ordinary you *have* heard, Franky. No matter how unimportant or small. And then, yeah, I'm gonna need you to deliver a couple messages for me."

Franky cradled the bottle to his chest like it was a teddy bear.

"I'm not gonna care much for this, am I?"

"If it makes you feel any better," I said, grinning, "they ain't gonna care too much for you, either..."

* * *

The crowd was tiny.

Later in the day, even a slow one, the place'd be crawling with patrons. The buzz of conversation woulda drowned out a falling bomb, and the parking lot woulda been more steel and rubber than concrete. Hadn't been too much quieter'n that last time I'd been here: even though it was after hours, and even though there hadn't been that many of 'em, the bulls and newshawks had been making more than enough of a ruckus for anyone's tastes.

But now? Early morning on a weekday? Place looked as though they oughta be throwin' a "going out of business" sale to move the elephants along. Was only a trickle of people passin' through the doors; a stream, at most. Nothin' close to the normal current. Hell, since a lotta folks were still making their morning commute, the passing sidewalks were a *lot* busier.

Mighta been that I didn't need to be here, that I was wasting time I couldn't be certain I had to waste. But I couldn't shake the memory that'd struck me a couple times already—back at Rosen's flop, for instance—and that I'd been reminded of again at Franky's place: so far as I could recall, I hadn't sensed anything powerful enough to be *Gáe Assail* at the museum. The more I thought about it, the more certain I was that the discrepancy was important, maybe even the key to this whole goofy fiasco. And that meant I couldn't rely on recollection of "probably" and "maybe."

I hadda be sure.

Gave some real serious thought to just walking in with the rest of the tourists and then sneakin' my way down. Odds were good I could be quick'n quiet enough to be done before anyone noticed I didn't belong...

On the other hand, "good odds" are still odds. Gettin' caught red-handed could seriously gum everything up, especially if someone called the cops before I had the opportunity to, uh, *talk* 'em out of it, or if the security guards were packing: I could wind up taking a few nights to recover, or cooling my heels under glass. Galway and the others who'd been bamboozled into taking orders from the Seelie sure wouldn't mind an excuse to put me away for a spell.

The other way, then.

The "gettin' in" part was the same. I paid for admission. Then it was just a matter of wanderin' a bit until I found myself a security guard near an exhibit that was still pretty quiet. The display where I finally found him was something about gems, if I recall right. They were blue.

Gink I eventually located was a tired, doughy-lookin' mug in uniform somewhere between a cop's and a postman's. He *was* wearing heat at his belt, though.

He didn't much appreciate being flagged down and talked to, either.

"What do you—?"

"Mick Oberon. PI. Consulting with the police on the recent break-in." Hey, it was only *sort of* a lie, right?

"I…"

Guess, on top of the talking, the guard hadn't been prepared for anything that might require, y'know, thinking.

"How do I know you're—?"

I slipped my PI ticket out of my wallet and thrust it at him. His brow furrowed, and I worried he might be planning to read the whole license.

But that was okay. I had him confused, the idea planted in his noggin, so now it oughta be duck soup as soon as…

He looked up. I dove in.

Into and through his eyes, easy as a pond, and I gotta say I had plenty of elbow room back there, if you get what I mean. I really didn't need to do much more'n a poke a few thoughts to make him nice and pliable.

"'Kay," he said dully. "So whatcha need?"

I hadn't actually planned to grill him at all, just use him as a walking key, but… "Mr. Lydecker been behavin' at all unusual lately?"

"Uhh... Well, yeah, a little. He's usually down in that basement for hours after close, but accordin' to Sal, last night was the second night he ain't stayed late. Guess the break-in spooked him."

It *could* be that simple, but I doubted it.

"Yeah, I guess. Right." I guessed this "Sal" was one of the night guys, and Officer Moron confirmed it for me. Also confirmed, as I'd figured, that Lydecker didn't come in this early.

"Well, thanks. Now if you could just show me downstairs, I gotta poke around a bit."

"Well, but... I should probably get one of the curators to—"

"No, you shouldn't."

"Nah, I shouldn't."

I *thought* he'd see it my way.

Gink got me past the "authorized" doors, and a few janitorial staff who mighta looked at me askance if I'd been alone.

I posted him in the hall, to keep me from bein' bothered, and I told him in no uncertain terms that nothing'd interrupted his day, that when he got back to his rounds he'd forget all of this. I think he mighta drooled in response. Sharp *and* silver-tongued, this guy.

I had no trouble finding Lydecker's workspace. Room was bathed in sickly light and an irritating buzz, just as I remembered. A few other people came in'n out, far across the room, but I encouraged 'em to assume I belonged here. Since I'd gotten through the door'n had my security-guard escort, it wasn't a hard idea to plant.

Lydecker's table held maybe half the number of tools and fossils it had on my last visit. I dunno if that was because the workload had lightened or just 'cause some bits were actually put away at the end of the workday. And I cared even less than I knew. I wasn't here to criticize Lydecker's organizational habits.

I held my hands over the table, shut my eyes, reached out...

Nothing. Just as I'd I remembered it. And that made even less sense than anything else I'd stumbled over on this job.

I felt the cogs startin' to turn deep in my head again, same as they'd done back in Elphame, but I didn't try to focus on 'em yet. Didn't examine what I was thinking too closely. I needed to be *absolutely* certain before I risked breaking that chain of contemplation.

So, I did more'n just reach out, groping blindly for a lingering aura of magic. I reached into my coat, held the wand, and drew power to me—a lot of it. I was careless with it; a few of the smaller fossils crumbled.

Until, finally, I had enough. That same energy, that same luck I'd just taken in, flowed right back out, carrying my sight with it, my touch, senses you ain't even got words for. Auras and power far too faint for me to ever normally detect should become clear to me now.

And they did, but not how I expected.

Still no sign of the Spear of Lugh. Nothing even close. Oh, there was a ceremonial bowl and dagger set in the next room that had a minor enchantment on 'em, and there was a remnant of power in a trilobite fossil that I admit confused (to say nothing of worried) the hell outta me. I was almost tempted to pocket that one.

But no trace of the spear.

If it'd been here, it was *stupidly* well shrouded.

I did, though, glom to something else, something I'd never've noticed if I hadn't been swinging so much mojo right then.

Fae.

Oh, not now. But recently, there'd been another of the Fae in this basement, maybe even this room. Couldn't say who or when, wouldn't have even come close to spotting an aura this faint without all the extra power. But there'd definitely been someone from the other side of the tracks in here not *too* far back.

Fae were here but the spear wasn't? Or someone could hide the spear but not themselves? Or…?

Goddamn it.

Was useful to know I'd been right, that there'd been no

trace of Gáe Assail here, but that didn't bring me any nearer to understanding what the hell *was* up with the spear. Or *where* the hell. Or why the Unfit thought what they were doing was *so* urgent it was worth losin' the race we were all running. All I knew was that the room contained absolutely no-room-for-error-*zero* trace of the spear.

Why? How? I'd sensed it elsewhere; why not here, in the one place we *knew* it had been?

We *did* know Gáe Assail had been here… Didn't we?

Or did we?

Lost in my own labyrinthine thoughts, startin' to fit all this into my mental puzzle, I collected Officer Moron and made my way back toward the stairs.

Can I just tell you how very surprised I was, when I got home, to discover my place was bein' watched? What's an amount less'n zero?

Wasn't Sealgaire this time, though I didn't doubt he was skulking somewhere near. (I could tell by the nine thousand and three spiders crawling along my spine.) Nah, this was a tiny rise, a slight hump in the overgrown, autumn-soaked grasses between two stoops of a neighboring greystone. Hadda be a *ghillie dhu*—or *leshy* or green man, if you prefer. Between the leafy skin and the grassy beard, no human woulda noticed him even without the glamour that lay over him, an extra layer of supernatural camouflage. Only reason *I* made him was that I'd lived here long enough to memorize even the smallest details; once I'd caught the change in the topography, it hadn't taken much to identify my new frond for what he was.

Yeah, I said it; maybe Pete was rubbing off on me. Deal with it.

He *coulda* been local, keeping peepers on me for the Chicago Seelie, but probably not. Most *ghillie dhu* are way too timid to get mixed up in this sorta thing, and I knew from experience that the ones who live around here all more or less fit that stereotype to a T. Odds were this one was an outsider, keeping tabs for one of the bands who'd come hunting the spear.

Either way, though, didn't really matter. I gave him a jaunty wave—kinda funny watching the lawn twitching in surprise—and headed on in.

I decided then'n there that the gink's name was "Mow." Whaddaya want from me? Gotta amuse myself somehow.

What happened after I got inside was a lot less funny.

After all the Colts and Tommies and all that, you wouldn't figure a twenty-year-old Winchester hunting rifle'd be all that scary.

And I wasn't scared, really, since I knew it wasn't gonna kill me. Didn't really feel inclined to resting up a few days to heal, though, so I was maybe concerned. Worried a touch. Startled, certainly.

Goddamn sick of having heaters stuck in my mug, too.

He'd been lurking in my office when I shoved the door open and flicked on the lights. Standing behind my desk—who the hell knows how long he'd been there?—and, I guess, just waiting for me to show.

Took a moment to chew myself out something good, if only internally. Gink shouldn'ta gotten the drop on me this way. The rifle was freshly oiled and its owner was sweating worse'n a constipated hog. Even stronger were the emotions rolling off him, fear and rage and helplessness and grief thick enough to walk on. I shoulda sensed him from the hallway, maybe even the stairwell, but *noooo*. Mick's too busy running through plans and schemes in his noggin, and thinkin' wildly confused and contradictory thoughts about a certain dame, to pay attention.

I mighta *finally* begun puttin' the pieces together, but if I'd seen my own behavior over the last few days, I sure as hell wouldn'ta hired me as a detective.

Anyway, yeah, lights come on and I'm staring down another

barrel. Only this one ain't quite steady. Not shaking so much it'd have much chance of missing me at this range, but not still.

Whoever this guy was, he wasn't a pro. But then, fact that he'd brought a hunting rifle to shoot me from across the room'd already made that abundantly clear.

Took me a bit to realize I knew the face behind the rifle. Old, worn, grey—more worn and more grey than when I'd first seen him a few weeks before. You coulda packed a vacation for a family of four in the bags under his bloodshot eyes, and if his hair'd even *seen* a comb in days, it was in a fever dream.

But as I said, I *did* recognize him.

I hadn't planned to tell him until everything else was over. Guess I shoulda expected the bulls'd beat me to it.

"Something I can do for you, Mr. Caro?" I asked.

Frank Caro—father of the late (and probably lamented by some) Miles Caro, and the man who'd hired me to find his son—uttered a hoarse, choked sob.

"Can I get you something? Water? Milk?"

"*You can get me my son, you fucking bastard!*"

Oh, brother.

"Sure. You want him in pails, or will wax paper-wrapped parcels suffice?"

I know what you're thinking, and you ain't wrong. I'm an ass at times. Poor guy's in mourning something fierce. What would it've cost me to be kind? Sympathetic? It ain't as though I haven't grieved my own loved ones often enough.

And that's not even counting the gat he had aimed at me.

I coulda commiserated with him. Reasoned, maybe. Pointed out all the reasons he didn't wanna do—and his son wouldn't have wanted him to do—anything stupid. Or even just stall him long enough to work my way into his head and flip a few switches.

Lots of options, and any one of 'em woulda been kinder, more humane. Woulda taken time, but I had time; nothing else was supposed to go down until later in the day.

But the thing is, it also woulda taken patience. And I was just. Plum. Out of it.

Scheming factions of the Fae. Uncooperative cops. Any number of aches and pains and injuries. And of course, Ramona. My tank was dry as a sand salad.

So while Mr. Caro choked and sputtered and wept and wilted beneath those words, I refused to let up.

"I didn't kill your boy, pal. I didn't plant the bomb, and I sure as hell didn't tell him to get caught up with Mob bootleggers! You got a beef, fine. Plenty of mugs to choose from. I ain't one of 'em."

"You were supposed to find him!" He was waving that damn rifle wildly, now, arms flailing and his whole body shaking. "You could've prevented this! If you'd done your job, if you'd done what we paid you to do, my son would—!"

"And if you and the missus had bothered keeping up with your son's life, maybe you coulda told me who Miles was involved with and I mighta had a chance of finding him. Or maybe he wouldn'ta gotten mixed up with the wrong kinda cats in the first place. You sure it's *me* you're sore at?"

If it sounds like I'd gone beyond "mean" to "deliberately pushing," well… I had. And once he was good and worked up, sputtering and screaming and accusing and sobbing, it was duck soup to step up and yank the Winchester outta his hands. One startled gasp and he went silent, gawping at me, lip trembling.

"You're angry and frustrated," I told him more calmly. "But you also know what happened ain't my fault. You ain't ever gonna find the bastards who did it—and I'll tell you, Mr. Caro, even if you did? They wouldn't defend 'emselves with *words*. Your wife already lost her boy; you don't wanna make her a widow, too."

Not even sure how to describe the sound he made, then. I hefted the rifle, worked the lever a few times until I'd ejected all the slugs, then handed it back to him. He held it like he'd forgotten what it was.

"Don't ever come back here," I said, "and I won't prefer charges over this. Go bury your son, Caro."

The old man fled, weeping. Me, I shut the office door, slumped down at my desk, and tried to ignore it when, some while later, I finally started feelin' bad for how I'd talked to him.

It was past noon, and I'd been mostly sittin' since Mr. Caro's little visit. Waiting.

Thinkin', at first. See, I'd finally pieced it together. I finally had a theory that made it all fit, and oddly, it was Caro's father who'd given it to me. Or rather, it'd been me rememberin' back on my encounter with the guy. Thinkin' about how, once I'd got him all riled, it'd been so easy to take his roscoe away.

You'll understand why that's a relevant notion later.

Anyway, yeah, initially I'd been prodding at the theory, poking it, lookin' for holes. But after that? Just waitin', tryin' not to think about much at all. Probably coulda used those couple hours for something more productive, but still, I'd waited.

Hadn't felt much of anything else was appropriate, and probably wouldn'ta been able to concentrate on it anyway.

And this time, when she slunk into my office, I knew it really *was* as a snake. Even if it was one I'd almost be willing to let bite me.

"Good morning. I think I've... Mick? What's wrong?"

Heh. Good one. *What's wrong?* How about everything, dollface?

I'd spent a lotta time bracing myself for this, even reinforcing my own will with luck and magic, and I still wanted to back out. The smile falling off her face was like the sun going out. Just about every part of me wanted to hold her, stroke her hair, tell her everything was gonna be all right.

But no. *Hell, no.* Not this time.

I leaned back in my chair, heels crossed and propped up on

the desk, next to a mug with a bit of creamy residue slowly congealing on the bottom. (I'd really needed a nip this morning. It was the last of the cream; even cut with milk, it hadn't gone far.) Point is, all nice and casual, 'cept for the dour expression I couldn't keep off my mug. Also meant she couldn't see the L&G in my left hand, hanging loose at my side.

"I been thinkin', Ramona."

"Yes?" She stepped closer, hands together—not quite wringing 'em, but near as—concern painted thick on her face like too much makeup.

"Was there actually a Ramona Webb before you came along? You take someone's place, or just make this grift up outta whole cloth?"

Gotta say, she was impressive. Ain't easy to go pale on cue.

"What are you talking about?"

"If I'd had half a chance to dig deep enough into your sob story, would there be a real Jeremy? A real Cliff? I'm thinking not, but you got me curious."

"What's wrong with you?"

She was starting to go all teary. I wish I could say it didn't bother me.

"Why are you—?"

"Not why. Who. As in," I continued, before she could ask what I meant, "*Who are you?*"

It was kind of a roar, honestly. Suppose I coulda been more subtle about the whole thing, but I was fed up with games.

She broke down, sobbing, begging me to stop it, to make sense, to explain what she'd done wrong. But it wasn't her words I was focused on… And now, I felt it.

My fascination with her, the need to protect her, my excitement over her; affection, infatuation, lust, all of it: it got stronger. *Heavier.* A front of pressure, pushing in on me from all sides. From *outside*.

That's why it'd been so surprisingly strong, so all-consuming. It wasn't real. I almost wished it was.

Big bad Mick Oberon. So damn confident, nobody's gonna mess with *his* conk without him sensing it. What a joke.

I was real glad I had the wand right then. Made her enchantment a whole lot easier to shrug off.

No. No, that ain't true. I didn't shrug it off. Felt it as powerful as ever. Maybe more. What I *was* able to manage was to put it aside enough to work through it.

I raised my arm, tapped the wand against my chin like I was absently pondering something.

Then, when I was sure she'd not only seen it, but understood the implication, I said, "Not buying what you're selling, babe. Not anymore."

Stubborn tomato, Ramona. She gave it one more college try.

"Mick, darling, please. Whatever you think I've done—"

"I tailed you downtown yesterday."

She drew herself up stiff, perfect picture of affronted dignity.

"You what? How dare you? I—"

I frowned around the wand, just givin' her my level-best stare. Her shoulders slumped.

"Damn *sidhe*. You always were way too mule-headed for anyone's good." Funny how the tears, the hurt, all of it just vanished in that moment. "What gave me away? You didn't just randomly decide to follow me."

"Started with the iron stool at Bumpy's."

That got a wince out of her.

"I was afraid of that. I wasn't sure if I'd need to defend myself from those Seelie galoots. I had you hooked good by then, though. You shouldn't have noticed."

"Almost didn't. Took me until after your other fuck-ups to suss it out."

"Oh?" She crossed her arms, emphasizing her curves in ways that weren't helpin' my focus any. "And what, do tell, were those?"

"First, Pete tells us about a guy following him—a guy who looks just like the mug who'd been following *you*—and you didn't utter a peep. Didn't register at the time, but lookin' back? Only tracks if you already knew who the gink was."

"All right, that's fair—and careless of me—but still pretty thin. There's got to be more to it."

"Oh, there is. You were too comfortable searching Rosen's place. Didn't quite jive with your hysterics. Still didn't prove anything, but it was enough for me to spot your slip after the old man's grandkid showed."

"Slip? You aren't…" She abruptly barked something real unladylike. "The spear. You asked her specifically about a spear."

"And you didn't bat one pretty eyelash, doll."

"Goddamn it. I must be more tired than I thought."

"Tell me about it."

She turned, grumbling, and plopped herself down in a chair.

"All right. So what now?"

"I just said. Tell me about it."

"Mick, I actually really do like you. That part wasn't an act. But if you think—"

I aimed the L&G and let loose. Not at her, at the door. Metal clattered as the lock more or less gave up the ghost, locking us both in here until either I fixed it or someone forced it.

Ramona looked back at the sound. When she turned her attention back to me, I'd wrapped my right mitt around the *other* surprise I'd had waiting behind the desk. Everything but her breathing froze as I lifted the old Spanish-steel rapier into view.

"You're good," I said. "I mean, amazingly good. Impressive enough you managed to whammy me—*me*—at all, but to keep me from even noticing for days… Damn. If it hadn't faded a hair anytime you were outta sight, I might never've gotten wise."

"Wouldn't *that* have been a shame?" she grumbled.

I kept right on. "I dunno if you're a mortal who's picked up some *real* potent tricks, or one of us. If it's the latter, congrats on some of the most convincing glamour I've ever seen. Either way, I got no intention of killing you unless you make me, but I'm more'n happy—and able—to injure you bad enough that this whole fiasco'll be *long* over before you're shipshape again."

Her sharp exhalation was almost a hiss.

"You wouldn't dare! You can't even be certain you *could*!"

Real slow, real deliberate, I put both feet on the floor and stood, sword in one hand, wand in the other.

"Try me."

I felt a sharp gust through the office, one that came outta nowhere, rustling papers and making the fan—turned off at the time—spin backwards. The lights in the office and the hallway flickered, couple of the bulbs even burst. I musta been closer to losing my cool than I thought.

Maybe because, even after all this, I still wasn't *completely* sure I had it in me to hurt her.

But whatever else it mighta been, it was convincing. Ramona looked unsure for the first time, and she nodded slowly.

"I represent a certain… political interest."

"Yeah, I got that much from City Hall." I sat back down, but kept both hands—and their contents—real obvious. "Who?"

"Someone who knows a good portion of what actually goes on in Chicago. Among other things, he's a collector."

"A coll… He wants the Spear of Lugh as a *trophy*?"

"Well, and to keep it from falling into anyone else's hands, but essentially, yes."

"And the fact that he fits the profile—rich, powerful, and wise to some of what goes on outside the mortal world—of a bunch of other mugs who've kicked off lately? I'm sure that's got *nothin'* to do with him wanting some kinda leverage."

"That… concern might also have come up in passing," she admitted. "Why, have you found a concrete connection? Proof the deaths were deliberate?"

I ignored the question, as I still had too many of my own.

"Who is he?" I asked again.

She leaned forward, fists clenched.

"No."

"Ramona…"

"I can't."

I started to stand again. Her fingers'd gone white.

"Mick, I *literally* can't, even if I wanted to. Enspell me, torture me, kill me. I *can't*."

All right, that coulda been on the square. I could think of a couple different magics that would bind someone that way. I settled back down, and she visibly relaxed.

"So the whole 'terrified client' routine was just about gettin' an in with me?" I asked.

"Pretty much. To start with, anyway. My boss is well informed, but he's not privy to everything that goes on in your world. I wasn't going to recover the spear on my own, and since infiltrating any of the official Court factions seemed a long shot at best…"

"You decided I made the best patsy."

Her grin was almost sheepish.

"If it makes you feel any better, I wouldn't have bothered if I didn't think you were good enough to have at least a chance of succeeding."

"Hey, surprise! It doesn't. Why such a complicated yarn, then? Why not just some jealous boyfriend coming after you?"

"Made it more likely to hook you. Kept your mind on me and kept us together long enough for me to work. Not as though I had complete power over you from the get-go."

No, just almost.

"And you knew I'd be too busy to really dig into it, while the hunt was still on."

"Mick, listen."

She scooted her seat forward with a piercing scrape, reached out to take one of my hands, then I guess thought better of it when they clenched on the wand and rapier.

"We can still help each other! Neither of us has the resources or numbers of the other factions, and we both know that the others are worse news than you or me. Work with me on this! When it's all said and done, you and I can decide which of us gets the spear like reasonable, rational people. And it'd give us a chance to work out... other issues."

Hmm. Either she didn't know I was in this on behalf of the Unseelie, however reluctantly, or she figured she could take the prize from me before I could deliver. (Hell, I kinda hoped she *could*, I still didn't wanna turn it over to Queen Mob.)

Or maybe she didn't know about Fae oaths and figured I'd never go through with delivering.

Or she *wanted* me to think she didn't know, or didn't think I'd go through with it...

I was gettin' dizzy all over again.

"Right," I said. "I'll go right on ahead and trust you, 'cause you've proven yourself good as your word up until now. Horsefeathers, Ramona."

"I'm trying to help both of us, you idiot!"

She actually sounded stung that I didn't trust her. The hell does *she* get off being offended?

"Nah. You're tryin' to help *you*."

She opened her yap again, and I raised a hand. Well, the wand, but it was *in* a hand.

"I'll tell you what, though. You're right that we could both use each other's resources. So here's the skinny. You're gonna have your mystery boss pull some strings for me. You get me what I need, we can feel our way from there."

"You don't know who I work for. How do you know he can pull the strings you need?"

My turn, now, to lean forward—glaring, unblinking, shoving everything but anger as far down as I could.

"I *don't* know. I hope. And Ramona? You want us both to walk outta here healthy, you better hope, too."

* * *

"Hey, uh, Mick? Did you know your door frame's busted?"

Sigh. "C'mon in."

"Okay, but..."

Wood slivers fell and hinges scraped as Pete pushed open the door—kinda a wooden curtain, now, really—and slipped inside, dodging splinters thrusting outta the frame.

Sigh. Again. "Yes, Pete."

I've done that trick with locks before. Suck enough luck from 'em that something sensitive slips outta joint. Later, feed it back—plus some extra—and jiggle a key in it for a couple, and the bits fall back into place.

I'd been pretty steamed with Ramona, though, and I sorta overdid it this time around. All the luck in the world ain't gonna get bits and pieces and broken tumblers to defy gravity and jigsaw themselves back together. So when I'd needed her to step out into the hall and get her boss on the horn, well...

"Yes," I repeated. "I'm aware. I'll get a carpenter and a locksmith in later. Unless you wanna fix it...?"

Dressed in his wrinkled civvies—he'd just come off a late-night-to-late-morning beat—Pete smirked.

"Pretty sure even if I had the know-how, right now I ain't really got it in me to operate a tool more complicated than a pillow."

"So you're down to, what, eighty percent capacity?" I asked.

"Cute."

"I thought so."

I was still ensconced behind the desk, where I'd been playin' statue. Pete offered Ramona a quick, appreciative glance, which she chewed up and spit back at him.

She'd been slouched in her chair where I could keep tabs on her, and she wasn't dealing with the stillness as gracefully as me. She'd told me, about forty minutes ago, while squirming uncomfortably in her seat, "I'm about ready to jump up and hop around the room screaming."

I'd told her to go ahead, it'd be a hoot. She'd decided against, and that was the last thing anybody'd said until Pete showed.

Pete recoiled from Ramona's obvious frustration, and then dropped a thin stack of papers and folders on my desk.

"I dunno what kinda miracle you called in to pull this one off," he said. "Six hours ago, orders from above were to not waste the piss it'd take to put you out if you were on fire. I thought I was half a step from losing my job. Now..."

I tossed Ramona a quick glance; she returned a tight, satisfied smirk. It seemed her boss really *did* have an awful lot of strings he could pull, if he wanted.

I *really* hadda figure out who this gink was, someday.

What I told Pete was, "I still got connections. This everything?"

"All of the last few nights—and be careful with 'em! I gotta get 'em back to Keenan in one piece! That other thing," he continued, "ain't ready yet. They were still waitin' for the warrant to clear when I left the clubhouse. Shouldn't be too long, though." Then, in a lower grumble, "Judge Meadors woulda had it done by now."

"Thanks, Pete. This, the other night... I owe you." I meant it, too.

"I know," he said.

Ramona snickered.

I started to flip through the files and reports, but something still ate at me.

"Keenan gonna catch any federal heat over this?" I asked. Whoever my fetching "client" worked for, his pull probably didn't reach higher'n the locals. And even if it did, it ain't like Áebinn or Raighallan were really FBI.

But, "Nah. Feds dusted outta there like their asses had gone cannibal, maybe an hour before the call came down that we should help you out after all. They musta gotten wind of something meaty."

Well how about that? Franky'd actually followed my instructions and come through. Least in part. I'd find out tonight if the rest had gone down as smooth.

The blower rang, out in the hall, and Ramona popped up to go answer—in case it was her mystery boss, I guess, or maybe she just didn't wanna rely on me telling her everything. (Sharp woman, if so. I'd shared basically the whole story up until now—she'd already known enough of it, anyway—but I had no *intention* of letting her in on any *new* information until it suited me.)

I made gently with the pages—so Pete could return 'em in ace condition, sure, but also so the rustling and crinkling wouldn't keep me from eavesdropping on Romana's half of the phone call. Turned out that it wasn't her boss, though.

"Call's for you," I told Pete, not looking up. "She'll be in here in two shakes to tell you—"

"Call's for you, Staten," she said, breezing back through the doorway.

Pete looked at me, looked at her, looked back at me, and headed out to pick up the horn.

Me, I kept skimming. The files were a waste of my time, and I knew it; I'd mostly needed the warrant. But I wanted to check the blotter *one* last time, make absolutely sure I wasn't missing something, that the redcaps really had been abnormally— almost ludicrously—inconspicuous. I finally had the germ of a working theory, and I didn't want a surprise bloodbath spoiling it for me.

Nothing. Nothing. Flipping pages punctuated the notes I was jotting down in my head. *Probably nothing...*

I heard Ramona's nails clicking against the seat of the chair.

"Pete get calls on your payphone often?" she asked.

I didn't look up. *Nothing...*

"That's basically my office line, doll. If Pete told Keenan where he was off to..." *That one might not be nothing; go back and double check...*

More nail-tapping.

"What're you doing?" she demanded.

"I'm reading the files Pete brought."

"Well, yes, I can see *that*. I meant why?"

"So I know what they say."

"Oooh, you...!" She groused herself into silence, then yanked out her pack of smokes. I'm surprised she even needed a lighter.

I kept reading.

Nothing. Maybe something. Nothing. Would seem to be something, but they caught the guy...

The door-turned-flap wobbled again as Pete returned.

"You were right," he said, almost accusingly.

"Yeah, well, I'm used to it."

His whole mug scrunched into a prune-ish glob of lines, but he kept on jawing.

"It'll be a bit before Detective Keenan can courier over the specifics, but he confirmed four separate deposits. Couple thousand berries each."

"Who are we talking—?" Ramona began.

I held up a finger for quiet, which I think mighta actually burned clean off my hand if I'd been much closer to the fire in her scowl.

"Swell. Uh, I need one more favor from you, pal," I said to Pete.

"Yeah, I'm used to it," Pete parroted.

"Nice." I handed over a folded scrap of paper I'd scribbled on earlier. "I need this tip to reach Vince Scola, and it's gotta go through channels he trusts. I figure, you know enough stoolies and snitches to—"

"C'mon, Mick." He looked pained, held the note with two fingers, as though maybe he figured on it biting him. "You know I don't like you gettin' mixed up with those guys."

I just stared, and even Ramona left off looking furious to look shocked.

"Pete," I said, "I got the Seelie Court looking to rub me out, the Unseelie Court using me as a puppet, Herne the Hunter and a whole mess of outsiders doing who-knows-what, all in aid of finding a prize that's a legend even to people you think of as legendary. And you're sore about me rubbing elbows with a few local wise guys?"

"They're trouble I can wrap my head around. And they'll still be here in Chicago when this is all over."

All right, he had a point there, but...

"I can dig that, but they're already involved. You get this to them, it'll be a big help in me gettin' 'em *un*involved."

Grousing, Pete pocketed the note.

"Get some shut-eye," I said. "You're gonna have a busy night."

I could literally see him decide not to ask. He said something or other in the way of farewell, and blew.

"*Now* will you tell me—" Ramona began. And then, "You raise that finger to shush me one more time, Oberon, I may break it."

I shushed her with a *different* finger and made for the hallway.

Didn't head for the blower first, though. Nah, before that, I stopped in front of the stairwell door, giving the frame a good up-and-down.

C'mon, redcaps are short bastards, where had he...? Ah!

It was dried, flaky, near invisible against the wood grain, but it was still there from when Grangullie'd leaned back against the wall. I scraped a bit of the old blood off with a fingernail and rubbed it into powder between thumb and forefinger, trying not to think too hard about who it mighta belonged to before it'd been soaked up into the hat.

All right, next step, upstairs for a few. I was gonna need a *lotta* luck, and since I didn't wanna hurt anyone or bring down the roof, that meant a little bit of mojo from a whole *bunch* of passersby.

And then, back downstairs. I couldn't put it off any longer. Nuts. I hated this next part more'n collecting the blood.

I picked up the receiver and tucked it between head and

shoulder, working at ignoring the sudden drone of a hundred mosquitos in my ear canal. I put one finger on the blower, drew and aimed the L&G with the other hand, and pumped every last bit of good luck I could manage into the phone. I stood still for minutes, just feeding it, more'n more, until I was afraid any further manipulation would start to damage the hallway.

Normally, even that wouldn'ta been enough, not with such long odds. But focusing it through Grangullie's blood—well, the blood from his hat, which wasn't his originally, but he'd staked a claim to it—should make all the difference.

Also normally, I preferred to go through the operator, as that meant I hadda have that much less interaction with the friggin' dingus. But somehow, I didn't expect too many operators would be keen on being asked to connect to a random extension.

So, wincing, I stuck my finger in the dial and chose numbers at whim.

Line rang without answer long enough I was startin' to worry it hadn't worked, and then…

"What?!" He sounded angrier that the horn had the temerity to ring than curious about who it was.

He also sounded more irritable in general. Least I wasn't the only one suffering with a phone to my ear.

"Hi, Grannie. It's Oberon."

"Ober… How the *hell* did you get this number?"

"Wild guess."

"*Wild*—?"

"Look, put Téimhneach on. I got a tip for him."

Grangullie's tone went solicitous—well, solicitous as redcaps get—right swift.

"I can pass on any message you need, Oberon. What's the story?"

"The story is: once upon a time, put Téimhneach on the fucking phone, happily ever after, the end."

I know it's hard to believe, but he got less solicitous again after that.

"I ain't some goddamn errand boy!"

"Well, you know, you sort of are, if you really—"

"Téimhneach ain't available. Tell me whatcha need to tell *him*, and I'll get it to him."

"I speak a *lotta* languages," I said.

"Uh, yeah? So?"

"So in how many of 'em do you gotta hear 'no' before it penetrates?"

The awful crunching I heard then turned out just to be the redcap's teeth grinding, but I swear I thought he might be eating the phone.

"I ain't askin' anymore, Oberon! You work for us, see?"

"Yep. And you ain't the boss. He is."

More grinding. I imagined this was how an angry cornmill might sound.

"I got all day, Grangullie. And I ain't the one you gotta answer to if Téimhneach misses his shot 'cause you couldn't be bothered to fetch him."

The horn clattered loudly where he dropped it, and I could hear that grinding and a frustrated pounding both fading into the distance as he stomped away. I waited, receiver as far from my cheek as I could move it and still be sure of hearin' if someone else picked up.

Someone else picked up.

"Forgive my other dog, Mr. Oberon," Téimhneach said in that fake highfalutin tone that made me wanna pound on him until he could taste his spleen. "Seems you both need some discipling."

"'Other' dog? What... Oh. Ha-ha."

"Indeed. What have you to tell me?"

"You know Oak Woods?"

A pause, there, probably while he decided if it was safe to admit any kinda ignorance in front of me.

"I know what oak wood *is*, obviously..."

"The cemetery, genius. Oak Woods Cemetery."

"Ah. I imagine I can locate it."

"Good. You want the spear? Be there at half past midnight. Don't be late."

"Now just a moment! You're going to have to give me more than—!"

More than what, I dunno, because that's about where I hung up on him. Then unplugged the payphone, just in case he had some means of knowing where to call back.

"That wasn't at all suspicious," Ramona growled as I returned to the flop. "Won't he suspect some sort of trick?"

Well, I'd figured she'd be listening in as best she could, so…

"Nah. I mean, yeah, he will, but it don't matter. He'll be there. That's what counts. C'mon."

"Oh? I'm worthy of your attention now, am I?"

"No." I slung my hat and flogger off the rack. "But I'm bein' magnanimous."

"Is this your idea of working *with* someone?" she demanded.

"Actually, it was your idea, wasn't it?"

I could just about feel her fingers on my throat from inside her mind.

Wasn't gonna let it stop me. I *had* to keep pushing at her. Was the only way I knew to keep myself from giving in and trying to make up.

"Where are we going?" she asked, all stone and ice, now.

"Got a few errands. Then Oak Woods Cemetery. I wanna be there by sundown at the latest."

"Why?" she asked, though at least she stood and started gathering her things while she yapped. "I heard you say the meet wasn't until twelve-thirty."

"I wanna be there early enough to see everyone else who decides to arrive early. And I figure most of 'em will."

"Them?"

She was right on my heels as I left the office. I almost turned outta reflex to lock the door, then shrugged and made for the stairs.

"Who's 'them'?" she persisted.

"'Them' is… Well," I admitted, "'them' is… kinda everyone."

"Oh, is that all? Convenient we'll already *be* in a graveyard when it comes time to bury us. Should save the undertakers some work."

"Yeah, well, I do my best not to inconvenience others. You comin' or what?"

"Yeah, yeah. Tell me, have you figured out how you're going to avoid handing the spear over to a bunch of homicidal monsters? Or are you playing that by ear, too?"

Damn, she just *had* to have the last word, didn't she?

The grass sprawled in all directions, an endless carpet that—at this time of year—probably woulda looked kinda wan in daylight, but gleamed in the drizzle and the glow of the cloud-veiled moon. And it *did* seem endless: place wasn't far shy of two hundred acres, stretching on for block after block between Sixty-Seventh and Seventy-First. Headstones in white, grey, rust, and black marble modestly bedecked the grounds between massive granite mausoleums and monuments with angel- or cross-topped spires reaching toward heaven. Wet, pungent breeze offa Lake Michigan rustled the leaves in a large copse's-worth of thick, lush trees, and sent ripples over the much smaller waters of the cemetery's four memorial lakes.

It's a nice place, is what I'm gettin' at. Woulda been real peaceful, if we'd been here to visit a graveside or stroll along the pathways or unwrap a picnic supper.

Instead, Ramona, Pete and I were crouched on the roof of the Fuller Tomb, largest in Oak Woods. Inside was a large sheet of granite, inscribed with the usual names and dates. The rest of the place? Had the blocky bases and ornate pillars and corrugated roof of the so-called Classical Greek. After the museum and City Hall, it just felt appropriate.

From up on top, on the western shore of Symphony Lake,

we basically had a slant on the whole graveyard. Or at least I did; I didn't think there was enough light for Pete to see, and I'd thrown in the towel on tryin' to figure out exactly what Ramona did or didn't need.

She shivered a touch in the soft wind and softer drizzle, but most of us coulda put on that particular show if we wanted. Wasn't proof of mortality. My cop buddy wasn't acting quite as chilly, but that coulda been because he hadn't stopped twitchin' since I called him and told him when and where I needed him to meet me. He seemed to be tryin' to read every headstone at once, and his hand clutched his piece like a security blanket.

Square, he probably didn't need to be here. Wasn't a lot he could do to back me up if things went sour, and it might be putting him on the firing line. On the other hand, I wanted to make a pretty clear statement to the Unseelie—and I didn't want him off on his own if those bastards decided they didn't care for what I had to say tonight and went lookin' to take it out on someone.

"Why in the name of sanity," Ramona asked through chattering teeth, "did you pick *this* of all places?"

She was asking mostly as a way of letting me know she wasn't happy, without actually complaining. I was wise to that, see, 'cause we'd been over it already. Twice.

I already knew the place. I knew they could find it. I knew it was open enough that I'd see 'em all coming, but with a good deal of cover and places to hide if unpleasantness ensued. And, at this time of night, it was somewhere I could be real sure that there wouldn't be humans around to get swept up in said unpleasantness.

I firmly decided not to noodle over what could happen in a cemetery, though, if any of the factions included a necromancer among 'em. They *probably* didn't...

"Hey," she said suddenly, leaning out toward the edge. "You hear something?"

Yeah, I did. Wasn't anywhere close to the twelve-thirty meet time; last I'd checked, it was only just comin' up on ten. But it'd never been a question of whether they'd show up early; just *how* early, and in what order? If we didn't have a full house by eleven, I'd have been gobsmacked.

My gob remained unsmacked.

The Seelie showed first. Paranoid as they hadda be, with strangers and the Unseelie—and, uh, me—in the mix, I couldn't say I blamed 'em.

They arrived in a small procession of cars that I assume were driven by charmed mortals, since I had no cause to think Áebinn or any of her crew were any more fond of flivvers than I was. Or maybe they were something else entirely, just dolled up to *look* like cars. The one at the forefront sure *seemed* to be a long-base Duesenberg Model J, deep cherry, extended hood cutting across the darkened cemetery driveway like a ship's prow. I couldn't help but notice, though, that the growl of the engine was less an engine and more an *actual* growl.

So, yeah. Maybe a flivver, but I wouldn't bet my bottom dollar on it. I suppose I coulda poked through the illusion, taken a gander at what was inside, but it felt like a *real* potent glamour. Woulda taken a bit of power, and I didn't know if I was gonna have any to spare before the night was through.

They climbed outta this vehicle and that, and clustered at the gate, until there were at least a dozen of 'em congregated there. Then they slipped the lock and marched in, a miniature parade along the twisting pathways, Áebinn all haughty and queen-ish in the vanguard. Raighallan followed behind, openly sporting a pair of big brass Elphame pistols. The rest of the Seelie "cops" came after, and all of 'em were alert, steady, and very armed.

"Is this an investigation or a war?" Ramona asked, whispering softer than a landing snowflake, lips so close they actually brushed my ear. If I'd shivered right then, it wouldn'ta been from the cold.

"Same thing, to them," I answered.

"Peachy. Any chance we might get accidentally shot in the crossfire?"

"Nah," Pete answered before I could. "It won't be by accident."

Well, he wasn't wrong.

They were yappin' as they approached, and why not? Wasn't as though they were trying to be real sneaky in the first place.

"...revolting little toad," Raighallan bitched as they stepped into hearing range.

"That and more," Áebinn said, not looking back over her shoulder. "And if this tip proves false, I will allow you to express your distaste for him in unmistakable terms. But he *knows* we're not terribly fond of him, and what sort of consequences we can bring about should his information prove deceptive. I think it a good possibility that this is legitimate."

Good boy, Franky! I dunno what he'd told 'em that had kept 'em gallivanting around all day and only showin' up here, now, but he'd really come through. I was gonna have to make sure nothing happened to him as a result.

Probably meant I really shouldn't beat the stuffing out of him, too. Suited me fine. You may not buy it, given some of what I've told you, but I don't actually enjoy roughing the guy up.

Áebinn and her bootlicker weren't saps. No matter how fond of 'em I wasn't, I'd needed to remember to never make the mistake of thinking they were. Soon as they got near Symphony Lake, half the group spread out, vanishing behind trees and headstones, creeping like they owed the clouds money. Every couple ticks, one or two would pop up from what coulda been a real convenient hidey-hole or ambush point, to wave their bosses the all-clear.

And then a couple of 'em started climbing a nearby mausoleum, scrambling on up with fingerholds you couldn'ta seen, let alone used, and I got wise that we didn't have a lotta time. Ramona and me were on the tallest mausoleum around, but eventually they'd get to this one—or they'd climb one of the ornamental spires and see us from above.

Either way, last thing I wanted was for them to assume we were waitin' to bum-rush 'em and start squirting metal.

Ah, well. Woulda been nice to stay unnoticed until everyone showed, get a good slant on who—what—I was dealing with, but it wasn't *essential*. I shifted my feet on the granite, ready to stand and announce myself when they got closer.

Turned out I didn't have to, though.

The Seelie heard 'em coming same time I did. They spun like they'd choreographed it, comin' to rest facing east, heaters and blades drawn.

The next bunch of guests came wading and swimming, cutting through Symphony Lake with barely a ripple. I dunno if they'd been shadowing Áebinn and company, or if they'd gotten wind of the rumors Franky'd been planting on the grapevine, but either way, they'd come. All fishy complexions and weedy beards.

No way for me to know if these *bagienniks* were part of the same faction the *rusalka*'d been bossing around or not, but the fact they were in Chicago right at this moment said they were hunting Gáe Assail either way.

Also either way, neither group was too keen to see the other. Ugly whispers and ichthyoid racial slurs were punctuated by the click of gat-hammers while the *bagienniks* burbled and hissed at each other like a *really* angry teakettle.

"Scram, slimebags!" Raighallan shouted, voice rising above the others. "You got no business in Chicago!"

One of the others, who I figured to be the leader on account of—well, on account of him answering, since the damn scaly things all looked the same to me—shouted back.

"Youuu ruuule here, maybe, but city is not youuurs." I'd have had to gargle a whole mug of ketchup to sound like that.

Áebinn raised one perfectly slender hand.

"They've not broken any of our laws yet, Raighallan. Leave them be. *Until*," she added, now addressing the water and its occupants, "they make even the tiniest flicker of a move to interfere with us. At which point you have my permission to spend the rest of the night fishing."

Raighallan and several of the other *aes sidhe* snickered nastily. The foreigners gurgled to themselves some more.

All of which was fascinating, but not so much I didn't hear the next group of footsteps crunching and squishing along the cemetery roadway. Way too loud and clumsy to be Fae—'cept maybe a troll or the equivalent—I figured instead it hadda be...

Yep. Seven or eight humans, all wrapped in long coats and most of 'em carrying heaters only about, oh, *half* the size of a bus. No sign of Bumpy himself, but I recognized his witch, Gina—the only skirt in the group—and even if *she* hadn't been there, I'd have known the type.

Guess Pete's snitches had come through, too. I mean, he told me they would, but still.

As for the man himself, he clenched up when he saw the trouble boys, tensed in a way he hadn't even when the spitting fish-folk had arrived. I could about *hear* his hand stretching out for his gat. Say this for Pete: he's consistent.

"Awright!" shouted the apparent leader of the crew, waving his Tommy in a way that was almost obscene, "Everybody grab some air! I wanna know what the hell... you..."

Gina whispered frantically in his ear, tugging on his shoulder, while pretty much everyone else there just studied him as if he was some mildly surprising but basically uninteresting bug. He didn't look nearly as scared as he oughta be—as he *woulda* been, if he'd really understood what kinda brodie he'd just committed—but at least he closed his head and stopped tryin' to blow out an imaginary fire with his piece.

Got nice'n quietly tense for a while after that, Seelie watchin' outsiders watchin' mobsters watchin' Seelie. Some of 'em jumped and twitched at every little movement; others stood so rock-still they might as well have been added to the collection of monuments and statuary. *Aes sidhe* demanded to know how *bagienniks* had found out about this place, where they'd gotten their info, why they'd come. *Bagienniks* hissed and gurgled at *aes sidhe*, offering nothing that could ever be mistaken for an answer. Humans demanded to know who *everyone* was, what the hell was goin' on, and were roundly ignored. Only total commonality was that nobody was even marginally relaxed. Whole thing was a tinderbox in a powder keg in a frying pan.

And that's when the fire showed up.

CHAPTER FIFTEEN

Ain't as if I hadn't known they were coming—I'd invited 'em myself—but that didn't make me any gladder to see 'em. They trooped into the faint light from Oak Woods' shade-shrouded south side; God forbid they use the same gate as everyone else, right? For a few minutes, they were nothin' but darker against dark, motion without source, silent except for the occasional harsh, rasping breath or low, malevolent chuckle.

If I ever forget myself enough to make fun of you lot for being scared of the Unseelie, remind me of this moment, savvy? Should shut me right the hell up. Ramona seemed to be having some trouble keeping her breathing anywhere near to calm or even, and I ain't entirely certain Pete was breathing at all.

Bumpy's pet witch paled enough to hide behind moonlight, and the whole crew began to back up. Sure, they had their gats up'n ready to shoot, but their peepers were mostly wider than the barrels, and I think the sound of their own guns mighta sent 'em packing. The *bagienniks* also retreated, not near as far, but back into the deeper waters of Symphony Lake. Wasn't much of a sanctuary—not all that wide or deep—but I guess they felt safer.

For their own part, the Seelie might as well've forgotten either of those groups existed. They only had eyes—and scowls, and snarls, and curses, and heaters, and wands; a few even hissed like snakes—for the newcomers.

Redcaps bubbled outta the darkness, as if they'd just shrugged it off. Short and hunched shorter, spread out in a wide front, they plodded heavy-footed across the grass. Now and again one of 'em would stop long enough to dig a finger through the soil covering a relatively fresh grave, licking the filth clean as they resumed their advance.

I knew one of 'em was Grangullie, but damned if I could tell which from here. Other'n the fact that some carried gats and some meat cleavers, they all looked alike.

Téimhneach appeared just a few seconds later, the night spitting him out like unwanted gristle. A black dog padded beside him, near shoulder height. Damn thing had paws the size of hubcaps, blinkers that blazed a hellish green, and a maw full of jagged teeth that gleamed sickly in the glow.

Capone and his people'd buried men in concrete that was less thick than the tension in the graveyard that night.

Áebinn, Raighallan, and their people barked orders, cited laws, made threats.

Téimhneach and *his* said nothing, letting their postures and their vicious grins and their unsheathed weapons do the threatening for 'em.

Everyone else, even those who didn't really need to breathe, held their breath.

Nobody wanted to be the one to set it off. The politics between the Courts, even when—*especially* when—it comes to open conflict are... let's go with "intricate." Every one of 'em wanted to tear into the other side, but nobody was quite sure of the repercussions of drawing first blood.

Figured that was my cue, if ever there was one. Everybody was wound, but if I got their attention now, I could head off any ugliness. *Still* wasn't sanguine about startin' up before I was sure everyone was here, but no help for it. I stood, raising a mitt and drawing breath to shout for attention...

Then one of the redcaps pulled a brass piece, plugged a *bagiennik* in the forehead, and all hell broke loose.

Do I gotta explain it? While it ain't exactly diplomatic, attacking a Fae outsider don't carry the same possible consequences as rubbing out a local. On the other hand, it's vicious enough that the Seelie "police" are allowed—some'd say obligated—to get involved.

The Seelie were grinning as vicious and ugly as the redcaps as the two sides smashed into each other, and the only thing that surprised me about that was the fact that it surprised me at all.

Bursts of blinding light and waves of smothering darkness swept the rival forces. Phantom howls and distracting shrieks; indistinct swarms of smoke and shadow; fires of every hue, burning or freezing or simply clinging; claws of dragons and serpents from the lake and free-floating agony without apparent cause. *Aes sidhe* and redcaps appeared where they weren't, disappeared where they were, taunted and laughed and stabbed from three places at once.

It was all illusion, of course, or nearly all. But our illusions are real enough, if you believe, and even if you don't, it ain't easy to figure which ones got real fire or real knives hidden inside.

Good fortune and bad swept back'n forth between the two groups in almost visible tides, an eldritch tug-of-war between ancient man-children to whom chance was just another toy they didn't wanna share.

I saw one of Áebinn's guys pull a knife and throw. It passed clear between not one but three pairs of combatants, riding a stream of impossible luck. A sudden breeze caught it, tweaking its trajectory just enough so that it sank into the arm of a redcap it shouldn't have come anywhere near. Even as the victim cried out, though, the thrower hit a muddy patch near the lake and wound up on his back in the grass—where another redcap gleefully jumped on him and started stompin' his noggin into the dirt.

Aes sidhe spun and pivoted, parried and thrust.

Redcaps launched themselves at their enemy, cleavers or big, shark-intimidating teeth sinking into flesh and bone.

And around the periphery, the leaders circled. Raighallan had thrown himself into the scrap; but Áebinn on one side, Téimhneach and his hellish hound on the other, drifted in a constant orbit, attentions locked on one another.

More Fae were still driftin' into the cemetery, more outsiders to the Windy City. I saw a couple *aes sidhe* I didn't know from Adam; a *ghillie dhu*, who may or may not've been Mow, skulked through the grasses; flitting will-o'-the-wisps tried to lead victims from both factions astray. There was a headless *dullahan* dressed not as a traditional rider in black, as Eudeagh's were, but instead as a Great War doughboy, complete with coat and pouches and a really long rifle; there was even a *huldra*, the flesh of her back split wide to show off the wood-lined hollow within. Hadn't seen one of *them* in the New World—on the mortal side of things, I mean—since the American Revolution. Apart from the will-o'-the-wisps none of 'em were throwing in yet, they just stood back and enjoyed the show. But it was just a matter of time before someone or something dragged 'em into the ruckus.

And, for that matter, only a matter of time until we drew the attention of everyone within a mile of Oak Woods. So far it'd been fairly quiet—you know, far as small-scale supernatural warfare goes. Not too many shots, no big explosions. We'd be getting one or the other soon enough, though, and even if we didn't, there was plenty of screaming, real and illusory.

As if she'd read my mind, Ramona asked, "Shouldn't we stop this?" No more whispering—she was still right up beside me, but felt the need to shout. To be fair, that's probably what it woulda taken for a human to catch her gist.

Thing is, I didn't think I *could* stop it anymore. My own magics are useful enough, but they don't lean toward the flashy. I thought about askin' Pete to squeeze a few slugs into the air, but somehow I didn't figure more shooting was gonna stand out in any useful way. Wasn't real probable I could get everyone's attention, then. I knew someone who maybe could, though, and while I hadn't spotted him anywhere, no way was I gonna believe he wasn't lurking, watching.

"Minute of your time, Herne?" I asked loudly. My old friend was used to not understanding what I was up to, but Ramona thought I'd lost my mind. I puzzled that out partly 'cause of her expression, but mostly because she'd muttered, "He's lost his mind." I probably wasn't meant to have heard that.

For a long spell there was nothing, until I couldn't help but wonder if I'd figured the guy wrong. If even *his* ears couldn't hear me past the hubbub, or if somehow he really wasn't around at all.

Then something landed atop the mausoleum right behind me. Pete's jaw dropped wide enough to catch bowling balls without losing a molar, and Ramona squeaked and near fell off the roof.

"I admit," Herne rumbled in that six-cylinder voice, "that even I grow weary of the smell of bloodshed. What do you want, Oberon? I would have thought you'd be content to sit back and watch the proceedings."

"Under other circumstances, maybe. Nix on tonight, though. Can you stop this?"

"Hmm." Herne stroked his chin, then shrugged. "Perhaps. But why would I want to? This ought to thin out the competition quite nicely."

"Yeah, you'd think so. You tail one of the other factions here, or did you hear a rumor on your own?"

"I tracked the *bagienniks*, who were trailing the Seelie. Why?"

"Just wondering if you thought it hinky that everyone got the same intel about tonight."

Then, when he was still mulling that over, I whispered a real brief summary of what I had planned for tonight—and why.

Which resulted in me being violently turned around by a big

honkin' meathook wrapped around my neck, while Herne's other hand held his spear nice and steady about a knuckle's width from my mug.

"You're a liar!" he accused.

I could just see Pete skinning leather and aiming at the Hunter. Either Herne missed it or ignored it; either way was better for Pete.

"Frequently," I croaked. "But not about this. You think I'd have gone through the hassle of getting everyone here if I wasn't sure?"

"You might, if you believed you had an advantage or an angle."

But he'd relaxed his grip, and while the spear remained in one tight fist, it was no longer aimed directly at anyone. By which I mean me.

"Very well," he said finally. "But speak convincingly, Oberon."

"Thanks, Herne. Any other tips while you're at it?"

"Yes. Learn to shut up."

"But if I shut up, how can I speak convinc—?"

The Hunter took one look at the tableau below, hefted his spear, and threw—almost straight up. It climbed, higher, higher, until it was lost in the dark of night. It reappeared a moment later, falling far quicker'n gravity could account for, and plunged directly into the middle of the fight.

Same time it hit, Herne let loose with a deafening howl— like a wolf, times eleven. It damn near drove me off the roof of the mausoleum; got no idea how the other two handled it. Between the scream and the spear, though...

Yeah, Herne'd gotten their attention all right.

I noticed a few of 'em stopped to study the spear up close before turning away, and I figured they were goin' through the same train of thought I had when the thing'd been chucked my way the other night. "Is this...? No, just a normal spear." Or, well, relatively normal.

"Thanks," I said.

Herne grunted. "Convincing," he reminded me. He then hopped down to retrieve his spear and took up a spot at the edge of the crowd. If he even noticed the angry looks cast his way, he sure didn't show it.

"Guess I'm up," I said to nobody in particular. Everyone was here, now, anyway. (Well, no sign of Sealgaire, but I didn't imagine there would be unless he wanted there to be.) I stepped nearer the roof's edge, where I was sure everyone could get a solid slant on me. And then...

All right. I shouldn't have. Couldn't help it.

"Friends, Romans, countrymen! Lend me your ears!"

If you're up on your ancient Celtic history, you might get why some of the Fae might find that particularly offensive. I'd say that wasn't deliberate on my part, but neither of us'd believe it.

"Oberon!" Was more'n a few voices remarking on me being, well, me. And it was more'n a few that went on to grumble or complain, but it was Raighallan who shouted, "Is this a game to you? We don't have time for your foolishness!"

"Lemme guess!" I called back. "You're all here on secret tips that more or less amounted to 'If you want the spear, you better be here tonight.' Yeah?"

"It would appear our information isn't as exclusive as we might have hoped," Áebinn sneered.

"Well, no. I hadda make sure word'd reach all of you, didn't I?"

I stood back'n smirked while I let them figure that out.

"You?" I don't even know who it was, that time. "*You* brought us here?"

"More *invited* you, but—"

"What trickery is this, Oberon?" Téimhneach demanded, practically spitting in rage.

"No trickery. I said if you wanted the spear, you oughta be here. And you *should*. I figured it out, see?"

"And why the hell would you share that with the rest of

us?" one of the foreigners asked.

"Well, if you dumb bunnies would stop interrupting with all the fool questions and just listen up for a minute, I might actually be able to explain a thing or two!"

More grumbling, and a few folks of various factions started to walk away, tried to talk their pals into going with, but most were too curious to turn around now.

Good thing, too, 'cause this city wasn't gonna be able to stand too many more nights of an absolutely fruitless scavenger hunt.

"Áebinn? Catch!"

I whipped a plain brown envelope out from inside my coat.

She caught it neatly in mid-spin. Then she paused just long enough to make it clear she was openin' it of her own accord, not 'cause I wanted her to.

Jesus.

She removed the torn squares of newspaper like they made her wanna wash her hands.

"What are these, Oberon?" she asked.

"Obituaries. From newspapers over the last month or so." Trackin' 'em down and cuttin' 'em out had been one of my errands during the day. I didn't think she'd believe me if I just *told* her.

"And I care about this why?"

"Recognize any of the names? If not, I'm sure you know at least one person back home who knows each and every one of 'em."

She finally looked, *really* looked—which was a truly peculiar thing to see, given her whole "empty sockets" thing. I won't say she got flustered; I don't think Áebinn *does* flustered. But certainly taken aback.

"This can't be. We would have noticed!" she said.

"Sure would've, doll. If you weren't busy with something else."

While I let that sink in, let her own gears start grinding, I addressed the others.

"Some'a you ain't from around here," I said. "I go by Mick Oberon. Yes, we're related; third cousin on my mother's side. Here in the mortal world, I'm a gumshoe—and a good one, no matter what a few of my buddies here would rather believe."

A few scoffs and snorts from the Seelie, but no outright denials.

"And lemme tell you what I've puzzled out about this whole damn circus: It's a whole load of malarkey. Horsefeathers, the whole kit'n caboodle."

Now I had their attention. Swear I actually felt the air pressure drop as damn near everyone present inhaled and opened their traps to start flinging questions.

I beat 'em to it.

"How many of you've come across lingering traces of magic? Signs that Gáe Assail'd been around, but not anymore?" Then, as everyone worked to catch up, "C'mon, it ain't as though telling me that's gonna give anything away."

Herne spoke first. "I have. On several occasions." I'd known he had, since there'd been traces in the building where we'd had our second face-to-face, but it was handy knowing there'd been others.

Slow at first, but then quicker, others answered. A lotta them still refused, but it was pretty clear each faction had run across a couple.

So I went on.

"Yeah. Me, too. Thing is, they were both *exactly* the same intensity. Any of yours different?"

Whispering, muttering.

"The point being what?" one of the foreign *aes sidhe* demanded.

"The point being," I answered, scuffing a foot across the stone as I stepped right to the edge, "if the glamour that was veiling the spear from all of us was breakin' down, some of those traces shoulda been weaker'n others. Just a nip at first, then more as the spell unraveled."

"You seek complications where none exist." Áebinn, snooty and dismissive as ever; I'd gotten her suspicions roused, but obviously I hadn't worked her around to "benefit of the doubt" yet. She wasn't shouting, didn't even really speak up, but her voice carried. Banshee, and all. "So the spell isn't disintegrating; it simply was never strong enough to entirely hide the spear. The power leaking through remains constant. You're a fool."

"Oh, gee-golly, officer, why didn't I think of that? How about, oh, I dunno, *because there was no such trace at the museum itself*? If the hole in the veil was constant, as opposed to slowly comin' undone, there shoulda been, savvy?"

Some of the mutters were sounding troubled, now.

"You could have missed it," Áebinn grumbled, but that was the downside of pipes like hers. I could hear the doubt creeping back, however she tried to swallow it.

"Don't take my word for it. Herne?"

The Hunter frowned so hard I thought his antlers might slide down his face.

"No. Nothing. I hadn't put it together…"

"Don't beat yourself up. You usually hunt different kinda game'n me."

Not that the big galoot's feelings mattered much to me, but there was still that whole "I'll kill you when this is over" thing I hadda talk him out of. No sense making it any tougher on myself.

Téimhneach spoke, which actually kinda surprised me. I'd figured him to stay dormy until I got to the best part.

"What are you suggesting, Oberon?"

"The whole trail was too straight. Too pat. Manetti, Rosen, Clanton…" Some of 'em looked confused, so I took a moment to explain the path I'd followed. "Exactly the sortsa people you'd need for a racket like this, all conveniently bumped off, all leading me to the next, but never to any real answers. Between that'n the fake traces of magic—and let's be real clear, if we've ruled out either a weak veil or a fading one, they almost *gotta* be fake—what we got left is a hell of a wild goose. Someone wanted to keep us busy, running around in a tizzy digging for a prize *that was never here*!"

I couldn't say much else for a while, or even shout much else, since the whole crowd was yelling and yapping like a bunch of gossiping Chihuahuas. Guess I couldn't much blame 'em for not believing; *I* hadn't wanted to believe. Hell, if you remember, I'd stumbled across the answer a couple different times during my musings about this whole fiasco, and rejected it.

It was only when Herne hefted his spear and demanded silence in the voice of an earthquake with a hangover that the hubbub quieted.

Mostly.

Raighallan, my absolute favorite *aes sidhe* in the whole world, kept right on yapping.

"This is sheer idiocy!" He couldn't seem to decide if he wanted to glare at me or address everyone around him. Ultimately, he settled on a burning glare. "How stupid do you think we are, Oberon? How gullible?"

He really didn't want me to answer that first part. As to the second…

"I don't think you're gullible at all," I lied.

"Did you think we wouldn't see through you? This is an attempt—and a pathetic one!—to trick the rest of us into giving up so you can find Ahreadbhar for yourself!"

I didn't bother trying to correct that particular wrongheaded idea. Even if he'd believe a word when I said I didn't want the damn thing, figured this wasn't the time to try and explain the specifics of my particular rock and hard place.

What I said instead was, "All right, Raighallan. You're so positive the Spear of Lugh's in Chicago? Why don'tcha tell us all why?"

Bastard opened his trap… And stopped.

"Rumor, right?" I asked.

"Well…"

"Guessing it was rumor dragged all of you here?" To the chorus of reluctant nods, "Rumors that coulda been planted by just about anyone? Course you're none of you jingle-brained. Wouldn't have believed rumor alone, right? Woulda blown into town, dug around some, and split. Except…"

Áebinn sounded as though she'd rather gargle molten iron that speak up, but give her credit; once she saw it for what it was, she didn't let her dislike of me stop her.

"Except we found everyone *else* had also heard the rumors, and we all stumbled across traces of some occult power throughout Chicago," she said.

"Bingo. So tell me. Raighallan, have you—have *any* of you—found one shred of evidence that the spear's even here, other'n rumor and a fake lingering aura?"

"You still ain't proved it's fake!" someone shouted from the crowd. "You're just supposin'!" A few murmurs of agreement followed, but they weren't too sure of 'emselves. I'd gotten everyone pondering, and they weren't happy with what they were coming up with.

"The curator!" Raighallan grinned all triumphant, mouth stretching beyond human. "The man saw the spear when someone tried to hide it in the museum!"

I'd known *someone* was gonna bring that up, but I can't pretend I wasn't extra glad it was him.

"You're talkin' about the break-in at the Field?"

"Of *course* I'm talking about—"

"The break-in that was perfectly timed to reinvigorate everyone's hunt, shore up those rumors, when a heap of you were startin' to give up on the whole shebang? Hell, it's almost as if someone was afraid you'd take your peepers off the prize and start payin' attention to somethin' else."

Murmurs were growin' even less happy.

"The human saw it," Raiggy insisted again.

"'The human,'" I said. "You mean Morton Lydecker? Assistant Curator. Older guy, looks like a brush?"

I could taste his frustration so bad I wanted to brush my teeth.

"You know damn well who I mean!"

"The same Morton Lydecker who's recently been paid close to ten thousand checkers from some secret admirer?"

Dead silence.

"Áebinn, I know the cops think you're a Prohibition agent. Feel free to check in with 'em, if you figure I ain't bein' square with you. It was all on the up-and-up. Got a warrant and everything."

I looked and smiled sidelong at Ramona, who was just sorta dazed at the whole thing.

"Thank your boss for me again, wouldja?" I said to her.

"Very well, Oberon." Herne took a single step, and the murmurings that'd been building again died out. "You make a compelling case. Nothing you offer is *proof*, but there's certainly sufficient..." He paused, groping for a word.

"We call it 'circumstantial evidence,'" Áebinn told him. He jerked her a nod in thanks.

"However," he continued, "I—and I'd expect these others, as well—cannot afford to simply give up this hunt on your suppositions, no matter how well they fit. If you cannot offer proof—"

"How's about I offer motive, instead?"

His eyebrow arched sharp enough to launch an arrow.

"You would have to know who perpetrated such a hoax to know that."

"I imagine I would, yeah."

Honestly? I missed this a little. Standing and talking at a whole captive audience of fellow Fae, nobles of the Seelie Court... Still wouldn't go back for the world and a sundae on the side, but it wasn't *all* bad.

I continued, "In addition to the info on Lydecker's bank accounts, I also got my mitts on police reports from across the city. You know how much random street violence's gone up in the last few weeks?"

"Why does this even—?" Raighallan began, but his own partner shushed him with a glare.

"Zip," I said. "Nada. Well, other'n the raid on Scola's place. And the car bomb that killed Manetti, but that's part of the scam. No big fires. No mass firefights or gang clashes. No rash of murders and disappearances. Nothing that coulda been the 'official story' to cover any sorta clash between Fae factions.

"There's only so many leads to follow. I've run into each faction here at least once over the course, some of you more'n once. No way you all haven't also run into each other. So tell me, how many of you actually bumped into the Unseelie before tonight?"

Téimhneach drew himself up—and as a boggart, that made him actually taller'n he had been a minute ago.

"I beg your pardon?" he said.

"*I* did," I said, "because you guys got something on me." Still didn't like to admit that, but I hadda make the point. I ignored a few accusing glances from the other Fae. "But other'n when you first dropped me off, it was only ever you'n Grangullie. You got over a dozen redcaps here, Timmy. Where've they been?"

"They've been searching, since we very clearly couldn't count on you to—!"

"Our guests," I said, sorta waving at the *dullahan*, the *bagienniks*, and the others, "wouldn't attack the Chicago Seelie outright. Too much chance of bringing down some unpleasant consequences on their heads. They wouldn't attack each other, for the same reason the Seelie wouldn't attack them without *real* good reason. Too much attention, and too much risk for not enough reward. But what're the chances that a buncha redcaps coulda met up with a big group of competitors, or been thrown in among a bunch of humans, and *not* started something? Hell, they did it just a few minutes ago!

"But nothing. No reports of mass violence. Not a one of you ever bumped into 'em. And why?"

I dropped from the roof, feet sinking a few inches into

the soft, wet soil around the mausoleum. Just a couple steps brought me to within spitting distance of Téimhneach.

"Because while we all been runnin' around with spears in our eyes and heads up our asses, Grangullie and the rest of Téimhneach's anklebiters've been off workin' their own angle. Áebinn? Would you tell everyone what I gave you a minute ago? For the folks in the cheap seats?"

"Obituaries. All 'accidental' deaths. All men and women of influence or power. And if the entire lot is consistent with the names I recognize, all men and women either with ties to the Seelie Court, or who know of us and choose to remain neutral. *Mostly* the former." By the time she hit the last word, I'm surprised the artificial lakes hadn't frozen completely over.

"Yep, that's about the size of it," I said. "Thanks. That's a nasty move against the Seelie, Téimhneach. Some might even call it a step toward open war. As if we didn't get more'n enough of that along with the humans, fifteen years ago.

"That why you hadda orchestrate this whole flimflam? To justify your presence and keep the rest of us occupied and lookin' the other way while you rubbed out the enemy's mortal power base?"

"You're insane," Téimhneach whispered, and I gotta say, I wavered there for a minute. Knock me over with a crow-feather if he didn't really seem to mean it. His expression, his posture, his tone, all of it *screamed* that he really had no notion what I was yammering about.

That's somethin' you always gotta remember about shapeshifters, though. For a guy who can stretch and twist himself up like a squid contortionist, reshaping an expression, a posture, even a heartbeat, is kid's play.

So I kept at him. "Ain't just here, either. Things're real tense back home, but nothin's actually *happening*. Like a whole lotta Fae are just busy elsewhere. You whacking all these poor people? Helluva blow, but not compared to the power of Gáe Assail. No way, *none*, you'd risk losing the Spear of Lugh—at all, let alone to the Seelie—in order to pull off your little series of secret murders. *Unless* you already knew they were never gonna get their hands on it!"

Say this for the boggart, he sure gave it the ol' college try. He'd begun ranting before I even finished my sentence.

"...absolutely unacceptable. I *will* be having words with Eudeagh about you, Mr. Oberon, and I rather hope she allows me first opportunity to..."

It didn't matter anymore. Everyone, and the Seelie especially, was pourin' enough hostility onto the shape-changing gink he shoulda drowned.

And then I got a good, solid look at the redcaps. Some were staring off into the wild blue, or at the grass, some nudged one another, tryin' their hardest not to grin, and—in a few instances, not many, but enough—failing something awful.

Of course.

"You're just as happy this is all comin' out, ain'tcha, Grangullie?" I said. "Weeks of bloody murders—and not just anyone, but your enemy's people—and you can't even brag about 'em? Gotta make 'em look like accidents? You must be bustin' at the seams to take credit."

I ain't quite sure how to describe the sound the redcap made in response, 'cept to say it was somehow a cross between an audible shrug and a snort. He was showin' just as many chompers as the rest of his crew, now, though. More grins'n redcaps, I think.

"Grangullie!" the boggart warned. "Do not even *think*—"

Unable to choke it down any longer, the redcap laughed.

The whole of Oak Woods echoed with it, an ugly, filthy sound. He guffawed, hard'n wet, spitting and drooling as convulsions brought viscous fluids I didn't even wanna identify up from his throat, to seep between his ragged teeth and spray between his lips. He doubled over, clutching at his gut, barely keepin' himself upright. Those arrowhead teeth, slimy and slick, glinted—even sparkled—in the muted moonlight.

And the other redcaps laughed with him. It wasn't the worst thing I'd ever seen, but in a lifetime of *thousands* of years, the fact it even broke the top fifty is sayin' something.

Téimhneach wasn't so amused.

"Stop this at once! Remember whom you serve, redcap! I order you to—"

Then, between one guffaw and the next, Grangullie turned and stomped on Téimhneach's knee, shattering the bone and bending the joint a good thirty degrees in the wrong direction.

The old man screeched, like a dying porcupine on a chalkboard, and collapsed. That kinda break would take me maybe a couple days to heal. For a shapeshifter like a boggart, it would probably take only hours, maybe even minutes. But that didn't make it hurt any less in the moment.

"You stupid fuck!" Grangullie shouted, spittle still spattering from his yap. "Nobody serves you in nothing! We just let you think we did! You ain't been in charge since you pulled that idiot move threatening Oberon's pet!"

"They know I'm standing right here, right?" Pete asked softly.

Ramona shushed him.

"Eudeagh didn't like hearin' about that, no. You just hadda push," the redcap shouted on. "Hadda prove yours were bigger'n his! You're the one who drove him to diggin', you stupid fuck! He shoulda just been spinning in circles, same as everybody else. *You* wanna warn *me* off givin' anything away? You're the reason we're *havin'* this conversation!"

Then, a lot more calmly—he even straightened his tie as he turned—"You're sharp, Oberon. Not enough to give *us* any trouble, you understand, but sharp."

He wasn't wrong, in this case. It was swell to be proved right'n all, but if I'd figured it out sooner...

"How many?" I demanded. "How many people did you slaughter during this little operation? I'm sure we ain't heard about *all* of 'em yet."

"All you gotta know—all any of you do—is *enough*."

His bestial smile looked like a great white had swallowed the crescent moon.

"Grangullie…" I was starting to sound steamed by then, much as I tried to hide it, but he just laughed again.

"What're you gonna do, Oberon? Threaten me? There's a few more of us than there are of you."

"Perhaps." Áebinn was at my side, now. It was nice to see that sneer and that anger directed somewhere other'n me for a change. "But as you might imagine, the Seelie are at *least* as curious as Mr. Oberon in this matter. And a *great deal angrier*!"

The Seelie began to spread out, forming a wide crescent on the grass. The redcaps, snarling, turned outward, ready to face an attack from any direction. The black dog circled, snapping at anyone who moved, while the out-of-towners backed away. I'm sure some of 'em wanted to get involved—Chicago or not, they'd still mostly be associated with one Court or the other—but it ain't good politics to jump into something like that. That's how wars between domains get started.

Trust me, nobody mortal *or* Fae wants that.

Grangullie snarled, and I swear his teeth got bigger. He pulled the cleaver from inside his coat with one hand, slapped the back of the blade into the palm of the other…

And it wasn't a simple meat cleaver anymore.

Some of you've read stories or legends about redcaps. You maybe been wondering what happened to those ugly, jagged pikes they're famous for, in the modern day'n age.

Turns out they still carry 'em; just usually in a much smaller form.

The weapon Grangullie wielded now was near twice as long as he was tall. The shaft was gnarled, knotted wood, ugly and thick. The blade remained a heavy, brutal thing, but now it took on a serrated edge and curved up at the tip. Looked like it could cut a horse in half in one swing, or peel open a suit of armor—or a flivver—with a thrust and twist.

A whole fusillade of *smacks* followed, as the other redcaps followed Grangullie's lead, and suddenly they were a jagged steel hedge, absolutely bristling with blades.

"You know this ain't gonna bring a one of 'em back," the leader sneered. "And even *if* you win, and *if* you take any of us alive, nobody's gonna spill nothin', about this job or anything else. You got nothin' you can threaten us with that's anywhere near what'll happen to anyone who talks. So how many, banshee? How many of your Seelie pansies you ready to sacrifice for squat?"

"You wish *us* to back down? It was you who shed first blood, you who committed crimes against us! I don't want your *answers*, redcap! I want your *head*!"

I *tasted* the fury pouring off Áebinn's aura; it tainted the air in every direction. I might not care much for her or her people, but I didn't wanna see 'em diced into Faeburger, either. And this was a fight that everyone was gonna lose, no matter who won.

I knew it was chancy, but I risked putting a hand on her shoulder.

"He's not wrong," I whispered. "It ain't worth the lives you'll lose. You know what they were up to, now, and you need to tell the rest of the Court."

Well, Ielveith had probably already done that, but it wouldn't really have been too helpful to explain that just then.

I kept at it, speaking fast and low.

"This is only an opening gambit of something, and now you know to watch for it. You'll have another shot at him."

"Yes," she sighed. "Yes, I suppose I will."

She shrugged my mitt of her like it was a cockroach, but she didn't follow it up with a threat, an insult, or a punch, so I figured our relationship was on the right track.

"Make no mistake, redcap," she hissed. "This was an act of war, and the Seelie Court shall reply in kind."

She refused to look at the Unseelie any longer. She just said her piece and walked away, her people falling in behind.

Raighallan went last, glaring enough for all of them.

The redcaps' pikes reverted to their cleaver forms with a series of peculiar *snicker-snacks*. Grangullie stuck his back in his coat, then crouched to meet Téimhneach's gaze. (The boggart hadn't bothered to stand back up, maybe wasn't even sure where he was.)

"By the way," Grangullie said to him, "don't think that kneecap was the end of your penance, ya shit."

Téimhneach didn't raise his face, just opened a slack mouth and one weak, watery eye on the back of his head to address his former underling.

"What... what is?"

Grangullie dragged him up by the belt until the boggart had no choice but to stand. Then the redcap kicked him in the same knee, and when Téimhneach crumpled, Grangullie's cleaver was there to meet him. Bit more'n a third of the old man's head landed a few feet away with a wet splat. Don't think even a boggart was comin' back from *that*.

"She left it to my discretion," Grangullie told the chunk of head, which was still blinking, not quite realizing it was dead. "Probably didn't mean anything quite this permanent, but if not, she shoulda said. And you always were a cock."

Then he, too, walked away, heading in the opposite direction than Áebinn had taken.

Uh-uh. Not yet.

"Hey, Grannie!"

The redcap stopped, visibly sighed, and turned.

"Stop calling me that, Oberon."

"Whatever. Why bring me in on this at all?"

That damn smirk was back. I wanted to wipe it off his face. With an anvil.

"You're the private dick. Why'd you think?"

I didn't hafta think; I'd already worked it out.

"Made the whole thing look real. Anyone who knows I owe you figures 'They wouldn't call that marker in if it wasn't important,' and anyone who doesn't still sees a guy who knows the city all caught up in the hunt. Either way, makes it more legit."

"Yep. Pretty much. Was that it, or...?"

Again, I couldn't keep the anger outta my tone. "That's why Eudeagh made the debt contingent on *finding*, not just lookin'. You all knew from the beginning there was no spear to find, so... this was never really *about* paying off a favor. You made me your sap, and I don't even get out from under, 'cause this whole thing was a deliberate scam. Am I right?"

His smirk was bigger'n his head, now.

"Like I said, Oberon, you're sharp. Too bad you ain't ever figuring this stuff out in time to do you any good."

It took everything I had to watch him go without throwing a punch or an enchantment that woulda accomplished nothin' but maybe getting' me beat up or zotzed. And I wasn't *quite* hot enough to make a move that dumb.

Not quite.

Anyway, most of the foreign Fae'd already vanished back into the shadows or the lake, which did me just fine. Saved me the trouble of telling 'em to scram.

The one that was left, I wouldn'ta told to scram anyway, least not in those words. He was still standin' by one of the trees, leaning on his spear, unwittingly tearing twigs off the branches with his antlers, and pondering on who knows what?

"Herne," I greeted him.

"Oberon."

"This whole thing looks to be over."

"So it would appear."

"I'm surprised you're not angrier with them for wastin' your time."

You ever seen a "powerful shrug"? He gave me one. Not sure how else to describe it.

"Not angry enough to declare war on the Unseelie Court of an entire city," he growled. "Now, should I catch any of

Eudeagh's minions alone, outside your borders..." The wooden haft of his spear creaked in his fist.

"More power to you."

I tried not to make it obvious I was tensing, but I was ready to go for the L&G in a pixie's heartbeat.

"Are *we* gonna have a problem?" I asked.

He gazed down at me, and y'know, maybe I been around you lot too long, but I'd forgotten just how unnerving that whole not blinking thing is when you're standing on the outside of it.

"Wouldn't serve any purpose," he said about six centuries later.

"'Bout how I feel," I told him. "Glad we're on the same page."

"I'll still kill you without hesitation if you get in my way on anything else. Ever."

"Uh... Okay."

"Be wary, Oberon. The Unseelie would not perpetrate a fraud this large, draw so much attention from the Seelie and outsiders both, without something *enormous* to gain. Whatever they hoped to accomplish by weakening the Chicago Seelie's foundations in the mortal world, it's only the start of something greater."

"Yeah, believe me, I know. I just said as much to our favorite Seelie cop. It'll be keeping me up for a while, lemme tell ya."

Herne wasn't wrong, but we didn't realize then just *how* bad it was. I knew we didn't have a complete list of their targets, that only the biggest names had made the news, but it was months before I learned just how many there actually had been, and that the Unfit'd been making promises as well as spilling blood. A whole bunch of the city's "neutral and powerful" were about to take sides in a war that shoulda stayed entirely in the Otherworld.

Definitely no way they coulda gotten away with all this if the Seelie hadn't been distracted.

But as I said, I didn't start gettin' wise to any of that until later, during the whole clambake with the wendigo and—well, that's a whole other story.

So, back to this one.

"Uh, Herne…" I had no good reason *not* to mention it, and it wouldn't hurt to get a little further on his good side. "Got a warning for you, too. The Hunt… They had someone here."

"I see. I shouldn't be surprised, I suppose." And indeed, he didn't sound surprised; more troubled. I assumed because he hadn't sensed 'em, but I didn't ask for confirmation.

"Thank you for mentioning it," he continued. A tilt of his noggin, not really a nod but not really not a nod, and Herne the Hunter leaped into the branches above. I didn't even bother tryin' to follow his progress, and after only a few seconds, the rustling and scraping stopped.

Which left, not counting the sorta shell-shocked Pete'n Ramona, just one last bunch.

Bumpy's crew'd waited on the sidelines, kept their yaps shut tight for the whole affair. Probably the wisest move they'd ever made. Or not made, really.

I thought Gina might up'n faint on me as I got close. The lead trouble boy aimed his piece at me, but his hands were none too steady.

I wasn't much in the mood to deal with bullet holes in my flogger. I gathered my will, just so he could feel the power roiling around me.

"That Tommy gun can be a lawn ornament, bo," I informed him, "or a suppository. You got a preference?"

Took a couple breaths for him to work out what I meant, and under most circumstances, I think his pride woulda made him do something jangle-brained. As it was, though, his heater hit the grass and mud with a combination of sounds similar to those I imagined a basilisk's digestive tract might make.

"Sharp move," I said. Now that I was less likely to catch a ribcage full of lead, "You'll go far in this racket." Then, peering around the headstones, "Well, not *too* far—maybe just a few plots over.

"So… *you*." I turned my attention to the blonde.

Gina flinched, almost stumbled. Man, witches used to be made of sterner stuff'n this.

Then I thought of Orsola, and decided I preferred 'em yellow-bellied.

I leaned in *real* close, until I almost choked on the cloying scent of her emotions.

"You got a look tonight—*just* a look, mind—at what's really out here. And, trust me, you ain't ready for it. Whatever you told Bumpy, however you think you've warded him, *he* ain't ready for it. None of you *ever* will be. You stick your schnozzola into our world again, it ain't gonna be pretty. Mosta this lot ain't as patient as me. At *best*, you'll get yourselves dead. Mess with the wrong thing at the wrong time, you'll get a lot of other people dead, or worse.

"So listen good, baby-witch. You're gonna make Bumpy understand he needs to stick to his own underworld. Be *real* persuasive. Because if I decide it's up to *me* to keep him outta this stuff, I'm gonna start by taking away his ability to detect it—and you'n me both know who *that* means. Savvy?"

Gina's throat bulged as she swallowed, as if she was tryin' to suck down a whole orange.

"Yes. Yes, I… I understand."

"Good. Now get the hell outta here. You bother me."

If they'd scampered off any quicker, in any more of a barely controlled panic, they'd hadda literally grow tails to tuck between their legs.

The breeze kicked up, washin' away the scent of fear and confusion—and blood—with the perfume of Lake Michigan. And I was alone again with Ramona.

Yeah, Pete was there, too, awkwardly clamberin' down the mausoleum wall. But for a minute or so, it was just me'n her in all ways that mattered. She was still standing on the roof of the Fuller family tomb, lookin' slack-jawed and confused and dizzyingly beautiful.

"Sorry you gotta give your boss such bad news," I called up to her.

She eased herself down, slow'n careful so she wouldn't fall, until she was perched on the edge, legs dangling over. Then she just shook her head, again and again.

"If you like," I continued, "I can help you explain it to him."

With that, a small grin broke through her bewilderment.

"Nice try."

"Hey, figured it couldn't hurt. You wanna at least tell me if you're human or not?"

It bugged me not knowin', especially since it ain't that easy to hide that kinda thing from me. I'd have thought damn near impossible, but... I'd been off about a lotta what's possible, lately.

"What do you want me to be, Mick?"

She wasn't serious, wasn't tryin' to make me think she was serious; just tiredly kidding around, takin' her next turn in the game we'd been playing for days now.

She wasn't serious.

I couldn't afford to let myself believe she might be serious.

"A bed."

I couldn't help but chuckle at her expression. I think she was actually shocked. I heard my cop buddy tryin' to stifle a coughing fit somewhere back behind the low building.

"Did... you just say you wanted me in bed?" Her voice'd gone higher but quieter, but I couldn't tell if it was outrage or—something else.

"Nah. I said I wanted you to *be* a bed. I'm friggin' all-in, and I'm going home to catch at *least* eight hours of doss. G'nite, Ramona."

"You're... What? Wait! Wait a minute! Mick! You get back here!"

I waved and kept goin', until her voice was lost behind me and the cemetery gates drew near up ahead.

Pete caught me up before I reached 'em.

"What'd she do to make you so steamed at her?"

What'd she do? Ha! *You don't have that kinda time, bo...*

The short answers, the curt goodbye, though... I wasn't *just* bein' irritable with her. If I'd given her more of a chance to talk, hung around for a longer farewell, I still wasn't sure I coulda left at all.

Apparently Pete figured out I had no want or plan to talk about this, 'cause he changed tack.

"You *are* gonna explain all this to me, right?"

"Bad guys work up big hoax to keep everyone busy while they kill a bunch of people."

"Gee, thank you *so* much. Yeah, I got that. I was lookin' for something a bit more specific."

"You want more detail, it's gonna have to wait. I'm headed home. I have *got* to get some bunk time."

"Oh?" Pete reached past me, pushed open the gate so I wouldn't have to touch the iron. It's the little things I'm grateful for. "Why?" he continued, more'n a touch sarcastic. "You got a big day tomorrow after takin' it easy all week?"

"Well," I answered, stepping past him, "I still gotta recover the spear, see?"

With one foot still in the cemetery and one out, Pete—if you'll excuse the expression—stopped dead in his tracks.

"What? But you just said—"

"I know what I said. I was there, and actually payin' attention to most of it."

"But... you... they... You *lied* to everyone!"

"Lower your voice some. You're about to break windows. No, Pete. Every word I said back there was true. It just wasn't the *whole* truth."

I hadda smile, even laugh out loud, at his expression.

"It's the reason I couldn't get the pieces to fit nicely. Whether the spear was here or not, some things didn't add up. But it *does* all fit if someone used the Unseelie hoax to cover the *real deal.* It's a thing of beauty in its own way, pal. The Unfit got hoodwinked as bad as the rest of us. Damn dingus really *was* here, and the guys tellin' everyone else it was here never even knew it."

"But... But..."

I don't think he was this taken aback even the day I told him he was gonna start turning hairy and quadrupedal every full moon.

"Who? How?"

The who, I hadn't actually sussed out yet. Was the only part of this whole Rube Goldberg scheme I hadn't figured.

It was gonna be *real* interesting to finally find out.

CHAPTER SIXTEEN

"What? *What?*"

Lydecker's voice shot up high enough to shatter glass—or maybe concrete. If he'd looked like a dandelion before, now he was more a dandelion after a short, sharp storm. His hair was mussed, standing out in cowlicks here, plastered to his skin there, and his suit was rumpled as though he hadn't just slept, but bathed in it.

"What do you mean 'no'?" he squeaked.

Raighallan, apparently not-so-devoted upholder of the law for the Seelie Court, sneered at the curator from across a worktable covered in brushes, small chisels, old bones, and some pretty spiral-shaped fossils. The overhead lighting was weak, flickering, casting 'em both in some pretty sickly shades. If Raighallan's contempt'd been any thicker, it probably woulda darkened the whole table in its shadow.

"What do you *suppose* I mean?" the *aes sidhe* demanded. "The word only really has the one definition."

"But the police are investigating me!" Lydecker wailed. He'd picked up one of the smaller fossils and was rolling it between thumb and fingers. Figure his situation *hadda* be upsetting if Mr. Fastidious was willing to play with the gewgaws that way. "They've been looking into my accounts!"

"Since I warned you of that a few days ago, it's a fact I'm well aware of. So?"

"So I need your help, damn it! Letting others learn of my complicity in this was never part of the deal!"

"Not my problem," Raighallan informed him coldly. "Now, if you'd kindly—"

"I did *everything*! Everything you asked."

"For which you were well paid, Lydecker. I owe you nothing. You, however, have still not completed your end."

The desperation on the curator's mug turned sly.

"You're right, I haven't. And I'll be happy to do so, once you've helped me come up with a way—"

"Don't. Even. Think about it."

Raighallan leaned over the table, knuckles pressed hard on the surface. He showed no emotion, no change in his expression at all, and his voice was harder'n deader than the fossils beside his fists.

"Renege on your word to me now, stand between me and what is mine, and I will lay you out on this table and *peel* you. Inch by slow, meticulous inch, until you beg to be allowed to hand it over, beg to die. And if you're truly fortunate, if my ire has cooled by then, I might just let you."

"I…"

You wouldn't figure Lydecker could get any more pallid, but he pulled it off with room to spare. He wasn't too far from glowing in the dark.

"I'll just go fetch it, I think."

"Wise decision."

The old man vanished into the winding maze of cluttered shelves, full of forgotten, half-finished or abandoned projects.

Raighallan fidgeted about as much as I did, of course, so for a while the place was more or less silent, 'cept for the occasional fumbling clatter from back in the darkness, or the irritating buzz of the cheap bulbs overhead.

When Lydecker reappeared he was staggering, sidling

sideways between the shelves so he'n his burden would both fit. Clutched to his chest was a long, narrow box; taller'n me, if it'd been set upright, but less than a foot in its other dimensions. Carved from a dark hardwood, it was absolutely covered in symbols, runes, and hieroglyphs from a dozen different ancient languages. Celtic, Norse, Greek, Egyptian, Minoan, Sanskrit, something outta the proto-Sino-Tibetan grouping... And all of 'em icons of power, all of 'em directed at whatever lay inside.

Not that it was all that tough to guess what lay inside. With *that* sorta mojo, was no wonder most of us hadn't managed to sense it.

I realized something *else* when I saw that box, too, but I'll get to that. For the moment, I decided this was my cue.

You shoulda seen Raighallan's mug.

He'd gone almost rapturous at the sight of the box, a religious fanatic receiving divine revelation—and from that straight to slack-jawed, chin-twitching, bug-eyed shock when I appeared across the room.

Lydecker just about passed out.

Hadn't exactly been eggs in the coffee to keep hidden, not from a fellow *aes sidhe*. It'd taken everything I could manage, a deep pocket of natural shadow and layer after layer of hallucinatory darkness laid over me with nerve-wracking care and slowness, knowin' that any tiny hiccup would've shrieked out to any nearby Fae like a siren. I've told you I don't perspire, but doing that even once, let alone for three nights in a row, sure made me feel as though I was about to break out in a cold sweat.

Yeah. Three nights. I'd figured somebody'd show eventually, but I had no way of knowing *when*. (Or who, for that matter.)

I gotta say, though, even if it hadn't been something this damn important, that look on Raighallan's face woulda made the whole thing worthwhile.

"Oberon! What... How could... Why are...?"

"Whoa, slow down, Raiggy. One question at a time. I ain't as quick as I used to be."

I moved fully into the light, making real sure they both got a good slant on the wand I pointed at 'em. Figure with my flogger hanging open, they probably both saw the rapier at my waist, too, but I do wonder what they thought of the dingus in my other mitt, hanging at my side.

I saw Raighallan tense, saw his gaze flicker toward Lydecker—and the box.

"As you just said, bo: don't even think about it," I said.

His shoulders sagged. I think he wanted to be angry, but still couldn't gather his wits enough to get there.

"How?" he asked me. "How could you *possibly* be here?"

"So, you see that hinged slab over there in the wall? That's called a door…"

He snarled.

I snickered.

"I gotta hand it to you," I said. "This whole thing was brilliant. Seriously. I'd almost be tempted to let you walk away with the spear, just outta respect for how you pulled this off." Raighallan started to perk up a bit. "'Cept, well, I don't want you to have it."

Less perking.

I kept on jawing. "Sorry, though, it wasn't quite brilliant *enough*. I didn't know it was gonna be *you*, until you walked in here—I had a whole list of possibilities—but I've known it was a double-blind for a while now."

"*How?*"

"First off, don't even take another step."

Lydecker, who I guess'd thought I was too wrapped up with his partner, froze in his tracks.

"In fact, why don'tcha move back a few paces? Yeah, good. Raiggy, your rumors and false auras mighta fooled almost anyone, but I don't figure it too probable that you coulda snowed the Wild Hunt. They slide right on through concealment and deception easier'n Santa through a greased chimney."

"That's *it*? *That's* what convinced you?" Raighallan sounded almost affronted.

And actually, he was right. Sealgaire bein' here in the Windy City? That just helped me confirm what I knew. Same with the stories that'd come to Hruotlundt from across the pond: evidence, but not proof. No, it'd been Adalina Ottati—restless, confused Adalina, who'd somehow sensed the thing through all its concealing magics, who'd talked to me in a language she couldn't know about a relic she'd no good cause to have ever heard of—who'd convinced me it was genuinely here. But I wasn't gonna mention her to Raighallan, dig?

"Well, that'n Mr. Lydecker here gettin' multiple payments. Ongoing 'gift' says ongoing *job* to me. If all he hadda do was stage the break-in, that woulda been a one-time thing, over and done. But if he was actually holdin' the spear for you, *that* makes ongoing payout fit. And it's a wise choice. Spear's less obvious in human hands, partly masked by the other gewgaws in the museum, and nobody's gonna look for it too close in the one place they 'know' it was stolen from.

"Didn't come to me until late—it really was a sharp scheme—but that was it."

Most of that wasn't even a lie: I'd only tumbled to the significance of Adalina's mutterings, and how they went against the whole rest of my theory, when I was settin' up the meet at the cemetery.

So, right. I had *most* of it figured. Raighallan'd gone about it all pretty brilliantly. Most mugs, they'da tried to set up a distraction somewhere else, get the Fae *outta* Chicago. But that wouldn'ta cut it. You ain't ever gonna get *everyone* outta here, see? especially not any of the bigwigs. And long as they're around... well, something like Gáe Assail can't stay hidden forever.

But you get everyone riled up, running around here looking for it, and then reveal it was all a fake? That's got potential. Store Gáe Assail at the museum until the Unfit are done with their game, pattin' themselves on the back for an ornate lie that was accidentally true. (And don't think for one second that I didn't know how impossible a coincidence all this woulda been—if I thought for even *half* a second it *was* coincidence.) Move it a few days later, and if anybody hears about it or senses it, they'll figure it's rumor or false magic left behind by the hoax. Nobody looks too close, and Raighallan gets to spring his new toy on everyone as a Yuletide surprise.

Wasn't too hard to work out *why*, either—with the kinda power the Spear of Lugh offered, it wouldn't be tough at all for Raighallan to work his way up in the Seelie Court, grab himself some titles and authority he'd never've gotten anywhere near otherwise.

But that still left me hangin' on two big questions.

"Your turn, Raiggy. How the hell'd the Spear of Lugh end up with Lydecker here in the first place? Damn dingus's been missing for centuries."

"I have friends and connections," he said stiffly. "I learned it'd been dug up and... called in a few markers to get it here. Wasn't too hard keeping it hidden in the wilds, where we're scattered. In the city, though? Where there's a whole population of Fae in Elphame, just a whisper away? Figured if I just marched in with the thing, I'd have half of the other Chicago on me in two minutes. This..."

I jerked a nod. "This buys you time and doubt. You might even be able to *use* it a time or two, let alone open it, before anyone starts really paying attention again. Right. Got that."

He was leaving an awful lot unsaid: I really wanted to know who in God's name'd managed to find the thing after all these years, and keep it secret to boot. And what sorta debts Raighallan coulda held that would be worth *that* trade. But I didn't guess he was gonna spill on that topic anytime soon, and the Seelie could work at getting it outta him after I handed him over.

But me, I was more concerned with the local than the global. I'd walked away from most of *those* concerns when I came to the New World and left the Courts behind. So I had a much bigger question—bigger to me, anyway—than who'd dug it up or gotten it as far as Chicago.

"All right, then," I said. "Just one last question, then we can start yappin' about what to do with the two of you. How in two worlds did you pull this off? The odds that Eudeagh'd decide to pull an Ahreadbhar-related hoax at the exact time somebody'd actually found the damn thing are so small they make zero look fat. And even if by some miracle it happened, you'd hafta have some way of knowing about it. The Unfit ain't exactly careless with their plans, and I don't think you've got any spies high enough in her organization to suggest a scheme this big. So tell me, bo, how'd you manage to make all this happen in—"

It wasn't much of anything. Raighallan was rock-steady, of course, not a blink or a breath to give anything away. But Lydecker... Lydecker was only human. He couldn't quite suppress it, the tiniest catch in his breath, the faintest flicker and dilation of his pupils as he watched me.

Me... And the room *behind* me.

I dove forward, and it was just luck—real luck, even, not "I'd wrapped myself in enough magic to make physics cry" luck—that I'd glommed Lydecker's tell in time. That was why the blade only slashed my back open, instead of punching straight through it to the more important bits.

I hit the floor, hard, and just barely managed to avoid a table leg as I rolled back to my feet. My whole back screamed as I bent and mashed it in ways it really didn't enjoy, and I left a thick smear of blood in my wake.

I shot thick swathes of magic from the L&G before I was even fully upright, not at Raighallan or back at whoever'd tried to dry-gulch me, but at the curator. I stabbed my will through his face like a dagger, burying his thoughts under a couple irresistible commands and an unholy, unreasoning, unmanning terror. With a high shriek that disintegrated into a dry, rasping hack, he turned and ran—carrying the case with him.

Raighallan was on him in less time than it takes for a satyr to forget your phone number, but that still gave me a second or two to recover, try to get my bearings.

See who'd just ruined another perfectly good coat, to say nothing of almost gumming up a perfectly good spine.

Huh. Okay, gotta be honest, I hadn't seen *that* comin'.

Grangullie the redcap stood where I'd been, grinning to show off his teeth like they were new babies. His pike was fully extended, with splotches and rivulets of blood that I really hadn't planned on sharing running down the glistening blade. I swear he licked his lips as he doffed his fedora and ran it along the edge, soaking up a goodly amount of the red stuff.

Redcaps're stronger, see, the fresher the blood soaking their hats. So he'd basically just fed offa me. Made me feel *real* slimy.

The *aes sidhe*'d just stood from where he'd tackled Lydecker to the floor, holding the rune-scribed case under one arm.

"Of course," I said, watching him and Raighallan both. The last bits finally clicked. One conspirator in each Court, working behind everyone's backs, hiding this and suggesting that, tugging on strings. "Lemme guess, Grannie. It was you who suggested the whole flimflam to Eudeagh?"

"Uh-huh," he gloated. "Never even crossed her mind I might actually have the genuine article."

Thoughts flickered through my noggin like a stuttering projector, now. I wasn't gonna get 'em to stop and explain their scheme, but the way I figured, it was a matched power grab. One of 'em uses the spear to take over his half of Elphame Chicago, then turns on the other Court. They get their keisters stomped for a while, until the other partner steps up with some plan or another to defend against their newly empowered enemy. And since they're actually workin' together, his plan works where others hadn't. The Courts go back to their usual stalemate, and two former no-names get to sit on the thrones.

Piece of me actually admired their ambition. Both of 'em were servants—useful, powerful, but in the end, nobody who'd ever end up running the show. Not without help, anyway.

But...

"There's absolutely no way," I said, "that you mugs can *possibly* trust each other to make this work. And you sure as hell ain't gonna oath-bind yourselves to each other."

They both grinned.

"It only works if we cooperate," Raighallan told me. He didn't seem real surprised I'd figured it out, or at least that I was talkin' as if I had.

"Hostage trade don't hurt, either," Grangullie added.

Yeah, that fit. Even the Unseelie—well, most of 'em—have people they'd rather not see rubbed out. If they'd exchanged friends or family...

"All right, here we are," I said.

Me and Raighallan and Grangullie, three sides of a lopsided triangle with a table full of fossils smack dab in the middle. Each of us had his meathooks wrapped around something dangerous, and for a couple breaths, not a one of us moved an inch.

"So what now?" I asked.

"You ain't all bad for a Seelie," Grangullie generously offered. "I got no real need to ice you, and you... whadda you care who's in charge in our Chicago? You spend all your days in this one. So blow. Walk away. We'll even take steps to make sure nobody tries to drag you into the fightin' once everyone's gone to the mattresses. Right?"

Raighallan looked less than thrilled with the compromise, but he made no objection.

The redcap tried to throw me a non-threatening smile, which is sorta like tryin' to shoot someone with a non-threatening slug.

"So whaddaya say, Oberon? Deal?"

Gotta admit, part of me was tempted. I was getting pretty well fed up with the politics and game-playing going on around me. I'd left my place in the Court to get *away* from all that hooey.

And it wasn't as if I cared much for the current leadership in the Chicago Courts. Buncha backstabbing thugs, every one of 'em. Raighallan and Grangullie wouldn't be any *worse*, right?

'Cept... Yeah, they would be. Redcaps ain't known for restraint, and the idea of either Grangullie or Raighallan wielding the power of Gáe Assail made my soul shiver. Who was to say they'd be satisfied once they were done? What domains other'n Chicago might fall into their hands thanks to the Spear of Lugh?

And in either case, whether just Chicago or beyond, how many hadda die to make it happen?

(Plus, of course, I had no reason to suspect they'd keep whatever promises they made me. It may've worked for them, but I ain't the hostage-trading sort.)

So really, I gave 'em the only answer I could.

A blast of magic rocked Grangullie off his feet, ripping luck and potency from his aura and channeling 'em to me. No way he was outta the fight that easy, not strong as I figured he hadda be, but it gave me an opening.

I didn't even bother goin' around the table. Two sprinting steps, a jump up on top of it, and then I hurled myself at Raighallan.

Raighallan who was, in that instant, fighting with the latch on the spear box.

I knew if he got the spear in his hands, I'd probably end up *so* dead I'd need a second corpse to hold it all. I might have tried to wrestle the box away from him, but he already had a pretty solid grip on it. So...

Remember I told you how, when I saw the box, I'd realized something? What I'd realized was *why* I'd brought the object I'd been clutching in my left hand this whole time.

I hadn't *planned* on bringing it. Was just one of those urges I get from outta nowhere that I don't really understand until later. Pure whim, same reason I'd asked for it in the first place. I'd just always figured, when the time came to use it, it'd prove vital 'cause of its symbolic value. Language of magic, and all.

Nope. Turns out it was mostly valuable 'cause of its *shape*, and 'cause the box was just the right width to make it work.

Even as I smashed into Raighallan, I raised the metal bracket—the old switch off the electric chair at Cook County Jail, which I'd gotten from Assistant State's Attorney Dan Baskin as payment for an earlier gig—and slammed it hard into the box.

Or, more accurately, around it.

Wood peeled, metal screeched, and just that quickly the hotsquat switch neatly clamped Raighallan's box shut as tight as any vise.

Yeah. Fae whims and destiny dance some strange dances together.

Raiggy looked about ready to cry, even as he wrenched and tore at the bracket. Slivers of wood showered to the floor with every yank, and I saw real clear that it wouldn't take him too long to work the thing loose.

But I had even less time to deal with him.

Grangullie was upright again, roarin' loud as a volcano spitting tigers, and pounding across the room at me. His heavy, iron-booted tread made the fossils jump'n dance with every running step, and he held his pike almost at the butt, more like a baseball bat than a spear. No way he shoulda been able to get any sorta controlled swing out of it that way, but I learned centuries ago that "should" don't carry a lot of weight with the Fae.

I threw myself backward and down, coiling my legs under me.

I hit the floor hard, back first. I woulda broken bones, or at least knocked the wind outta me, if—say it with me now—I were human.

I ain't human.

Even as I landed, I kicked out with both heels. The heavy table left the floor, tilting sharply as it toppled. Tools and fossils skittered across the room, wise enough to flee a situation I was too mule-headed to leave. The redcap's pike sank into the table with a nasty crunch, blade punching almost all the way through. But "almost" was just swell—it bought me the few seconds I needed.

A sharp roll and flex of my shoulders landed me back on my feet. Before the room'd even finished spinning and righting itself around me, I tossed the L&G to my left hand, squeezed a *massive* blast of magic through it, and drew my rapier with my right.

That magic surged and crackled over the bracket I'd jammed around the box. Reaching deep into the metal's lingering aura, far into its past and the histories it represented, I drew its spiritual nature to the surface.

As I said, it was *mostly* useful for its shape, not its symbolism—but not *entirely*.

The traitorous *aes sidhe* reached out, grabbed the bracket again to give it another yank, and fell back screaming, dropping the box with a loud clatter. A sharp, ugly crackling swept through the room as a spiritual echo of the thousands and thousands of volts that'd snuffed out so many lives now poured through the bracket itself. If I'd gone right then and given Raiggy a thorough up'n-down, I wouldn'ta seen a trace of burning or injury, but that didn't make the pain any less real.

Then I couldn't focus on him or the box anymore.

The already damaged table split in half beneath a nasty kick and Grangullie stormed through, pike leveled more like a lance. I spun aside, sword twisted into a downward parry, and he pretty much swept right by me. Metal screeched on metal as the blades slid past each other, and my sword—my whole arm—shuddered.

This rapier? One of the best ever forged by human hands, savvy? Good, solid Toledo steel.

But it ain't Fae-made. Ain't enchanted. I'd deflected the pike, but no way my blade'd do anything but shatter into a zillion pieces if the two ever met head-on.

Not without help, anyway.

I shifted into a dueling stance, rapier before me, wand raised back'n over my head as if it were a parrying dagger. Even as I faced the rabid redcap, I was suckin' power through the L&G, drawing on the luck and energies around me, and funneling most of 'em straight back down into my sword. (Most of 'em—I saved some for myself, since I ain't *quite* that dumb.)

Grangullie let the haft of his weapon slide through his mitts until he gripped it more in the center, the way you'd normally wield the thing. Again, we both locked stares, each waitin' for the other, each casting quick glances aside to see how Raighallan was managing. I caught him trying to use a small pair of pliers that'd spilled from the table to hold the bracket—and saw him fall back, cursing and screaming, as the tool did him no good whatsoever.

Then Grangullie lunged.

We circled, danced, blades flickering and clanging and bouncing aside before flickering out once again. It was impossible, how swift he was with that thing. The weapon was frickin' bigger'n he was, and he had the control of a surgeon with it. He had reach on me by a good few feet, and he was stronger'n I was. Even if I hadn't felt it in the impacts, I'd have known by the freshness of the blood that glistened on his hat and occasionally ran down one cheek.

On the other hand, Grangullie, same as most redcaps, relied on brute force. He didn't have the know-how I did, and that was enough to keep me from decorating the edge of his pike.

Barely.

It was startin' to wear on me, though. If I'd *just* been dueling him, that'd be one thing. But I was also constantly feeding mojo through my sword to keep it in one piece, and tryin' to keep half a peeper on Grangullie's partner.

Time to try something new, then.

The next time the redcap took a poke at me with the razor-tip of the pike, I moved *into* the thrust while twisting aside, instead of out. Sorta spun along the haft of the weapon like it was a yo-yo string, until I was good'n deep inside Grangullie's reach, way too close for him to cut me.

On the down side, I'd also underestimated his lunge, so I was too close in to comfortably use the rapier.

Ah, well.

I dropped the sword, grabbed the pike, and shoved it sideways hard'n fast as I could. The back end swung inward and gave Grangullie a nice solid rap across the ribs.

Wasn't too solid a blow, but he grunted and staggered a step, and that did me fine. I moved in the last couple inches and started landing punch after punch—wand still wrapped in my left mitt, now channeling extra strength and extra *pain* through my knuckles—around his mug and throat.

'Cept near his mouth. Don't ever take a poke at a redcap's mouth. Might as well try to survive a bear attack by clogging up its gullet with your head.

Blow after blow, I kept him reelin', didn't give him half a breath to get his bearings. He took a few wild snaps at my fists, to trap one or maybe bite it off, but he was dazed enough to telegraph. I saw each one coming long before teeth got anywhere near skin.

My meathooks were startin' to smart, though. Even with the extra magic *oomph*, I wasn't gonna beat a redcap to death with my bare hands. Hell, I'm not sure I could beat a redcap to death with the Sears'n Roebuck clock tower.

One more poke; I dropped my shoulder into a half-crouch so I could land one in his gut, putting every last bit of extra sensation into it I could. Grangullie doubled over with some horrid combination of a groan, a growl, and a gag. I kneed him in the forehead, then grabbed him by the collar as the impact straightened him back up. *Another* surge of magic and extra luck, this time to me, and then I lifted him with one hand and hurled him straight *through* several of the shelves.

I hope none of those fossils or samples were irreplaceable, 'cause by the time the crashing and shattering stopped, a guy couldn't hope to tell the bone fragments from the plaster fragments from the wood fragments.

Pain.

Agony washed over me. Felt like something was shredding through my aura, ripping away the bright spots of my life, scraping at the edges of my soul.

Raighallan. Bastard'd just shot me in the back with his wand.

I dropped to one knee, teeth grinding, and tried to counter him, tried drawing power from around me to replace what he'd just torn away. And if I'd started fresh, I probably coulda pulled it off, but I was already suffering, already drained. I couldn't focus enough on the L&G to counter him; I just stem the tide a bit.

So I let myself fall forward, and land in a heap where Grangullie'n me'd been sparring.

Oh, and where his pike'd fallen from limp fingers while I was pounding the stuffing out of him.

Came nowhere near actually *hitting* Raighallan. Even if I wasn't already weak and suffering an acute case of bad-luck poisoning, damn thing wasn't exactly made for throwing, was it? Still, he flinched back as the pike I'd hurled spun over his head, and one man's flinch is another man's opportunity.

This time the L&G fired first.

Instantly I started to feel better, draining away and reclaiming some of what he'd taken. I kept shooting, blast after blast, knowing if I let up for half a breath, he still had his own, stronger, wand ready.

He groaned, and swayed. I hit him again. He staggered. I hit him again, draining as much luck from him as I could, so that when he staggered a second time…

Zzot!

Gotta be careful where you put your hands when you got something nasty like that bracket lyin' around, Raiggy.

He folded and collapsed like a sack-full of… well, nothin' really. Me, I made for his side of the room, ready to get my mitts on the dang thing and get the hell out of—

Wood shrieked, strained, and splintered with an unmistakable *crack*! A shadow, huge but faint in the poor lighting, slid over me, wrapping me in an unwanted embrace. One of the shelves—massive, solid wood, weighted down with all manner of tools and samples—toppled toward me, inexorable as an avalanche. Pretty sure I heard Grangullie yelling "Timber, you fuck!" from somewhere behind it.

A quick "whip-crack" of the L&G snagged as much luck as I could from Raighallan and the room around me; several of the fossils crumbled to dust, the random chance that had allowed 'em to survive the eons suddenly drained. And then, with a mutter that mighta been a prayer, if I'd had anybody specific in mind to hear it, I jumped.

At the falling shelf.

Through the falling shelf.

Bits and pieces and gewgaws bounced off my noggin and shoulders, a rain of stone and metal hail, but it only stung. None of 'em were big enough to do me any real hurt. The thick wood—the sides of the shelves, yes, but also the two shelves themselves—scraped by me so close, as I passed between 'em all, that it damn near yanked my coat off my shoulders. There was *barely* room for me between those slats—took an astonishing amount of luck pass through unscathed.

But I *had* an astonishing amount of luck. And *aes sidhe* reflexes ain't to be sneezed at, either.

That same leap carried me higher still, so that I reached the top of the next standing case right about the same time the falling one hit the floor and broke apart.

Grangullie, who really looked better'n he should have after the broderick I'd given him, had stepped aside after he set the case to falling, moving back toward the next row, where I'd launched him through a few shelves of his own. I'd only gotten a slant on him for a blink or two, at the height of my jump, but that'd do. I snagged the top of the shelf with both hands, vaulted up and around without ever setting foot on the wood, and hurled myself heels-first at the gape-jawed redcap.

We both went tumbling good, but I definitely got the better of it—mostly 'cause I wasn't the one who'd just had an *aes sidhe* dropped on his collarbone. Grangullie struggled upright, but he wobbled, arms windmilling and grabbing at anything around him in hopes of keeping steady.

I rapped him across the temple with the wand, once again drawing everything good and useful from his aura that I could, filling in the gaps with disorientation and misfortune and pain. The redcap collapsed backward, slamming into the half-cracked ruin of one of the shelves I'd tossed him through earlier.

It was a low but terrified cry that distracted me from pounding Grangullie's face into something resembling peanut butter and jellyfish. Raighallan was making for the door at an awkward waddling jog. Over one shoulder, he hefted the box—keeping his grip good and distant from the bracket. Over the other, he carried the limp and whimpering curator, head bobbing and bouncing, fingers reaching almost idly for anything that might save him.

Well, shit. I hadn't the foggiest idea what Raiggy had in mind, but I sure as hell wasn't about to let him outta my sight with the spear, no matter how well sealed it was. I jabbed the L&G hard into Grangullie's throat, physically and magically both, and hadda hope that was enough to keep him down. Then I was running full out, half-shredded flogger flapping behind me. Think I about tore the door off its hinges, since I just turned my shoulder to it instead of stopping to push it open.

Footsteps echoed, vanishing up the stairwell and I pounded after 'em. But, of course, he heard me clear as I heard him. I dunno if Raiggy'd been making for anyplace in particular or if he'd just wanted to put some distance between us. Either way, guess he figured he wasn't too keen on me catchin' him up on the stairs. Just as I'd dashed past the landing on the ground floor, I heard another door slam open a flight'n a half above me.

Next stop, main floor: birds, Africa, Egypt, and scuffling Fae come full circle. It kinda fit, honestly.

I blasted through those doors, too, just in time to spot Raighallan crouching beside one of the free-standing displays. Couldn't really see what he was up to, but he had the box in his hands, and Lydecker's feet were sticking out from behind the small pedestal.

He heard me comin', started to turn, clutching the box under one arm and drawing his wand with the other...

I didn't bother stopping to use my own magics. I just threw myself at him in a tackle I'm pretty sure woulda been illegal on any rugby or football field. I wrapped my mitts around him as we rolled, and leaned aside to steer us a little. He smacked me once in the ribs during that tumble, sending a shock of pain all through me, but I wasn't gonna let it slow me any. I came outta the roll back on my feet, hefting the bastard in both hands, and hurled him hard as I could at my old elephant buddy's tusks.

What can I say? The trick hadn't worked with Herne, but I felt it still had some potential.

Unfortunately, if it did, that potential wasn't realized tonight, either. Even as Raiggy hurtled on his way, I could feel the spiritual wound from his wand, the gobbet of raw luck he'd ripped away from me.

And with that extra luck, he managed to raise the box over his head, now braced with both hands (though at least he'd hadda drop the wand in the process). The long wooden crate slammed hard into both tusks, cracking one of 'em—and more importantly, keeping Raighallan from being impaled on either, or even from hitting the big bony head between 'em.

I charged, aiming to grab his wand, see if I could make this more of an unfair fight. He dropped to the ground in a half crouch just as I neared, but there was no way he could get to his weapon before I did...

'Cept he didn't try. Instead, he gripped that damn box at one end and clocked me something fierce with the other.

The end with the bracket, of course.

Zzot.

My whole body went stiff and limp, burnin' and freezin' at once, and if that don't make any sense to you, imagine how *I* felt. I hadn't even realized I'd been thrown or staggered back until I crashed into the wall between two massive archways. Not sure how I'd kept hold of the L&G, but I wasn't complaining any.

Well, you know, about *that* part of it.

I thought the faint sizzling was all in my head, at first, leftover from the phantom shock I'd just got, but no. My thoughts cleared some, ears stopped ringing, but it was still there, loud as day (um, so to speak): the drunken honeybee buzz of the bracket's awakened power.

I righted myself, pushing off the wall with one palm, and it was then that I saw just why Raighallan had scooped up poor, dumb, greedy Lydecker.

The curator—or former curator, to judge by the open, sightless blinkers and slowly blackening splotches on his skin—was bent around the bracket at the waist. Raighallan wrenched the body back and forth, basically using Lydecker as a real large and awkward oven mitt.

No, I can't tell you why the energy didn't conduct through the body the way it had the tools downstairs. It wasn't real electricity, after all, just sorta a spiritual equivalent. Maybe once it got grounded in flesh or soul it didn't pass through any further? What the hell do I know?

I knew it was working, though. I heard more scraping on wood, saw the prongs sliding back and forth. Slow going, sure, but given a minute or so, Raighallan was gonna have the damn thing open.

So, no finesse. No careful manipulation of chance. I aimed, braced myself, and blasted him with every last bit of agony, mental darkness, and sheer power the L&G could take in a single shot.

Raighallan arched back, screaming, stumbling—and since I hadn't been mucking with things, I can only call it *genuine* good luck that Lydecker's limp body crumpled one way while the box toppled the other. Even if Raiggy could gather himself, he couldn't reach both at once.

I didn't really mean to let him gather himself, either.

No running, now. I advanced on him at a steady walk, and with every other step, I shot him again. Again. And again. He reeled back, and I kept coming. He fell. Crawled. Whimpered as he dragged himself across the floor, desperate to escape the pain I kept pumping into him.

And you know what? I'm honest enough to say I enjoyed it. Reveled in it, even. He had it comin' to him, this and so much more.

Maybe, in that moment, so did I.

In my advance and his crawl, we'd moved past the box and the body, see? Not far, just a few paces, but far enough.

I heard Grangullie's scream of fury, spun in time to see the pike rise up, up, only to come crashing back down.

On the bracket.

The redcap staggered back from the phantom shock, but the damage was done. The impact of the enchanted blade knocked the metal from the box, sending it flying amidst a flurry of wooden splinters.

I was on him before he could even catch his balance, parrying the pike aside with the flat of my hand, stabbing at him with the L&G like it was a dagger. Everything I'd thrown at Raighallan a minute ago, I used to pound Grangullie now, made just that little bit worse by the physical blows. The redcap was already looking pretty well pummeled from our dust-up in the basement. His efforts to push me back, land a punch, or bring his pike to bear, were pretty feeble and growing weaker.

And a damn good thing. I could be in a *lotta* trouble, here. Now that the box was vulnerable, I hadda keep 'em both reeling, put 'em down before either of them got their hands on...

From behind, I heard the click of a latch opening.

It wasn't an impressive sound, nothing unique or important

or scary, but I swear the whole world went quiet. Grangullie's rapid breathing, not to mention my own; the distant echoes of traffic from outside; light rain on the skylight overhead; the soft hum of the minimal nighttime lighting. All of it paused as Raighallan, battered as a used cake pan, reached into the box and hefted its contents for all to see.

You know, it didn't actually look all that impressive. Was a tad shorter'n I'd expected—the box hadn't needed to be quite as long as it was—and not real ornate. Functional, undecorated wooden haft that had frankly seen better days; and a simple leaf-bladed tip of iron, with a couple feathers and an unevenly shaped stone or two, dangling from the base of the blade by tangled twine.

That's how it looked. How it *felt*...

Everything in my head glowed, lit by something that wasn't any kinda light you'll find leaking from a prism. Memories cast shadows; thoughts changed color. It was a spotlight, a note, a dream of places and people long forgotten or never known.

It was beautiful. And terrible. It was life and death, and it valued neither over the other.

Gáe Assail. Ahreadbhar. Among the most awful creations of the Tuatha Dé Danann.

The Spear of Lugh.

Raighallan lifted the spear, and the spear, like an overeager hound, leapt to the call of his hatred.

I don't think he even meant to use it, not yet. He didn't know how, didn't know what he was doing; it hadn't finished telling him. If he had, I wouldn't be here to jaw about it. But from his emotions alone, the anger and pain and humiliation, the spear took purpose.

And it took steps.

The whole room *rippled*, swept beneath a wave of pure mystic force. One glass case shattered; another merely cracked, but from those lines it began to *bleed*. The elephant's tusk repaired itself, which wasn't *too* big a deal, but the thing also turned its head to a new angle, which kinda was. Stone dust drifted from the ceiling. Behind me, in the various hallways, power flowed through exhibit after exhibit. It left most untouched, but some it shattered, some it shook. A few bones turned into rocks, a few rocks to fur or ice or just other rocks. Several bits of ancient metal tools melted, shrinking away like butter in the summer sun.

As for me? The blast lifted me clear off the ground, but I didn't know it at the time, because even the fundamentals of "me" were in question.

I am a worm, crawling, wriggling, digging, ignorant of everything but the soil ahead. But then how do I know "I"? I am a human, infant, squalling, suckling, all of life ahead and none behind. But then why do I remember?

I am a beast, I am a bird. A fish, a flower, a corpse, a kid.

No! I am none of these! I am—

I hit hard, crashing to the floor way down one of the smaller halls. I skidded to a halt, angry and aching—but I was still myself.

Because whatever else the spear's magic tried to make me, above all else, I was—I am—*aes sidhe*. Older than many, older than most of you could ever fully understand. Tuatha Dé Danann, when that was a title to shake the earth and set armies to rout.

I carry the weight of millennia in my memories, and unless I wish otherwise, they are immovable, immutable, as the foundations of the earth.

Fuck Raighallan *and* Lugh is basically what I'm sayin'.

I braced my hand on the wobbly glass front of an exhibit, using the leverage to stand. From behind the transparent barrier, I locked stares with of one of the Tsavo man-eaters, and even though I know they're stuffed animals with glass eyes, I swear it glared at me for being so grabby and careless with its pen.

"Sorry," I muttered. Oddly, it didn't really look all that mollified.

I trooped through broken glass, keeping to a low crouch, to retrieve my wand. I'd apparently finally dropped it somewhere about halfway through my abbreviated flight.

Then I ducked back behind an exhibit of antelope, turtling my head just out of sight when Raighallan appeared at the end of the hall, silhouetted against the larger main chamber, spear in one fist, wand in the other.

He was laughing, maniacally, a high, harsh barking sound that made me think of a consumptive clown.

A twist of his arm, a flick of his wrist, and he hurled the damned thing. It was casual, almost gentle, but the spear launched forward like a *real* big bullet. More display cases shattered in its path, filling the air with a glittering, crystalline shower. The spear sank well over half its length into the back wall, then just as swiftly leapt back out, reversing its flight to slap snuggly into Raiggy's waiting mitt.

"Shall that be your end, Oberon?" he called out to me. "Cored through by Gáe Assail? Not bad, as deaths go. All I— *we*—need do is see you for the spear to follow you, though you run for all your days!

"Or perhaps you prefer fire?" The tip of the weapon crackled, a lot louder'n my bracket'd done. "Shall I feed you to the storm?"

Why do they always get more flowery and purple once they're exposed as the bad guy?

I was tryin' to decide if it was safe to answer him—to try to keep him booshwashing while I figured out what the hell to do—or if just my voice'd be enough for Gáe Assail to pinpoint me on the next throw, when Raiggy made it real obvious he didn't care to wait for my reply. The lightning flash at the tip of the spear began to spread in every direction, a few inches at a time, longer and farther with each flicker. Faster'n faster, until individual forks of electricity turned into a spider-web of energy, growing every second. Some of the broken glass around Raighallan's feet started to fuse, and I could feel the first waves of heat even where I was crouched.

The lightning flickered again, painting an intricate net in the air a good couple yards across—and then it caught fire.

The web of ozone-stinking, crackling electricity *caught on fire*.

Smoke poured from the edges and from the very tip of the spear, and I figured it was time to go. No way I could handle this head-to-head now, not on my own. I hated the notion of giving Raighallan longer'n he'd already had to fiddle with the spear, to understand and to master its powers, but I didn't see that I had any option. Only possible way to beat him now'd be to take him by surprise, and since he knew exactly where I was, what I wanted, and what I was capable of, surprise didn't really look to be part of tonight's agenda.

I tensed up, ready to make a desperate leap from cover, to try to vanish into the other hallways and take the run-out before he got wise to what I was doing. Gáe Assail cracked and thundered even louder, as though it knew what I was thinkin' and didn't much care for the idea. Raighallan took a step nearer, spitting taunts or questions—or, hell, singing psalms, for all I could hear over his deafening toy.

And then I got sharply reminded that if "surprise" was on the agenda, it wasn't really a surprise, was it?

Raighallan shrieked, arching backward sharper'n your average longbow. His wand clattered to the floor and bounced off to the side.

And more importantly, so did Ahreadbhar.

The thunder and the flame vanished the instant it left his grip, snuffed out like a cheap matchstick. It spun partway across the room, not just dropped but hurled by the bastard's sudden flailing, eventually rolling to a stop by the farthest free-standing display case.

Seems to me now that I shoulda checked to see what was *in* that exhibit, just to see if there was any sorta symbolism—or irony—but it never occurred to me at the time. I don't even remember deciding to stand up from cover, frankly. Just sorta found myself creeping back toward my opponent and the main hall.

Still bent backward, stumbling, Raighallan clawed over his shoulder and around his waist, trying to reach something behind him. Finally, gurgling, he twisted to one side and fell to his knees, giving me my first clear slant on what'd just happened.

An old knife—and I mean *real* old, coulda-come-from-its-own-exhibit old—was sunk deep into Raiggy's back, nice'n centered. The hilt was wound in fresh cloth, but enough protruded beyond the makeshift wrapping for me to guess its age, and even though I couldn't see so much as a hair's width of the blade, I didn't even *hafta* guess at its composition. I could feel the pure iron from here.

All of which wasn't near as bemusing as who it was who'd been *wielding* the knife.

"Ramona?"

Even in the middle of everything, her smile remained breathtaking.

"You didn't really think I believed this was all over, did you?"

The old grey matter was already past that on to other questions. Big one being, had she wrapped the handle in cloth just for a better grip—or to keep from touching the iron herself?

Even weirder than her being here, though? Way behind her, near invisible in the gloom and the shadow of the fighting elephants, was someone else. Someone I couldn't make out, 'cept for his general shape…

And the dull glint of his sunglasses.

Which, of course, opened up a whole new floodgate of questions in my noodle. But this wasn't the time to pick at 'em.

Ramona'n me looked aside almost simultaneously. Even floppin' like an amorous salmon, blood pouring from his mouth, Raighallan followed our gaze. From across the hall, leaning hard on a display case to keep himself upright, Grangullie stared, too.

All of us locked on the same sight, still right where it'd ended up after Raighallan flung it.

Well, almost all. I got no notion of *what* Sealgaire mighta been doing.

It was almost a weird game, for a minute. I'd watch the spear, then one of the others, who was watching the spear, then one of the others or me... Our eyes danced like we were attending a table tennis match played by ambidextrous octopuses.

We waited for something, though I dunno what. If this'd been half a century ago and a lot farther west, I'd have expected a tumbleweed.

"You're just gonna have to fork it over if you get it, y'know," Grangullie gloated, albeit weakly.

"Not really," I told him, offering a sweet smile. "You told me this whole task was a sham, that it'd never really had anything to do with my debt, remember? If you wanna go fetch Eudeagh so she can call in her marker *again*, you go right on ahead and be my guest."

The redcap howled. And maybe that was the signal we'd all somehow been waiting for, 'cause everyone broke at once.

I swept out with the L&G, not at Grangullie or Raighallan, but at Ramona. Felt a little rotten about it, but it made the most sense. A quick jerk on luck's strings, and she tripped over the crawling Fae's legs even as she tried to step over him, her ankles getting tangled up in his. She toppled forward with a sharp gasp, slowing the both of 'em down for...

Oof. Ouch.

Well, slowing herself down for a moment, and Raighallan more or less forever, seein' as how she landed on the knife hilt still jutting from between his shoulders. Bone cracked, the blade scraped on the floor beneath him, a fine red mist sprayed from his mouth'n nose, and then he shuddered and went still.

My whole gut went cold, not like ice so much as dull, heavy rock. No matter what he'd done, or planned to do, I couldn't celebrate the death of another *aes sidhe*. So many centuries of knowledge, sensation, sheer *life*, stolen from the world, just like that. And there's so few of us left, compared to what we were…

Regret didn't stop me moving, though.

Grangullie'd been farthest from the fallen spear, and he wasn't at his swiftest, not after the pounding I'd given him. So even after my belated start from dealing with the two Rs first, he was a good couple paces from the damn thing when I tackled him, once more stabbin' with my wand.

Yeah, I don't got the same issues with redcaps dyin' as I do certain others.

Gotta give it to him, though, he was a tough little fucker, even compared to most of his people. I'd pumped enough pain and misfortune into him over the course of the evening to kill a troll. But Grangullie was still kickin', still fighting—as a solid sock to my temple and a small chunk bitten outta my arm made all too plain. Woulda been a lot more'n a small chunk if I hadn't pulled away so quick. As it was, the sleeve of my coat now perfectly matched the gaping rents in the back.

Funny the details that occur to you while you're shaken by a good smack to the brainbox.

I heard running from behind me. Ramona was back up.

I spun away from Grangullie, who wasn't in any shape to try'n stop me, and dove for the spear.

But I'd left it too late. Ramona was just that extra step closer'n I was, and I could see right off that that'd make all the difference…

Sealgaire appeared behind her, pretty much outta nowhere. Ramona jerked hard to a stop with a sharp yelp as a big frickin' meathook snagged her by the collar.

My own mitts closed around a long haft of ancient wood…

Fire. The conflagration that ignited in my head, searing the edges of memory, blackening every thought to cross through, was brighter than the ambient lighting by a hundred-fold. A thousand years of civilization and restraint burned away to ash; pride and hatred and wrath flared high, pillars of flame reaching to the farthest vaults of mind and soul.

I don't remember makin' a choice. I don't even remember having an urge. All I remember is seein' the hall through a haze of rippling hatred, hefting the Spear of Lugh, and shouting something harsh and awful in a language that was dead before the first of you discovered writing.

The lightning flared, tiny flames rippling along the sides of the snapping, flickering bolts. Grangullie danced, twitched, spasmed, dangled on the strings of a puppeteer having a seizure. Smoke poured from his nostrils and ears, his eyes bubbled and boiled in their sockets. His skin blackened, cracked open, revealing only the glow of the lightning, painting horrid pictures in brilliance and shadow.

Then he was gone.

A pile of ash, the metal soles of his boots, and a fedora slowly curling and shrinking as it burned.

He was gone, and I was me again, gazing sickly at the ugly death that was the reason I'd come to my senses. Wasn't that I'd killed Grangullie, savvy? I'd been more'n prepared to do that already.

It's that I'd rubbed him out without thought. Without conscious decision.

Casually.

I hadn't been that casual about killing since before I... For a long time. The notion of goin' back to that, to giving as much thought to ending a life as I do to tossing out a newspaper? Not even the Spear of Lugh could make me okay with *that*.

I got no idea how Ramona'd reacted to my magic redcap-ending tantrum. By the time I turned back to her'n Sealgaire, she wasn't even lookin' my way anymore.

Tryin' to calm down, I took a gander around, a few deep breaths. Looked at the huge mess, the broken displays, the shattered artifacts, the scorch marks, and snorted. They'd close for a few days to clean up, give the newshawks some innocuous cover story, and that'd be that. I'd done enough tonight; wasn't about to worry about the clean-up.

"I thought you were just observing!" Ramona snapped at Sealgaire, drawing my attention back right quick. "That you weren't going to interfere!"

"That's about the size of it, ma'am. This wasn't interfering. This was me makin' things right *after* gettin' in the way."

"What on Earth are you talking—?"

I broke in. "How did you know I'd be here, Ramona?"

"The little lady's been on your trail like a bloodhound since the cemetery, son."

Since she looked too busy snarling to expand on that, I turned Sealgaire's way. For a short spell, at least, I was too beat-up, too tired, and too Spear-of-Lugh-having to be afraid of him.

"I been real careful," I told him, "to lose any tails every evening. I'd have either noticed her or lost her."

"Oh, you did. She was getting right frustrated with it, too. Always picked you back up the next morning, lost you again come sundown. Ain't nobody loses *me*, though. I'm afraid tonight I slipped up good. Let her spot me following you, and let her follow me. Right careless of me."

Ramona stomped away, muttering angrily, and I couldn't really blame her. It'd be easier to tail me to Avalon than to tail Sealgaire from bedroom to kitchen. She was only just now getting wise that she'd been bamboozled, that he'd led her here in time to help me keep the others from winning the prize, then corrected his "mistake" by stopping her from snatching it up herself.

Which left only…

"So why'd you want *me* to have it?" I asked him.

He looked hard at me, and there was nothin' even vaguely human about the expression he half-hid behind those cheaters.

"Because, boy, we got no pressing desire to hunt your city, and you the only one in this mess who might have the brains to make the right decision."

"The right…?"

ARI MARMELL

"'Bout what you're gonna do with the thing now you got it."

And you know something? He was dead right. No way either of the Courts could get hold of Gáe Assail: the result'd be chaos. Even worse if it was some random Joe, whether human or Fae. I didn't much care for the idea of Herne throwin' the cycles of the Wild Hunt outta whack, let alone taking enough control to bend the Hunt to a personal agenda. And I sure as *hell* didn't wanna *keep* the thing! I had no notion of how to destroy it, and wouldn't have even if I could, not this big a piece of our legacy.

Which meant I hadda find someone not involved in the politics of the Court, someone who wouldn't care about wielding the spear's power, and who wouldn't be a whole lot worse with the damn dingus than they already were without it.

Sound at all familiar?

Actually, I was glad I had a good reason for handing it over. 'Cause see, if I hadn't? Either he'da made me, or I'd have killed him with the damn thing and had the Hunt on my ass for the rest of my real short life.

I turned my wrist, holding the spear perpendicular in fronta me. Presenting it, basically.

"Take the fucking thing outta my town," I told him.

Ramona barked something that was probably a protest, but I wasn't listening.

Sealgaire reached out and took the relic about as casual as if I'd been passing him a cuppa Joe. Then he smiled, and I got pretty good view of wolfish fangs that I *know* hadn't been there the last time he opened his trap.

"Smart move, boy. Much obliged." He tipped his hat, made to step away, stopped again. "Keep an eye on the girl, too, or you'll wish you had."

I glanced at Ramona, but Sealgaire shook his head.

"Not that one. Adalina."

"What? *What?*"

He was already walkin' away. I followed.

"What does the Hunt know about her? *Why* does the Hunt know about her?"

He kept walking. And I basically forgot who I was talkin' at, or else stopped caring that I didn't have the spear to back me up anymore. I reached out for his shoulder, good'n ready to *make* him stop and answer some questions...

And he was gone. Between one step and the next, a sudden blur of motion—and I mean *blur*, so that even I couldn't make out a damn thing—and then nothing.

I didn't take it real well.

"I don't even know what some of those curses *mean*," Ramona said as I finally drifted to a stop.

"They weren't all in English."

"Yeah, but I don't think I even got all the ones that *were*. Why's this Adalina so important?"

"Who do you work for?"

"I already told you I can't tell you that, Mick."

"And I can't tell you about Adalina."

"*I'm* bound by magic not to. What's your excuse?"

"I'm bound by not wanting to tell you."

She blinked twice, then laughed. It was almost musical. I wish I'd been in a better mood to enjoy it.

"I suppose that's fair."

I didn't much care for the softening in her tone. Or rather, I cared for it a lot, which is what I didn't much care for. I turned my back; it didn't much help. *Don't get distracted, not again. Gotta figure out what Queen Mob's endgame mighta been. Gotta go check up on Adalina. Gotta—*

"We should talk," she continued.

"Don't got a lot to say, doll."

Petulant as it may've been, I not only didn't turn around, but stuck my hands deep in my pockets.

Her hand, which just sorta appeared on my shoulder, didn't help—though it mighta been more effective if I didn't hurt like hell at the lightest touch.

"I think we do."

"Never do run outta lies, do you?" I grunted.

"Mick…"

Don't believe the hitch in her voice. You can't afford to believe it.

"It wasn't all a lie. It was supposed to be, I guess, but…"

"You manipulated me. I'm impressed, but that don't make me square with it."

"Yes, goddamn it!" She hauled me around so I had no choice but to look at her. "Yes, I manipulated your feelings. I had no choice."

"Tell me another—"

"But I didn't *create* them, Mick! Not all of them!"

She gazed up at me, expression wide and open. I thought I might break in half with conflicting needs.

"I am not in love with you," I insisted, even though part of me—the part she still had her mitts on—woulda argued that.

"I know."

Okay, not the answer I'd expected.

"But you could be," she continued. "And you *do* care about me. What do say, Mick? Can't we give it a shot?"

I was leaning in before I knew it, got so close I could taste her lips on mine even though we never… *quite*… touched.

All the travail and effort of that night, and the hardest thing I did—without contest—was turning away again.

"Why?" She kept the quaver out of her voice; I heard it anyway.

"Because I can't trust you, Ramona. I'd never really know how mucha what I felt around you, *for* you, was bunk. Something you'd foisted off on me. If I wanted that back, I'd go home to Elphame."

"I can try to turn it off…"

"How would I ever be sure? No. Maybe… Maybe someday. Not now."

My shoulder got real cold as her hand slipped from it.

"Maybe. I guess… I'll see you around, Mick."

I swore I wasn't gonna say anything more. She'd about reached the stairs before I changed my mind.

"Wait a minute. At least tell me *what* you are!" 'Cause I was damn certain now the answer wasn't "human," no matter how well she looked the part.

I dunno if she'd just put her mask back on, or if the last few minutes'd just been another performance. But she not only smiled again, she threw me a look so smoldering, it mighta washed out the Spear of Lugh itself.

"If you tail me long enough, maybe you'll find out."

I was still deciding what I could possibly say to that when the stairwell door slammed shut.

FAE PRONUNCIATION GUIDE

Áebinn [ey-b*uh*n]
aes sidhe [eys shee]
Ahreadbhar [ah-**rad**-bawr]
bagiennik [**baig**-yen-nik]
bean sidhe [ban shee]
boggart [**boh**-gahrt]
brounie [**brooh**-nee]
Claíomh Solais [**kleev**-soh-**lish**]
coblynau [kawb-**lee**-naw]
Credne [**kred**-naw]
cu sidhe [koo shee]
dullahan [**dool**-*uh*-han]
dvergar [**dver**-gahr]
Elphame [**elf**-eym]
Eudeagh [ee-**yood**-*uh*]
Firbolg [**fir**-bohlg]
Gáe Assail [**gey** ahs-**seyl**]
gancanagh [**gan**-kan-aw]
ghillie dhu [**ghil**-lee doo]
Goswythe [**gawz**-weeth]
Grangullie [gran-**gull**-ee]
haltija [hawl-**tee**-yah]
Hruotlundt [**hroht**-loondt]
huldra [hool-dr*uh*]
Ielveith [ahy-**el**-veyth]
kobold [**koh**-bold]
Laurelline [**Lor**-el-leen]
Luchtaine [**lookh**[1]-teyn]
Lugh mac Ethnenn [**lugh**[2] mak **ehn**-nen]

Oberon [**oh**-ber-ron]
phouka [**poo**-k*uh*]
Raighallan [**rag**-hawl-**lawn**]
Rusalka [roo-**sawl**-k*uh*]
Sealgaire [sal-**gayr**]
Seelie [**see**-lee]
Sien Bheara [shahyn **beer**-*uh*]
Slachaun [**slah**-shawn]
sluagh [**sloo**-ah]
spriggan [**sprig**-*uh*n]
Téimhneach [tey-**im**-nach[1]]
Tuatha Dé Danann [too-**awt**[3]-h*uh* de[4] **dan**[4]-*uh*n]
Unseelie [**uhn**-see-lee]
Ylleuwyn [eel-**yoo**-win]

---

[1] This sound falls between "ch" and "k," as in the word "loch."
[2] "Gh" pronounced as "ch," but more guttural.
[3] This "t" is *almost* silent, and is separate from the following "h," rather than forming a single sound as "th" normally does in English.
[4] Strictly speaking, these "d"s fall somewhere between the "d" and a hard "th"—such as in "though"—but a simple "d" represents the closest sound in English.

MOBSTERS OF CHICAGO

While none of the characters who *appear* in this series are historical figures—at least thus far—a great many of those *referenced* are. If you're at all interested in learning more about them, this ought to be enough to get you started.

BATTAGLIA, SAM: A typical (but successful) Chicago gangster, Battaglia joined Torrio and Capone in the Outfit in the mid-1920s. After Capone's era ended, Battaglia remained a member in good standing of the Outfit, and went on to hold substantial power in the organization.

CAPONE, ALPHONSE GABRIEL "AL" (ALSO "SCARFACE"): Perhaps the most infamous gangster in American history, Capone rose from being a small-time hood to a lieutenant of John Torrio's, and eventually succeeded Torrio. A member of the Outfit, Capone was actually never "in charge" of the entire city, as many people believe, but as the man behind what was arguably Chicago's largest—and certainly most violent—gang, he might as well have been. Capone was eventually imprisoned in 1931 for charges stemming from failure to pay taxes on his criminal profits.

MORAN, GEORGE CLARENCE "BUGS": One of the biggest Irish gangsters of Chicago, Bugs Moran ran the Northside Gang from 1927 to (roughly) 1935. Violent and hot-tempered, Moran himself was one of the main causes for the constant conflict between the Northside Gang and the Outfit.

MUDGETT, HERMAN: Also known as H. H. Holmes, Mudgett wasn't actually a gangster, but was in fact one of America's earliest serial killers. From 1888 to 1894, Mudgett murdered an estimated 200 or more victims. Many of these were killed in his "Murder Castle," a hotel with secret rooms where victims could be suffocated, asphyxiated with gas, or tortured to death, before their bodies were disposed of in the sub-basements through careful dissection or submersion in lime pits.

NITTI, FRANK "THE ENFORCER": One of Capone's lieutenants, Frank Nitti went on to serve an important role in the Outfit after Al's arrest: specifically, that of a figurehead. While he did have *some* voice in the running of the organization, he was primarily a mouthpiece for the "Board of Directors." Although often portrayed in fiction as a chopper-toting psycho, Nitti was actually a bookish, white-collar criminal who rarely, if ever, got his hands dirty with violence. His nickname came from citing and enforcing Outfit rules at various meetings and sit-downs.

NORTHSIDE GANG, THE: A largely Irish gang based in Chicago's north side (obviously), this group was often at war with the Outfit over territories, routes, and the like. Capone's infamous Valentine's Day Massacre was targeted at Northsiders.

OUTFIT, THE: The hub of organized crime in Chicago, the Outfit was the organization/syndicate to which Capone (among many others) belonged. After Capone's time, the Outfit's leadership took on a very corporate form, with a Board of Directors and no single person in charge. The Outfit frequently cooperated with the Commission (a similar organization, based out of New York) and other Mafia organizations.

POPE, FRANK: A member of Capone's organization, he eventually went on to manage many of the Outfit's gambling interests on behalf of the Board of Directors.

TORRIO, JOHN: A powerful gangster during the rise of organized crime in Chicago, Torrio pioneered many of the bootlegging tactics and routes that would be used throughout Prohibition. It was Torrio who brought Capone into the fold, and eventually turned over power to ol' "Scarface."

VOLPE, ANTHONY: Volpe was one of the Outfit's gangsters who eventually rose to a position of some prominence, handling the group's gambling interests alongside Frank Pope.

ACKNOWLEDGMENTS

This book would not have been nearly as good—it might not even have been finished—without the support of a great many people.

My wife, George, for her critique, her reassurance, and for putting up with my crap.

Sam and the other folks at JABberwocky Literary Agency—and Cath, Natalie, and the other folks at Titan Books—for thinking Mick's almost as cool as I do.

Rhiannon, for beta-reading and for thinking I'm almost as cool as I... think Mick is.

And all the above, plus Sara, Rose, Joe, Miranda, Colin, Angelique, Erin, Jaym, Brian, Laura, Hannah, Scott, Crystal, Naomi, Carole, and Roger for helping me find some light in a very dark place. For you, and to everyone else who's stood by me and propped me up, I am more grateful than I can say.

ABOUT THE AUTHOR

A RI MARMELL would love to tell you all about the various esoteric jobs he held and the wacky adventures he had on the way to becoming an author, since that's what other authors seem to do in these sections. Unfortunately, he doesn't actually have any. In point of fact, Ari decided while at the University of Houston that he wanted to be a writer, graduated with a Creative Writing degree, and—after holding down a couple of very mundane jobs—broke into freelance writing for roleplaying games. In addition to the Mick Oberon novels, with Titan Books, his published fiction includes *The Conqueror's Shadow* and *The Warlord's Legacy* (Del Rey/Spectra), *The Goblin Corps* and the Widdershins Adventure series (Pyr Books), and *Agents of Artifice* (Wizards of the Coast), as well as several others and numerous short stories.

Ari currently lives in an apartment that's almost as cluttered as his subconscious, which he shares (the apartment, not the subconscious, though sometimes it seems like it) with his wife, George, and a cat who really, really thinks it's dinner time. He is trying to get used to speaking of himself in the third person, but still finds it awkward and strange.

You can find Ari online at www.mouseferatu.com and on Twitter @mouseferatu.

For more fantastic fiction, author events, exclusive excerpts,
competitions, limited editions and more

VISIT OUR WEBSITE
titanbooks.com

LIKE US ON FACEBOOK
facebook.com/titanbooks

FOLLOW US ON TWITTER
@TitanBooks

EMAIL US
readerfeedback@titanemail.com